To Helen —

On coming to P9-EGD-341
her old friend (oh for those Thursday
lunches!) from her current job —

From her friend who's very
glad she's here —

Love,
Marina

On Being Told That Her Second Husband Has Taken His First Lover

On Being Told That Her Second Husband Has Taken His First Lover
and
Other Stories

By

Tess Slesinger

Quadrangle/The New York Times Book Co.

Library of Congress Catalog Card Number: 70-130393
International Standard Book Number: 0-8129-6242-7

THIRD PAPERBACK PRINTING, 1975

To My

Mother and Father

Publisher's Note

THERE is something unspeakably sad about the premature death of an artist: all the promise that will now go unfulfilled, the good work that will never be seen, the unique vision closed off and sealed forever. Tess Slesinger, who died in 1945, cut off by cancer at the age of thirty-nine, was such an artist. Of Miss Slesinger, her friend Lionel Trilling has written:

"She was, I have no doubt, born to be a novelist. Her talent, so far as she had time to develop it, invites comparison with Mary McCarthy's. She had a similar vivacity and wit, although rather more delicate, and similar powers of social and moral observation, which, like Miss McCarthy's, were at the service of the impulse to see through what was observed. In her satiric enterprise Tess Slesinger was gentler than Miss McCarthy; her animus, although it was strong, was checked by compunction. This was partly because the literary practice of the time still imposed certain restraints, but chiefly for reasons of personal disposition."

Tess Slesinger was born in New York City in

1905 and grew up and attended school there. In 1928 she married Herbert Solow, a political journalist and later an editor of *Fortune*. The marriage thrust her into that ambit of New York Jewish intellectuals gathered around the figure of Elliot Cohen, then managing editor of the *Menorah Journal* and later founding editor of *Commentary*. In 1934 she published her first—and what was to be her only—novel, *The Unpossessed,* which enjoyed a decent commercial success and a more than decent critical reception. Although the correspondences between the characters of *The Unpossessed* and the members of what may be called the Cohen circle are by no means exact, it is fairly obvious that she drew heavily on them for her sympathetic yet finally devastating portraits of intellectuals.

What must have been equally obvious to *The Unpossessed*'s first readers was that its author, at twenty-nine, was the real thing, an authentic writer. Although the novel is not without its flaws as a work of art, that it is the work of an artist is unmistakable. A legitimate argument could indeed be made that the various chapters of Miss Slesinger's first novel detach very well as separate short stories. (One such chapter is, in fact, included in the present volume.) Which is perhaps a roundabout way of saying that Tess Slesinger was consummate in the short story form.

One need read only the first lines of Miss Slesinger's title story to know that hers is a unique voice, one that captures its readers right off. It is, those who read further will find, a wholly feminine voice—compelling, shooting off insights, sure of its tone, searching after the feeling behind appearances, and everywhere finding it. Professor Trilling has written about Tess Slesinger's essentially feminine wellsprings as a writer, and though he finds reasons for complaint in its use in *The Unpossessed,* he is surely correct in designating her style in the tradition of "the bright controlled subjectivity of a feminine prose manner inaugurated by Katherine Mansfield, given authority by Virginia Woolf, and used here [in *The Unpossessed*] with a happy acerbity of wit superadded."

The stories in this collection—with the exception of "A Life in the Day of a Writer," which was selected by Martha Foley for her *Fifty Best American Short Stories, 1915–1965*—first appeared in 1935. After their appearance Miss Slesinger, now married to the producer and screenwriter Frank Davis, went off to live in California, where she had two children and wrote the screenplays for, among other movies, *A Tree Grows in Brooklyn* and *The Good Earth.* In California her production of fiction diminished, though she occasionally published a short story in such magazines as *Vanity Fair* and the *New Yorker.* Notebooks with jottings for future novels and stories, now in the possession of her son, show that she intended to get back to writing fiction. But it was not to be. Ten years after she left New York, she died, leaving behind only her single novel and this collection of short stories.

Tess Slesinger's novel has since been republished, and it is with special pride that Quadrangle now reissues her collection of stories after it has lain out of print for more than three decades. The original title for the collection was *Time: The Present*, a title chosen, doubtless, to denote that they are all set in the 1930's. We have changed that title in the belief that Tess Slesinger's stories transcend their setting and are immensely readable in our own or any other time.

Contents

*On being told
that her second
husband has taken
his first lover*

On being told that her second husband has taken his first lover

WELL (you think in a sprightly voice) this is no surprise, at least *essentially*. So it's nice my dear, that you are always so clever; and sad my dear that you always need to be. Time was when a thing like this was a shock that fell heavily in the pit of your stomach and gave you indigestion all at once. But you can only feel a thing like this in its entirety the first time, after that it's a weaker repetition. Nowadays you go around automatically expecting the worst all the time, so that you can only be pleasantly surprised by the exceptions. Pretty nice to be so clever, Cornelia my gal, *pretty sad too*. Now when the message is shot out to you you've got a nice little lined glove like a catcher's mitt for it to fall into, more or less painlessly, more or less soundlessly. Oh sure, the details, falling like pepper into a fresh wound, sting a bit. And of course the confirmation, the *dead-certain* confirmation, of what you were clever enough to *know* and clever enough to keep away from knowing, does wrap you round in a sort of strait-jacket for a minute . . . But no nausea comes.

No nausea. No sharp pain. A mild disgust, and a quick defensive rallying of your forces. Your wits are keyed to concert pitch, nothing can escape you, you are intensely self-conscious. You have utter and absolute control over all your nerves. You go right on lying there in his arms letting what must have gone rigid inside you with his words go rigid away inside your skin, so his arms can't sense the difference, can't feel the animal flinch that maybe after all you couldn't avoid.

You observe the lines in his face, his weakness, his male pride which even in his moment of confession he cannot hide even from himself, and at the same time you are marking infinitesimal notes on your own emotions. Implacable logic comes and sits in your head. Your associative processes, like your wits, are functioning brilliantly, you are intensely, even thrillingly alive with the tingling call to battle in all your veins. Your past thoughts and observations, fragments from his conversation, kaleidoscopic pictures of his facial muscles scarcely noted at the time yet registered indelibly somewhere deep in the consciousness, stand out like well-framed entities of a jig-saw puzzle, only they cease now to be entities, and under your courageous and all-seeing eye they fit together and form a large bold map omitting nothing.

Oh, you could talk about the thing, in Proustian vein, forever. Show him where he was weak, analyze his emotions for him, tear him to pieces like a female lion. Time was, with Jimsie, (ah, *that* pain can still come, and it is not that Jimsie ever was more to you than Dill is now, it is because Jimsie was the first, and that pain was the first, his news was a blow the heart will never recover from—never) time was when you brilliantly talked, explaining away everything, for two whole days, while Jimsie stayed home from work to listen and neither of you so much as dressed nor saw another person but the boy from the delicatessen bringing sandwiches and cigarettes at intervals, and at last vichy-water when you fell to drinking. But you have learned a lesson. You know that you cannot handle these things as though you were giving a lecture course. No, no; no matter how much he acknowledges with his mind, there will be no satisfaction for you ultimately, and no sensitive revelations for him, unless you become at the same time an artist and an actress (or else of course an impulsive human being, but that is not possible.) Of course, you could go on forever, apparently relieving your mind of all its stored-up bitterness and grievances (some of them you never knew you had, some of them you had only against Jimsie and not against Dill at all), but a stream like that is futile and self-multiplying; you must be a highly selective artist, Mrs Dill Graham formerly-something-else; a gently restrained actress, *née* Cornelia North.

It is a delicate matter you have on your hands, my poor Cornelia, unless, that is, you choose to toss it down quickly with a drink and never look it in the eye again. But what's the use of doing that? Why make infidelity a painless operation and take from it its only possible lasting virtue, a possible binding closer together of the original two partners? Besides, there's something cheap in painlessness, something too modern-generationish. Go in for recriminations, gal, but on a modern scale; you can't of course go on lying there in his arms (and it's cowardice that keeps you so, even now) and mutter things about honor and weep, because you know too well that honor has nothing to do with it, and you don't feel in the least like weeping, in fact you couldn't manage it right now thanks. No, it has nothing to do with honor, it unfortunately has nothing to do with anything but human nature, and how can you take a man to task for that—not to mention *two* men?

He has the gall to ask you whether you feel "through" with him now. No, you answer, the thing has been going on right along and I've been happy enough—I'm not one to look back now that I know I've always had t.b. and say God how I have always suffered. "Well, but is it going to make any difference to you, from now on?" How in hell should I know? At the moment I have no desire but to keep my head above water and say funny things. And I can do it too, by God. (Like the time you wandered into the wrong room at a party and found him with his arms around that girl What's-her-name in no uncertain manner—ah, you put on a swell act that time, old girl! Just before being sick in the bathroom you managed a hearty laugh and said, O dear Lord, it looks so funny when you're not doing it yourself! How mad Dill was. But how he loved you for your wit. Still, if he had known about the mess in the bathroom which you so carefully cleaned up, *mightn't* he have loved you more? and *mightn't* you have prevented this other thing . . . ?) "Is it going to make a difference to you, Cornelia, now that you know?" "If you must be a gay deceiver, honey, for God's sake, be a *gay* one! My goodness, isn't adultery more fun than *that*?"

Suddenly you are filled with power which makes you light as air, which goes to your head like champagne the last night on shipboard. You have somehow got rid of something, somehow picked out his weakness in chiaroscuro. His triumph is smaller now than his guilt; his guilt you will reduce to sheepishness. I can do anything, my little man: now give me something *hard* to do. Besides, it occurs to you suddenly (elated as you are) that the thing is impossible. Simply and utterly impossible—it hasn't happened at all. Does he actually exist when he leaves your sight? Does he actually exist when . . .

Ah careful there, Cornelia; the ice is thin that way, Mrs D. Graham; watch your step dancing on those there *particular* eggs, Miss North—for the visual inner eye is a keen thing, a sharp sadist, a talented beast of an artist, an old devil of a perverted surgeon . . . delete that diagram, my dear, quick, before it stains the heart's plate permanently . . .

And then you reason (philosophical now, the body gone cold in his cold hands, the mind gone cold in your own cold skull) it *is* impossible, elementally and fundamentally impossible—impossible on the level of real values. For you are YOU, therefore if he loves the real YOU he cannot *love* anybody else; and if, on the other hand, it is not the real YOU he has reached down and found to love, why then, the hell with him altogether—you don't want to be loved for what you have in common with other presentable women: for your decent hair, your fine teeth, your eyes, your neat little figger. No. You want to be loved, not really even for your wit, but for the whole tricky pattern of all these things and the mysterious something else besides which spells in the end YOU and you alone. So then, since he loves you in this way, Dill does (of that you are sure, both warmly and coldly), since he really *loves* you, since he loves the real YOU— what can it possibly matter if he touches her with his hands, not the real HER, and not with the real HIM, suppose he does say to her . . . laugh with her . . . kiss her. . . Ah, ah, that way the ice is thin again, that way leads not to pain but to the terrible presentiment of pain. . . Ah, cold philosophy! denying the body, consoling the brain! Philosophy is senility to the young, religion to the starving, a dictionary to a baby, a fine silk purse to a pig . . .

To hell with philosophy, in short. "But what are you going to *do*?" he says, Dill says, and you discover that he too is lying without moving, as afraid as you that if a muscle twitches or a breath catches, something, or the whole of everything, will go smashing to small pieces in this life you share. What are you going to *do*? To *do*? Why, lie here, I suppose, for the rest of our married life, in your arms gone cold, in our bed gone cold, my heart gone cold as a philosopher's. What am I going to *do*, you think. It is a good question. One of the best questions, for there is never any answer to it.

Certainly, you think, you have a legalistic right to go out and get even . . . But you did that once, you matched Jimsie amour for amour, and what happened? Why, the string between you wore out, it got like old elastic and finally, because it would never snap any more for deadness, each of you let go his end and wandered off, too empty to feel pain, too dead to feel anything. You merely destroyed something that way, Cornelia, you didn't even save your self-respect when that bank closed. No, that's painless dentistry again, remote control, the Machine Age, Watson and the reflex, the Modern Generation. To derive *full* value out of anything, one must pay the price in pain; full beauty consists of pain as well as joy—and halving the pain cuts the joy in two. Let us not compromise, you think strongly; God send me pain again, God let me feel.

"I mean, can you love me in spite of anything?" If I love you at all, you think, if there is such a thing as love at all, then I suppose it is in spite of anything. "Oh sure," you hear yourself saying like a girl scout, but it sounds like the kind of records your grandfather used to play on his gramophone. "And how about you, my gay deceiver, would you love me in spite of anything, Dill? Would you now?" Impossible, clearly, to speak without lilting; try a drop of pallid humor first thing in the morning, nothing like it to aid digestion, avoid those in-fidelity blues, that early-morning tremolo.

"Anything, *but no gents*," he says, with fear piled up in his eyes and a sort of anticipatory hatred. "Don't ask me why, I don't *know* why, but it's different with a man."

He says and has said and will go on saying, *But no gents* for you, my girl, one gent and I am through. He will go on saying it until there has been one gent. (And the first is the only one that counts. After that, the elastic begins to stretch and go dead—we found that out between us, Jimsie and I.) Then it is a toss-up what he will do, when there has been one gent. But one thing is clear, Cornelia, you shrewd and calculating woman, one thing is clear: one gent, and you will have lost the large part of your power over him. For it is not true that men despise what they possess or what they have exclusive rights over; what is true is that they cannot love (in normal, masculine fashion) what they must share. No, there is no point to your going and doing likewise, not as long as there is any point to your relations with this man, this philandering second husband, this gay deceiver who tells the truth and looks so far from gay about it. As long as he can lie there with fear written on his face and say to you *But no gents,* you have a power which nothing can destroy. You gain thereby an integrity which exists not merely in his eyes, but which is actual, which is a fact. You become a whole person even in your sadness, while he stands before you, however male, a split one. He will know it, you will know it.

"The old Dolly Gray complex," you say. And evidently every man has the germs of it in him somewhere, the little woman waiting at home. It is even a little perverse that he can feel this way about you when he considers you were a bum (as he called it) out and out before he met you, ever since Jimsie in fact, and realizes that you were one on the very night he met you. But that's nice; that's what appeals to him; the very perversity of these strange facts: that you were a bastard (in his own language) and that now you sit at home and wait for him. He could not bear it if you were straight-out Dolly Gray, for he is a modern young man. But you have that whole rich background (rich! and supposing you have children and then grandchildren, would that story about falling asleep in a fraternity house with two "brothers" be the kind kids would like to hear from dear old Granny?)—but you have it, and he can never quite forgive you, and this is enough to tease him and please him for the rest of his life; you can never be quite Dolly Gray in his eyes because you can never shake off your past and his memory of your complaisance (to put it mildly) on the very night on which he met you. All right, let him have the joy of reforming you, of capturing what was free and keeping it in a cage, of owning what used to belong to nobody. At least let him for the time being. See what happens. You can always go back to being a bum again. Hallelujah, bum again! "I couldn't stand it if I thought this changed things," says Dill—and of course he knows it has changed things, what he means is he can't stand it if it's going to change your staying at home and waiting for him.

"Ah let's get up, nothing is changed, why should it be," you say quite gayly (and feeling it too), and spring stiffly out of his stiff arms. Well, it isn't quite the same as yesterday, it never will be. There is none of that pleasant, early-morning family-feeling now. You feel wicked a little as you run about with your pyjamas falling off one shoulder, getting breakfast but taking care to be rather attractive about it today as though you and Dill were not married yet. Ah yes, it is a very flirtatious breakfast that you have, flirtatious and a little bit precarious, for if the toast burns you might cry, and if the coffee is not done properly today he might fling it to the floor in a rage. But no, no; everything comes out all right because it *had* to come out all right, even the eggs get poached quite nicely instead of slipping out of their shells and allowing themselves to be parboiled—the toast turns out like the toast in a suave English comedy, and the coffee has never been better (you taste all this with your mind, with your weighing-machine, for your tongue has ceased to give a damn, and your alimentary canal is working like a derrick without a soul.) In fact the whole thing passes off rather like a fine English play, in which the husband has just murdered the child because he found out his wife had it by the butler, the wife is scheduled to murder the butler immediately after breakfast, and meantime the butler serves them an impeccable breakfast over an impeccable table with unimpeachable manners, and the husband and the wife delicately break their toast and wonder if the season will be a good one, if the Queen has got over her cold. Oh yes, yes, yes, it is all very nice, Dill flips over the pages of *The Times* (why is he wearing his good blue jacket and his natty grey trousers, he never starts that until May and here it is only April) and Cornelia does the wifely thing, she keeps his plate stacked with fresh toast and wipes the corners of her mouth (which she has rouged before breakfast, for a change) very nicely, with the edge of the fringed napkin (which belongs to the linen set they don't usually use when they are alone).

And it is all very nice (and a little bit formal), only that the house looks queerly different to you now, no longer quite your own, it no longer holds you as it held you yesterday. Yet there have been days when those four walls were so dear to you, too dear, times when they hemmed you in until you felt like a caged animal. Today you rather wish they pressed in closer. But the walls seem all made of doors today. Now the boredom that weighed pleasantly yesterday is gone. Why did you not whisper yesterday, while there was still time, why did you not shout it yesterday while you still had the voice—that that boredom was a good thing, let us preserve it, Dill, it is good, it is warm, it is real; it cannot be said today. No, no, and a good thing too, for this is life, life as it is spoken in the Twentieth Century, will you have a little toast dear? No? really not? then how about a second cup of coffee, well for heaven's sake, those politicians! when will they leave off cutting one another's throats?—all so very delicate and stilted, all so very fine and quiet, so civilized, so neat, the corpse inside in the bedroom but the play's the thing and let's not forget our very fine modern manners. (And why, with that impossibly gay suit, has he chosen that impossibly gay tie—a bow tie, does he think it's Spring?) but why in such a hurry, Dill, Dill darling—"You've left half your coffee, it's cold, Dill, let me pour you another cup? it's still hot." And you have the specious joy of seeing him stay against his will and drink his second cup of coffee, which he clearly doesn't want.

So he wipes his mouth and puts his fancy napkin down and stands there smiling at you quite politely. This is the moment for you to rise and casually murder the butler and come back and help your husband with his coat. But you can't make the grade. For you see it all suddenly, you see it there in his face, reluctant as he is to hurt you. He does have an actual existence outside of you, and he is anxious to leave you now and enter it. You see it in his face. It is clearer than any of the things you told yourself—and he cannot help revealing it to you. He will be lost to you the minute he walks out of your sight; he will be back, of course, but this time and forever after you will know that he has

been away, clean away, on his own. You see it in his
face, and your heart, which had sunk to the lowest
bottom, suddenly sinks lower.

"Don't go yet." It is time to murder the butler,
but you walk instead—or lilt, for you cannot trust
yourself to walk—to your husband, and you begin a
wretched game of opening up each button of his
coat after he has fastened it. You go on playing the
game together, both of you laughing, it may be a
little ruefully. He lets you get all the buttons un-
done at last, and then when you press yourself
against him like a very small girl suddenly, he puts
his arms around you and holds you—oh *fairly* tight,
you think, but you can feel his arms relaxing, you
can feel goodbye in his fingertips. You indulge
yourself anyway for a mad whirling second, you
steal what he doesn't want to give you, the illusion
of comfort against his apochryphal chest, the illusion that he is holding you so tightly that he will
never let you go. And then you give up, quite nicely,
and stand back surveying him with your head on
one side. Very definitely you refrain from asking
him why the Spring suit, the bow tie. Quite loudly
you do not ask him what time he will be home.

He tells you, though, he tells you everything.
"I'll be a little late," he says; "I've got to stop off
someplace for a cocktail or something." I'll be a little late, he tells you, with his gay-deceiver's troubled
eyes, with his blue serge coat and light grey pants,
and with the tiny pause he gives his words, I'll be a
little late because I've got to stop off for a cocktail

or something—with my girl; because I'm helpless, Cornelia, helpless, caught in as strong a web as your misery makes for you . . .

In a minute now the pain will go tearing and surging through the veils, drop the curtain on the polished comedy—but hold it for another moment. "Oh then," you say, reaching up, quite coy, quite gay, "you must let me fix your tie in a better bow, if you are stopping off someplace for a cocktail or something." Tweak, tweak, like an idiot, at his gay bow tie. "Which will you have, my darling, my blessing or my cake? And always remember, little one, that everything you do reflects on me," but this is bad, you realize, and turning with your hands raised in a rather silly gesture that is meant for mocking admiration, you wave him off, "There, there we are, now off with you in a cloud of dust."

B plus for that one, little sister, you tell yourself wearily, as you stand there hearing the door slam, and you wait there a minute but he doesn't come back, he isn't coming back, and if he were going to telephone you from the corner drug-store he would have done it by now, and you walk back past the laden table and you do not sweep the cups and saucers off the table, nor do you scream nor do you turn on the gas nor do you telephone the boy that used to take you dancing (though you think of all these things), nor do you fall in a heap sobbing on the empty bed (though that is what you thought you wanted to do)—you merely stand at the kitchen sink letting the hot water run to grow hotter, and you say to the cold walls reproachfully, "Oh Dill, Dill . . . oh Jimsie, Jimsie . . ." and when the doorbell rings at last you know that it is not Dill and not Jimsie but merely the man collecting last week's laundry.

1935

After

the party

After the party

MRS COLBORNE had given three cocktail parties a week in honor of various celebrities, ever since her nervous breakdown back in 1930. The doctor had told her then, when she was convalescing, that she must get interested in something; he suggested dancing (she felt she was too old), social work (but she shuddered, she had had dreadful experiences, really dreadful), writing a novel, going round the world, being psychoanalyzed in Vienna, studying economics in London, taking a course in sculpture, endowing a hospital, adopting a baby, breeding dogs, Christian Science (he was very broad), collecting early clocks, marrying again (oh dear no, Mrs Colborne said, that was as bad as social work), starting a publishing house, running an interior decorating shop, moving to the country, or learning to hand-paint china. But Mrs Colborne twitched her head, in that odd way that was part of her neurosis, to all of these suggestions; and at last they had settled that she should give parties, parties *for* people, in order that she should feel she had some contact with the world still.

They had talked over what kind of people Mrs Colborne should give the parties for, and many interesting things, both about people and about parties, were revealed. For instance, Mrs Colborne said, if she had musicians they would just come and stand about not talking and looking like Poles; you had to *push* musicians, Mrs Colborne said, to make them go, at a party. If she had painters, they would line up in factions, the surrealistes against the muralists or whatever you called that radical·new crowd, and simply shout each other down. There were obvious difficulties with actors, and dancers were always hungry and homosexual; Mrs Colborne thought earnestly for a while of establishing a salon for critics only, music critics, dramatic critics, book-reviewers, and thus correlating the arts—but there would be scarcely any turn-over that way, for most of the columnists she knew of had apparently been appointed for life and their sons seemed slated to inherit after them. Suddenly Mrs Colborne brightened; there were the writers!

The writers would supply her with an ever-changing list for guests of honor and guests of honor's friends. The author of a best-seller this Spring would be the author of a critical survey of Russia or the New Deal in the Fall; this would bring in an amusing variety of guests, as the famous writer's circle changed. Then too writers seemed more like other people than most types of professionals—lots of them made money, they weren't inclined to be too temperamental, and many of them came from quite good families. And finally, even the very stupidest writer was, from the nature of his profession, able to talk—and after all, you select a good caterer for the sandwiches, you hire waiters to mix and pass the cocktails, but it is still talk, good old-fashioned talk, that makes a party. Mrs Colborne twitched her head in that funny way she had developed during her breakdown, and smiled at the doctor. She would get well, she would give parties; she would get well in *order* to give parties.

Everybody said that Mrs Colborne made a marvelous recovery, considering. She would never be absolutely well, she must rest a great deal, and she could neither eat nor drink at her own parties. But by sheer effort of will she did manage to reëstablish her life. And she had had a dreadful time, a really dreadful time, enough to drive anybody to a breakdown, and Mrs Colborne had always been rather sensitive. Of course, if it hadn't been for *Henry* Colborne. . . Mrs Colborne had been an angel with him, a perfect martyr; and the funny part of it was that no one knew a thing about Henry Colborne, no one thought of him as queer, or cruel, or stupid, until *after* Mrs Colborne left him. Then, of course, the whole thing came out.

All of Mrs Colborne's friends were horribly shocked. Oh yes, said Mrs Colborne bravely, she had always known that Henry was a *Socialist,* at heart—in principle; he had been inclined that way even when she first met him, when they were both at school. Wore old clothes, in those days, wouldn't take her to the best places to dine, professed to be ashamed of his father's wealth—and all that; but that, Mrs Colborne said, was all right, it was Youth and it was even attractive. Later, when they were married, he insisted on certain things like living in an unconventional part of town (Gramercy Park) and drew the line at butlers, parrots, and things like smokadors—but otherwise he was all right, he was all right at parties even though he wouldn't play bridge, and it turned out that the Socialists he picked up were really very presentable and gentlemanly and could be invited anywhere, just fellows like himself who had been to Harvard or, at worst, sons of New England clergymen. No, it was not the Socialism that Mrs Colborne objected to, not in the least; she thought herself that it was what we were all drifting toward in the long run *anyhow*, the New Deal and the N.R.A. and after all the Republican Party was out, everyone was down on the bankers and about half the brokers had already committed suicide. No, no, *Socialism* was all right. It was particularly nice, Mrs Colborne said, for people who hadn't any children, who *couldn't* have any children (Mrs Colborne had had to have a very sad operation in the first years of her marriage, the women of her family were very delicately complicated inside)—for then these childless couples could feel that they were doing something for the future of other people's children anyway.

No, it wasn't the Socialism, Mrs Colborne said unwillingly; and gradually the whole story came out. Henry Colborne had grown increasingly moody ever since the event of their discharged chauffeur. Henry said he was sick of being driven

about by a flunkey, it was *chi-chi* (as he termed
everything from Aubusson carpets to remote control) to have a liveried ape at the wheel; there was
no reason in the world why both of them couldn't
learn to drive. Mrs Colborne didn't mind in the
least, most of her friends drove their own cars, and
she really found it fun. So they fired the chauffeur
(with a month's extra wages, and presents of old
clothes for his whole family), the chauffeur gave
them an ugly look and came back a month later to
rob them. Fortunately he was caught, unfortunately
it was discovered to be his second offense, and in
the end he was given—despite Henry's efforts to get
him off—several years in jail. Of course Henry had
undertaken to support the chauffeur's family—but
that was all right too, Mrs Colborne said, only fair
indeed, since they were the victims of social injustice and all that. But Henry had begun to grow
moody then.

He began to keep Mrs Colborne up all night
talking, and torturing her with tales he picked up,
the Lord knows where, about the suffering and
starvation of the city's poor. He seemed to derive a
peculiar morbid relish from making these tales as
harrowing as he could. Some of them Mrs Colborne
felt he rather exaggerated; others were, we all know
too well, she said, lamentably true. But what could
they do about it, Mrs Colborne said, what *more*
could they do about it, that is, than they were
doing? They gave plenty of money away to anyone
they heard about needing it, they supported the

chauffeur's whole family, and they were already "carrying" members of their own who had never recovered from the War. Well? Mrs Colborne asked him; what about Socialism? aren't we Socialists after all?

Socialism! Henry flung back at her. I'm talking about the working classes, do you think they're Socialists? have I ever brought a bricklayer in overalls home to dinner? I should hope not, Mrs Colborne had said complacently; after all, we've all read that play of Shaw's about the lady that made her family wait on the servants one day every year and the servants were as miserable as the family, we all know those things don't work, they belong in the realm of Idealism. It was Barrie, not Shaw, who wrote that God damned drivel, Henry had simply shouted at her, flung out of the house, and for the first time in their twenty years of married life spent the night away from her.

After that things went from bad to worse. He refused to accompany her places, forcing her to go to dinners by herself and to account for his embarrassing absences as best she could, and either maintained a disagreeable silence or shouted unpleasant things when they had guests at home. On one occasion he mortified her by refusing to dress for a welfare ball, and another time he insisted on coming to the opera early, before the overture even, because he said he was curious about the beginnings of operas, nobody had ever heard one and he half suspected that they hadn't any. Ridiculous things like that. Another night when they were coming home from the theater he sat on the little side-seat and left the window open allowing the night-air to blow down her neck, so that he could talk to the taxi-driver—and of all things, he asked him about his whole life, about a taxi-driver's pay, and if they had a union. Mrs Colborne said of course the taxi-driver looked at him queerly. But the worst thing was his shaking hands with a waiter one evening and calling him Comrade—Goodnight, Comrade, he said with the strangest smile—and after that (after the humiliation of seeing the waiter "indulge" a half-cracked customer), after that Mrs Colborne frankly told Henry that she preferred not to go out with him at all.

Obviously they were headed for disaster. Mrs Colborne began to feel shooting pains that she knew were not neuralgia, in the cords of her neck, at the back of her head. Henry said unfeelingly that the pains came from having been "stiff-necked" all her life and that he wouldn't be surprised if pretty soon her chin began to ache from holding it so high in the air. Then he fell to talking to her very earnestly, almost like a clergyman, about her *soul*. He said wasn't she tired and ashamed of the empty life they led. Empty! Mrs Colborne tried to show him where he was wrong, tried to point out that they not only kept busier than many people but actually *did* more—she cited the chauffeur's family. It was not her fault, she said pathetically, that they had not had children; she had always wanted children

—two. No, no, he kept saying, that wasn't what he meant; what he meant was, wasn't she tired of their living so easily and well when other people, *most* other people—and then he went on with his harrowing tales about the poor and the sick and the starving. When she put her hand to her heart one night (in the midst of one of his stories) and said quietly that she had a terrible pain there and did he think she ought to try psychoanalysis before she had another metabolism test, he said, listen, maybe what's hurting you is the same thing that's hurting me, my conscience.

But when the stock market fell in the Fall of '29, Henry seemed to take a turn for the better. He became more normal, Mrs Colborne said. He worried to death, like anyone else. He stopped torturing her with his terrible stories, and seemed as eager as she to visit their friends and exchange information and hunches and advice. He figured all night, like everybody else, how to save their investments— and he was cleverer than most of their friends, in the end he saved nearly every penny both of her fortune and his own. Mrs Colborne said that despite the financial worry, she had a happier time then with Henry than she had had for over a year. This was because, although he drank pretty heavily that Winter, and his hair turned a little grey, he *did* seem normal again, as though he had got both feet on the ground once more. And Mrs Colborne felt much better, she was able to get up for breakfast again, and the two of them had a happy time worrying and adding and subtracting together like any decent married people in that Winter. The 2nd stock market break in the Spring sent, not Mrs Colborne, but Henry himself, to bed with symptoms of the flu and nerves, and Mrs Colborne's nerves and pains left her completely for three weeks, so that she could nurse Henry well again.

And then, then of all times, after their happy interlude, after Henry had saved an incredible amount of both their fortunes, came the tragedy. For Henry came out of his illness another man. He was very quiet and abstracted for a week or so, and one night said to her quite clearly that they must have a talk. He had been doing, Henry told Mrs Colborne, a great deal of thinking during his depression illness. Of course, Mrs Colborne said understandingly; one comes close to death and it does things to one; it changes one's whole horizon. Henry said yes, that was just what had happened to him: only that *he* was planning to change the horizon himself, change his whole way of life—and Mrs Colborne said she asked him if he would like to adopt a couple of children.

Henry smiled quietly—afterward Mrs Colborne said she thought there was something a little mad in that new quiet smile of his—and said, no, he couldn't afford two children, nor even one. Mrs Colborne said that was very selfish of him, he wouldn't have to sacrifice anything to support two children. Henry said no, he couldn't afford even one child, or one anything—because, he said, with that mad smile, he was *giving away every cent of money he had in the world.*

Purely selfish, Henry went on that awful new smile—just to save his soul. He said that $500,000 was the new low for souls since the Depression, and his present friends wouldn't take a cent less than all he'd got. He was giving a small income to the ex-chauffeur's family, and sums outright to his brother, who had crashed with the market, and some of his father's cousins' children; that, he said, was pure malice on his part, for these people either hadn't got any souls or he (Henry) had no interest in what became of them. For himself, Henry said, he was keeping nothing, nothing at all; and Mrs Colborne had her own money in her own name. As for the rest of his soul's price, Henry said, he was distributing it to defense and propaganda organs of —*the Communist Party.*

He had discovered, Henry went on to explain in that super-rational tone of one completely mad, that as long as one possessed money, one was primarily concerned with it; that he had only just discovered, through his illness, that he himself was not immune from this universal fact, and had only caught on to himself thoroughly with a contemplation of the past strange Winter, when all his ideals and principles and feelings had been subordinated to the passion of saving his stocks. That he had become at the end of the Winter a nervous invalid as a result filled him with nothing short of horror, and left him utterly convinced that his one way of salvation, or survival even, was to remove, permanently and irrevocably, every cent of temptation that he had so cleverly salvaged for himself. In the same way, Henry said, he had become disillusioned with the tactics of the Socialists, who hoped by compromise and persuasion to win over kindly converts like his former self to sacrifice portions of their incomes; he knew too much about his own class, Henry said, to believe in it; and hence he believed that for the larger good of humanity, that class must be wiped out once and for all, and by nothing short of revolution. The Socialists, he said, were a halfway house, a stepping-stone; the Revolutionists were the ultimate Party. And there was absolutely nothing she could do or say about it, Henry went on to Mrs Colborne, for he would as soon die as continue another week in the life they had always lived.

Mrs Colborne said she was sure that the origin of those pains in her throat was sitting there that dreadful evening and keeping herself from screaming. For she saw everything in her whole life crashing in little bits about her feet; it seemed to her that Henry was taking a quiet, mad pleasure in smashing her life before her eyes. She couldn't speak. She just sat there silently, gently shaking her head as though she were pleading with him, Oh no, Henry, no, no, no.

It seems he offered Mrs Colborne a chance to "save her soul" too, and named the entire sum of her fortune as the only price. She should be flattered, he said, that her soul brought in so much, and that he thought enough of her not to allow it to be marked down. Mrs Colborne said that she just went on sitting there helplessly shaking her head (that motion that became so strangely exaggerated during her breakdown later) and not knowing what to do or say to bring him to his senses. She said that he looked to her, with that quiet glow in his eyes, like a man utterly *possessed*.

Then, it seems, Henry abandoned all pretense of levity, and grew terrifyingly solemn. Look, Helene, he said, let me show you something; what is the newest article of clothing you have on, and what did it cost? Mrs Colborne was so bewildered that she told him the truth: a crêpe de chine petticoat trimmed with hand-made lace from France; it had cost twenty-seven dollars. Henry described the conditions under which the French peasants had made that lace, and said the reason for those conditions was simply and directly Helene's fault: because she would pay no more than twenty-seven dollars, some of which went to the United States customs, some to the wholesale importer, and considerable to the retail department store where she had bought it. The French peasants who had made it in the first place, Henry said, were now, thanks to Mrs Colborne, miserably starving and living under thatched roofs through which the ice and sleet dripped in on their new-born babies. Nor was that all, Henry said (though Mrs Colborne was sure she had turned pale as death and her heart was beating painfully), for they must not forget the woman behind the counter who sold the finished petticoat to her—undoubtedly either a middle-aged woman with varicose veins or a skinny little girl with pernicious anemia from undernourishment—who made at most seventeen dollars a week. Nor must they leave out, continued Henry with relish, the truck driver and his kid assistant who delivered the parcel to their Gramercy Park home, whose scant salaries also came out of that twenty-seven dollars and robbed the original French peasants of still more—and meantime the peasants' eyes were giving out because it was such very fine work, and of course there was no insurance and no pension for blind and aged lace-makers—and for all this, said Henry, and much more, you, my dear, and I, are *criminally responsible.*

Mrs Colborne's head shook mutely from side to side as though she were saying *No, No, No,* to some invisible ally.

Now all these people, Henry said, the French peasants and their friends the stokers on the boats which carried the imports, the truck driver and his friends the million other truck drivers, the salesgirl and her numberless colleagues—and hundreds of millions more for we have forgotten such tribes as the miners, said Henry, not to speak of the factory hands, the underpaid navy, and the great unemployed—are leaguing together to finish us off. Their class, Henry said, the class he and Mrs Colborne so ably represented, was in the very small minority, and as soon as the important majority, what he called the working classes, got themselves together and organized and learned enough about fighting and methods of communication with each other all over the world, they were going to rise in a body and smash the handful of capitalists—ruthlessly, Henry said, and justly.

No, No, No, said Mrs Colborne's poor aching, shaking head.

There were then, Henry said, two courses for members of the upper classes to pursue. Either they could hang on for as long as they could and go under when their time came; or they could become human and see that their own decency was identified with the welfare of the masses. For his part he was going to join the masses and fight his own class; he hated his own class, and his whole heart and brain and soul wanted to be in this fight to finish it off and end its centuries of barbaric domination. Of course, Henry said, he would be looked upon with suspicion by his new comrades for a time; but after all, he was giving them his money, his soul, and the rest of his life; and once he was without a checking-account the important differences between himself and them would be dissolved. Besides, he owed them a huge debt, an unpayable debt, for his forty years of capitalism, and a little mental unease was not too much interest to pay. To this life, Henry said with madly glowing eyes, he was looking forward happily; he felt that his life was only beginning. . .

Here he broke off, Mrs Colborne said, and turned to her again, earnestly pleading with her to change her way of living too. When the Revolution comes, Helene, he said, there will be guns pointed at all the things you love most in this City, the great department stores, the fine churches, the skyscraper apartment houses; you will hear their roar from the Battery to the Plaza, from the subway to the Bankers' Club on the top floor of the Equitable Building; the gutters on Fifth Avenue will run with blood; Washington Square Park which we see now strewn with the living unemployed, will be covered with the dead and dying of our own class; in the end the guns will be pointed at you. But right now, Helene, before those guns can be manufactured and distributed, before the working-classes dare to shoot, there are fingers pointing at you, pointing from all parts of the world, hundreds of thousands of them, fingers of French peasants pricked by their needles, bloodless fingers of rachitic babies, trembling fingers of beggars, fingers of factory hands, miners, all of them, Helene, lifting and pleading and in the end threatening, it will then be too late to turn the other cheek for the fingers will be on all sides, pointed at you. . .

Mrs Colborne heard no more. She had begun to scream, and her head, which had been shaking first in helplessness and then in anger, now shook in terror before the millions of pointing fingers which came at her suddenly out of the air, till the whole room, the whole world, became filled with them, and Mrs Colborne was their sole target. She kept turning her head this way and that to escape them, but there was no escape, and although the fingers were disembodied and never touched her, she could feel their millions of sharp little pricks nevertheless all over the surface of her brain. What happened of course was very simple, the doctor said later; Mrs Colborne being a person of great sensitivity and imagination, had temporarily taken over her husband's delusions and made them her own. By the time the doctor arrived, summoned at once by Henry, Mrs Colborne had been carried to her bed and was lying there sweating and trembling, shaking her head weakly on the pillow at the many dim and angry fingers which had followed her up to her bedroom. When the doctor soothingly asked her if she could rest her head for a bit, Mrs Colborne answered wearily, "No, for I must turn the other cheek."

Mrs Colborne was in bed for three weeks turning the other cheek and was delirious on no other subject. From her sick-bed she continued to order the house quite properly, saw to it that the drapes were taken down and the summer curtains hung, dictated the correct complaints to erring butchers, florists, and second-floor maids, arranged with her lawyer for a divorce—but all the time spoke confidentially to the doctor and the nurses about the beggars who continued to point their fingers at her from the walls. At night the fingers stood out more clearly, and Mrs Colborne's nurse cleverly turned

round her schedule so that Mrs Colborne slept during the safe, light day, and did her household figur-
ing by night, when terror prevented her sleeping.

Gradually the delusion faded, the fingers re-
ceded; for a while they came only at night, and at
last only when Mrs Colborne was over-tired. She
had stopped shaking her head in that frenzied way,
though it still twitched a bit every now and then
as if she suddenly remembered to turn the other
cheek. But of course by now it was merely a tic, the
doctor said, and was no more summoned by the
delusions. Recovery was imminent, and after a restful trip to the mountains, Mrs Colborne was so
much better that the doctor told her it was now
time to look for a new interest in life. Henry was
gone, one read his name in the papers occasionally
as being arrested for picketing or speaking without
a permit, and so there would be no real home to
devote her time to. It was then that the doctor suggested dancing, social work, writing a novel, going
round the world, being psychoanalyzed, studying
economics, endowing a hospital, etcetera . . . and
that finally, after much thought, it was settled that
Mrs Colborne should give cocktail parties, and after
still more thought and consultation, parties for
celebrated writers.

In the beginning Mrs Colborne's parties were for
the authors of articles in the liberal weeklies, or
novelists of the *succès d'estime* rank at best, to whom
she found it easy to obtain introductions; every-

body knew somebody who wrote on the Plight of the Farmer or the latest medical discoveries or the lives of the Medicis. These early parties were not very good, and Mrs Colborne was discouraged; there was not enough drinking, the women were "interesting looking" and correspondingly dull, and the men appeared to be present only on sufferance—those early parties broke up at seven at the first brave sign of anyone's leaving. But Mrs Colborne was making contacts, even at these parties; among the guests that the dull article-writers suggested her asking there were always the names of half a dozen really celebrated writers, and of those half a dozen, three or four often accepted, and of the three or four who accepted, one was quite likely actually to come.

This celebrity Mrs Colborne would quietly corner, let him talk himself out on the sale of his current book and the possibilities of the next one, and finally she would say, quietly, kindly, and firmly, "I am going to give a party for *you;* shall we say the twenty-second?" (She had her dates accurately in mind.) "You must mail me your list of guests by the twelfth, so that I can get out the invitations a week in advance; my secretary takes care of all that. You had better invite seventy-five people and I shall invite seventy-five more, for fifty people make a good party, and I have found that an average of one-third of the invited guests are able to come to a party." Then when the celebrity was leaving, Miss Rand the secretary (who had already been informed of all the details) bade him, not "good-bye," but "auf wiedersehen on the twenty-second," and shaking her finger at him admonished him not to let temperament get the better of him and post-pone his turning in his list later than the twelfth. "Here, let me write it all down for you," Miss Rand would say humorously, "you authors, I guess I know you never remember a thing but your own ideas. And if you have any suggestions to make, you know, your favorite canapés or a little music or some special cocktails, just give me a ring some time before the twentieth, in the morning, between ten and twelve."

But the guests of honor seldom had suggestions to make, they always said they were content to leave the whole thing in Mrs Colborne's hands, so all the parties were managed pretty much alike, except that now and then there was incidental music for a nation-wide best-seller, or an informal song or dance number for a prize-winner. There were al-ways quantities of canapés, little sandwiches, nuts, ripe olives, and petits fours, and guests were always offered a choice of Martinis and old-fashioneds.

Mrs Colborne and Miss Rand had to run on a schedule, built up about the parties, in order to get everything done on time, and they made a great point of writing everything down and never slip-ping up on a detail. From ten to twelve every morn-ing Miss Rand was at her desk tabulating guests and filing their little address cards with the dates on which they had attended parties—for they were

careful to change the list of Mrs Colborne's own
guests so that the same people should not too often
be meeting together; then there were a series of little
cabalistic marks, understood only by Miss Rand and
Mrs Colborne, to remind them of each particular
guest's characteristic behavior at parties—there were
good mixers and poor ones, heavy drinkers and
total abstainers, certain critics who should not be
brought face to face with certain writers, couples
who were too newly divorced to be asked to meet,
and a set of single young ladies of no exact literary
persuasion who could always be counted on to come
and look smart and click glasses with gentlemen
one didn't have to bother introducing them to.
This file Miss Rand brought strictly up to date the
morning after each party, based on the post-party
discussion she and Mrs Colborne held after the
guests had gone home the night before, while Mrs
Colborne had her dinner in bed and Miss Rand on
a table alongside. On mornings that there was to
be a party, Mrs Colborne stayed in bed until twelve,
when Miss Rand brought the whole filing system
up to her room and showed her the tentative lists
she had drawn up for the coming parties; on non-
party days, Mrs Colborne was up and sat with Miss
Rand, working with her. Both of them wrote and
filed every suggestion that was ever made between
them, and one of the index cards was called
"Miscel." for Miscellaneous, and this section con-
tained ideas found impracticable thus far, but filed
for future use.

Eleven days before each party, Miss Rand telephoned the guest of honor if the guest of honor had not already telephoned her, and reminded him that his list was due tomorrow. Sometimes the prospective guest would say he'd been thinking it over, and after all why should there be a party given for *him,* who was he anyway, and besides most of his friends were out of town and he was terribly, terribly busy on his new book. In these cases Mrs Colborne was called in, and gently encouraged the modest one, assuring him that in ten days it would all be over, Miss Rand had him down for the twenty-second and if he wanted to change the day maybe *that* could be done, but all the arrangements were made and Mrs Colborne just wouldn't let him off. In the end the modest one always capitulated, explained how really he'd love a party given for him, but had just thought he wasn't important enough, and he'd send in his list tomorrow though he didn't think he could bring it up to seventy-five. Miss Rand and Mrs Colborne would smile swiftly at each other. They had never lost a guest of honor.

Then twice more during the week Miss Rand telephoned the prospective guest on some pretext or other, just for the purpose of casually mentioning the date again, and urging him to come early; in the case of the modest capitulators she always added encouragingly, "Mrs Colborne and I are *so* excited about your party; we're looking forward to it *particularly*," so that there might never be a last-minute lapse of memory or of courage. The system with caterers and liquor stores was equally perfect, and there was absolute harmony even with the men who brought folding-chairs and took them away again three times a week.

And so for four years before the particular party which is to be described, Mrs Colborne's parties were a going concern. Everybody in New York had been to at least one of them, and to some persons they were a regular institution. The majority of publishers and critics had ceased to come because they would only meet for cocktails the same persons with whom they had been having lunch; but they generally sent a representative—an assistant or an editorial reader. Most of Mrs Colborne's parties were neglected in the book columns, because there were so many of them; but there was mention of them in the cases of new arrivals in the world of fame or remarkably brilliant successes. It was in the former category—that of new arrivals—that this particular party was mentioned; and on Tuesday, the seventh of May, 1935, the top item in three literary chat columns read: "This afternoon Mrs Helene Colborne will give a party for Miss Regina Sawyer, whose recent novel, 'The Undecided,' has already won a place on the best-seller lists of New York City."

It was funny about Miss Regina Sawyer. She had come to one or two of Mrs Colborne's parties in the past, her name appearing toward the end of some guest of honor's list—before she had published her novel, presumably while she was still working on it—and nobody had paid the slightest attention to her. She was quite small, Mrs Colborne and Miss Rand remembered, and not bad-looking; but she dressed very inconspicuously, either in too-plain tweeds or a too-fancy and too-obvious "cocktail dress"—Miss Rand was not sure which. Miss Rand had approached her once and murmured something pleasant, and asked her to excuse her poor memory but what (this was for the sake of the files)—*what* did she do? Miss Sawyer had gulped at her cocktail, which she held along with a cigarette and a fancy napkin in her left hand, and tried to dispose of a sandwich, a purse, and a pair of gloves in time to free her right. Miss Rand remembered that Miss Sawyer had had to clear her throat before answering—nobody had been talking to her, and it seemed that she might be testing her voice first to make sure of it—and then said, "I don't do anything, really." Someone—the editor of one of the smaller magazines—standing nearby had turned and exclaimed kindly, "Why Regina Sawyer, you damned little liar! She writes, Miss Rand, and very nicely too." "Yes, I write," Miss Sawyer had said meekly. "Oh well, then," Miss Rand had cast about vaguely for someone to attach the nice little thing to, "then you *must* meet Mr Graham, Mr *Judson* Graham—Mr Graham, this is Miss Sawyer whom we are expecting such wonderful things from." Mr Graham, widely known as a literary playboy, had barely nodded, and Miss Rand had no other recollection of Miss Sawyer at the party. Mrs Colborne was not sure that she had ever spoken to her, though she recalled a quiet and rather wistful face.

Then one day in the middle of April, almost a month ago, Miss Rand had clapped her hands in surprise over the morning book-review section, for there was a review of "THE UNDECIDED, by Regina Sawyer, $2.50." "Well, will you listen to this!" she exclaimed to Mrs Colborne. "Regina Sawyer . . . hmm hmm . . . vivid . . . hmm . . . portrayal New York intelligentsia . . . hmm hmm . . . promising newcomer . . . daring witty penetrating compassionate . . . hmm hmm . . . well, for goodness' *sake!*" she had cried to Mrs Colborne. But Mrs Colborne had scarcely listened, for she had reached the book-review section of the other morning paper and burst into exclamations herself: "Regina Sawyer . . . intellectual claptrap . . . hmm hmm . . . wordy nightmare . . . vicious and not very clever portrayals . . . hmm hmm . . . trite dull unimaginative cruel . . . hmm hmm. . ." Miss Rand read on from her paper: "Prose perhaps a little crude, uneven. . ." Mrs Colborne burst out over hers: "Prose, however, rhythmic and poetic . . ." "Brilliant characterizations," read Miss Rand. "Characters so many puppets coldly illustrating thesis," read Mrs Colborne. "Unfortunate that such a book will probably fail to achieve success," read Miss Rand. "Will probably sell widely because of specious air of 'truth-telling.'" Mrs Colborne wound up triumphantly.

"Well, for goodness' *sake!*" they both exclaimed.
"Little Regina Sawyer!"

After that they had scanned all the papers and
clipped every mention of Miss Sawyer's name and
waited to see if "The Undecided" would really catch
on and sell. To their surprise the Sunday papers
carried a two-column photograph of Miss Sawyer,
and there was their neglected little mouse of an ex-
guest looking as snappy and sporting as many an assured author of three best-sellers. Four days after
publication Miss Rand found a publicity note stating that the first edition of Miss Sawyer's book was
sold out and the second in preparation—and she immediately phoned the publishers and insisted that
they dig her up a first for Mrs Colborne. Mrs Colborne and Miss Rand were very much excited and
ımused; and, really thrilled for the new little
author, they held their breaths and read their clip-
pings and waited to be sure.

Luckily the reviews were widely at variance with
one another, someone started a controversy and
Miss Sawyer responded immediately in an open letter somewhere—an interview appeared on Miss
Sawyer's impression of the still-younger generation
than herself—and gradually her name crept out of
the literary columns and into the chatter columns
as having attended parties here and there and there
was even a vague rumor that Hollywood was Interested. Finally her name appeared toward the end
of the city's best-sellers—she never made the prov-
inces—and that Monday morning Mrs Colborne

and Miss Rand, who rather felt that they had discovered her, decided to give a party for Miss Sawyer.

"My dear Miss Sawyer:" Miss Rand wrote at Mrs Colborne's dictation; "Miss Rand and I are so thrilled with your glorious success! May we offer our belated but nonetheless sincere congratulations? And I hope you will permit us a little secret pride, for we knew the celebrated author "when" —and we always predicted great things for you among the literary "stars"! We were both disappointed that you found so little time for us, but now we understand that you must have been working away on your splendid book! Paragraph. Now, Miss Rand and I have been wondering if you would allow us the privilege of giving a little party in your honor—we would be so pleased! You needn't go to a bit of trouble, I can imagine how rushed you must be these days!—just send us a little list of about seventy-five friends—or more if you wish—and we will attend to all the "gory details". Paragraph. Do let us know what date would be convenient for you. May I suggest the seventh or the tenth of May? Paragraph. Once more, we are so proud of you, dear Miss Sawyer! Most faithfully and cordially yours, Helene Colborne, per Fredrika Rand, sec'y."

The Regina Sawyer party was already in progress when Mrs Colborne, who disliked the tension of the beginnings, came downstairs. Groups were already forming, and the waiters had begun to circulate with the cocktails among the early arrivals, who, as usual, consisted of interviewers, photographers, and critics' assistants, for whom it was more or less a business to be prompt. The guest of honor was just arriving, attended by Mr Judson Graham and those two young men who looked just like him, wearing flowers in their button-holes—as Mrs Colborne herself swept down the stairs. Mrs Colborne saw with relief that little Miss Sawyer had learned to dress at cocktail parties—she was wearing a strictly tailored suit that was anything but pour le sport, of a fine wine-velvet which belied the severity of the cut; a shoulder nest of three gardenias offset her smartly groomed hair, which curled in little clusters behind her ears—and which, Mrs Colborne remembered, had been perfectly straight the year before. Miss Sawyer was laughing merrily and seemed to be holding all three of her escorts by the arm, and as Mrs Colborne modestly approached to greet her it became clear that little Miss Sawyer had no recollection whatsoever of her hostess and also that she was a little bit tight.

"—but I never forget a face," Miss Rand was assuring a young gentleman who had what looked like a false black beard—as Miss Sawyer's procession tripped a little over the threshold, and Mrs Colborne who had decided to remain incognito meekly sought an inconspicuous entrance behind them. "And here is our guest of honor!" exclaimed Miss Rand turning from the false beard and running with little cries to Miss Sawyer. "So *grand* to see you again, Miss Sawyer! Ah, Mr Graham! so you have captured Miss Sawyer already, have you! Well, you will have to give her up for a time, everyone is *dying* to meet her."

Mrs Colborne wandered quietly and contentedly through the growing little groups, and saw that more than the average fifty would soon be at the party. It had not been a mistake, after all, to give a party for Miss Regina Sawyer. Everything was going well; the folding-chairs lining the edge of the room had been properly pushed out of place and now reclined, properly unoccupied. The waiters skillfully made little paths through the standing groups, going away with empty glasses and quickly returning with fresh ones. The few critics who had come had retired comfortably to the alcove where the drinks and sandwiches were laid out upon a table, and were holding their usual tired, pleasant stag. The non-literary "extra girls", the helpful "party girls", who were oddly so much prettier than the average run of writing-girls, were smartly turned out and making themselves agreeable to the men, in particular the charming older men, and being pleasant about it when they were abandoned for the plain celebrities. Mr Judson Graham was lying on a couch with his arms mildly embracing two middle-aged lady authors who chatted briskly over his knee with one another. Miss Regina Sawyer was doing beautifully, repeating her own jokes to guest after guest whom Miss Rand brought up, and raising her voice a little or laughing and gesturing gracefully when it seemed possible that someone was not recognizing her as guest of honor. Miss Sawyer was drinking steadily and kept up a stream of what seemed to be irresistible merriment, and Mrs Colborne would have worried a little about her being intoxicated except for the thoughtful look Miss Sawyer's blue eyes assumed when, every few minutes, she would glance hurriedly about the room, keenly survey the critics' group, take in Mr. Judson Graham and his platonic embraces, and concentrate on older celebrities who had not yet made their bows to her. No, Miss Sawyer was doing exceedingly well, and Mrs Colborne felt grateful and warm toward her. As for Miss Rand she was, as usual, not neglecting a thing; she saw to it that the right people met each other, that groups were broken up when they started a too-earnest conversation; and with her infallible memory she was greeting everyone, by name, or face, or book.

Mrs Colborne felt soothed by the steady hum about her, by the richness of the flowers nodding on the mantel, by the subdued and yet colorful assemblage gathered in her home, by the perfect, clock-like regularity with which every detail of her party functioned. She moved contentedly through the crowd, wandering from the balcony at one end to the long windows giving on the Park at the other, and occasionally someone spoke to her and said what a nice party it was, and frequently people who had been there before came up and warmly shook her hand. Mrs Colborne spoke mildly in return, and pressed them all to go right back and join their friends. Once Mrs Colborne gained the windows and stood there smoothing the drapes a bit, where they had got wrinkled from someone's leaning against them and for a minute she saw the sun settled peacefully in Gramercy Park. She would soon be taking those heavy drapes down for the Summer, she thought, perhaps in time for Mr Forsythe's party on the twenty-first, it would be nice to have the transparent gold net up by then; she must remember to speak to Miss Rand. Behind her the hum was pleasantly gathering as the crowd swelled and the drinks began to mellow all the voices. Ah, here were some more people climbing her steps from the street, strangers evidently, for they glanced hesitatingly at the number before coming along up. Mrs Colborne let the Winter drape fall back in place and turned again to her party, to traverse it in her leisurely way from windows back toward the balcony again.

In one corner Miss Sawyer was posing for the photographers, and Mr Judson Graham had roused himself to come and stand beside her. Miss Sawyer smiled and pointed her foot, and Mr Judson Graham posed like a debonair poet, drawing her hand through his arm. Their friends came and stood laughing and drinking about them, until at last the photographers took them all in a group. The older critics had turned their backs on everybody and were standing and patiently drinking, and looked, Mrs Colborne thought, rather like men who preferred to be playing poker when they were not shut up by themselves reading away at their new books. Mrs Colborne was glad that she had not limited her parties to salons for critics only, for she thought them a serious-minded lot, excellent for the background of a party but less successful in the stellar rôle. She had reached the other end of her party by now, nodding composedly when she was nodded to, and graciously extending her hand when it was asked for, and now she slowly turned, and started on her pleasant ramble back toward the windows again—when Miss Rand dashed up and took her arm.

"Dear, it's going so *well!*" she whispered. "Miss Sawyer is a darling! And listen honey, you know the one with the black beard, there, the young one, well . . ." and here she whispered the result of some of her researches into Mrs Colborne's ear. "And Mr Kilpatrick, don't forget to speak to *him,* we've two more open dates in May. And Miss Beardsley, what do you think, dear? we might consider—perhaps in June . . . And 'Reckless Lady' is the name of his book, no dear, not Mr Kilpatrick's, Mr *Wallace's,* the young man with the black beard . . ." Excitement had brought a flush to each of Miss Rand's hardy cheekbones and Mrs Colborne thought affectionately how nice she looked. "I'll remember everything," she said obediently, "and Fredrika dear, I'm *so* glad you wore that, you look just lovely." They squeezed each other's hands and parted; their real fun would be afterward, when they would pick everybody to pieces over Mrs Colborne's supper-in-bed.

Two of the "extra girls" who came to all the parties, danced up to Mrs Colborne. "Such a *swell* party, Mrs Colborne!" they said; "and Regina Sawyer's such a *duck*. My, she looks about eighteen!" and Mrs Colborne, glancing down, saw that each of the "girls" before her must be thirty at least, though she had been thinking of them for the last four party years as twenty-five. "So nice to see you both again," said Mrs Colborne kindly; "so nice of you girls to come to all my parties." "I may just have to run away early, Mrs Colborne," said one of them quickly, "I have a 'pressing engagement' for this eve—" "That's quite right, my dear," said Mrs Colborne, "enjoy yourself while you still can." And she nodded to the "girls" and moved gently on.

And there was Mr Wallace, momentarily free. Mrs Colborne advanced and cut off his forward motion toward the fireplace. Mr Wallace, apparently not seeing her, side-stepped mechanically to his right, and Mrs Colborne side-stepped to her *left*, which brought them face to face. "Mr Wallace, I *do* want to congratulate you," Mrs Colborne exclaimed, "on the success of 'Reckless Lady.' And such a fine press as it got! Miss Rand and I were simply delighted!" Young Mr Wallace murmured his thanks and said he wondered that he was recognized behind his new beard. "Miss Rand and I never forget a face," Mrs Colborne assured him vivaciously; and then grew firm with him. "You must let us give *you* a party, Mr Wallace. May we put you down for the twenty-fifth?" "But what have *I* done?" murmured the young man shyly. "Nonsense," said Mrs Colborne crisply; "may I put you down for that date, may I, Mr Wallace? Miss Rand will arrange everything. Come now," said Mrs Colborne winningly, "it is only one afternoon."

On her way to Mr Kilpatrick, Mrs Colborne encountered Mr Forsythe, whose hand she clasped warmly. "So glad you could come today," she said; "Miss Rand and I are *so* looking forward to the twenty-first" (it was a policy with Mrs Colborne and Miss Rand never to miss an opportunity to remind a prospective guest of his date) "and Miss Rand tells me you've been perfectly fine about making up your list." And then Mrs Colborne smiled and dropped his hand, for there was Mr Kilpatrick, standing with a mousy little woman who wrote popular novels about detectives' wives.

"Oh Miss Pierson, you must help me persuade Mr Kilpatrick to let me give a party for him! Now, I won't hear any of *that,* Mr Kilpatrick! What have you done, indeed! What has the author of 'Pearls into Swine' 'done' to deserve a party! My goodness! May I put you down for the twenty-eighth, Mr Kilpatrick? Come now, make him say yes, Miss Pierson. The twenty-eighth then! Fine! Oh no—it's *I* who am flattered! Miss Rand will arrange everything. So nice to see you, Miss Pierson, some day you must let me give another party for *you.*"

Making her way complacently toward Miss

Beardsley, and wondering about the empty month of June, Mrs Colborne got wedged temporarily behind a group of happy drinkers, who resembled the strangers whom she had seen hesitantly mounting the steps. Mrs Colborne could not move for a moment, for a waiter, standing with his back to her, forced her up against the strangers. "And I don't know which she is," said one of them, "but the story's killing. Regina says she's just like the head waiter at Tony's, you know, you bow if you happen to remember, but it doesn't really matter—" "And wasn't there something about the husband being an anarchist or something?" "I think so, and Reggie says the most heaven-sent *material,* but only God can make a plot—" The waiter moved on, and Mrs Colborne said "Pardon me" to the stranger group, and managed to get past. There was Miss Beardsley, but she looked dull, Miss Rand had only said to *think* about Miss Beardsley, and Mrs Colborne was aware of feeling rather tired, rather numb. Besides, the rest of May was taken, and in June perhaps she and Miss Rand might run up to the Mountains for a little rest. The city grew so warm in Spring, the room was quite stifling with the people and the smoke and the reflected afternoon sun, and Mrs Colborne found herself leaning against the window again, thinking about the Summer drapes, and giving up Miss Beardsley altogether.

People were beginning to drift homeward now, and quite a number made their way to Mrs Colborne to say goodbye. Mrs Colborne felt wan and a little absent, but she brought her mind back with an effort, and remembered to sort them out correctly: "Don't forget Mr Forsythe's party on the twenty-first," and "You will be receiving an invitation to Mr Wallace's party on the twenty-fifth" or "Mr Kilpatrick's party on the twenty-eighth," and even, with a burst of initiative "Oh Miss Fitch, couldn't we give a party for you some time, perhaps in June," for it suddenly occurred to Mrs Colborne (she felt tired) that they might *combine* Miss Fitch and Miss Beardsley and thus kill two birds with one stone.

The hum was thinning, floor space grew visible again, and the room looked lovely in the deep May light. Mrs Colborne stood and dreamily watched the people leaving. But she had two more duties to perform, before the end of the party.

Mrs Colborne found Miss Rand in the hall before the hospitably open street-door, having formally taken her station there to bid goodbyes. Mrs Colborne got to her an instant before Mr Wallace, and had time to whisper briefly, "Mr Wallace, the twenty-fifth, Mr Kilpatrick, twenty-eighth, I'll talk to you later about Beardsley." Then she beamed at Mr Wallace, and stood listening pleasantly while Miss Rand shook the young man's hand in farewell: "And Mrs Colborne said the twenty-fifth was all right for you, Mr Wallace, so if you will let me have your list by the fifteenth, I should say about seventy-five names or so—and if you have any suggestions at *all* just phone me some morning between

ten and twelve—but let me write it all out for you,
you authors!" "Goodbye, Mr Wallace," called Mrs
Colborne softly, "or rather—auf wiedersehen, on
the twenty-fifth!"

That was the first of Mrs Colborne's last-minute
errands. There was one more. And hurrying to the
bookcase she found the paper-jacketed first edition
of "THE UNDECIDED" by Regina Sawyer which
Miss Rand had left sticking out a little on the top
shelf. Miss Sawyer was still standing merrily with
Judson Graham beside her, bidding people goodbye and extending her hand now and then to be
kissed, and Mrs Colborne made her way smiling
toward them.

"Miss Sawyer, my dear," said Mrs Colborne
gently, "if you would just autograph my book, I'd
be so pleased! I know it is a bore, but I should love
it so."

Miss Sawyer looked up brightly, recaptured her
hand from a passing biographer of Cato. "Why,
sure! I'd love to. Ah, a first edition! Aren't you
lucky!" Mrs Colborne piloted her gently to a little
desk, where pen and ink were standing ready. "I
hate to steal you from the guests, Miss Sawyer, but
only for a minute." Little Miss Regina Sawyer,
whose eyes were a trifle blood-shot now with liquor
and laughing, dipped the pen politely into the ink-
well and reverently turned the pages of her own
book. Suddenly the pen dropped as Miss Sawyer
was reading to herself. "Look at this, it's marvelous! Hey, look at this, Jud, you poor fool playboy.

. . . Oh God, I'll never do anything like it again, never, never! It's got everything in it I ever saw or thought or felt . . . Christ, will I ever do anything again? will anything ever mean so much again?" Tears were gleaming in Miss Sawyer's eyes. "God, finding my own book at a lousy party! it's like running into a mirror when you're naked, or seeing your mother suddenly when you're cockeyed drunk. . ."

"Reggie, pull yourself together!" Judson Graham stood over her, man-of-the-world with a flower in his button-hole. "We haven't time to stop for a crying jag now, honey, hurry up."

Regina Sawyer looked up again at Mrs Colborne with her eyes brightly glazed. "Playboy takes care of me," she said; "year ago he wouldn't speak to me at parties. Now I'm a catch. Next year he won't speak to me either. What do you want me to write in this God-damned book? What name shall I put?"

Mrs Colborne was about to tell her, but Judson Graham said angrily, "You drunken little idiot! It's Mrs Colborne, your hostess. She's just cock-eyed, Mrs Colborne, don't mind her, of course she knows you."

"Mrs Colborne! My God, of course," murmured Regina Sawyer blushing miserably. "Why my dear," said Mrs Colborne soothingly, "that's perfectly all right! You've had a difficult afternoon, poor child! And Miss Rand tells me you've been perfectly fine about it."

Regina Sawyer bent over and wrote in haste, and

Mrs Colborne saw one tear roll down Miss Sawyer's cheek and fall on the fly-leaf of her book. "Thank you so much, my dear," said Mrs Colborne, taking it up; "and—*now* the guest-book, if you *don't* mind?" and she drew out the Venetian leather folio which lived downstairs only during parties. "Thank you *so* much, dear," said Mrs Colborne. "Thank *you* so much," murmured the frightened Miss Sawyer, "you must forgive me, I mean, you work and you work like hell on a book and all you know is that book and then suddenly—oh, you just go haywire, I suppose." Judson Graham was guiding her deftly toward the door. "And you must try and come to Mr Forsythe's party on the twenty-first, both of you, the invitations have not yet gone out," said Mrs Colborne in farewell. "Goodbye, goodbye, and thank you again, Miss Sawyer, you've been perfectly *fine*."

Mrs Colborne did not like the dwindling ends of parties any more than she did their beginnings, and feeling tired, feeling also a pleasant sense of accomplishment, another party gone and future parties set and to be planned at cheerful leisure, the guest-book signed again and a new autographed first edition, she slipped unobtrusively up to her bedroom. Let Miss Rand stand nodding in the hall, bidding the guests goodbye. Let the fine living-room slowly empty itself until only the furniture and the hired waiters remained. The party was over. Mrs Colborne was needed no more.

In her room the bed had been turned down, waiting to receive her, her nightgown and bed-jacket were laid out cordially across the pillow, and the windows were opened wide to the Spring twilight rising from the Park. Mrs Colborne stepped slowly and contentedly across the carpet (the air was heavy and lush, inviting quiet movement) and sat at her little mahogany desk where the street lamp threw a beam across the blotter and the mother-of-pearl desk-set. She set down the guest-book and "THE UNDECIDED" and slowly drew out her memorandum book, Venetian leather like the guest-book. Very carefully she printed the dates for the new parties: May 21, 1935, Robert Forsythe; May 25, 1935, Julian Wallace; May 28, 1935, Richard Kilpatrick. Under the first day of June she wrote in pencil, very lightly, "Fitch-Beardsley, unsettled, confer F.R.—or should we go up to the Mountains?" she added dreamily, and laughed to see how funny the words looked on the business-like page, before she erased them neatly.

She really had taken care of everything, the book, the dates, the few necessary details—she must still place "THE UNDECIDED" on the shelves of autographed books, perhaps beside David Crane's book, the colors would harmonize—and it was certainly her time for undressing slowly and waiting in bed for her light dinner to come up, for Miss Rand. . . . But Mrs Colborne felt she couldn't hurry. A pleasant apathy descended on her limbs, so that she did not move to press the lights, not even the little mother-of-pearl desk-lamp that Henry's mother had given her (*Henry!*) so many thousands of years ago. She sat there by the window, waiting to place Regina Sawyer's volume, and meantime holding it absently on her lap. She was mildly curious about the inscription, and tilted the book so that she could read it by the street-lamp: "To Mrs Colborne, with my very best wishes, Regina Sawyer, May 7, 1935." Oh, how nice, thought Mrs Colborne, the very same thing that Henrietta King had written in her "Preambles and Constitutionals"—and what was it David Crane had written to her? Which was David Crane's book? A moment ago she had seen it in the bookcase, but it was too dark now, and the air was too lush and mellow for one to want to move; presently Mrs Colborne would rise and push the button and flood the room with light, and look into David Crane's book; he was a charming man, they had given him his party some time that past Winter, he had written a book on either Mexico or Lewis Carroll. Miss Rand would know.

But meantime Mrs Colborne sat content in the window, Regina Sawyer's best-seller in her lap, watching the afternoon grow old and listening to the last sounds of the few lingering guests. Soon the folding-chair men would arrive, the waiters stack the glasses in the kitchen; her own servants would clean up; they would bring her supper on a tray. Soon Miss Rand, Fredrika Rand, would have given the last orders below-stairs, and would come and join her beloved friend and employer. Soon too the city Summer would be heavy upon them and perhaps they had better put off the Fitch-Beardsley party till the Fall and run away to the Mountains. They had better go soon, thought Mrs Colborne, catching her breath in a sudden panic, soon, soon, everything had to be soon. For it was growing late. It was growing still. It would soon be too dark to see. She did want to find out, thought Mrs Colborne, *before it was too late,* what David Crane had written to her in his book the Winter before. She did want to look through the guest-book and count up the names again, the last time she had counted there were one thousand and twenty, including guests and guests of honor, and that was three weeks ago, after Mr Carleton Fisher's party, no, Susan Delaney's—but Miss Rand would know; odd that the book which was the record of Mrs Colborne's life bore her own name on no page. Of course it was because she had not put on the lights that shadows began to beckon from the corners, from the fireplace, through the window from the Park; of course it was because she was tired that Mrs Colborne's head began to shake from side to side, pleading *No, No, No* to all those shadows, to the many lifted fingers that suddenly pressed against her eyelids. They must go to the Mountains, she must remember what David Crane had written to her in his book, she must arrange about the Fitch-Beardsley party . . . For it would soon be too late, too dark, too still. Regina Sawyer's book slipped to the floor as

Mrs Colborne turned the other cheek to day, to
night, and rose to light the lamp that Henry's
mother once had given her.

1935

The times

so unsettled are

The times so unsettled are

THE little Austrian girl Mariedel, sitting numbly in her deck-chair (they were passing Ellis Island now and soon would dock), had not cried for twenty years, since she was ten. Then they had brought home the body of her brother, killed on the Italian front, and Mariedel and her mother had wept unceasingly for three days. Her mother had virtually never stopped; meals and sleep and occasional bursts of gayety were merely interludes for Mariedel's mother, for her real life had been given over for almost twenty years to weeping. But Mariedel had never had a tear again—not for her father, horribly wounded toward the end of the War, nor for her second brother dead of some mysterious disease in the trenches; not even for her sweetheart Heinrich who had died two months ago, shot down on the parapets of the Karl Marx Workers' Home which he had always predicted would some day serve as barricades. Heinrich is dead, they said to her very gently—her weeping mother, her crippled father, her friends—Heinrich has been killed, Mariedel, don't you understand, don't you hear us? Yes, said Mariedel over and over again; I understand; Heinrich is dead—and I am going to America; the Amerikaners, Richard and die schöne Mahli, they always asked us to come, but now Heinrich is dead and so I am going alone; excuse me, but I cannot weep. For she had cried herself out in 1914, and no tears were left for Heinrich, whom she loved the most.

What had died really for Mariedel was Vienna, her beloved city. It was not the Vienna her parents had known, of course—all her life she heard them tell sadly of the music now withdrawn from the cafés, of the balls and excursions and military splendor that were gone forever. But that was not Mariedel's Vienna. Mariedel's Wien was a tortured little city with the bravest and saddest and oldest young people in the world. Night after night they sat in the cafés, Mariedel and Heinrich and their contemporaries, and talked of Vienna's future, so bound up with their own—and most of them looked to Socialism as their parents had to God. Five of their number had killed themselves—one apparently for love, the others for vaguer reasons; yet no one was particularly shocked, reasons were not sought for long; they all understood, the rest of them, meeting again to drink coffee in the Herrenhof, that Karl or Mitzi or Hans had been pushed just so much farther than he or she could endure, and that at any moment it might happen to one of the surviving coffee-drinkers. The times are so unsettled, they said, explaining to themselves, and to the childishly emotional Richard and Mahli from Amerika; and nodded much as their elders did, and went on drinking their coffee.

They had gone in, too, their little band, for resolutions to leave Vienna, to strike out for Berlin which they hated, or America which they feared. There things always seemed to go better; one could have a job that might lead somewhere; one might marry and raise children; one might take part in a government less deadlocked than their own—there might perhaps be a future more vital than drinking coffee in the same Café-Haus every night. But none of them ever left. And when the Amerikaners, die schöne Molly (who signed her letters 'Mahli' when she wrote to Mariedel, because that was Mariedel's way of saying it) and Richard, came and were taken into their midst for the brief and lovely month of their honeymoon, and begged them all to come to America and start life over again, they had all of them laughed and shrugged their shoulders and said "vielleicht" and known very well that they would never leave Vienna. Richard and Mahli had laughed too, and said that when they came to celebrate their golden wedding, they would undoubtedly find their old friends in the same Café-Haus, at the same round table in the corner, the men with long white beards—all laughing and promising to come to America and ordering another cup of coffee: with Schlagobers when they could afford it.

Richard and Mahli had been particular friends of Heinrich and Mariedel, even though Heinrich was never gay and always distrustful of strangers, especially tourists, especially Americans, of anyone who was not a Socialist, in short. But they were so warming, Richard and Mahli, so happy together, and so much in love that everybody fell in love with the pair of them—just as they fell in love with everyone they met and the whole little city of Vienna, which they never tired of comparing with their own New York. They talked German so badly, especially Mahli, and so eagerly—it was so funny to hear them addressing each other as "sie" because they could not learn the ramifications of the personal pronoun. And they looked so hopelessly, so ridiculously American—Mahli like a tall American chorus girl in the pink and blue peasant Dierndel which she wore about their rooms, with her boyish hair-cut and her tiny American breasts which scarcely bulged above the apron; and Richard, attempting on Sundays to resemble his Viennese comrades on their Ausflüge, continued to look like a cartoon of an American in his baggy knickers and shoes with saddles, and his horn-rimmed glasses through which his eyes looked so straight and pleasantly clear. The most disillusioned of their little band had fallen in love with these Americans, even Heinrich, bitten with distrust and worse (for Heinrich had stopped believing in God more suddenly than was good for him) —even Heinrich had let the Americans laugh at him and tease him, and sometimes he was almost able to joke back, just like Mariedel.

The Americans had chosen Heinrich and Mariedel for their particular friends because they saw that they too were in love. But Mariedel knew that theirs was a different sort of love; they had been brought up, Mariedel and Heinrich, in too much poverty and change, and their love was more of a refuge than a source of gayety to them, it was a necessity as bitter as the need for bread. They loved each other in the way that sole survivors on a ship must love—and they did not doubt each other, but they doubted themselves and everything about them. For in a shipwreck such as theirs, where brothers turned on brothers and fathers against their sons, how could they be sure even of their love enduring? And Heinrich was so bitter that he even doubted love—in his mind, that is; in his bitter mind; for his heart (which Heinrich believed as poor a word as God) had really never failed her. No, Heinrich, snatched from the University and forced to earn a living for his widowed mother and his sisters, who hated him for supporting them and hated him for being a Socialist, starving and living in wretched, disease-ridden quarters, could not allow himself to be happy in the "unsettled times". He could enjoy nothing that was not whole and lasting, could trust nothing that was not severe.

He had been an ardent Socialist; but when the Socialists took over Vienna, had Heinrich permitted himself to be really happy? to rejoice? Not for long. There were his Socialists, doing all the things he had wanted them to do; they taxed the rich; they housed the poor—but Heinrich was never satisfied: they must tax the rich ever harder, they must house the poor better and faster, they must carry on the fight in the country outside Vienna, or Heinrich predicted their downfall. Mariedel and Heinrich would wander arm in arm through the fine courts of the Workers' Houses, where the poor were quickly learning the cleanliness and healthful habits of the rich, they would look into the community stores lining the streets below, they would visit the charming practical apartments where sunlight and plenty of heat entered every room—and Mariedel had felt happy, happy as she had been in her childhood before the War, when everything was good and gay and plentiful. Look, Heinrich, look at the little children wading in the community fountain—two months ago they would not have known what it is to have a bath. Look, Heinrich, the mothers, so proud of their new homes, their clean children; how well they care for the gardens, they who a short time before saw only a potted flower now and then. Look, Heinrich, at the new building going up over the hill, how fast it rises, the workmen love what they are building, the bricks fly into place as though they loved it too. Everyone, everything, working together, Heinrich, for the poor, at last, for the majority, the real people, look, Heinrich, is it not beautiful and gay? But the lean look never went from Heinrich's eyes, not altogether; yes, there would be pride in them as he saw how swiftly building after building mounted the old streets, how each house was better than the last—but he would run his hand along the parapets above the courtyards where the children played: "Some day these all will be barricades, Mariedel, it cannot be done through peace, we must have more blood-shed, Mariedel, before the

rich will permit such houses to stand for the poor."
His eyes would sweep the dingy sections of old
Vienna, spread below them. "All that must be
wiped out and built over, Mariedel, work must be
done faster, we must be stronger, more inexorable,
like the Communists—too many of our Socialists
are dreamers, and these houses, they are so few,
Mariedel, they are built on dreams instead of
power." He would not take transient happiness; in
the same way he would not really take her love.
Perhaps he was waiting till the world too should be
wiped out and built over, a fit thing to house their
love.

"But you poor silly children," the happy Mahli
had cried, out of her own joy and love; "you are in
love, you live together when you can, why don't
you get married and do it properly?" Mariedel and
Heinrich laughed and shrugged their shoulders;
naturally Mariedel would have married Heinrich
any time he said, but in her heart she knew it was
wrong as long as either of them had a reservation.
She too longed for a whole country that could live
and eat in peace and security, a world which could
wipe out the memory of a brother brought home
dead from the Italian front and causing a little sister to shed the last of her tears. "Oh, Mahli," she
had said often in her faulty English, "the times
here so unsettled are." And Richard and Mahli had
laughed at her English and hugged each other and
hugged Mariedel and Heinrich, and sung over and
over again, "Oh Mahli, the times so unsettled are."

"But you ought to come back with us!" Richard and Mahli had cried together. "We'll find jobs for you somehow, Richard, your father, darrling—you could live right next door to us, we'd find them a place, wouldn't we, darrling—you bet we would, beloved—and then you could be married and live the way we do, the way you ought to. Vienna is lovely for a honeymoon (thank you, Richard darrling) but for young people starting out it's dead from the neck down, isn't it, beloved? Of course it is, darrling. So do come back with us," they cried together, "Mariedel and Heinrich, won't you, couldn't you really now?"

Mariedel had smiled softly across the table to Heinrich. To tell him that if he went to America of course she would come too; to tell him that if he stayed behind in Vienna and spent the rest of his life fighting and being underfed, she would stay with him anyway; to tell him that she loved him. Heinrich had always the same answer to make in his precise, cold, studied English—but smiling, for he loved these Americans and their contentment was infectious: "If Vienna is dead, then Mariedel and I are dead too, Vienna is our city. We will live with it or die with it. If we do not marry, it is because we do not believe in marriage; marriage does not stop a husband from being killed in war or revolution, it does not stop a wife from having too little to feed her children, it does not even ensure love. Yes, we would like to be married, if it would mean that we could live as we believe people should. But, for us in Vienna, we must fight and keep on fighting. . ." And Mariedel, loving him and aching for him, painfully wishing to be loyal and to be thought loyal in the eyes of the Americans, would look across at Mahli and try to make her understand by making her laugh: "With us, it is so different, Mahli —the times so unsettled are."

In the end, of course, everything that Heinrich said was proven right. The Socialists had not lasted, their dreams had been put down by blood-shed, blood-shed in which Heinrich himself, who loved peace and wanted peace more than anything in life, more even perhaps than he wanted Mariedel, in whom he sought it, had voluntarily taken part. And he was right too, it was as well to be still young and to lose one's life-long lover as it would have been to lose a husband; however it was, Mariedel, on hearing her father and her mother and all her friends murmur gently, Mariedel, Heinrich has been killed, can't you understand?—Mariedel could not weep. It was as if she had wept for the death of Heinrich almost twenty years before, when she wept for the death of her brother. The old folks went on weeping when once they got started—Mariedel's mother had never left off again; but Mariedel was still of that younger stock, that had shed their last tears with their first, and Mariedel could not weep, she must go on living somehow. Almost at once the memory of Mahli and Richard had come back to her like a little island of safety in the middle of all the chaos. She would go to America. They would revive that

little month in which she and Heinrich had been
so nearly happy with their American friends; and
in any case, Mariedel would find something to
shock her from this numbness. And so she had written to Mahli, saying that Heinrich was dead; saying
to forgive her for not writing in nearly three years
but that the times so *very* unsettled had been that
there had seemed somehow little use; and that now
Mariedel would like to come along to America—
since the Socialists were finished, and many of her
friends now dead or scattered, and Wien, as Heinrich had prophesied, as the lieber Richard had said
too, was dead as well. Mahli's cablegram had been
prompt, the first thing after Heinrich's death that
meant anything to Mariedel: "Come soon as you
can arrange so sorry about Heinrich visit me as
long as you like love Mahli." She had even remembered to sign her name "Mahli!"

So it was all over with Heinrich and Vienna and
the Socialists, thought Mariedel, sitting numbly in
her steamer-chair when they told her they would be
landing in thirty minutes now. She thought she
would never go back, unless it were to die. And she
remembered that last sight of the crumbling Workers' Home—which would now, her old father said,
be turned over to the rich to do anything with they
liked, while the poor would be thrown out on the
streets again—where Heinrich had met his death.
Broken glass and legs of furniture lay scattered on
the ramparts; there were blood-stains on the parapets which Heinrich had rightfully seen as barri-

cades. She had stood there, as numb as she was now in her steamer-chair, with twenty-years-old tears frozen in her throat. They had all hoped that the sight of the ruined Home where Heinrich had died would make Mariedel weep again; they wanted her to weep, to weep as she had when she was a child, because they thought that was nature's way of healing. Mariedel had wanted to weep too. But she could only stand there, wondering if Heinrich had been right—that the Socialists should have trained an army and fought with the weapons of their enemies, even though their end was peace; and wondering too if Heinrich had been right about that other thing that he always so passionately declared, that there was no God, that the sooner people knew it the better it would be for them.

For Heinrich, of course, with all the unhappy youths of his age, had been a violent atheist. Mariedel herself never went to church, not since they had been to the funeral of her second brother; and she knew that her mother went only to find another place in which to weep and remember, and weep more hotly. No, Mariedel did not believe in any sort of church-God; and yet she never brought herself to curse the thought, as Heinrich had. It was as if Heinrich, expecting things from some King of Kings, turned his disappointment to denial that that King had ever existed. Mariedel expected very little, except perhaps Heinrich's love—and perhaps that was it, for her, perhaps that was why in the inner parts of her brain, or her heart (which Hein-

rich never let her talk about, because it sounded
synonymous with God) she nevertheless held some
sort of belief in something. If it had been Mariedel
who had been killed, she felt now, instead of Heinrich, then Heinrich would have seen in her death
still further proof that there was no God; but Mariedel, not even able to weep for Heinrich, knew
that there had been *something* between them,
which no chemical could account for and no revolution wipe out—something in their hearts which
not even Heinrich's death could end. She had it
still, she had his love for her and her love for him,
and sitting there in her deck-chair, not speaking to
a soul on board, remembering numbly how her city
and her lover and all that they had stood for were
dead, she still could not say there was no God, she
still felt that something went on which outwitted
death and outlasted life . . . And perhaps it was
this that she was really going to America for, to find
it again in the lives of Richard and Mahli and keep
it somehow vicariously lighted in herself through
them.

Now the great city of New York was in her sight
for the first time, and again she thought that there
must be something, *something*, beyond greed and
restlessness, which led people to building up great
towns ιand preparing for so much life. The city
looked to her like a city of closely packed cathedrals,
and she imagined that the streets must run like dark
little aisles at their feet. And this was where Mahli
and Richard belonged, probably they lived back in

the heart of the magnificence somewhere, out of sight of the sea and the dividing rivers, protected forever by these looming towers. Heinrich's words about the barricades came into her mind for a moment, as she stood with her hand on the rail, and she thought perhaps some day all those many windows might be crenelles, the buildings fortresses. Perhaps she was slightly dizzy, as the boat ceased motion. For the buildings swayed a bit before her eyes, and for a moment looked less like cathedrals than like spears, like bayonets, marching in line over the heads of dead and living soldiers . . .

"Mariedel, Mariedel!" Richard and Mahli, her dear Americans, were kissing her one moment and lightly weeping the next—they were unchanged in these seven years, Richard with his mild steady glare through his horn-rimmed spectacles, and Molly, tall and American as ever, with a gentle fringed bang to her eyebrows now, and her bright mouth painted redder than before, and her wonderful chic clothing that made her look like a mannequin. Mariedel stood dazed, allowing herself to be kissed and wept over—how easily happy people wept, either for joy or for sorrow!—and then stood with her hand through Mahli's while Richard did wonderful American things to find and get rid of her luggage. "This is a real reunion," said Richard, coming back, and speaking unconsciously a little louder to Mariedel as he always had, as Americans were always doing, as though foreigners must be slightly deaf, "a real reunion, and we ought to celebrate—in a real American Café-Haus, Mariedel?"

"In the Childs, in the Childs," said Mariedel eagerly remembering, "where you said you would some day show Heinrich and me, the very table where you sat and figured on paper napkins how you could marry and you forgot to leave out for the laundry, do you not remember, Richard and Mahli?"

"But—" began Mahli. They hesitated a bit, those dear Americans of hers, and Mariedel felt she guessed the reason. "No, no, you think I am sad, that it will make me sad, because of Heinrich, but it will make me gay—it is what I have come to America for," she begged them; "I want to see where Richard told Mahli, and Mahli told Richard, and about the laundry, and the lady making jack-flaps in the window—"

"Flap-jacks, you darling," said Mahli, hugging Mariedel again. And Richard said, "A real reunion, Molly, we might as well do it up brown," and Mariedel felt again their delicacy, their shyness with each other in her presence, because they didn't want to hurt her. She must explain it to them, how she had come all the way across an ocean to see them with each other. Richard said again, "What do you say, Molly?" and Molly, taking Mariedel's arm, cried, "Off for the reunion in Vienna!" So then everything was beginning to be all right again, and they found a taxi and Richard said solemnly to the driver, "Childs, on Fifth Avenue, where the best paper

napkins are," and Mariedel sat between them holding both their hands and chattering briskly to put
them at their ease about her and looking out at the
strange streets and feeling thankful to God that she
was here with them.

They came into the big clean restaurant, Mariedel
dancing on her sea-legs, and because it was late
afternoon it was fairly empty, and Richard and
Mahli were able to find the same table in a corner
that they had sat at years ago. "It is a reunion, a
reunion," Richard kept saying, with his steady clear
American eyes on his Molly—and Molly was beginning to look at him, and Mariedel felt happy that
her Americans were remembering things and perfectly happy to be left out for the moment. "Only
I am going to have a cocktail this time," said Mahli
gayly, "just think, Mariedel, in those days one could
not drink cocktails except in practically cellars, and
now, right here in Childs. . ." "I wish you would
take just butter-cakes and coffee," said Mahli's Richard softly, "then it would be a real reunion. . ."
"Reunion, reunion, who's got the reunion," said
Mahli merrily; and Mariedel knew it was an American joke of some kind and laughed in order to be
one of them, and then saw that neither of them was
laughing as Mahli turned to the waitress and repeated firmly, "Yes, a Manhattan, please."

"Tell us, Mariedel," said Richard gently, "about
your poor Heinrich, how terrible it must have been
for you."

"No, no," cried Mariedel, "I do not want to talk

about Heinrich, I want to talk about Richard and Mahli, I want to hear again how you say Darrling to each other, and then there was something Richard used to say—"

"Oh, don't talk about *us*," cried Mahli, tipping her little velvet beret deeper over the fringe, "we want to hear all about Vienna, so terribly sad, awful about those beautiful houses and everything—"

"But I do not want to talk about all that," Mariedel explained to her Americans, "I want, I have come such a long way, just to see two people happy once more. Do you see, I have remembered so much, it gives me only joy to see you two happy, just as in Wien seven years ago . . . Always Darrling this and Darrling that—and that other word, Richard used to say—"

"I think I will have a cocktail too," said Richard suddenly. "How are the Manhattans, M—Beloved?"

"That is it, that is it—Beloved!" cried Mariedel, clapping her hands joyfully. "Ah, now it is like the old days! Heinrich and Mariedel, Richard and Mahli. . ."

"The Manhattans are swell, Darrling," said Mahli quietly. "Here's to you, Beloved," said Richard, lifting his little glass and staring at her through his spectacles. "To you, Mariedel darrling," said Mahli, but her eyes were returning Richard's gaze, and Mariedel could see that the two of them, Richard with his level eyes and Mahli with her red mouth made up for laughing were growing soft and misty again. Because this was where they had come,

Mariedel thought happily (refusing herself to drink anything but coffee), this was where they had come and figured on paper napkins how they could make do, with Richard's little salary. It was not much like the Herrenhof, where Heinrich and Mariedel had come every night and figured on the marble table-tops how they could *not* make do—but it was lovely and clean and gay, and Richard was looking at his Mahli, not *quite* as Heinrich had ever been able to do, but surely as he had wanted to, as he had been meant to, if only so much misfortune, so much un-settledness. . .

But her Americans had put down their glasses and remembered her again. "And what do you think of our skyline, gnädiges Fräulein," Richard was trying to say.

"Ah, do you not remember her, Richard," cried Mariedel, waving his nonsense away, "do you not remember her as she must have looked that night? In a blue sweater, you said—?"

"Yes," said Richard, nodding gravely. "Yes, she was wearing a bright blue sweater and a bright blue skirt, and it was summer and both of us had come out without our hats. She looked rather remarkably beautiful that night, if my memory doesn't play me tricks—"

"Though he couldn't have possibly seen me, Mariedel," said Mahli, "because he was so nervous he kept taking off his glasses and wiping them and doing tricks like making the cream stay on top of the coffee—"

"Whereas she, Mariedel," said Richard, "she was so calm and poised that she spilled most of hers all over that bright blue skirt."

"I did not, you fancy liar, it was you, you admitted it."

"Always a gentleman, Beloved."

"How silly we are, how boring to Mariedel," murmured Mahli.

"No, it is lovely," said Mariedel, "please, you have not come to the part about the laundry yet." She saw how the drinks were making them grow less shy before her, how each time they started speaking to her and ended by addressing one another as though they had no audience. "It was a terribly hot evening," she helped them out, "there was Donner und Blitzen," she prompted Richard. . .

"and she pretended to be frightened"

"and we went on drinking coffee even though it was so hot because we didn't want to ever go home and end that evening"

"we sat through three shifts of waitresses, Beloved"

"I must have journeyed to the Ladies' Room four times"

"and when we'd checked through telephone bills —and were going to save by using candles instead of electricity—"

"then suddenly we discovered about the laundry, Darrling"

"and Beloved do you remember I said something about how I wanted a dependable wife" "and I was simply scared to death Darrling, I almost burst out crying, I thought you were going to tell me I wouldn't do or something."

There was a mild diminuendo in their sweet gay American *Tristan*, and Mariedel saw that they both had tears, these Americans, as volatile as children—even Mahli with her bright red lips not made up for crying at all.

"And there was that frightened little moment after we had both said yes to each other when we thought that we would never again have anything to talk about"

"Oh, it was terrible, Mariedel," said Mahli, wiping her eyes, "we sat there and were afraid to look at one another—"

"and then—" said Richard.

"and then luckily we both started laughing at the same moment and that saved the day, Darrling"

"we confessed to each other, Beloved, how scared to death we were"

"and then we weren't any more, because we knew that—"

"because we thought—"

They were silent for a moment and Mariedel sat poised and expectant.

"We thought we could always laugh together in the bad moments," said Mahli softly.

"We nearly always did, Beloved."

"Only of course there are some things, Darrling."

"Yes, there are some things, Molly."

There was a curious hiatus in their song now,

coming, thought Mariedel, in the wrong place, just as they had been mounting to the allegro—and she sat perfectly still, feeling that perhaps they were going on with it silently, between themselves, in some other, private realms she mustn't enter. They looked at each other for a long time, and then looked away at the same moment. "It wasn't our fault," said Richard, setting down his glass. "No, it wasn't anybody's fault," said Molly, the tears rolling down past her bright red lips and falling into her empty cocktail. "Shall we have another drink, Molly?" said Richard, leaning across the table as though he were asking her something else. "No, I think not," said Molly, lifting her head and beginning to blink away her tears, "I think then nobody would be able to laugh at anything any more." And as Mariedel sat bewildered, out came Molly's purse and from it a little red stick, with which Molly painted on another laughing mouth. "Heavens above," cried Molly gaily, "what awful fools Mariedel must think Americans are—and here we sit and sit with all of the sights ahead of us still, we must think what we would like to do this evening, Mariedel darrling—"

"Shall I—" began Richard, taking out his watch but looking at Molly instead.

"Yes, please, Richard, I think it would be better," said Molly smiling brightly through her new red lips.

"I guess you're right," said Richard, and to Mariedel's surprise he cheerfully whipped his watch back into his pocket again and rose and tossed his paper napkin on the table. "It's been a beautiful reunion, Mariedel, hasn't it?"

"You—you are going?" said Mariedel, feeling suddenly frightened and lonely.

"Why yes, I have to be going," said Richard easily; "but I'll see you again, Mariedel, for sure."

"You have to *go*?" said Mariedel, feeling stupid and shy.

"Yes, he has to go, Mariedel," said Mahli gravely. "Goodbye, Darrling, it was a beautiful reunion."

"Goodbye, Beloved. Goodbye, Mariedel."

"But what is it," cried Mariedel, feeling as she had twenty years ago when her mother had opened the telegram from the War Office, black apprehensive despair and her limbs gone hollow, her heart beating like somebody else's heart—"what is it," she cried again, feeling she was a stupid Austrian girl, that perhaps her life, the death of Heinrich, everything, had unhinged her more than she knew.

"It wasn't anybody's fault, Mariedel," said Molly, putting her too-red lips to the empty cocktail glass. "It wasn't her fault and it wasn't mine," said Richard, standing now and putting his hands on both their shoulders—almost impersonal he was, Mariedel thought, as though he wished to comfort them, to apologize, for something none of them could help. "It was just as you used to say, Mariedel," said Molly, smiling and grave—and Mariedel could hear Heinrich telling her bleakly, through his bitten lips, that there was no God, that marriage did not ensure food, or peace, or even love—"here in America too—the times unsettled are."

Suddenly Mariedel was crying, crying as she had when the first thing went out of her life, for now the last thing was going too—and Molly with her red mouth not made up for crying, was crying too, and comforting her, as Richard walked away.

1934

Mother

to dinner

Mother to dinner

KATHERINE BENJAMIN, who had been Katherine Jastrow for something less than a year, said Goodafternoon to the groceryman and, stooping to the counter, gathered two large and unwieldy packages close to her body, balancing one elbow on her hip so that the hand, crawling to the top, could hold sternly separate the bottle of milk from the package of Best Eggs. The thin, one-eyed errand boy who sprawled on an empty packing-box near the door leaped to his feet and opened it with a flourish and a "hot, isn't it?" And sliding past him, curving her body to make a nest for the projecting bundle, she heard the screen door swing lightly closed behind her, flutter against the wood frame in a series of gently diminishing taps.

Why did one say Goodafternoon instead of Goodbye to tradesmen and teachers, she wondered, following her packages as they bobbed evenly down the street before her, recalling (as she adjusted her gait to her burden) countless times when she had waited, in middies and broad sailor hats, for her mother's comforting "Good*morning*, Mr Schmidt," and Mr Schmidt's answering "*Good*morning, Mrs Benjamin, *good*morning I'm sure." And now Katherine, no longer in middies or accompanied by her mother but modestly wearing a ring on her left hand, heard herself kindly bidding Mr Papenmeyer Goodafternoon, and feeling, as she said it, very close to her mother, feeling almost, as she nodded firmly to him, that she was her mother. (Gerald predicted with scorn that it would not be long before Katherine would speak of Mr Papenmeyer as "my Mr Papenmeyer" and he suspected that she would even add, in time, "he never disappoints"; but she was not to suppose, he said, that he would glance benignly over his *Saturday Evening Post* as her father did, and listen.)

Katherine hugged her packages like babies; in them lay, wrapped in glossy wax paper, in brown paper bags, in patent boxes, the dinner to which Katherine's mother and father were coming as guests . . . The dinner over which Katherine would frown at Gerald politely insulting Mrs Benjamin; over which Mr Benjamin would cough and insist on the worst cuts of everything . . . She hoped nervously that Gerald would not be insolent and argumentative, that her mother would not be stupid. . . . She must protect them both. . . And she began to dread the strangeness which always oppressed her on beholding her mother in a house which was her home and not her mother's. . . . Ridiculous, she said brightly, I'm not going to let *that* happen again . . .

The spire of the church on the corner raised itself in the form of a huge salt-shaker against the mild, colorless sky. The sun, a blurred yellow lamp, glimmered palely behind veils of soiled cloud; it might rain, for the air was sodden, the leaves on the tree before the church hovered on the air with a peculiar waiting indifference, like dead fish turned over on their backs and floating in still water.

And for years to come she, "Mrs Gerald Jastrow," would walk, heavily laden with her thoughts and her packages, in Fall, in Winter, and in Spring, from Mr Papenmeyer's meat-and-grocery store through these same streets, past the church with its salt-shaker spire, past the row of low brick houses, past the tall india-rubber apartment with the liveried doorman shuffling his feet under the awning, stretched like a hollow wrinkled caterpillar to the curb, to her own home, which she shared with Gerald, of whom she had never heard two years before . . .

Katherine's fingers, tapping the sagging bundles, reviewed their contents. Meat—Mr Papenmeyer's recommended cut for four—bread, milk, corn, tomatoes—without her asking, the clerk had passionately assured her they were firm—two large packages it amounted to, one small slippery one under her elbow, and her purse. By a minute flexing of her left hand she could feel the key tucked neatly in her glove to save her trouble when she reached her door. An absurd ritual, that, said Gerald; one which in the sum total could not save her much trouble. You've picked up all these damn habits, he said, from your mother: they're a waste of time, they take more time to remember than simply to leave out; be careful, Katherine, before you know it you will be keeping a platinum-framed market-list. But these little rituals made doing the things fun, Katherine argued; when she remembered, at the grocer's before picking up her packages, to tuck the key in her glove, a horde of vague recollections, almost recollections of recollections, unravelled pleasantly in her mind. They gave meaning to what would otherwise be just marketing; they formed a link not only with yesterday and tomorrow, but with other women squinting at scales and selecting dinners for strange men to whom they found themselves married; with, if you like, her mother, who had been doing these things every day for thirty years. You may say pooh Gerald, she said, but there are many things which you, who are after all a man, cannot be expected to know; why two years ago you didn't even know *me* . . .

Were the flat faces she had left haggling over green peas and punching cantaloupes aware of the waiting uncertainties, the uprooting, the transplanting, the bleeding, involved in their calmly leaving their homes to go to live with strangers? Strangers—husbands—Gerald A. Jastrow—I met a boy named Gerald A. Jastrow at a party, he asked to take me home—I am sorry, I am seeing a boy named Gerald Jastrow, he has a cowlick which trembles when he argues—but mother I am seeing Gerald tonight—Gerald says, Gerald thinks—I am going to be married—his name? (*whose* name?—oh, the Stranger's)—his name is Jastrow, Gerald Jastrow

—I've been married for eleven months—my husband's name is Gerald Jastrow, no I don't know him, he's a Stranger to me, but I put away his male-smelling underwear. . . . Katherine reached the sidewalk just in time to avoid a cab which sped down the street in front of her house.

She smiled brightly at the elevator man, an expert, busy, kindly smile; she felt again like her mother. "Wouldn't be surprised if a storm blew up," Albert said to her shrewdly, resting his hand in a friendly way on the lever. (A storm, she didn't want a storm, Katherine thought, suddenly frightened; Gerald might say what he liked about the risk of motoring being greater than that of flying, and the chance of being murdered in sleep greater than that of being struck by lightning: she *wouldn't* fly, and she cowered before thunder and lightning.) "Oh do you think so?" said Mrs Gerald Jastrow, and she looked in awe at the elevator man, as if it was all in his hands whether a storm came or not. "Oh I hope not," she pleaded. The elevator stopped on a level with her floor, her door was before her, familiar, with its arty streaks, its brass knob and keyhole, the number 21 in black painted letters. Albert, slamming the door of his cage, determined to go the whole hog. "Well I wouldn't be surprised," he said, and dropped suddenly out of sight.

Katherine could not bear to drop a single one of her burdens, now that she had come so far; she made a series of supreme efforts, balancing, juggling, squirming, forcing her key out of her glove with fractional, inch-worm motions, still carefully separating the bottle of milk from the package of Best Eggs, evoking a new muscle to keep the small package from slipping.

And then she was in, in her own house, with the door shut behind her, and the yellow curtains dancing on the window panes, the stove standing, homely and patient, in the small kitchen, the chairs sitting in friendly fashion, as if themselves guests at a tea-party, just as she had left them . . .

Suddenly she was overcome by a swift engulfing depression. She stood at the door of the yellow room and was unable to put down the packages in her arms. The air in the room stood hot and heavy, waiting, like Albert, with melancholy assurance, for storm; the curtains flapped treacherously.

What nonsense, she said crisply, amazingly comforted by a slant of faint sunlight which quivered through the gloom. Look, she said, it is my own house . . . Reassured, she dropped her packages on the kitchen table. But someone should be there to greet her, she felt, to rise from one of those friendly chairs and say to her: What did you buy? How was Mr Papenmeyer the butcher? Was the one-eyed errand boy there today? Come in, take off your hat and gloves, I am glad you are home . . . A year ago she would have stood at the door and shouted *Moth-er,* where *are* you? And if Mrs Benjamin had not come in haste at her call, a white-aproned German maid (Mrs Benjamin chaperoned

their love-affairs so successfully that they generally
stayed with her for years, like obedient nuns) would
have come and said, Oh Miss Katy, your mother
said to tell you she went over to your Aunt Sarah,
your uncle's not feeling just right.

But she would call *up* her mother, she thought
gleefully, running to the telephone: He*llo*, mother,
what do you think I bought for supper? The
butcher said . . . Do you think there will be a
storm, mother? . . . As she lifted the receiver from
its hook she thought she heard faint steps behind
her; Gerald, she thought in a flash, and slid the receiver back to its place. Of course it wasn't Gerald,
at four o'clock in the afternoon, of course it wasn't
anybody; but suppose he had come upon her tele-
phoning her mother: she could hear him say, as he
had said last Sunday, catching her at the telephone
(and of course one thought of one's mother on a
long Sunday), Oh for God's sake, Katherine, like a
two-year-old baby you are always running home to
mother . . . Cut off from her mother. Yet Gerald
was right, she mustn't, she mustn't.

Loneliness surrounded Katherine like a high
black fence. Then why not call up Gerald, why not
rush to the telephone and call Gerald at his office
(where she could never visualize him); if only she
could call him up and say to him: I have just come
home to our house. It is pleasant and cool, the curtains are still yellow. I shall take off my dress and
read. Then I shall cook dinner, for you, for me, for
my father and mother—you haven't forgotten they

are coming? you'll come early?—*Gerald, what are you doing?* But she knew his firm "Jastrow speaking," and she could guess, if she dared to go beyond it, at his business-like: "What do you *want, dear?*" Well, what *did* she want, she wondered impatiently, and strained to discover whether that was thunder or furniture moving.

Probably Gerald was right, she thought wearily —for he was so often "right" in a logical, meaningless way—that thinking about every small thing, attaching significances to every moment, wishing to communicate every small thought, was, besides being sentimental, "an imbecilic waste of time." Gerald railed against sentimentality, and, charmingly, disarmingly, gave way to it at moments. When the moment passed Gerald shed it like a wet bathing suit, and emerged cool and casual, forgetful and untouched. But with her mother, these moments grew into comfortable hours, never forgotten, linking one with another, remaining always, a steady undercurrent, ready to rise and fill them at the lightest touch.

And sliding the bread into the shining modern breadbox she felt a strong nostalgia for the worn-out tin that had stood for years on her mother's shelf. This cold affair of shelves and sliding doors, glittering knobs and antiseptic lettering suggested too much newness, too little use and familiarity; her mother's loomed in contrast, a symbol of security, almost a refuge from storm. And yet Mrs Benjamin, with the vision of that old, battered, loyal thing in the back of her mind, had come with Katherine graciously, gayly even, to buy this tawdry substitute. (My little girl, she had said to the clerk, smiling ironically at him and drawing him into her sympathy, would like that Modern Breadbox. It was as if she had said, My little girl has tired of her old mother, she wants the latest thing in young men, one that can scientifically explain away the fear of lightning.) Feeling warmly bound to her mother, she caught herself opening and slamming the little door a second, unnecessary time, an old nervous habit of her mother's. For a moment she felt purified, intensely loyal, as if by this gesture she had renounced the new for the old. She walked from the kitchen with her mother's tired, elastic step, the step of a stout woman who has shopped all day, whose weary body will neither submit to rest nor ignore the stern orders of fashion. It was a step singularly unsuited to Katherine's slimness, but it was comfortable now, familiar; she slid gratefully into it, like one falling into a cushioned rocker which is too large for the body but provides, nevertheless, a warm and comfortable harbor. And so she bent her body back from the waist and became her mother, balancing her stout body, carrying the heaviest part bravely before her. (Your mother navigates like a boat, Gerald had said to her once. Katherine, ruefully succumbing to the justice of the description, had come starkly awake on the edge of falling asleep that night, and cried bitterly, not because Gerald, whom she hated for sleeping soundly beside her, had said it, but because she had laughed.)

Oh of course Gerald was "right," she told herself. And yet, this coming home eagerly, her arms aching with pleasant weights, delighting in facing those yellow curtains again, with no one to greet her, and unable to telephone because what she had to say to her husband was irrelevant—her mother wouldn't like it, she felt. But between two people who lived together, why should anything be irrelevant? nothing she could ever say, she knew, would be irrelevant to her mother: how eagerly Mrs Benjamin had awaited reports of adventures no more important than a shopping expedition, a subway jam, a lunch engagement. (Oh but that had been stupid, stupid—inadequate. You told your mother insignificant things because you knew she wouldn't understand the important ones. Gerald's words: but true, true.) But Gerald himself had so *little* concern for the small things she did all day that she refrained from telling him anecdotes which she passionately feared might bore him, but which, nevertheless, she collected like bouquets of precious flowers to lay before him if she dared. Looking about the empty room, Gerald's desk standing solidly in one corner reproved her; she became irritated that her mind flew so often to thoughts of her mother. . . .

Like a human shuttle she wove her way between these two, between Gerald and her mother, the two opposites who supported her web. (Why couldn't they both leave her alone?) When she was with her mother she could not rest, for she thought continually of the beacon of Gerald's intelligence, which must be protected from her mother's sullying incomprehension. And when she was with Gerald her heart ached for her deserted mother, she longed for her large enveloping sympathy in which to hide away from Gerald's too-clear gaze. From sheer hopelessness and irritation, tears filled her eyes. . . .

She was glad to escape from the kitchen, for she had begun to hate Mr Papenmeyer's excellent foods, which would merge artfully and serve as the camouflage of a family battle. As long as the dinner lasted, she knew the conversation could be kept meager and on a safely mediocre level. But Katherine, sitting between her mother and father, and eyeing her husband with apprehension, would know that around her own table, consuming food she herself had prepared, a victim would be fattened for slaughter, a victor strengthened for battle. And whoever won, Katherine lost . . . Oh come, she told herself, exasperated, this isn't the Last Supper . . .

But that wasn't furniture moving, she told herself grimly, crouching on the window-sill and regarding the street which was lying quietly in its place before her house—not twice, she said, that's Albert's thunder. It rumbled from a great distance, as though it were in hiding.

Certainly, she thought, her mind returning, like a dog worrying a bone, she lived with Gerald on a

higher plane—if her misery was sometimes more
acute, her pleasure, in proportion, was more poign-
ant. While they had felt nothing deeply, Katherine and her mother, as they had built up, over tea-
tables, simple patterns of thought, simplified ways
of looking at things. What if Katherine had had to
stoop her mind so that they might stay together? at
least they could talk, at least they kept each other
company. (Gerald said their talk was no more than
gossip; he said that Katherine and her mother had
shut themselves up in a hot-house, talking and comforting each other for griefs that could never come
to them while they remained in their lethargic half-
life.) But in a world like this, thought Katherine,
where thunder-storms can creep on one ruthlessly,
why shouldn't two people who love each other hide
away and give one another comfort?

Thunder rumbled more constantly now. Katherine, suspicious of it, in spite of its distance, detected in its muffled rolling a growing concentra-
tion, as if it were slowly gathering its strength, as
if it were winding itself up for a tremendous spring.
Should she telephone Gerald?—no.

The thought of Gerald frightened her. He led
such a curious existence apart from her every day
from nine till six. Katherine and her mother had
always known exactly what the other was doing, at
almost every hour in the day. It was a comfort to
stop suddenly, look at one's watch, and think
"Mother's at the dentist's now" or "I should think
mother would be on the way home now." But there

were times when Gerald was in the room with her, sitting beside her, lying beside her in bed, when she didn't know exactly where he was. . . .

Gerald said—and with some justice, she admitted to herself—that she and her mother had lived like two spoiled wives in a harem kept by a simple old gentleman who demanded nothing of them beyond their presence and the privilege of supporting them. But because of his docility one could not take seriously a possible injustice to him. Beside his work downtown, Mr Benjamin mailed their letters, called for their purchases, or did any of the little errands which they had spent the day in pleasantly avoiding. If he entered the room where Katherine and her mother were talking, it had seemed quite natural for Mrs Benjamin to say, "Dear, we are talking"; it seemed natural because of the peaceful expression with which Mr Benjamin picked up his *Saturday Evening Post* on the way out of the room. All Katherine's uncles were disposed of in the same way by her aunts.

Gerald referred to the Benjamin men as "poor devils," as "emasculated boobs". You resent me, he said to Katherine, because you have a preconceived idea of the rôle to which all husbands are relegated by their wives; you'd like to laugh me out of any important existence. (Indeed, it was only at moments when he was away and when she was performing, in his absence, some intimate service for him, that she could look upon Gerald as her mother looked upon her father; with ease, with possession, with a maternal tolerance touched by affectionate irony. Here were things of which she could be certain: that he rolled his underwear into a ball and dropped it on the floor, that he left his shoes to lie where they fell, that he draped yesterday's tie around the back of a chair. But she could never achieve this intimacy in his presence: when Gerald was with her, when she *thought* about Gerald, it faded; there was more strangeness.) Gerald again! She was aware of a wish to sink Gerald into the bottom of her mind: she was too much aware of him; when she read, when she visited, when she noticed things, it was always with the desire to report back to Gerald: nothing was complete until Gerald had been told.

She and her mother had discussed and reported everything. But she could no longer be alone with her mother, for it seemed as though Gerald sat in taunting effigy between them, forcing Katherine for her mother's sake to deprecate him, for his sake to protect him, from obscurity, from misrepresentation, from neglect . . .

His presence, even now, while she was alone, sat heavily, reproachfully, in the empty rooms, forbidding her to call him up, forbidding her to recall comfortably past days she had spent with her mother. This was not living, Gerald said, to spend one's hours in introspective analysis, to brood over the past. Katherine's flights he called "a worthless luxury, like the visits of the rich to Palm Beach or

Paris." But it was living, Katherine knew unhappily; she was living most acutely.

The room darkened suddenly. Something of the
tension which would be upon her later, as it always
was when her mother and Gerald were in the same
room, came upon her now, as she sat straining for
the sound of thunder, watching shades of gloom
silently lay themselves in the hot room. Katherine
held her breath waiting for thunder, for rain, anything. Voices of children floated reassuringly up
from the street, and in a moment the sunlight reap-
peared, tentative, tempting one to believe in it for
all its faintness. The thunder sounded like the chop-
ping of wood in a far-off field. Katherine longed for
her mother. She wished she were not so near the
heart of the storm.

She hated herself for thinking of her mother. But
not to think of her demanded a complete uprooting, demanded a final shoving off from a safe dock
into unknown waters. Besides, she felt guilty toward her mother, she brooded over her as one does
over a victim, pitying him, resenting him and utterly unable to forget him.

For against her mother Katherine felt that she
had committed a crime. She had abandoned that
elderly lady for a young man who, from her mother's
point of view, had been merely one of several who
had taken her to dances, to dinner, who had kissed
her in the parlor, with whom finally, inexplicably,
she had come to have more dates than with any

other. She had abandoned her mother, left her sitting at home with no more evening gowns to "take in", no one to sit up for, no young men to laugh about in the bathroom at four o'clock in the morning when Katherine came home. She had left her to sit opposite an old man at dinner every evening, she had imposed upon her the tragedy of being a guest in her own daughter's house; she had reduced her to a stranger.

But a little bit her mother had the advantage. She had seen Gerald, after all, in the absurd rig of tuxedo and stiff shirt, calling upon her daughter with flowers, with books, leaping to his feet when she (Mrs Benjamin) entered the room. She had watched Gerald for a year politely talking parlor politics with Katherine's father, posturing ridiculously when he held Katherine's coat, becoming perforce friendly with the elevator boys in the Benjamin apartment, slinking shamefacedly before a doorman who had seen him too often. Nothing, Katherine reflected, could be more unreal, more unconvincing, than a young man in the act of courting. She could never forgive Gerald for having let her mother observe him in that rôle. (Equally she could never forgive her mother, blameless as she was, for having seen him.) Her mother could never take seriously, surely, a marriage which had grown from love-making in taxi-cabs which had been reported to her with amusement by Katherine, brushing her teeth in the bathroom. She had not shared with her mother the tortuous transition which had left her no longer an amused observer, but a help-less, suffering participant. All the indication Mrs Benjamin had had of Katherine's growing need of Gerald was a burst of hysteria and a state of nervous irritability which had succeeded the usual calm of Katherine's disposition—before suddenly one eve-ning, preparing her charity report in a black lace dress, she was confronted by two embarrassed young people who declared their ridiculous intention to marry.

This, Katherine felt, she should have spared her mother. She should not have caused her, so heart-breakingly, to drop her charity report on the marble table and to look suddenly at her daughter with reproachful eyes, saying, half-humorously, What, daughter, tired of your old mother already?

She had left her parents for no reason, they had given her no cause to leave them, she had left them for no better reason than that when Gerald said to her that he would never again ask her to marry him, she had been seized with panic lest he meant it.

Gerald, who two years before had not existed. Whereas her father and mother had fed her por-ridge, given her blackboards, measured her growth against a door, for a long period of twenty years during which Gerald had never heard of her. She was unsafe, she cried internally. She was living with a stranger in a strange land where storms evolved closely about one. She was living with a stranger who had no knowledge of the first twenty years of her life, the major portion of her life. She was living in a strange land where her childhood had no existence. It was unreal, it was unsafe, it was terrifying. Gerald liked to hear her tell stories of her childhood; but it was as if, when she told him little things she remembered, she and he were together contemplating the childhood of a stranger. She held tightly to the arms of her chair, but the slippery wood was repelling. Suddenly everything was reduced to an absurdity. It was, to Gerald, as though she had not begun to exist until he had noticed her two years before, at a party, and asked to take her home; but suppose she had not come to the party—she had come only out of boredom; or suppose, to make it more ridiculous, she had not worn the particular blue dress which had caught Gerald's eye? and he hadn't asked to take her home? Their life together seemed no more than the result of a series of insignificant accidents. Could it be real? Could she share the rest of her life with a stranger whose eye had casually fallen on a blue dress? With someone who had known her for only two years out of her twenty-two?

Katherine felt herself to be struggling somewhere in the middle, between two harbors, unable to decide whether to swim backward or forward, tempted almost to close her eyes and quietly drown where she was. Shuttle, shuttle, she murmured to herself, miserably, exasperated at her weakness, her helplessness.

Smoking in the yellow room, she waited with

unhappy certainty for Albert's storm which would surely come now. The air was oppressive, sullenly pregnant. It was as if an evil thing crouched in the room, waiting for birth. Dark was gathering in shades, permitting still a faint yellowish gloom. Wind was dead. Katherine, fearing and hating the coming storm, nevertheless feared and hated the moments of waiting even more. A clock on the mantel slowly ticked off the moments she would have to wait; it was in league with the coming storm. Her body was chill in the midst of heat.

She was weary already with the nervous effort she would make to bring Gerald and her mother close to each other, with her own struggle to remain equally close to both of them, simultaneous with her desperate attempt to conceal from each the affection she felt for the other. Gerald and her mother sitting and eating in this room, which now was the home of the storm, would be a cat and mouse, quietly stalking each other under cover. (Was this true? or did their struggle for supremacy take place merely in her own mind? Because she must know, she must know.) Katherine would twist herself this way and that to keep the evening characterless and blessedly dull, rather than immerse them all in the horror of an argument, in which their superficial sides would represent symbolically their eternal, fundamental resentment. Katherine must take no sides, Katherine must flit nervously from one side to the other, breaching gaps with hysterical giggles, throwing herself into outbursts of hysterical affection, making a clown of herself in order to distract these two who fought silently for her. She was loathsome to herself.

Her mind struggled with a remote memory. Something—perhaps the slumbering quality of the air which sheltered the coming storm so that its pent-up evil would suddenly roll forth and smother the world—reminded her of a thing which seemed to have happened when she was a child. Frowning, she gazed into herself to recall. And it came back to her. She had cried one day for her mother and they had told her that Mrs Benjamin had gone to Atlantic City for two days and that this young lady would take care of Katherine while her mother was away. Katherine kicked and screamed, but Miss Anna proved so entertaining—she showed her how to make a whole family of paper dolls live through a day's work and play—that she forgot her mother and was surprised to hear the next day that she would be home in an hour. Suddenly she hated Miss Anna, and when Mrs Benjamin came home she found her daughter crying angrily, Miss Anna bewildered, murmuring, But she seemed so happy, she seemed perfectly happy. . . I was not happy for a minute, Katherine screamed, I was waiting the whole time for my mother to come back.

Enraged with herself, she wondered whether she retained somewhere the idea that because her life had begun with her mother, it would end with her, whether some childish part of her could not accept their parting as final and looked upon her life with

Gerald as no more than an interlude. Oh Gerald, Gerald, she sobbed, I am worse than unfaithful to you . . . I hate my mother, she is a venomous old woman who tries to keep me from you. . . . The injustice to her mother overwhelmed her. She hated herself. She felt like the child of divorced parents, driven from one to the other and unable with either to make a home.

I have been married during every month except June, she thought, lifting her head and quietly looking, as if to remember, about the room. She was comforted by Gerald's desk, which had been with her during eleven months. Thunder, blasting the earth in a distant place, filled the room. She had been married for eleven months and had never told her mother anything but housekeeping troubles. Why? A second roll of thunder sounded.

She was surrounded, she could not escape. She was suspended, she could take refuge with neither Gerald nor her mother, she was caught fairly by the thunder . . .

Deception had begun with her engagement. One had to keep one's eyes constantly glowing, however terrifiedly they looked at the approaching cliff, one's words constantly gay and effervescent, lest one's mother look searchingly at the prospective bride and say, But are you sure, Darling, absolutely *sure?* Of course one was not sure. One was suspended, even as now, with thunders rolling in from all sides. (I ought to start the dinner, I ought to start the dinner: I *can't*, I can't.)

During a wedding trip one was awakened to innumerable things, most of them delightful, all of them terrifying. A longing had filled Katherine intermittently to be back from this trip of surprises: she pictured herself talking to her mother all day for many days, sharing with her, not details, but the contemplation, of intimacies. It seemed to her the most delicious part of the trip, that she would return and talk about it to her mother. Gerald's jealous allusions to her mother she had accepted with a tolerant smile; his analyses—for it was then that he had violently expounded his harem theory —meant nothing to her, they seemed to have no connection with reality. "Dearest mother," she had written, "all the things I have to tell you! I can hardly wait to see you . . . So many things have happened. And of course, Gerald being a man . . ." (Was that lightning, or was it the mere lifting of the curtain by the wind? The dinner, the dinner was waiting to be cooked: I won't *touch* it.)

The awful farce at the station, where Mr and Mrs Benjamin had come to meet them, came to her vividly now. Mr Benjamin, having screwed his courage to the point of making Katherine remember his presence long enough to kiss him, retiring to help Gerald, competently wasting time with the luggage in the background, mother and daughter swaying in a series of embraces—Katherine was suddenly lost, locked, imprisoned, in the body of a

stout, fashionable stranger. Why doesn't she look
at me? she thought, all she wants is to hold me, to
squeeze me, to choke me to death, it never occurs
to her to look in my face. Sweeping her daughter
to one side, Mrs Benjamin sprang forth to smother
Gerald. She had no right to, cried Katherine wildly
to herself, as she turned from her father's vague
embrace, and all the things which Gerald had said
of her mother came back to her and they seemed
true. And at the same time she felt passionately that
Mrs Benjamin must not expose herself to Gerald's
unsympathetic eye; horrible embarrassment arose
in her, when, thank God, she saw that Mrs Benjamin in her eagerness had missed her aim; her kiss
floated on past Gerald's clean indifferent cheek—
he at least was unsullied, and at the same time her
mother was protected from nakedness. Mrs Benjamin, discarding Gerald, threw her arms around
Katherine once more, with force and meaning, and
kissed her in great wet gulps. "Katherine, Katherine," she sobbed, rocking her great body from side
to side, "I've got you again, darling. Let's leave all
these men and go off together, darling." Katherine
felt fastidious, she drew her body back delicately
from the impact of her mother's.

Mrs Benjamin shook off the two men, she carried
Katherine off to a tea-room—their old favorite tea-
room—for lunch, a confidential lunch it was supposed to be, but Katherine had grown to hate
tea-rooms, a month with Gerald had taught her to
hate shrimp salad. . . Mrs Benjamin, suddenly

squeezing her hand under the candle-lit table, looked into her eyes, her own eyes fatuous, confident, worried and questioning, "Katherine, darling Katherine, now tell me the 'many things' you wrote about." Katherine, looking into her mother's avid eyes, knew that she could never tell her anything again.

How horribly she must have hurt her, thought Katherine, gravely hurt herself at the recollection. In bed beside Gerald that night she had lain, trying to make the night go faster, so that she might see her mother and change what she had done. She thought of her mother lying sleepless, even as she was, beside a sleeping husband, thinking, bitterly thinking, of the thing that had happened between them. But Katherine could never undo the thing that was between them, for it was Gerald who stood between her mother and herself, just as her mother stood between herself and Gerald.

Well, *was* Albert's storm coming or wasn't it, she thought impatiently, and beat out her cigarette on the window-sill, dropped the dead stub and watched it hurtle past awnings and window-boxes and land haphazardly in the gutter. (And what about the dinner?)

A clap of thunder brought her trembling to her feet. It had traveled with treacherous silence from a great distance to burst like a shell in her ear. And now lightning quivered across the pewter sky in a blinding streak. Katherine, trembling, holding to the mantel, felt all the elements of storm gathering closely about her. The intense heat and stillness in the room vibrated with suppressed force. She had a sense of something evil, something unhealthy, waiting beneath the table to be born. The room was alive, awake, crouching before the storm, waiting in every sense for its approach.

She laughed aloud, nervously, when the thunder sounded next, meek and far-off; it rumbled for a few seconds, then it rolled toward her with increasing force until something cut it off sharply in the height of its passion. The storm was playing with her; it was here, but it played at hiding, it retreated and advanced so that she could never be sure of it.

What was she to do, what was she to do? Should she, could she telephone?—*no*.

Thunder shook the house. Malicious streaks of lightning drew themselves across the sky, lighting up the gloom until the day shone for a second like steel. Suddenly night came. Winds came alive and tore drunkenly down the street. Another long reverberating crash of thunder, incredibly near and ear-splitting. There was a moment of suspension, while only the wind moved. And then the sky retched and large cold drops of rain like stones pelted the windowpanes . . .

Panic seized Katherine. She rushed to the window to escape. She was afraid of the room. It rocked with unhappy speculation. She stood at the window facing in, and saw how the storm was fed from within her room. The lightning lit it like quick fire, the thunder sounded in it long after it had died outside.

The thunder bounced about the room, striking at corners, rolling over furniture, shaking the walls, groveling derisively at her feet.

It seemed to her that before the next clap of thunder she must have reached a decision or she would die. But what decision, she cried, striking her fist against the window? What decision? about what? The problem was obscure. (She imagined her mother struck by lightning, her stout body collapsing with dignity under a tree, she heard herself telling Gerald with triumph as an overtone to her grief, My mother is dead, I have only you now.) And if the problem was obscure, how much more obscure the solution. (She imagined Gerald struck by lightning, a look of hurt surprise in his eyes as he fell beneath a tree, murmuring something about scientific chance, she heard herself telling her mother, strange relief mingling with her sorrow, Gerald is gone, mother, I shall have to come back to you.) And the next thunder rolled down a hill, louder and louder, faster and nearer, and fell to the bottom, bursting into cannon balls, exploding with insane crashes, and in a thousand voices splitting the earth in its center. Katherine burst into passionate tears.

Now everything was the storm. The storm, which had circled about the room, wished for closer nucleus, and entered her body. The lightning pierced

her stomach, the thunder shook her limbs, and retreated, growling, to its home in her bowels. There
was no escape for her; she was no longer imprisoned
in the storm: the storm was imprisoned in her.

She stood in a shaking lethargy, she had no will,
no feeling. She was frozen; she was a shell in which
storm raged without her will. All the world had
entered the room . . .

It came to her slowly that there was a new sound
in the air, a sharp metallic ring that repeated itself
at intervals. She had no idea how long she might
have been hearing it in the back of her head before
she took notice of it. Now it rang again, sharply,
there seemed to be fright in it, or anger, she could
not tell which. On stiff legs she ran down the hall
toward the door, by reflex knowing that it was the
doorbell which had sounded. But with her hand on
the knob something held her back. She could not
force herself to turn the knob, to move her hand,
even to call out, Wait, wait . . .

Was it her mother, or was it Gerald? Which, in
the midst of storm, did she want it to be? It seemed
to her that she could not open the door until she
knew. A great ball of thunder followed her out of
the room she had left, hurtled down the hall and
broke beside her, and in the midst of it the terrified
bell rang repeatedly, in small staccato notes, shrill-
ing through the depth of the thunder, prodding . . .

She did not know. She knew only, as she closed

her eyes and slowly turned the handle of the door, and drew it in toward herself, that she wished that one of them, Gerald or her mother, were dead.

1929

Relax is all

Relax is all

SHE rode Comanche badly, sitting him with no sense of ease or mastership, she let him jog her this way or that as he wanted, and when he turned his captious neck homeward, because if he couldn't keep up with the others he would rather get back and brood by himself in the corral, she let him have his head for several yards before she could succeed in guiding him back to the narrow, sandy path that edged the lake. He despised her anyway because of the way her citified old-maid bottom bounced up and down on his back, sliding her weight first to this side, then to that, of the saddle. But chiefly he despised her because she rode him so far behind the others; he wanted to be up in front with his kind, he wanted to spatter them with sand when he bounded suddenly ahead, he even wanted sand and water splashed in his own rheumy eyes when he fell behind; he wanted to nose his big head between Piute's slim, mustang rear and the great, powerful hind quarters of Coyote, he wanted to dash playfully beyond Chiquita who was ridden by Bud, and then when Chiquit', who was an old lead horse and could bear no more than her cowboy rider to be anywhere but in the lead, spurted leaping and panting past him he wanted to flick her good-naturedly with his tail, side-step in a cute way he had and elbow Chiquita and Bud gently into the water. But not with bony, down-east, old-maid gal on his back, who held him in (through fear, God knows: she would have given up her pōsition in New York to follow them once, be one of them on their mad gallops down the beach) while the others dashed off the minute their hoofs met the hard sand.

Ethel Blake knew that she enjoyed no respect from her horse, although she had learned to saddle him herself and did so tenderly, being careful not to fasten the cinch too tight round his great belly, and although God knew she more than obeyed Bud's injunction never to run a horse till he dropped. But when she entered the corral she imagined Comanche's face fell, that he eyed her gloomily and shied away as though hoping against hope that she would change her mind about catching him. In the beginning, before his spirit was broken and before he had grown ashamed to look his fellows in the face, he had fought her; once he had set the bit and run with her clinging to the pommel, her feet clasping his belly, the stirrups flying wild, while he dashed over rocks and leaped sage until she was frightened nearly to death. A better rider, Bud had said afterward, would probably have fallen. But Miss Blake—you ride so stiff, can't you relax more, he kept saying (his blue eyes wandering to Mrs Montague who sat her horse like the upper part of a centaur) can't you just take it easy; relax is all, he said.

Relax! Back east in New York Miss Blake had a desk, she had an office; there was Winter, and Spring, Summer, then Fall; and in all those seasons except just for two months of the Summer Miss Blake could be found behind her desk and in her office— and what would happen if she relaxed? Relax, the cowboy said (who despised her as much as her horse did). Imagine Ethel Blake "relaxing". Why, her name would waltz off the printed letterheads, her files would tip over and spill out their carefully catalogued contents, mixing the cases which needed immediate attention with the cases she had marked with her own red pencil "Closed—E. B." Imagine Dr Stratton coming for the Monday afternoon seminar held in her office and finding *Miss Blake* relaxing!

But the very thought of Dr Stratton (after a decade of sitting side by side and nodding intellectually behind their glasses at lectures on neuroses, on conditioned reflexes, on sublimation, she was sure they had come to look alike)—the very thought of Stratton, and the Decade Report she was supposed to be working on while curing her asthma, filled her with disgust. She had shoved it all back in her trunk the second night on the ranch and she would have blushed with shame if any of the others had stumbled upon it. She wished she could have laid away her glasses on top of the pile of folders. But she couldn't see to the lake without them.

The others of course were riding a quarter mile's run ahead of her, along the curve of the beach. It was a short distance, especially when viewed with blinking eyes across the blazing Nevada sand, which danced a little with heat waves in the air. But it was an insurmountable distance to Miss Blake, who had shut away her real life in a trunk, who could read Proust in French and had been wishing all Summer that she couldn't, who would now gladly have sold her diplomas and her printed articles and her scholastic reputation to catch up just once with the others, to hear Bud say once, Hot diggity, gal! how you can ride! to have Comanche turn round and nip her affectionately on the toe of her boot.

The thing was, she thought, she had made of her horse a symbol, a something to conquer. If she could not control a horse then how on earth was she to control that more shapeless thing, her life? Yes, she had published her modest articles on pedagogy, she had seen her name in print (and Stratton told her her articles were more than meaty, they were brilliant, he said), but none of it mattered any more, and it had stopped mattering the very first day when Bud had helped her to mount Comanche for the first time and she sat there getting the feel of him in her unaccustomed limbs while Bud stood on the ground beside her, grinning: Now all you got to do is just sit back and relax, let yourself go; relax is all.

It seemed a sort of madness when she thought of how she talked all day with the little boy Jimmie (her only friend on the ranch; she *did* have a "way" with other people's children, and the fat little boy and herself were always together being left out of things) about sitting a horse and grooming a horse and how Bud had said Jimmie held his feet well in the stirrups and that Miss Blake was beginning to put her shoulders back and how a horse caught cold in the corral if you didn't walk him home to cool him off. And then she would fall asleep and wake in the night screaming or trying to, because there would be Comanche in her dream, looming twice his height with his head (rather human, and his lower lip stretched out like Bud's) carried toward her on a neck that stretched longer and longer as though to attack. So it's come to this, she thought, sighing and putting her hand forward timidly to touch Comanche's neck; I came out with work to do and books to read, and I have thrown them all away and my past life too because I have fallen in love with a horse who does not reciprocate . . .

But the others, a quarter mile ahead, were deserting the shore-path and cutting across the broad sandy beach toward a rocky formation a hundred jagged meters high, topped by the accidental perfection of an Indian's profile which gave it its name: Indian Head it was called, and it was said to contain a mysterious cave if only one were lucky enough to find the entrance. She could see them going slowly at last, because Bud at this point always reminded them that the soft sand was bad to canter over, the horses' legs might double under them. She had heard him say it in his drawling voice a hundred times, and he always added, "Now old Chiquit' here, she got stuck one time with one of her forelegs and where any other horse would have gone haywire and thrown her rider and busted her own leg, Chiquit' here just pulled herself up by the boot strap and laughed; laughed is all."

She tried to prod Comanche into moving faster. But she had developed a sullen horse, and each time she prodded him he broke into a small, deceitful trot which he abandoned the second her heel left his flank. And so they approached the group, walking stiltedly until they reached the point where the hoofs of Comanche's friends turned up, leaving their little hollowed prints in the soft sand. And then because he was so glad to see his fellows again, Comanche without any warning and totally disregarding the danger to his own legs, sprinted forward, exposing her to his difficult, jouncy trot before the eyes of his kind and her kind.

Already the horses were standing in their patient, restful line, each one with the rein of his colleague behind him slung over his own pommel, and his own rein slung over the pommel of the friend who stood before him. Ethel Blake dismounted in her awkward way, and watched while little Jimmie threw her rein over the pommel of Chiquita's saddle.

They were sprawled leaning and lying against the great rock, handing the canteen that had been carried round Chiquita's neck from one to another. Now Mrs Montague passed it with a kindly gesture,

handing it to Bud and nodding upward toward Miss
Blake. But Bud with his insolent grin lifted it as
though he would drink a toast and tilted it to his
own lips. She watched him as he sat drinking with
his eyes closed and the long sun-bleached lashes
coming down on his cheeks like a baby's, his ridiculous cowboy hat pushed far back off his sweating
forehead. She took in the boots that were the pride
of his life with the green butterflies stitched on the
sides; the hot baby tattooed in color on his chest,
left bare under the theatrical knotted handkerchief
round his neck; the ring with the big Nevada tur-
quoise, bluer and greener than a stone of any value,
on his brown finger; the gaudy snake-skin band on
his hat. She discovered that he was cheap as well as
stupid; a Nevada edition of a Broadway go-getter.
Then he passed the canteen on to her, and the thing
felt warm on the outside, and it smelled horsey a
little, from the sweat on Chiquita's neck. She
thought she detected a salty taste of Bud's healthy
spittle around the canteen's mouth, and although
it disgusted her sharply for an instant, she put her
lips around it nevertheless and felt comforted by
its warmth which was the warmth of another person.

"Let us be up and doing!" cried Mrs Montague.
"Let's explore! now that we've rested and drunk."

Bud had come prepared with a flashlight for the
inside of the cave, and now they all caught sight of
a sheath knife hanging from his belt as well.

"Good heavens, what's the knife for?"

"Rattlers is all," said Bud, shooting his blue gaze

at them all and smiling because he was too stupid to understand fear: he thought it a dude affectation.

"Rattlers!" Mrs Montague's eyes brightened. "But not for my little boy. Jimmie, you are staying here with the horses."

The little boy with his fat, freckled, brooding face, looked as though he would have wept then and there if he hadn't been ashamed before Bud. Miss Blake thought: what is it to me if I see the inside of an Indian cave? what is it to any of them if I go in with them or stay outside, on the outside, with my damn brains and eyeglasses and thin legs and my admirable way with other people's children? So she said, "I'll stay with you, Jimmie, we can tan our legs and keep old Midnight from rolling in the sand."

"What a gal," said Bud. "See you don't do anything I wouldn't do, Jimmie."

Mrs Montague, relieved, flashed her dazzling smile: "Oh Miss Blake, you're a darling! I wouldn't dream of letting you, only I know how you and Jimmie simply adore being together!" Down over one eye she pulled her scarlet beret, and then she was up and over the rocks following after Bud and the others.

They could hear their voices as they skirted the rocky base, seeking entrance. Somebody shouted, and they were alone in the world, an old maid, a little boy, and half a dozen horses.

All the horses stood together, now and then rubbing a nose against the backside of a friend, now whisking a tail, now sleepily rolling a great stupid eye toward Jimmie and Ethel Blake. Then there was commotion among them; all of them were realizing that it was a longish rest and they settled down to it, turning round as far as their bridles would permit, until at last they stood, broken into pairs, almost static, Midnight and Piute standing flank touching flank, and Chiquita's long neck stretched in peace over Comanche's thick and sturdy one.

"Don't you think Buddy's just great?" said Jimmie with a little tremor in his voice.

"Yes," said Ethel Blake absently.

"I wish I could ride with a silver dollar between me and the saddle, like Bud. I wish I had a nickname. Do you think I'll be anything like Bud when I grow up, Miss Blake?"

She had never before gone back on Jimmie or on any child. But suddenly it seemed that she must assert herself in some way, if only by being rude to a youngster.

"How foolish you are, Jimmie," she said sharply; "why Bud is nothing but an ignorant cowboy." She tore her eyes from the boy's hurt gaze to look out and out over a lake that filled her chest with pain. The bitterest sense of frustration came over her. It was as though she had never believed before that this was she, this pinched old-maid lady, who spent her evenings wearing herself out at seminars and meetings to keep herself from ever having a moment in which to feel something. The trouble with this desert climate and this western life was that they made one dizzy with a sense of potentiality and weak with the knowledge of it squandered. She felt it in her lungs, in her breast, in her brain, in the very muscles of her legs, the knowledge that she might have power for the first time in her life, and that it was bottled up tight in her because no one came to draw it out.

"I think you're a fine little boy, and you'll be a fine man, Jimmie darling," she said sadly. But he was hurt beyond repair.

"I wish they'd hurry, don't you, Miss Blake?"

They waited sadly beside the rock. Miss Blake felt that she would never recover from the failure that she had learned herself to be this summer. Chiquita stamped a foot in her sleep, and Comanche, stirring and shifting his weight, whinnied softly; Miss Blake wished for a good friend who would whinny to her.

"I hear them!" said Jimmie at last.

"Oh, the scariest place! Spiders . . . Bones . . . not white because they've been in the dark for dear knows how long . . . an arrow-head for Jimmie . . . perfectly fascinating, Miss Blake. . ."

"My hatband!" said Bud in a squeaky voice. And took off his large and idiotic cowboy hat, and sure enough his snake-skin band, brand new, was gone. He kept twirling the hat round and round on his finger but it wasn't there.

"Someone will find it next century," said Mrs Montague.

"I'm going back to find it *now*," said Bud.

"My God, get another, silly," they all cried.

"Someone's got to come in and hold the flashlight," said Bud obstinately.

And "Nobody's going to go back with you," they all cried, "what a fuss to make."

"I'm going to find it is all," said Bud, "I'm not going back till I've found it."

"Well, nobody's going to wait," they cried, moving toward the horses.

All but Ethel Blake. They didn't *get* him, she saw that. She was used to children; she understood them; she had a way with them. Here was a twenty-nine-year-old child who had lost his snake hatband; he would never be happy again if he didn't find it; if he found it he would forget it tomorrow, he would be dreaming about the green butterflies on his boots or a dirty scene he wanted tattooed on his thigh. But if he didn't find it he would have a lost place, a hurt place, inside of his chest forever, he would be thinking all of his life (and even if he didn't know it himself, Miss Blake couldn't bear knowing it for him) of the hatband lying abandoned, lying rotting in a dark cave, maybe waiting, maybe feeling hurt, for him to come back and save it. He would be thinking how all his luck had changed for the worse since the day that he had lost it; how for the two days he had had it he was the luckiest cowboy in Nevada. He frowned now, he was sulky, sullen, angry. But she knew he frowned because if he didn't look that way he would weep before them all.

"Well, I'm not tired," she said calmly. "I'll go back in with you and hold the flashlight."

His blue eyes rested on her in astonishment. "Will you? Say, that's mighty nice."

She thought as she turned to follow him that Mrs Montague gave her an amused look; but she stared right back, grave and a little stubborn, and then she thought Mrs Montague's look became definitely kind and not in the least malicious. She followed Bud around the rocky base and when she saw him at last put his great boot on a ledge and start to climb swiftly without a thought or a backward glance for her she wondered if she dared to follow him further. But something seemed to be driving her so that she could have stopped no more than a ball rolling down hill. Her foot with surprising ease found the ledge, her second foot came after, and there was Miss Blake (oh terribly afraid of high places; who had almost taken Dr Stratton by the arm once in Carnegie Hall because her breath faded away when she looked down), there was Miss Blake stepping calmly over crevices that revealed long slits of distance between herself and the ground, and running to catch up over narrow plateaus that held their breath on the edge of steep walls which dropped sheer a hundred feet. But she wasn't in the least afraid now. There was real danger, so she wasn't in the least afraid now, besides, she *couldn't* have stopped.

She saw him stoop; his legs went down; he was lowering himself, and coming after, she saw that here was the way in. She followed him down and they were in sudden darkness until she clicked the flashlight. Crouching all the time they climbed round and in, deeper into the heart of the rock; all the time the passage grew damper and darker, and looking back she could see the hole of daylight above them growing smaller and farther away. Round and round the path wound, every minute farther from reality, from day, from air, till the hole of light was a speck and then nothing. Round and round, like a path into the heart of a magnified sea shell.

"Flash it lower," he called brutally. She flashed the light round and round, expertly, while she watched him stoop and snoop and cover every inch of the ground with his nose down like a hound following out a scent. "It wouldn't have been here," he said. "Flash it over on the left. Not here, damn it."

It was not there and it was not there. Miss Blake shared his sorrow. But they climbed farther in. She was frightened of the place. But she was very happy. Wherever her light flashed it illuminated spider webs with spiders as large and coarse and fierce as crabs. A bat whirred past her ears. There might be snakes. But she hoped their sojourn in the cave would never end.

"God damn it," he whined, near to crying, although surely he didn't know it himself. "God damn it, we're nearly through, we'll be coming out soon, and I haven't found the God damn thing."

Ethel Blake knew suddenly that they must find it. If they didn't, then her Summer was surely the total loss she had been thinking it was and her life an irretrievable failure. She would crawl back home to New York and let her body droop and let herself go quietly to pieces until she died. She must find it and she must give it to him.

She saw it. It looked pathetic, lost, unwanted. For the thousandth time in her life she thought how an inanimate thing had a quality, borrowed a something of its possessor, like a woman or a child. The band lay curled with sweat, partly on its side, very lonely and brave and scared.

It was directly ahead of Bud, caught on the side of the wall. She flashed her light quickly on the opposite side. He was crawling ahead faster now, he was miserable, bitter, he had just about given it up.

She held her breath.

He was safely past it!

She waited a moment because her heart was beating terribly. "I've found it, Bud," she said.

"What? you've *got* it? Are you *sure?*"

She held it swaggeringly above her head and with her other hand flashed the light directly on it.

He looked at it and reached out for it. Suddenly, and perhaps for the first time in her life, Ethel

Blake grew coy, she dangled something and she withheld something, she felt her power come true and she let a man's eye rest on a thing she held in her hand and then deliberately she stuck her hand behind her back. The cowboy started laughing; it was a game he knew, a game he played, as easily and naturally as he swooped down from the back of a running horse and picked up a fallen bandana. He could afford to stand there laughing, because he knew Miss Blake could not withhold for long. And as for Ethel Blake, she became female and powerful, she felt as she stood there putting her head on one side and smiling that she must even, for the only time in her life, look *cute*.

"Give it here, gal." His voice was taunting. His blue eyes gazed laughing into hers.

She had no practice in this sort of thing.

"Wouldn't you really like it, though?" she said shyly, and loved herself for being so hard and so soft all at once.

"Will you lissen at the gal?" said Bud.

"Try and get it," said Ethel Blake faintly.

"Can't hit a gal with glasses," said Bud.

She almost brushed them off.

"Now put down the flashlight."

Trembling she put it down.

"Bet you can't," she whispered.

And then he was holding both of her wrists in his hands. But she hid her right hand behind her back, clutching the snake-band in a fist which would open only when the right time came.

He twisted her wrist. He bent over her and his laughing became panting as they struggled. His breath came in her face, went down her neck. She never stopped laughing, not for a minute, but it was serious laughter as laughter should be; laughter at something real and something really gay.

Her wrists burned, and when the cowboy reached around her back and found the hand that clasped his band nestled tight against the small of her back, her fist relaxed because it knew it was time. He unfolded every finger of her hand slowly, with a tortuous and tactical strength, a strength that held itself in check only because it was biding its time. One by one her fingers died pleasantly in his grasp, and then he wheedled the snake-band out of her palm and at the same moment kicked the flashlight so that it rolled over and went out and left them in the dark.

He was stuffing his snake-band into the back pocket of his jeans with one hand but with the other he held her firmly. Their laughter stopped. His right hand came back and traveled rapidly to her heart, while he took his lips away from her mouth to whisper slyly: "You'll never guess what I've found." She smelled horse on him, she smelled Chiquita, his other love. She smelled sweat and she smelled the clean desert dust on his jeans that had grown there through a whole Summer, because he said to wash blue jeans was to shrink them so they would never span a saddle again. She felt his legs wrapping strongly about hers with those muscles that were used to hugging the flanks of a horse, and she felt with her bold fingers the strength in his neck which was stout and hard, stubborn, like the neck of Comanche when Comanche was going to have his way with her. Then his lips came down hard over hers and with her last conscious, verbalized thought she imagined him drawling, Relax, gal; just let yourself go; relax is all.

They came out into the world again, and Chiquita and Comanche were standing there together, Chiquit' with her head across Comanche's neck, and both of them fast asleep with their eyes wide open and each with one foot curled delicately at rest. Chiquita lifted her head and saw Bud, rolled her nostrils bitterly and waggled her ears like a wife who had had a perfectly good time but was going to give her man hell nevertheless.

Bud went straight to the fastening of his snakeband onto his hat. But Miss Blake, who might have helped him, who might have leaned over and reminded him of her presence under Chiquita's jealous eye, was filled with strength and pride and a desire to show Comanche. So she tossed his bridle free of Chiquita's pommel and tightened the cinch which had come loose around his belly, tucking in the end so it would not dangle and brush against his legs. Bud meanwhile sat by, intent upon his hatband, murmuring conciliatingly, "Chiquit', old Chiquit', hello Chiquit' old gal," as Chiquita angrily stamped her foot. He scarcely saw Miss Blake until she had slipped her foot into the stirrup and leaped up over Comanche's back. Then he looked up in surprise, remembering, and cried out: "Hey, wait a minute there, gal! wait for Bud!"

She laughed and dug her heels into Comanche's flank. Comanche didn't believe it. Comanche was for waiting for Chiquita and he couldn't see Ethel Blake not waiting for Bud. So he stood still stubbornly. She pressed her heels again, hard and sudden as though she meant business, and Comanche started in surprise across the soft sand. When they reached the path that ran along the lake he took the little leap over the bank and then stopped dead as much as to say a joke's a joke but this one has gone far enough; but Ethel Blake, hearing Bud's taunting laugh from across the beach, would have none of it, and she kept kicking and kicking her horse until she had kicked him into spirit again, kicked him out of surprise and into a nice even canter on the hard sand.

Rocked in the valley between his great hillock of a behind and the uptwist of his thick, sturdy neck, she sat with her legs strongly outspread embracing his sides, her body following his rhythm as easily as though they had been a pair of expert tango partners. Beside the large forward movement there was a smaller motion of rolling, backward and forward, too gentle to be sliding, backward and forward and very gently up and down, almost circular, a lilting motion, powerful and very gay.

Ethel Blake and Comanche heard them coming

up behind. Ethel Blake seized the end of her bridle
and stung Comanche as far back as she could reach
and at the same moment she dug both of her heels
into his flanks, and when Comanche shook his
head to show her that she was still like a city gal
holding him in with the reins, she caught on suddenly to the art of riding and gave him his head with
a thorough confidence that she had mastered him at
last. He broke into a full run, leaping over the little
bays on the shore's edge or splashing through the
water because he had not time to slacken his speed
or to waste going around the little scallops. Chiquita
came dancing in their rear, her breath coming angry
and joyful behind them, until she was so close that
her nose snuggled against Comanche's backside,
and "Faster! Faster!" cried Ethel Blake, and slapped
Comanche on both sides with the end of the rein
and kicked him with all her strength.

Now for Miss Blake there was no motion, nothing at all but sitting tight and flying through space
with the ecstatic assurance that she would be caught
and beaten; so paralyzed with joy and with terror
and with a kind of unbearable excited suspense that
she thought she would die when the horses came
parallel.

The path was too narrow for two great horses.
Chiquita nudged Comanche out of her way,
sprinted forward; there was a wild whoop from Bud
who reached out suddenly and touched her shoulder, and then the two horses were exactly parallel
and Bud and Ethel Blake were riding side by side

like lovers, and Ethel Blake knew that this was the finest moment in her thirty-five years of life.

For a few seconds the horses ran abreast, and then Bud dashed ahead on Chiquita. When Comanche saw his friend beating him he sprinted desperately, but Chiquita was an old lead horse as against his having been brought up to round cattle, so he decided to be game, and side-stepping in that cute way he had almost forgotten, he elbowed Chiquita gently into the water. Chiquit' stumbled and splashed, righted herself under Bud's expert guiding hand, and when she had regained the path she was already ahead of Comanche. So there was nothing for Comanche to do but to stretch his neck and ever so lightly nip Chiquita's hind parts and then fall behind, which is where a cattle horse belongs.

Miss Blake pulled him out of his gallop and helped him to subside back into his jouncy trot. And then they walked slowly together like friends. In Ethel Blake's heart (which was still pounding furiously from the run and the terror) there was a peace which she had never guessed existed, almost as though she had died, but died such a brilliant death that it didn't matter if she never came alive again. But Comanche's sides were running with sweat, and his whole big frame was collapsing and swelling with his quick and happy breathing; every few steps his legs shot out from under him as though he would be off again on a run, although there was no strength left in him. Ethel Blake put out a hand on his hot neck and spoke to him softly, to calm him. "There, Comanche; take it easy, darling. Simple and natural, relax—relax is all." He quivered. Then her touch and her voice succeeded in soothing him. Turning his long head with a kind of solemn humor he nipped gently at the toe of her boot. And then he threw up his head and laughed; laughed is all.

1933

Jobs
in the sky

Jobs in the sky

IT MEANT that you wanted to hold your job
like nobody's business if you managed to get in
ahead of Mr Keasbey whose name had been first
in Mrs Summers' section-book and the section-
books of her predecessors for a noble fifteen years.
Mr Keasbey signed in daily at eight-forty (ten minutes before the deadline), and on the dot of eight-
fifteen on pep-speech days (a good ten minutes before Mrs Summers reluctantly counted you late)
—and daily, after removing the cover from his table
of Important New Fiction and flicking his books
with his private duster, stood with his fine white
head bowed, waiting reproachfully like the best
boy in the class. But on the day before Christmas,
the Monday which was the last day of the Christmas rush, 1934, and the morning for which Mr
Marvell's Christmas speech had been announced
(Mr Marvell being the 'M' in 'M & J'), Joey Andrews, No. 191–23, 167B, who had been till three
weeks before without a number in the army of the
unemployed, wrote his name and number on the
top line of Mrs Summers' fresh page at exactly
eight-eleven. Mrs Summers asked Mr Andrews if
he had fallen out of bed; she said it was nice to see
some face beside Mr Keasbey's so early in the
morning; and she said she had sat up in the bath-

room all night (not to wake *Mister* S) going over her records and trying to make them tally. . . And Mrs Summers, who limped before nine and immediately after five-thirty because there was not, she said, very much sitting on her job, limped off with the salesbooks for the hat-girls who were also part of her section.

Once more as Joey Andrews looked down from the mezzanine onto the great sleeping main floor below he felt in his stomach the dull ball of fear which a lover experiences when he recalls how nearly he missed going out on that particular Tuesday on which he met his love. But propping the biography of Dostoievsky against the Memoirs of a Grand Duchess on his own table of History and Biography, Joey Andrews felt that any recollection of his eight-months' nightmare among the unhired was unworthy of No. 191–23, 167B of a great department store. And wondering to what table Jane Eyre belonged (for surely it was not a biography?), "I must forget about the Washington Square gang," he scolded himself, "I don't belong with them any more;" and went to lay Jane Eyre tentatively on Miss Bodkin's table of Classics.

Downstairs the perfume girls were drifting in; the floor-walkers adjusting their button-holes and their smiles, moved here and there with dignity. Having arranged his own table, Joey Andrews looked about his beloved book department for some way to be helpful, some way to live up to the Christmas spirit of M & J. He didn't quite dare to fix Miss Bodkin's table; and he was just pulling the long white nightgown off Mr Keasbey's New Fiction when Mr Keasbey himself walked in—it was the dot of eight-fifteen—and, forewarned by the section-book violated, bearing another's name before his own, gave Joey a haughty, suspicious look and began flying around his table making kissing sounds until his fingers came safely to rest on the handle of his very own duster.

Now the cosmetic girls were mounting stacks of cold cream on their counters while near the doors the cheap stockings stretched coyly over amputated limbs. On the mezzanine behind the book department the hat girls in their drab black dresses and exquisitely sheer-hosed legs began clapping the hats on stalks like flowers. Mrs White who kept the lending library at the back came next; the Hierarchy permitted Mrs White and Mr Keasbey to bow with formal recognition of mutual virtue— Mrs White had been with M & J a noble twelve years to Mr Keasbey's noble fifteen—before Mr Keasbey hurried to return Rebecca of Sunnybrook Farm, which he borrowed every night that it had not been taken by a customer, for his mother who was eighty and had stopped sleeping. Mrs White began driving the hair-pins into the pretzel high on her head; and when Mr Keasbey laid Rebecca on the table before her, pointed her mouth like a pencil and made a check-mark with her head: down— one, two; hold; up—one, two—and Mrs White and Mr Keasbey part for the day.

Miss Paley of the Modern Library and movie-editions, to whom the Hierarchy does not permit Mr Keasbey to bow, mounts the mezzanine stairs with a look of resigned bewilderment on her melancholy face. Two decades of teaching school have left her permanently surprised at finding herself daily entering the Commercial World (and how had she ever, in the teeth of Mr Neely the Principal's disapproval, made the Change!)—and also there have been rumors breathed by Miss Bodkin that Miss Paley's life in the Commercial World is to be very brief indeed, and it may be that some of these rumors have even reached Miss Paley. Yet here she is, daily from nine to five-thirty, not selling children's books, as surely, she complains to Joey Andrews who rushes forth to help her with her jungle of cheap editions, as surely she had, after two decades of teaching little children, every reason to expect? had she not, as Mr Neely (who put things so well!) had put it, a gift for understanding children? But Mr Neely warned me, she whispers through her closed white mask, that the Commercial World was something else again . . . and drawing out the handkerchief (given her by the best-speller's mother) from her place in the Modern Library copy of the Old Wives' Tale which she reads at idle moments in the day, Miss Paley dismisses Joey with a kindly, authoritative nod as though he were the first-grade pupil who had just collected the rulers. And Joey, rather glad to get away, for ever since Miss Bodkin breathed the rumor, Miss Paley has been touched for him with some infectious germ, takes up his stand by his table of History and Biography.

Miss Willows the buyer trips over to her desk and lays her hat in the bottom drawer. But as yet no Miss Bodkin. Miss Willows bites at her pearls as she makes a hasty survey of the book department, arranges Christmas calendars with her head on one side like a bird. Still no Miss Bodkin (Joey Andrews hates to think of no Miss Bodkin.) "Heavens knows," murmurs Miss Paley to Mrs Summers on the subject of varicose veins in which they both specialize; and Miss Bodkin's chum Miss Rees slips in on the stroke of eight-twenty, the deadline, and carelessly pulls the cover off The Young Girls Series for which Miss Paley would cheerfully trade her miniature set of Proust; and "*I* know as well as Heaven," returns Mrs Summers humorously, and she has forty minutes more of the luxury of limping. Beautiful Miss Fern Stacy who is so dumb (according to Miss Bodkin) that she can hardly make change, takes her place behind the stationery counter—Mr Keasbey had fought bitterly against its ignoble presence in the book department, even for the Christmas rush week. Mr Keasbey stands with his arms folded, his head lifted; a fit citizen in the world of M & J, fit door-man to the gate of Heaven: perhaps one day Mr Marvell will pause and glance at his noble mien, his professorial posture, and will think to himself, What a man! what a faithful employee. . . And there suddenly is

Miss Bodkin, having signed in fraudulently in the space left blank by her good friend Miss Rees, a Miss Bodkin defying a gullible world to imagine that she was not present at least as early as Mr Keasbey, and that she does not every Saturday of her life make off with a first edition hidden away under one of Mrs White's lending library covers . . . Joey Andrews feels waves of purple sliding shamefully down his spine at the sight of Miss Bodkin's goose-berry breasts squeezed tight under her black satin dress; he remembers that it has been a long time since he has dared to ask a girl for a date, and that tonight is Christmas Eve.

Eight-thirty; and Mr Keasbey, for the fifteenth annual successive time, leads his class as though he were the monitor, down the mezzanine stairs for Mr Marvell's Christmas speech.

"and Mr Marvell who needs no introduction has come all the way from White Plains at this early hour to give us one and all his Christmas message." (Mr Sawyer of the Personnel speaking—O thank you, thank you for nothing, murmured Miss Bodkin, her small face expressing sarcastic devotion; Mr Keasbey delivered a withering glance; and Joey Andrews, though sick with admiration for her goose-berry breasts, moved away from her contaminating influence, for Joey, having had a Job for only three weeks was still more in love with the job than he was with Miss Bodkin.)

Beyond where the shoe-clerks were gathered a

white-haired man rose and bowed. "What a fine face," whispered Miss Paley; "he has Mr Neely's eyebrows exactly." Faint applause, led by smart clapping of department heads, while the great man smiled dreamily.

"My friends. (Mister God in person, murmured Miss Bodkin mouthlessly; and Joey Andrews stared for comfort at the graveyard of boils on the back of Mr Keasbey's neck.) I only wish it were possible to know each and every to shake each and every to wish each and every but—the.femilay.of.M & J.is. too . large. (Laughter, the lingerie girls throwing themselves in fake passion against their shrouded counters; under cover of the polite sounds Miss Willows the buyer leaned across Joey Andrews and hissed Miss Bodkin kindly stop that talking. The white hairs in Mr Keasbey's ears bristled sexagenarian triumph.) My friends, a spaycial responsibility toward your countray, your fellow-men the femilay of M & J have you ever stopped to think how the department stores contribute to the good cheer of this heppy holiday come rich and poor alike gifts for his loved ones differences forgotten all men are equal at Christmas and who has the honor the privilege the blessing (Bring on the castor oil, groaned Miss Bodkin.)

"Who.but.you.my friends. And this year in especial when so many renegades and complainers of course a bad year but take the good with the bad life wouldn't be moch fon if we didn't have our ups and downs like our good friends the ladies of the elevators here—and our slogan is down with the complainers friends, we don't want 'em here why up at Princeton we used to wash out their mouths with soap maybe we ought to enlist the parfume gehls to do the same thing here. (Haw haw roared the shoe-clerks remembering public school but the book department merely smiled condescendingly, such humor was beneath them and they knew was meant to be.) Bear in mind my good friends a job for every good man or woman in this countray if you don't like this countray you can go to another if you don't like your job here you can leave it always plenty only glad step in shoes.

"One word in closing to the new friends taken on to help us in this merry busy season. We wish we could permanently retain each and every make a permanent member of the femilay of M & J each and every but let me say to each and every WE will do OUR BAIST if YOU will do YOUR baist . . . and this is YOUR big chance to prove yourselves invaluable to US, on this last day of the Christmas rush when SOME of our friends unfortunately MUST BE DROPPED (the book department glances briefly and guiltily at Miss Paley, who continues to stand with her hands clasped as though Mr Marvell were the Principal leading assembly.) And I say this not merely to our new but it applies also to our old this is the day for EACH and EVERY.

"In conclusion it is good-will that counts good cheer is the baist policy the spirit of Christmas all year round is our slogan we are one big femilay and we spread our good cheer our customers expect it demand it PAY for it and now my friends I wish each and every a merry and profitable Christmas KEEP ON YOUR TOES ALL DAY OUR PROFIT IS YOUR PROFIT IT MAY BE THAT YOU CAN WIN YOURSELF A PER-MANENT POSITION my friends I thank you each and every one."

Smatter of applause, Mr Keasbey clapping on and on like an old Italian listening to the opera, while the section managers turned back toward their sections; but a thin man in a striped tie (Gadowsky who edited the monthly M & J Banner) leaped to a counter and cried: "Just one moment, friends. Let's give Mr Marvell a hearty send-off to show our appreciation—altogether now, M and J 'Tis of Thee . . ." The song straggled out across the floor; heads craned for a last glimpse of Mr Marvell, but Mr Marvell was on his way back to White Plains; the song died.

O God, if the gang could see me now, thought Joey, taking his place for this day of days before his careful table of History and Biography. (Y'oughta forget that bunch, y'don't belong with them any more. And look around, look around, Jesus it's like heaven to be working.) Now there steals over the book department, the hat department, the entire floor below, a period of hurried hush, of calm excitement; a poised expectancy, denoting the birth of the Store for this great day. Now the aisles lie flat and virgin, waiting, breathless and coy, for merry and profitable defilement. (Remember Pete . . . passed his examinations for the bar . . . in between starving he handed out grocers' handbills . . . and Dopy Simpson, turned down a job for $11 . . . said he wouldn't stay straight under $25 per.) Now you can hear Miss Bodkin whispering with Miss Rees about the rumored romances of Miss Fern Stacy the stationery girl: "when she said *three* I knew she was lying, there aren't three men in the city fool enough to propose to a girl a depression year like this." (Remember Rounds . . . been a scholarship boy at a swell prep-school until the Depression cut down the scholarship fund . . . went around saying over Latin verbs to himself . . . Dad said I'd meet swell fellows in New York, but he didn't think I'd find 'em on a park bench.) Now the large clock over the entrance doors jumps to eight-fifty-three; Miss Paley stands sweet and serious like a school-teacher—and God, it's as safe as being in school again, thinks Joey, coming here every day, nice and warm, watching the clock jump like that on its way to nine . . . Mrs Summers, her eyebrows dancing like harassed ghosts, limps like a nervous shepherd among her flock; only seven minutes more of that limping, Mrs Summers! M & J expects courtesy health good cheer of its employees, the customers expect it demand it *pay* for it . . .

Now Miss Paley closes the Old Wives' Tale with the best-speller's handkerchief in her place, and

stands lifting her melancholy mask like a lamp
waiting to be lighted. Behind her you can see tucked
over a row of books her pocketbook, another of her
many crumpled handkerchiefs, a pocket-comb; for
Miss Paley has moved in (despite the rumors), Miss
Paley has settled in (she has not heard the rumors),
among the cheap books, as she had for two decades
in her class-room, this is YOUR day, Miss Paley, to
prove yourself invaluable, and YOURS too, Joey
Andrews, and YOURS and YOURS and YOURS,
each and every . . . (Remember Jonesy, a real
bum, Jonesy . . . turned Christian and left the
gang, went and hung about with the Christers on
the Y breadlines . . . pan-handling and spending
his pennies on Sterno, which he converted into al-
cohol by filtering it through his handkerchief at the
horse-trough at the end of the Bowery . . . in his
Sterno he thought or pretended he thought he was
Jesus. But Rounds who had been a scholarship boy
said he'd go Red before he'd stand on a breadline
or sing Onward Christian Soldiers like Jonesy.)
Now you can hear Miss Bodkin: "I hate this God-
damn place, they fix the quotas high so nobody can
possibly make a commission except the week before
Christmas." Foolish Miss Bodkin! a daughter of the
femilay of M & J: doesn't she know when she's well
off? take care, Miss Bodkin, this is YOUR day too.
(Remember fumbling in the ash-can for a paper
before turning in—those nights you hadn't the
wherewithal for a flop—turning in on the grassy
center of Washington Square, surrounded by those

beautiful houses . . . dreaming and planning with Rounds the One Perfect Hold-up—can Mrs Summers read the mind? . . . remembering, because you couldn't sleep, how long it had been since you had had a girl . . . remembering, because you couldn't sleep for the drunks singing at the other end of the park, *If you've said your prayers Joey my son no harm can come to you*.) Now Mr Keasbey stands at the top of the mezzanine stairs with a dignity like the dignity of a Painless Dentist, his arms folded, threatening and somber, as he turns and prepares for his victims. Miss Willows herself descends from her desk and takes a position in the middle of the floor sucking her beads, a débutante hostess waiting, leaning forward from the hips, to greet the crowds that must be stamping outside in the Christmas cold. Now the outside entrance doors are thrown open and you can see the waiting customers pour into the vestibule sliding and coming to a stop like beads in a box. Now the big clock jumps to eight-fifty-eight; Mrs Summers can limp for two minutes more, and she limps from clerk to clerk, her eyebrows dancing, begging everybody to remember the Christmas spirit, and that extra pencils will be under each cash register.

(*You can get anywhere in this country with an education my son* said his father . . . oh gee pop, you were right, if you could only see me now! *I want you to have a high-school diploma son*.) Now the aisles below lie flat and smooth like roads, and the customers stamping in the lobby are a frenzied herd of cattle. "Watch the customers sharply," said Miss Willows; "and remember there are plenty of store detectives in disguise all over the store *watching every move you make*." Remember there are plenty of detectives, remember this is YOUR day, remember the Christmas spirit . . . remember they stood on a corner of fourteenth street where a young man promised them a bad Winter and Rounds said "I'd sooner go Red than stand on a breadline," and Joey Andrews shook in his thin-soled shoes for he knew he'd starve sooner than stand on a breadline and he felt he'd stand on a breadline sooner than go Red . . . remember KEEP ON YOUR TOES ALL DAY THERE WILL BE DETECTIVES WATCHING EVERY MOVE YOU MAKE THIS IS YOUR BIG DAY TO PROVE . . . remember Washington Square Park. . .

Where a bench was turned permanently outward, making a cosy little entrance to the grass hotel, a gateway to the open-air sleeping quarters for which no rent was charged, to which one came democratically without luggage, without even a full stomach. Remember you stood at the gateway, fumbling in a refuse barrel with your head well in, select a *Times*—the Tabloids are better reading but too narrow for practical use—for your blanket, mattress, pillow, bedlamp, water-carafe and chamber-pot. On the grass you chose a spot among the reclining forms and lit your good-night butt. "Lousy flop-house joints," your neighbor murmured; "a plate of soup, a free wash—who in hell wants a wash?" Bug-Eye the one-leggeder from the World War had to show off by springing over the fence instead of coming in nicely through the revolving doors. "They say he can still feel that leg . . . do you believe that?" "Shut up and give me a Chesterfield—oh well, a Lucky will do." "Amo, amare . . . amas, amat," murmured Rounds regretfully, as he picked himself up to go again to the toilet at the side of the park; he was having serious trouble with his stomach, no green vegetables. . . . "there'll be pie in the sky by and by," sang Dopey Simpson. "Shut up, there, lights out, no more talking."

Stars in the sky overhead, pie in the sky, moon in the sky, dreams, girls, pie, jobs in the sky too.

"Move over." It is Jonesy the Christer, lit on Sterno. "If you believe, believe, believe on the Lord. . ." "Smart Aleck, dirty sucker, hanging around the Y . . . mamma's boy. . ." *Papa can anybody in the country be the president?*

Three drunks sitting on the bench too happy to go to bed (sitting in the lobby of their swell hotel, drinking, guzzling, gossiping.) "Yesh shir, the mosht turrible thing in thish country is the bootlegger liquor . . . all the lovely young college boys going to their raksh and ruinsh. . ." "If you believe, believe, believe. . ." *Yes my son and remember Abraham Lincoln was born in a log cabin and Our Lord was born in a Manger.* "In the war we had such nice warm mud. . ." "Shut up, Bug-Eye, what'd it get you?" "In the war we had such nice warm blood

. . ." "If I wash preshident of the United Statesh, firsht thing I'd do I'd forbid the lovely young college boys. . ." *Just close your eyes Joey if you've said your prayers nothing can happen to you.* "Such nice warm mud. . ." "Sometimes I think Bug-Eye's just plain nuts." "I lost my leg in Avalon. . ." "Onward Chris-tian so-o-oldiers" . . . "When we ask them for something to e-a-t . . ." Rounds came back from the toilet: "I can't remember a deponent verb, I hate to forget all that." "If you believe, believe, believe. . ." *Do I have to eat spinach mamma? Yes Joey think of the little Belgian boys who haven't any—and it will make you big and strong.* "Work and pray, live on hay, there'll be jobs in the sky by and by." Rounds said all the comfort stations in the world wouldn't bring him comfort any more . . . he needed steamed vegetables . . . he said he'd go Red before he'd stand on a breadline. "Work and pray, live on hay, there'll be jobs in the sky. . ." "Onward Chrisssstian Soldiers. . ." One of the drunks on the bench was putting into action an experiment he had heard of: thoughtfully tapping one knee with the side of his hand to see if he was still alive. He was not. He toppled over onto his cold bed beneath the stars and if those gay boys sitting up and singing in their open-air dormitory thought they weren't spending that night with a corpse they were making just one hell of a mistake. . . Remember how that morning, remember how all that day, remember . . . REMEMBER THIS IS YOUR DAY, JOEY ANDREWS. . .

The bell rings, it is nine o'clock. Miss Willows wets her lips against the first polite speech of the day. Mr Keasbey goes rigid with desire. Mrs Summers stands erect at last on her varicose legs.

The heavy doors swing open. The mob in the vestibule surges and squirms, animals stampeding in panic inside a burning barn; then breaks suddenly, spilling like thick syrup down the aisles.

The machinery starts with a roar; unorganized come into conflict with organized; the clerks are over-powered, the floor-walkers swept along with the stream of customers; the aisles are drowned; arms reach like fishing-rods into the piled bargains on every counter. But gradually the frantic haphazard customers are subdued and controlled by the competent motions of well-trained officers, who reason, who separate, who mollify and implore. Still mad, but under direction at last, the crowd settles around counters screaming to be fed.

The mezzanine grows tense with desire for invasion.

The first customer toys with one foot on the stairs; pinches her pocket-book and climbs laboriously upward. Miss Bodkin's short, smart legs run to capture; but over Miss Bodkin's black banged head Mr Keasbey has already made a dignified assignation; like one hypnotized the customer makes her way surely and pointedly toward those grave commanding eyes. Miss Bodkin turns back in anger; meets Joey Andrews' admiring eye, and irresponsibly sticks out her tongue. Joey Andrews feels his confidence in No. 191–23, 167B slip a little as he sees with a pang Miss Bodkin guessing he is absolutely no good with girls.

"Mrs Summersss sssign please!" Miss Bodkin bags the day's next sale.

Surely these determined ladies and gentlemen (or are all the gentlemen detectives?) are not the same race as those tentative unhurried customers who loitered and weighed two weeks ago. Now they hurried fiercely, became insane people at indecision, rapidly bought two if they could not decide upon one. After favoring her customer with a cheap Lorna Doone from her classics table, Miss Bodkin with malice and caution sells her the latest detective story right off Mr Keasbey's beautifully stacked table, right under Mr Keasbey's bristling but dignified nose. Mr Keasbey bending his stately professorial back takes out his feather-duster and gives his books where Miss Bodkin has ravaged them a quick indignant flick. Miss Bodkin retires with the slyness of a nun to her own table.

A lady grazing close to Joey Andrews is captured by Mr Keasbey two strides ahead of Miss Bodkin who retires viciously blowing her bang off her eyes, and in passing murmurs, "If I printed what I thought about the sixty-year-old teacher's pet, it would make a book too awful even for my own Classics table." But all the lady wanted, and she said so too frankly, was a ninety-five cent copy of Robinson Crusoe for the kids and when Mr Keasbey lost out trying to explain the value of the three-fifty illustrated issue on his own table, he turned her over in haste to Miss Paley; because Christmas is here, and Miss Paley's cheap editions are petty game at this season to an old hunter like Mr Keasbey. . . But Miss Paley receives the gift gratefully and looking at Mr Keasbey's dignified face, who knows but she forgets for a minute Mr Neely. Now Joey Andrews has his day's first customer, and he will never forget her kind eyes and brown fur coat as she stands eagerly waiting for him to wrap her package with the Christmas twine. Miss Paley on her knees hunting and hunting for Robinson Crusoe which is hard to find because it is exactly the color and size of the Romance of Leonardo da Vinci, lifts a face modestly benign with the joy of laboring to catch her breath, for Miss Paley knows from her last decade's experience that if she rises too quickly she is likely to get the least little bit of swimming in the head.

The invisible electric wire carried rumors from clerk to clerk. Free lunch would be served in the basement; twenty minutes to eat. A hat-girl had been arrested for stealing change. A shop-lifter had been caught downstairs. The man in the gray felt hat was a Store detective. The Store had already done one-eighth more business than it had done by eleven-thirty of last year's Christmas Eve. Miss Bodkin's sales were higher than Mr Keasbey's. Miss Stacy had run out of Christmas stickers three times. Mrs White had sent down a twenty-dollar bill to be changed (no clerk was permitted to make change of anything higher than a ten out of his cash register) and the bill had not come back, after thirty minutes.

The first batch went to the free lunch at eleven-forty-five. They came back. They talked. They conquered. There was no second batch, except Miss Paley who went for a cup of tea. Miss Bodkin said the lunch was made of pieces of wrapping paper from returned purchases of 1929.

Mrs Summers asked Joey Andrews if he thought he could make out without any lunch. Joey Andrews said sure and dashed off to his next customer.

Joey Andrews was drunk. If for a moment he found himself without a customer he ran up to one lady after another like a lost child seeking its mother.

Miss Willows forgot that for the last two years she had been buyer for the book department; the fire of selling caught in her veins again; she sold passionately. Let Miss Bodkin take the credit down in her salesbook, let Mr Keasbey receive the commission—but let Miss Willows sell again! Her pearls caught on the edge of a table; scattered underfoot —Miss Willows laughed; turned to a customer and kicked the pearls recklessly out of her way. Miss Willows too was drunk.

Miss Bodkin whispered that her sales had reached $150.

Miss Willows greeting customers at the top of the stairs had lost her débutante coolness and become a barker for a three-ring circus.

Mr Keasbey broke down a reserve of years and squeezed Joey's arm as he pushed him out of his way.

Miss Paley, weak from no lunch, brushed her hand across her eyes and smiled until her whole head ached.

So it went on, and Mrs Summers passed among them, conspicuous for her white head, for her customer-like lined face, and in the back of her distracted eyes lurked worry like guilt.

Who shall say that even Mr Keasbey was actively, consciously motivated by the few cents' commission he was piling up? Each one was simply part of a great selling team, schooled and trained to perfection, each part functioned perfectly. All the time the crowd was changing, but imperceptibly; the stream which fed it must be flowing as fast as the stream which ebbed away. Now one was handing fifty-seven cents change to a gentleman with a green tie, now one was looking through the crowd for the lady with the feather.

In all his life Joey Andrews had never been so happy. His day was measured by customers, not by sales. He was mad with the delight of being necessary to so many people at once, with being efficient for his great team, with knowing exactly what part he had to play.

Miss Willows' voice grew hoarse, strangely naked she looked without her beads too—this way for calendars, this way for the latest fiction—Miss Willows was selling herself and was lost in passion.

But worry was growing out of Mrs Summers' eyes. She hovered for a brief second about Miss Paley as she stung open the drawer of her cash register. The invisible wires hummed again: Has Miss Paley, maybe Miss Paley, it looks as if Miss Paley. . . But Miss Paley, blind and dazed and cheerful, still flies among her cheap editions, still makes her way mildly in the Commercial World.

Still the crowd filled the aisles, covered the floor. Only now the incoming stream was heavier than the out-going, complemented by clerks and secretaries from Brooklyn to the Bronx. There was no slack, no shading. Even as there was no telling how the crowd melted and swelled again, there was no telling whether one's feet hurt or did not hurt; not only did no one attend to bodily functions, it was as if they had ceased to exist.

To get to your cash register now meant a hand-to-hand battle. The little bells rang as clerks shot out their drawers, counted rapidly, slammed them shut again. Joey Andrews clicked his open; good God, the bills under the weight were rising mountainously. He wasted a second of M & J's time: he felt with his finger the soft resistant pad of bills.

Mrs Summers with her kind and tortured smile, her worried eyes, her dancing brows, hovered briefly about Joey Andrews' cash register. Mr Andrews . . . Mr Andrews . . . Joey Andrews gave her a bright child's look with eyes which looked swiftly away, beyond her, in liaison with his next customer.

Feet were like rubber tires now. Bodies were

conveyors of books. Minds were adding machines. Fleeting glimpses of strained and happy faces—it might be Christmas, it might be the warm contact of body with body, of air made of the mingling of human breaths, it might be the happy exchange of one human tribe with another, the excitement, the warmth, the continuous roar of sound. . .

There was a slight lull, as there is sometimes a lull in a storm. Joey Andrews, running like a mountain goat, caught Miss Bodkin's round black eyes, caught Mrs Summer's level worried look . . . and then he found the eye of a lady with a scar on her throat, who was holding out a book to him, begging, begging for the kindness of his service. . . And then there was a flurry of ladies with anxious faces and Boy Scout nephews in small towns; Miss Rees had a sudden success with her Green Mountain Boys and Joey Andrews deserted History and Biography to take on her overflow. And the human storm was loose again, wrapping them all together in an efficient human mass. . . Mrs Summers stands like a bird of ill omen hovering over Miss Paley's cash register.

The invisible electric wires are humming again. Six hat-girls are going to be dropped, three of them old employees, three of them just taken on for the Christmas rush. They don't tell them, says Miss Bodkin viciously, until the last minute—so they'll keep on selling to the end. Miss Bodkin knows everything before anyone else. Paley's going to get hers, too, I know it, says Miss Bodkin—and Joey

Andrews wonders what Miss Bodkin is doing to-night, on Christmas Eve, he wonders if he might have the nerve. . .

Five-twenty-five. Joey Andrews flew to his cash register, back to the customer with the scar on her throat, back to his beloved cash register. "Well," says Miss Paley to Mrs Summers, "it can't be helped and it can't be helped." It has happened. Miss Paley's got the sack. They've told Miss Paley they're letting her go. This is Miss Paley's last day. What do you think, Paley's just been fired. Jesus, poor old Paley . . . Joey Andrews has a customer who wants something in green to match her library curtains. "Heaven knows," Miss Paley said, "I cannot understand, cannot comprehend. . ." and everybody knows that Miss Paley is using big words to keep from crying, and to show that she was a teacher for twenty years. Joey Andrews' customer would prefer something a shade darker; maybe that Oscar Wilde. Mrs Summers with her eyebrows going like an orchestra leader's baton: "I just feel terrible about this, Miss Paley, just terrible, I knew it last night and I couldn't sleep, they don't let us tell you till the last minute." Joey Andrews' customer doesn't see why they don't put out a Shakespeare in green suede—or even a dictionary.

Someone wants to buy Miss Paley's copy of the Old Wives' Tale. Such a nice lady, Miss Paley would like to tell her how much she loves that book. "Next to my Jane Austen," she almost says, holding her side as she graciously hands over the book. "The

Commercial World," says Miss Paley, reaching over for the wrapping paper. "My principal told me," Miss Paley said. "A natural teacher. Born, not made. He told me in so many words. . ."

The clock jumps to five-twenty-seven. Three minutes more in the Commercial World, Miss Paley. Three minutes more of non-limping, Mrs Summers. Three minutes more of being a human being, Miss Willows!

Mr Keasbey is smiling like a boy. Christmas Eve —he hasn't missed one in sixty years with his mother; bought her a shawl, he had, on the third floor, got the employees' discount; had it for her in his locker. Good cook, the old lady, probably'd spend the whole day getting up his Christmas dinner. "My principal told me," Miss Paley said; "he is a man who never minces words. Myra Paley, he told me. . ." Joey Andrews flies back to his cash register, he does not like to look at Miss Paley any more, Mrs Summers is standing tentatively: "Mr Andrews, oh Mr Andrews." Joey Andrews eyes her with his bright-eyed look, punching at the buttons which make the drawer slide out and tap him gently in the stomach: "Mr Andrews—I see you are too busy now." "My job at the school," Miss Paley says, "is gone; it's gone, my principal told me." Mrs Summers is off again, non-limping her last two minutes, like an unwilling bird of ill-omen off with her little messages—the hat-girls now.

And at last the closing bell rang and customers clung where they had been indifferent before and sales-clerks turned cold who had been themselves leeches ten seconds earlier, and customers would not, could not, tear themselves away until Stars Fell on Alabama was sent to Arkansas and the Motion Picture Girls to Far Rockaway and until they had made ab-so-lutely sure that the price was erased from the Grosset and Dunlap edition of The Bridge of San Luis Rey—and Joey Andrews, making out a final sales-check, catches Miss Bodkin's eye on him at last, kindly at last, friendly at last, as if at last she were perceiving him, and Joey Andrews' heart leaps with the thought of Christmas Eve and the chance, the bare chance, that Miss Bodkin, with her gay little bobbing breasts. . .

"My principal told me," says Miss Paley, not sitting as she had last night, on a counter and girlishly swinging her legs as she added up her sales —but standing off a little, apart from them, as the great store empties, as the people whom the employees of M & J have served all day go home and leave the Store to the clerks, to whom it properly belongs, Miss Paley stands all by herself, while Mrs Summers (avoiding her now, for Miss Paley is dead) moves like a plague from hat-girl to hat-girl, infecting them, six of them, with the poison from headquarters that has killed Miss Paley. Miss Bodkin, although she has higher sales than anyone else with the possible exception of Mr Keasbey (who bends his hand over his salesbook as though he fears someone might copy his sums) subdues her joy in her sales as a man uncovers his head for a passing funeral—and there is no doubt about it now at all, Miss Bodkin is definitely smiling at Joey Andrews as if she liked him.

They handed Miss Paley her handkerchiefs and pencils in silence. For all they were kind to her, and patted her shoulders, they were really hurrying her a little, too, hurrying her out of their lives—Miss Paley was bad luck. "Maybe your next job will be a sitting-down one, honey," said Mrs Summers, limping at last. They all wished Miss Paley would hurry. It is not nice to see someone dead. "Goodbye, all," Miss Paley said, and with a last bewildered look set her feet on the stairs to make her exit from the Commercial World. And they watched Miss Paley float out with her handkerchiefs, her pencils, and her varicose legs, and all of them knew they would never see her again—and Joey Andrews, turning back with relief to his salesbook, gathered courage to return Miss Bodkin's smile.

Mrs Summers is bearing down upon Joey, smiling too, suddenly everyone is smiling at Joey, Joey Andrews is a good boy and everyone is smiling very kindly at him and Joey happily smiles back. "different with you, you are young," Mrs Summers is saying. Young, yes, Joey Andrews is young as hell, and Miss Bodkin evidently thinks she has smiled at him too boldly, for now she lowers her eyes to her salesbook again. "You are young and life holds many opportunities," Mrs Summers says, smiling and smiling. "They don't let us tell them till the last minute, I tried to tell you but you were so busy, you were so happy, but it's different with you, you're so young," says Mrs Summers, smiling pleading for forgiveness. Of course I am young, thinks Joey Andrews, impatient with the old, with the white-haired Mrs Summers—and he tries to catch Miss Bodkin's eye again and signal her, We're both young, tonight's Christmas Eve—but the old will never have done talking to the young, and Mrs Summers goes on: "and so if you will leave your things tonight on my desk, and come for your pay-check next Thursday. . ." Nobody is smiling at Joey Andrews now, everybody is looking down very conscientiously at his own salesbook, he feels without knowing quite why that they are anxious to have him go, he hurries through counting the sales he scored for M & J, he stands apart a little as Miss Paley had, and when Miss Bodkin, not smiling any more now, comes and asks him in a low voice if he would like to come to her party tonight, just a few friends, just Miss Rees and herself and a few of the fellows, Joey Andrews says stiffly, "Thanks very much, I have a date," for Joey Andrews knows now why Miss Bodkin took to smiling at him so suddenly, Miss Bodkin knows everything ahead of everyone else—and Joey Andrews is not going to hang around people and be bad luck.

1934

White
on black

White on black

ONE OF the private schools attended by the "nice" children of the West Side some twenty years ago followed not only the liberal practice of mixing rich and poor, Gentile and Jew, but made a point also of including Negroes. Not many, of course—just enough so that when the eye of a visiting parent roved down the rows of pink and white faces collected for the Harvest Festival or the Easter Play, it stumbled complacently here and there—perhaps three or four times in all the auditorium—on an equally scrubbed black one sticking out like a solitary violet in a bed of primroses. For, except in the case of two sisters, or of a brother and sister, these black children never made friends among themselves, seldom even to the extent of choosing seats side by side in assemblies.

I suppose that the effect upon the rest of us was, as it was intended to be, on the whole good. It must have taught us well-bred little boys and girls at the least the untruth of the common slander that Negroes have an unpleasant odor; for certainly none of the Wilsons and Whites and Washingtons in our school ever smelt of anything but soap. And we were brought up, through weekly ethics lessons and the influence of the inevitable elderly lady teacher who had never got Harriet Beecher Stowe out of her mind, to the axiom that all men were created equal.

The few scattered colored children in clean clothes, then, contributed practically to our liberal education. But what effect we, in our more than clean, our often luxurious clothes and with our pink and white faces, had in turn upon them, it is impossible for one of us to judge. Although I can tell you today what has happened since to a number of my old schoolmates, even to those in whom I have long ceased to be interested, and although I run every year across gossip concerning still others, none of us has any idea what happened to our colored classmates. Some of them left school before the high-school years were over; some of them were graduated and stood at our elbows with their rolled-up diplomas; but all of them have equally dropped out of our common knowledge since. Where are they now? Did they drift back to Harlem, those Wilsons and Washingtons and Whites? How do they look back upon their ten years' interlude with white children? I cannot imagine. But I remember vividly the school careers of the two who were in my class.

The Wilsons, brother and sister, joined us in the sixth grade. Paul was exquisitely made, his face chiselled and without fault; a pair of delicately dilated nostrils at the end of a short fine nose, and an aureole of dim black curls. Elizabeth was bigger, coarser, more negroid; darker, her lips were thick, her nose less perfect; but still she was a beautiful child, luxuriously made, and promising to develop into a type of the voluptuous Negro woman at her best. Elizabeth was older than Paul; but her brain, like her nose, was less sharp, and both were put into the same class.

For the first week or two our kind teachers paid them the surplus attention which was always extended to Negro, or crippled, or poverty-stricken children. They suggested that Paul be chosen when the boys were choosing up sides; they asked the girls to take Elizabeth as partner. The children stood off from them no more than they stood off from any newcomers. We were not adultly snobbish; we merely glared at all newcomers in our world until they should prove themselves worthy. But by the end of the month, there was no longer any question of choosing Paul: Paul himself was the chooser and the permanently chosen; likewise Elizabeth was besieged with requests for the seats on either side of her in assembly, and it became an honor to have a seat in the same row; and the teachers turned round, and were given rather to suppressing the colored Wilsons than to bringing them out.

For after a certain natural humility had worn off, Paul and Elizabeth were not merely taken into the group; they took over the group. Including the faculty. They were a smashing success. For one thing, they feared nothing; furthermore, they proved marvelous athletes; and they were born leaders. Electing Paul to the captaincy of the basketball team was a mere formality; even if he hadn't richly deserved it, he would have permitted no one else to hold it. Elizabeth was as strong as a horse, less skilful, less graceful than he, but easily outshining, by her animal strength and fearlessness, all the white girls in the class. Beside their athletic prowess, which alone would have won them popularity in a class of eleven-year-olds, both of them were gifted with an over-powering jubilancy and a triumphant bullying wit, which inevitably made them czars.

They ruled the class with a rod of iron, chose their intimates, played with them, dropped them, and patronized the teachers. Their power spread to politics; by the end of the first year Paul was president of the class, and Elizabeth, who could not spell, secretary. Their class-meetings were masterpieces of irreverent wit and bedlam, subtly dominated by the tacitly authoritative Paul. The teachers turned over to them the difficult business of controlling the class after recess, and Paul, in his double capacity of legal president and illegal czar, easily succeeded where they had long failed. Even his sister, who was no small power among the girls, feared and adored him. If her authority was for one moment questioned, she had only to say, "I'll call Paul . . ."

I remember myself—and probably not a few others of the dazzled little white girls did the same in secret—going home to dream about marrying Paul and taking Elizabeth to live with us. I remember a moment of certainly unprecedented and of almost unsurpassed voluptuous pleasure on an occasion when Paul, twisting his wiry body into one of those marvelous knots from which he unrolled himself to shoot a basket, stretched so far that his shirt left his trousers and revealed a few inches of coffee-colored skin glistening with sweat, which caused me to gasp with delight. We girls chose to play against the boys of the class rather than among ourselves, and I was surely not the only girl who had voted favorably for the pure delight of being tossed on the ground and swung round the hips by the jubilant Paul, who had, beside his lovely body and fierce little nostrils, not the slightest inhibition.

For two years the noisy Wilsons demoralized the entire class into a raucous group that was never tired of wrestling, playing basketball, shouting jokes, and merrily defying the teachers. Not even the famous Seventh Grade Trouble, which involved the Wilsons as central figures, subdued them. Not even the visit, upon that terrifying occasion, of their mother. All of us made a point of walking past the principal's office to view Mrs Wilson, who sat there, dressed in black and with her face held low and ashamed as though she were the culprit herself. We whispered afterward, among ourselves, of what a lady Mrs Wilson was; we had never before seen a colored lady.

The high-school years loomed ahead. We were to be joined by another section of the same grade, and we were determined to maintain our solidarity with Paul at our head. Our reputation as a champion class had preceded us; but with it, we soon noticed, a reputation for rowdiness. Paul was instantly elected captain of the basketball team. But he was just nosed out of the presidency by a white boy belonging to the other section, who must have gained some treacherous votes from among our own. Although the other boy occupied the chair, Paul managed, for half a year, to bully even the new section into slowly waning submission to the last echoes of his power.

Elizabeth's popularity remained limited to the girls in our own old section. The others adopted her at first as a novelty, but they had not been trained to her loud hearty jokes and her powerful wrestling, and soon tired of her and left her to her old companions. These dwindled slowly, as we girls gained consciousness of our status as girls and wished to dissociate ourselves from anything rowdy. Of course it was our fault—we could have pushed Elizabeth forward and remained loyal to her—but we had so many things to think of in those days. And I think something of the sort was bound to happen to Elizabeth anyway; she did not have the native personality to warrant and sustain the unlimited popularity which had fallen on her partly because of her strength and partly because she was her brother's sister. There was a quiet girl in our class, less mature than the rest of us—who were, in that first year of high-school, more fiercely mature than some of us are today, which is ten years later. This girl, Diana, fastened upon Elizabeth as a chum, and from now on the curious pair were inseparable.

I remember the early days when it became the thing for the boys to take the girls to the corner soda-store after basketball games, and for each boy to treat one girl to a fudge sundæ. We couldn't help noticing that the boys, so eager to rough-house with Elizabeth in the classroom, hesitated among themselves as to which should treat her, and that the same one never treated her twice. We noticed too, that the soda-clerk stared at the dark blemish in our small white group. Elizabeth never seemed to notice anything; she developed a habit of kidding the soda-clerk in a loud professional voice, and soon our indignation was shifted to her, and we told her to lower her voice and not fool around with soda-clerks. Toward the end of the year Diana and Elizabeth dissociated themselves from our group, and began to occupy a little table by themselves in a corner. Here they would sit and pretend to be alone, and we could hear them giggling and whispering happily. Paul, of course, was still too young and too "manly" ever to join these parties.

In the course of that first year in high-school many things beside the soda-parties happened to us. Wrestling between boys and girls was outlawed, the girls began to loop their hair in buns over the ears, and the boys began to appear in navy-blue long trousers.

I remember Paul in his first longies. Instead of navy-blue, he appeared in a sleek suit of light Broadway tan, nicely nipped in at the waist, which harmonized with his clear mocha skin and showed off his dapper little figure to perfection. But it didn't quite fit in our school. I noticed that day, standing in line behind him to buy lunch tickets, that he wore brand new shoes: they were long and very pointed, and polished a brilliant ochre; they were button shoes, with cloth tops; they squeaked like nothing else in the world. I remember staring at them, and wondering where I had seen shoes like those before: was it in the elevator at home?

We were so grown-up that year that instead of shooting baskets in the twenty-minute recess that followed lunch, we got one girl to play the piano and the rest of us danced. Only about half of the boys were bold enough to dance; Paul still belonged to the group which stood in a corner and laughed and imitated their bolder friends, waiting for younger girls to be imported into the high-school department next year. With one boy to every pair of girls, it was not surprising that Elizabeth danced more than half of her dances with her friend Diana. The rest of us paired off with our girl-friends equally often.

But for no reason that anyone could see, Elizabeth's friends still diminished week by week. She had occasional spurts of her old popularity, but these were chiefly occasioned by reaction against some more stable idol, who would soon be restored to her post. Elizabeth's one permanent friend was Diana, the quiet little blonde girl who had no other friends. As far as I know, Diana was the only girl

who ever invited Elizabeth to her house, and it was
rumored that Diana was the only one who had seen
the inside of the Wilson house, but Diana could be
made neither to say whether it was true, nor what
it was like if she had seen it. As for the rest of us,
we were a little uncomfortable about omitting Elizabeth at afternoon parties at our homes; but somebody's mother settled it for us by saying that she
thought it would be an unkindness to the little
colored girl to invite her to a home where there
would be none of her own people. This conflicted,
of course, with the lesson of our ethics classes, but
we were thirteen-going-on-fourteen, and we had too
much to think about, so we let it go at that.

Meanwhile Paul, who had remained captain all
the first year, failed to be elected for the second.
Some of his classmates started propaganda to the
effect that, while still their best player, he was no
good as a captain, and they self-righteously elected
the second-best player in his stead. Paul took out
his anger in refusing to coöperate with the team,
and developed into a poor sport, that worst of
anathemas in school, successfully hogging the ball
so that no one else had a chance. The epithet poor
sport began to be whispered about the classroom,
and when class elections for the second year were
held, Paul was not even nominated for an office.
Our section had sworn to stand by him when we
had suffered defeat at the beginning of the year, but
when the time came we simply sat and held our

tongues, and elected another boy from the hostile section.

When the Wilsons returned for the second year after vacation, they looked a little different to us. Paul had turned into something resembling an uptown beau, and Elizabeth's face had grown coarser. Elizabeth joined her friend Diana at once, and their companionship remained unbroken. Paul, however, held in considerably less esteem, remained aloof, making no effort to regain his lost popularity, and pursued his way sullenly and almost defiantly among us. He met our reproaches with indifference.

That year evening dances broke out among us. For the sake of girls who might never be asked, there was a rule that everyone must come unescorted and unescorting. It was easy enough, of course, to break the rule. Most of the girls came regularly attended by boys from the upper classes. Elizabeth came the first few times with her brother, which was as good as coming unattended. Paul stood in a corner with the stags; Elizabeth sat with the other girls who had come unattended or attended by brothers, looking very dark and strange in her short-sleeved light dresses, and accepted gratefully her few opportunities to dance.

There began to be whispers among us of what we would do if Paul asked one of us to come to a dance with him, or offered a treat to a soda. We admitted to feeling uncomfortable at the thought of being seen on the street with him. At the same time we realized that what we were contemplating was horribly unfair. But Evelyn—Evelyn, who led our class in social matters because at fourteen she wore rouge and baby French heels—said, "School is school; it's not the World; it's not our Real Lives," and we let it go at that. As we had tacitly adopted policies toward Elizabeth, we now officially adopted one toward Paul; we were to be extra nice to him, but not in the way that one treats a boy; and we were to dance with him when he asked us, but very kindly refuse his invitations to escort us anywhere outside the school walls. Fortunately for our peace of mind, ethics lessons were that year changed to weekly lessons in elocution for the girls, and public speaking for the boys.

But none of us was given the chance to refuse him. So far as I know, he never asked a girl to go anywhere with him, never left the stag-line at our Friday night dances, and after the first half-dozen, he never even came with Elizabeth. He scrupulously avoided even the careless physical contacts in the elevator, of which the other boys took modest advantage. Also, when we followed our policy of being nice to him in school, we found ourselves politely ignored. Paul grew increasingly sullen, even occasionally rude, and one girl reported that he had passed her on the street and pretended not to see her, neglecting to lift his elegant tan felt hat.

In the middle of that year Elizabeth's friend Diana was withdrawn from the school by her parents and sent to a boarding-school in the South, rumor said to get her away from the black girl and teach her a proper sense of color.

With her friend gone, Elizabeth picked up smaller fry and dazzled them, because, unlike Paul, she seemed to want never to be alone. But even with these she learned to disappear at the school door, or at most to walk no further with a white classmate than the end of the school block. There, making some excuse about having to hurry, or going in another direction, she would dash away with a good-humored smile. I remember watching her running away from us once and wondering to what strange world she disappeared every day after school.

Of course, not one of the nice girls in our school would have dreamed of hurting Elizabeth's feelings by suggesting that she leave us on the street, but there must have been some hesitating on the corner before Elizabeth so effectively learned that her position with her white schoolmates ended with the school door. Or could it have been that dark lady, who had sat in the principal's office with her head lowered as though she were the culprit, that time of the Seventh Grade Trouble? But no matter, we were in our third year of high-school now, and had forgotten the seventh grade as we had forgotten the famous trouble, and were used now to seeing our dark classmate hurry off after school and run down the long block, leaving us standing on the corner, discussing our this and that, which was so awfully important to us. . . .

In the third year of high-school, Paul simply did

not appear. We were, I suppose, faintly relieved, in so far as we thought about him at all. He removed, after all, such uncomfortable questions as playing other schools with a Negro on our first team. And our own old section, our merry, rowdy section, of which Paul had once been undisputed king, had imperceptibly melted away, the boundary line was wavery, our old loyalty vague, a thing of the past; Paul, so far as he was anything in our minds, was a memory belonging to our lost section. When we asked Elizabeth what had happened to him, she told us he was going to another school because he didn't like girls and considered our private school sissy. She carried it off rather well, I think. One or two of us suggested that he might have been fired, because we all knew that his work had gone off badly in that last year.

Elizabeth herself, in those last two years, toned down considerably. Her prowess in studies had never been great, and she seemed now to be devoting more time to them. Her athletic ability had not lived up to its promise, because she had been after all primarily interested in rough-neck play, and seemed unable or unwilling to tame her strength and spirits into rules and skill. She abandoned the bright colors she had worn as a child, and came to school in neat and modest dresses. She dropped without reluctance into the common order of students, learned to toady as she had once been toadied to, and managed to keep up a decent sober reputation which ensured her a mild amount of companionship, restricted, of course, to within the school walls. On committees Elizabeth volunteered for unpleasant jobs and carried them out cheerfully and efficiently. She grew generous and sweet-tempered, and a little like a servant; and like a servant, she was thanked for her services and forgotten.

Paul had dropped out of our existence.

The last time I saw either of them was at our graduation dance. Elizabeth had long ago given up coming alone to our dances, but she came, of course, to this one, looking rather too burly and black in the prescribed white dress, with bare arms which hung like bones from her ungainly shoulders. She was the whole of the committee on refreshments, and all during the first part of the evening she stood behind a table with her diploma tucked on a rack over her head—nobody from her family had come to see her be graduated—and cheerfully dispensed sandwiches and ice-cream.

Everybody was mingling proudly in the big assembly room, waiting for the chairs to be removed for dancing; everybody was very nice to Elizabeth and even took down her address as a matter of form, but in the rush of taking addresses that really meant something and comparing notes about future colleges, she was forgotten, and if it hadn't been for a teacher who came to her rescue, she might have been completely alone. When the dancing began, the teacher led her away from the buffet table with her arm around her, to bring her to the row of chairs where girls sat waiting for partners.

Some of us must have had compunctions—I know I did—floating by her in our partners' arms, for on that night the least popular girl had achieved a faithful escort, if only by importing boys from classes below who felt it an honor to be there at all. But none of us felt badly enough to urge our partners to leave us and dance with Elizabeth. Later one or two boys danced a waltz with her, because a waltz was the least difficult thing to sacrifice. She sat all evening and talked cheerfully to the teacher. She looked uncomplaining, as though she had quietly learned her place. She even seemed to enjoy watching the rest of us dance.

The evening broke up on a high-note of "See you again," "Don't forget," and "Oh, the most marvelous time!" and I remember emerging from the dance-room in a fever of happiness, walking on winged feet I pushed my way through the gay crowd outside the door. Somebody tapped me on the arm: "Miss!" I turned and saw, for the first time in three years, Paul Wilson, the king of our old section! I smiled eagerly, delighted to see him again. "Why Paul!" I exclaimed, holding out my hand.

He was as beautiful as he had been three years before, but his face was different, hardened perhaps, so that the dapper tan clothes he wore made him cheap and flashy. He still wore pointed button shoes with cloth tops. He was standing by the wall with his hat pulled down over his eyes. "Why, Paul!" I said.

He looked up, caught my eye, and shifted his away as though he had failed to recognize me. He looked down at the floor and spoke in a low voice. "Miss, would you mind finding my sister Elizabeth Wilson inside and say her brother is waiting for her?" He stuck his hands suddenly into his pockets with something of his old sullen gesture.

I remember turning from him with an over-powering sense of guilt to spare him embarrass-ment, and going back with tears burning my eyes to find Elizabeth. I left him standing there against the wall, with his hat over his eyes, snubbing his former classmates, while they passed their former god and leader, some of them too happy to distin-guish his features under that hat, others no doubt turning from him to prevent his embarrassment, and even, on that happy night, to spare themselves. . . This should have been his graduation.

1931

The
Mouse-trap

The Mouse-trap

MISS BETTY CARLISLE, Mr Peter Bender's secretary-receptionist, came through the outer office with a sheaf of Mr Bender's letters for his signature—remembering, of course, to switch off the light over her typewriter as an example to the "human mice" as Mr Bender humorously called them. She was gracefully conscious of herself, as though she were still home in Kansas watching a smart New York secretary in the movies floating, brisk and yet charming (just as her clothes were both tailored and soft), through the maze of desks and telephones and tables, while the mice turned up faces friendly but a little respectful, a little envious, wholly admiring; she liked to smile poignantly, the letters at her breast, at Fred Dickinson—one of the "super-mice"—who always eyed her sheepishly over the waist-high partition round his desk. The outer office, Mr Bender had told Miss Carlisle, resembled a miniature city-room. The mice, who went scrabbling on all day behind Miss Carlisle's back where she sat facing the entrance with her Fifth Avenue tailleur and her Main Street, Topeka, smile, consisted of the three stenographers, the two young checking boys (who were better at finding scandal in the papers than Bender, Inc., Advertisements),

Gracie the telephone girl, and Willy and Jasper, the little errand-boys who looked as though they'd forged their working-papers. With the super-mice, lined round the edge of the room at semi-partitioned desks, were Joe Murphy, the copy chief (an Irish smart Aleck who thought he was the brains of the agency, reflected Miss Carlisle, and yet let anyone down to the colored office-sweeper call him Joe)— and his fellow-copy-writers: Nicholls, who wrote up office supplies; and an old maid who covered household furnishings and had published two poems somewhere; Fred Dickinson, who managed production; the art man, Mr Furniss; the two slick salesmen—"account executors"—who were never at their desks, and old Mr Partridge the book-keeper, whom they all called The Monitor because he kept tabs on everybody. Miss Betty Carlisle, remembering how Mr Bender said of the lot of them that some people were just born to be mice, smiled kindly as she passed, guiding her tailleur gently between the switchboard and a filing-cabinet, and always holding Mr Bender's letters as though they were a bouquet that she was bringing him. It was only when she emerged from behind the switchboard and started down the aisle of tables which led to Mr Bender's door—Peter T. Bender, PRESIDENT, *Private*—that she noticed, or rather *sensed,* sort of, that something was wrong today in the Mouse-Trap.

For they all, except Fred Dickinson, who dropped his eyes at once to his illustrated folder, were not greeting Betty Carlisle so much as they were staring

at her. All of them, from the art man down to Willy
and Jasper; especially Joe Murphy with a cigar in
his mouth; especially Mildred Curtis, the stenographer Mr Bender didn't quite "trust"; especially
Gracie, with her wreath of telephone wires quivering on her head; especially Sandusky the Polish
checker—in short all of them (except The Monitor,
who went on clicking righteously at his adding-
machine) behaved as if Betty Carlisle's switching
off the light over her typewriter and passing down
the room among them interrupted something that
might have been going on all the afternoon behind
her back.

It made Betty feel uncomfortable, sort of. She
was really on the friendliest terms with them all,
and before Mr Bender and some of the "accounts"
had started taking her to lunch she had gone along
with any of them to the cafeterias and cheaper
restaurants. Were they speculating on her relations
with Mr Bender, she wondered? But they had had
plenty of time for conjecture on that score; in fact
the girls had laughingly congratulated her on her
conquest, and seemed, the prettiest of them, curiously indifferent to Mr Bender's charm. "Hello
there," Betty said nervously to Mildred Curtis who
was screwing up her eyes like an artist measuring
the landscape; "how's every little thing?"

"Oh, just *fine*," said Mildred Curtis, grinning;
and for some reason Joe Murphy seemed to regard
Mildred Curtis's answer as something by way of a
joke. Mr Partridge looked up at their laughter and

fell to clicking again with irritated passion—while over in his corner Sandusky broke a rule and lighted a cigarette before the open files. Betty heard one of the little errand-boys delivering himself of a Bronx cheer behind her back as she opened Mr Bender's door at last and shut it on the human mice, to breathe in the pleasant cool pent-house atmosphere with reverent relief.

"Hy-a, Baby, done already?" Mr Bender was probably the handsomest and pleasantest boss any secretary-receptionist from Kansas ever had. However well-dressed and aristocratic Betty Carlisle might feel in the outer office, with the underlings, she always felt a little shabby in Peter Bender's presence. There was a certain tacit richness of air that he wore, in his clothing, his nostrils, his elegant carriage, which no amount of Fifth Avenue tailleuring could supply to Betty. She never had the feeling, not even in her smartest suits, that she could relax (like the horsey young matrons in the cigarette endorsements)—she always thought of herself as she had looked trying the suit on, or standing before the mirror that morning: remember to hold the stomach in, one hip a little raised, left foot drawn to the right so that her legs (still rich with the basketball muscles from home) resembled an advertisement for hosiery; there was no "at-ease" stance in her repertory, not in Peter Bender's presence. But back of the discomfort there was a slight and curious thrill: as though it were really rather exciting to remain a slave to Peter, to be shabbier than he was,

to wear out her manicure doing his work on the
typewriter—while he sat taking his whiskey "snif-
ters" and phoning for news of the stock-market or
the tennis courts.

She liked his friendly arrogance (as though he
felt the thrill himself, from *his* side of the desk) as
he held out a lazy hand for the letters. She liked
seeing how the white pages that she had taken such
pains with were made to look instantly casual and
ten times more potent, under Peter Bender's well-
kept tennis hand—each sheet came out resembling
him, careless, a little rumpled, but expensively
tailored to begin with. Betty was proud of having
been tailor to those handsome pages.

She watched him blot each one as though he
stamped it with the royal seal, and then he set them
in a disordered pile upon his desk. Betty took them
up reluctantly; she didn't want to leave—she did
want him to ask her to dinner again. "Oh say," she
began breathlessly, "I put up that sign you told me,
you know, in the Ladies' Room—and every time I
think of it I go in and switch off the light."

"The sign? oh yes. Do any go-o-od?" Peter Bender
was yawning absently.

"Well, not much. I was thinking, Mr Bender—"
she couldn't bring herself to call him Peter, not in
office hours—"I could take out the electric bulb
altogether, they can see well enough by the lights
from across the court, and *I* wouldn't mind—"

"Oh hell no, don't bother," said Peter Bender
pleasantly. "It doesn't come to anything, really,

even if they leave it on all day. It's just a kind of symbol, I mean, always let 'em know we keep our eyes open, that's all."

"And how about the light over *my* desk?" said Miss Betty Carlisle, flirting bravely with the boss but wishing she could let her stomach out, for just a minute. Oh *please* ask me to dinner, she prayed, thinking of her windowless kitchenette; I'm so homesick, sort of.

"Oh, you!" said Peter Bender lightly. "You've got attention-value, baby, you're the 'hook'—we need you in the limelight. . . ."

But no dinner invitation, thought Betty sadly. She turned to go, feeling still trim but dejected, as if for no reason in the world her tailleur had suddenly begun to droop—and found she hated to face the Mouse-Trap without a happy assurance in her smile. And then she remembered the hostility, or whatever it was, in the outer office as she had come through.

"They looked so funny out there this afternoon, sort of," she said—humbly, for her motive was only to stay a little longer and give him another chance to ask her to spend the evening.

"The mice?" said Peter Bender, yawning. "They always look funny, they eat too many hamburgers. But especially today?"

"Oh, they looked, I don't know exactly, but I *sensed* something—"

"You *sensed* something?" Peter Bender was at once a different man, rather like his signature, firm and keen, very upright and aware, a glorified photograph of the rising young business executive. "I cut that little Gracie this morning—still, she wouldn't have the spirit exactly—"

"I think Mildred Curtis," said Betty on a hunch, "Mildred and that Polish checker, and Joe Murphy—"

Peter Bender sat for a minute, tapping his teeth with a pencil, the way he did when he was rebating a commission to hatch a new account. "Murphy's a racketeer," he said, contemplative; "I'm not afraid of Murphy. But those other two, I'd just as soon be rid of them. Sandy's a foreigner, and I don't quite like the way the Curtis does her hair, I hate that type." He walked to the wall which held a little shutter giving upon the outer office. "Hmm, look at that," he said to Betty.

The copy-writers had left their partitioned desks and were standing in a tentative group about the switchboard, behind which Gracie looked very small and frightened, wearing her telephone wreath like a crown of electric thorns. Mildred Curtis and Joe were doing all the talking, while young Sandusky stood by flexing his muscles as if they were all he had to talk with. The art man hovered on the edge with his hands in his pockets, and Mr Partridge, at home in his glass cage, did his accounts furiously. The desks and the typewriters abandoned by the stenographers looked surprisingly blank and ominous—but everything was canceled out for Betty by the fact that the boss, standing shoulder to shoulder with her at the little window, had lightly put his arm around her waist.

"Tell you what, baby," said Peter Bender, shutting the window on the mouse-trap and growing tall and strong and curiously gay, "we'll catch the mice in their own trap, see, we'll spring it while they're setting it for us. Stick around, Betty, I'm going to put on one swell show—and then we'll make whoopee tonight in celebration."

"My, I think you're wonderful, Peter—" Betty Carlisle's heart was singing at the prospect of sticking around and making whoopee with Peter Bender; and she felt so elated by his touch that she called him easily by his first name now, even though it was still an hour short of closing time. "You don't seem upset or anything!"

But Peter Bender was extracting his whiskey bottle from a built-in cellar and whistling merrily. "Take it in my stride, baby," he said, grinning. "No, I get rather a kick out of it, to tell you the truth; I like having something to buck. Reminds me of the good old days at college when we went out strike-breaking and had the time of our lives with the scabs' daughters . . . some of the boys took the other side, after all, strikers have daughters too. Here you are, baby, have a snifter with me." He held his glass toward hers. "To the best-laid plans of mice and men!" he said. "And how about a little kiss—for luck?"

Feeling naughty but terribly gay, Betty leaned over the desk to kiss the boss. She was somehow

afraid to let herself enjoy the kiss, it didn't seem
suave—so all she really liked was the idea, the idea
that Mr Bender wanted to kiss her. She had never
known a man whose first kiss was so prolonged, like
any Kansas fellow's third or fourth—and the end
was as abrupt as the beginning. No, not abrupt
either, he wound things up like an artist, a caress
here, a murmur there, a polite renunciation in the
way his hand finally left her brow—but while Betty
was still recovering, still flushed from not letting
herself enjoy the kiss, Mr Peter Bender was finished
and putting away the whiskey, and looking like a
business executive again. "Thank you, honey!" he
said merrily, "you've got the softest touch system of
any secretary I ever had, that prize committee didn't
lie about you, back there in Topeka. Topeka, Topeka," he said, patting her lightly, "sounds like a
port in Japan or something. . . But business before pleasure, Bender! Let's go, honey!"

Betty Carlisle was terribly excited as Peter Bender stepped ahead and opened the door for her (the
outer office was a bedlam!) exactly as though she
were one of his lady accounts or his fiancée. She
had never felt prouder in her life, not the day when
the high-school principal back in Topeka had announced that she had won the stenography contest,
not when the girls in her class presented her with
a fitted suit-case for coming to New York. She
walked out of Peter Bender's office at Peter Bender's
side, thinking, "Betty Bender, Betty Carlisle Bender, Betty dear you were wonderful this afternoon,

it gave me ideas about how we could be partners for life, how about it, baby?" She could not resist giving her head a little toss as Peter Bender's sudden appearance startled the mice into frightened silence, and she hoped, standing at his side before them all, that she looked, as she felt, like his bride.

"Well, well, well," said Peter Bender, and his voice rolled like a smooth ball into his employees' midst, "what have we here, a football huddle or a family picnic?" There was an embarrassed silence, while Mr Bender allowed his eyes to rest coolly on each mouse in turn (Dickinson scraped an uneasy foot up the leg of his pants; Joe Murphy screwed up his face in a "clever" way—but more, Betty thought, to show that he was *equal* with the boss than really to go against him—while Mr Partridge, still bottled in his glass office, stared indignantly over the top of his comptometer). "Or is it a guessing game, do you think, Miss Carlisle?" he said, and stood and waited for the laughter which didn't come.

"We've been doing some guessing ourselves," said Mildred Curtis; and the mice stood awkwardly, glancing from their leader to their boss. "Listen, Carlisle," said Mildred Curtis bluntly—and Betty drew in her stomach and her chin and moved a little closer to the boss, "there's just one thing we want to know—are you with us or against us? Did Mr Bender raise your salary just to put out lights behind our backs, or also to spy on us?"

"Certainly not, Mildred," said Betty, flushing at

the brusque "Carlisle" in Peter Bender's presence. "Naturally I noticed, I *sensed*, that you-all were acting funny all day, and naturally, we all work together after all, so I spoke to Mr Bender." Her heart almost skipped, it felt so good to say "I spoke to Mr Bender," really as if she were already *Mrs* Bender! "And both of us wondered what it was all about."

"It's 'about' wages," said Mildred Curtis—and Betty flinched at "wages", it sounded so like a chambermaid. "And you'd better think twice yourself—how much does Carlisle make, Sandy? twenty-five, and has to dress like a million. How do you do it, Carlisle?"

Betty thought of the sales she attended at eight o'clock on business mornings, sometimes standing on the pavement with other receptionists in search of sample bargains from seven o'clock until the doors opened; also of how she got on without breakfasts to pay for having her hair done. "I know how to buy," she said coldly.

"Gracie knows how to buy too," said Mildred with a short laugh; "only she doesn't know what to do it with since this morning." There was a ripple of laughter over the office, as though Mildred had given the mice a bit of her nerve. Gracie blushed at her switchboard till her cheeks were almost as red as her eyes.

"Why Gracie!" said Peter Bender pleasantly. "Are you with grievance, my dear?" There was a burst of timid laughter, on the other side now—

shot through with reluctance, and here and there (you couldn't put your finger on it) a stir of indignation. "I *thought* you looked a little pale," said Peter Bender, as Gracie turned almost purple under her trembling telephone wires. Betty Carlisle shook with laughter, Fred Dickinson caught her eye and grinned meekly, Miss Pierce, the pretty stenographer, stuffed her handkerchief into her mouth like a school-girl. But there was a wave of restlessness from somewhere, Sandy flexing his muscles and Joe Murphy murmuring something like "let 'em eat cake"—and Peter Bender, *sensing* it, grew lightly grave. "But seriously, Miss White, Gracie, do you think this is quite fair play? Now if you have a complaint to make, my dear girl, why don't you come to me directly? instead of whining behind my back—" Gracie covered her face with her hands.

"That's not fair play, either, Mr Bender," said Mildred Curtis. "We've *all* got complaints—this isn't Gracie's fight, it's all our fight." Sandy and his fellow-checker nodded.

"Fight?" said Peter Bender, underlining the word incredulously. He stood there with his hands in his pockets, very boyish and puzzled, glancing from one face to another. The faces remained blank and hard, set against him. Peter Bender stepped forward to become one of them, and Betty saw how his hand rested in a friendly way on the shoulder of Jasper, the littlest errand-boy. "Look, my good people, this is so much nonsense. To hell with the happy family racket, you all know I've never pulled anything like that, that's factory stuff—if you people have any complaints to make, I'm sorry and surprised as hell to hear it, I think you're a pretty swell bunch of people and I always thought we got along like nobody's business." He shook his head, rather hurt. "But, good Lord! I want everybody to be satisfied! There's no question of any fight! Now look," he concluded, brisk and kind, "we'll get much farther if you all come into my office, one at a time like gentlemen—and let's have a drink and talk things over privately—"

"And get the can privately too," said Sandusky insolently, "like a gentleman, with a drink—no, thanks."

"Be quiet, Sandy," said Mildred Curtis. "It's too late for that, Mr Bender. We've got a lot of complaints in common and we're all going to stick together—either you meet our terms or we quit in a body."

"Quit? Terms?" said Peter Bender, brushing his hand over his brow as though he couldn't have heard correctly.

"Cold," said Sandusky, grinning.

"The curtain rises," said Joe Murphy with relish.

"It's all too much for me," said Peter Bender, weary and sad. "All right then, sneak out like servants, give notice like a bunch of servants, and I'll treat you all the same way. Two weeks' wages, and of course I can't conscientiously recommend you as loyal—"

"We're not sneaking out like servants, Mr Bender," said Mildred Curtis dryly. "We're *walking* out—we're giving you the works this time: a strike."

"Heh, heh, heh," said Joe Murphy, with a humorless laugh like a poor comedian.

There was silence then, all over the office, and you could hear Sandusky lighting a cigarette and Dickinson scraping his shoe on his pants. The air in the Mouse-Trap, thought Betty, was charged with something odd and sultry. For a moment terror landed in her heart, she didn't know what to expect—but a glance at Peter Bender, standing lazy and composed, assured her: he was taking it in his stride.

"Strike," said Peter Bender, dilating his handsome nostrils as though he had come across a hair in his soup. "Strike!" he said, turning it gracefully into a rather graceless joke. "Strike!" he said, almost baby-talking it, kidding it, turning it round in his mouth like a teething-ring and sticking it between his teeth to show he didn't fear it.

"Egad, you got it!" said Joe Murphy, "Strike's the word." "With all the fixin's," said Sandusky, grinning. The younger checker unwrapped a bundle of cuts and sent them spinning across the floor. The little errand-boy freed himself from Peter Bender's stroking hand and ran giggling to his partner—and one or the other of them made a noise like an aborted Bronx cheer. There was a strange tension now, Betty felt, as though the silence were made of suppressed sounds—not sounds of battle exactly, but a hushed and hurried cleaning-up of weapons. You could hear Gracie White sobbing quietly with her head on the horizontal switch-board keys.

"Of course you all realize," began Peter Bender slowly—when suddenly Mr Partridge slammed shut his desk and came wheeling his old book-keeper's body righteously toward the boss, his brief-case in his arms like a baby. The striking mice drew back and made an aisle for him, as though a leper passed too close.

"Mr Bender, Mr Bender, I just want you to know sir, I am totally dissociated from these unfortunate events in the office, I have grieved for you sir, since I learned the facts. I have been helpless to offset the general Bolshevik spirit—"

"That's all right, Partridge old man, I appreciate your attitude," said Peter Bender a bit hastily, for The Monitor was an incorrigible old wind-bag.

"And I just want you to know, Mr Bender," said Mr Partridge, trembling, "that I cannot brook this scene, I beg to be permitted to go home, as you know I have never left before till after closing time. And you may count on me, Mr Bender, if there is anything I can do, through thick and thin, come what may—"

"Sissy!" breathed the younger checking-boy. "Why don't you marry the boss, scab?"

"I understand perfectly, Mr Partridge," said Peter Bender quietly. "And thanks, thanks." ("Tableau," breathed Joe Murphy, "ole Black Joe and young Marse Henry reaching across social chasm to

wring each other's hands.") "And there *is* one thing
you can do for me, Mr Partridge—take these young-
sters home, get them out of this nightmare." He
pointed, stern and kind, to Willy and Jasper, who
stopped chewing their gum in united horror. "Go
home, Willy, go on home, Jasper," said Peter Bender; "think of your parents, you two kids—Jasper,
your dad is living on city relief, I think? and your
mother is having another baby, Willy? Well, now,
don't act like a couple of spoiled kids playing
hookey, there aren't many offices in town that'll
take on a pair of young monkeys with no training
at all, you don't want to break your parents' hearts,
do you?"

There was a cry from Sandusky: "He's bribing
you, kids, don't fall for that stuff, stick to your
guns." But the youngest checking-boy, Sandusky's
partner, looked scared, he was not so old himself,
and this was the first job he had ever had.

"Let's try and keep our voices down, Sandusky,"
said Peter Bender quietly; "and don't shout the
whole night-school vocabulary at a couple of innocent little kids." ("Women and children first,"
murmured Joe Murphy around his cigar.) "Go on
along with Mr Partridge, you kids," Peter Bender
was advancing on the frightened little boys and
patting their bottoms in the direction of the elevator. "Let me know when that new baby's about due,
Willy old boy, we'll see if we can't give it some kind
of welcome party. . . . See that you buy 'em each
a soda, Partridge, and charge it to wear and tear.

. . . Run along, son, if you want to keep your job. . . ." Mr Partridge went trembling on his way, the little boys, with a backward glance at Mildred, followed sheepishly.

"Now that the kindergarten has retired," said Peter Bender, "do you people realize that you're trying to do something that will absolutely brand you? This—this—what do you call it, Sandy? this *strike* of yours," he said, pronouncing it like something in a very poor nursery rhyme, "of all the uncivilized performances! No, listen," he said, sad and grave, and addressing particularly the super-mice, "we're all experts here, professionals. You, Nicholls, a writer! Miss Heald, I think you've published poetry. Dickinson, Furniss, an artist—and you, Murphy, have you thought of your wife?" Everyone glanced briefly at Joe, for it was commonly known that he had married above his class, a fine girl who demanded the best of everything. "And all the rest of you," said Peter Bender, shaking his head as though they had all become demented, "all the rest of you—haven't I given bonuses to the entire staff for slogans? My God," he said, becoming more and more deeply alive to their tragedy, "why, you people are behaving like a bunch of, of *factory* hands!"

"Why not?" cried Mildred Curtis. "We get paid like factory hands, don't we?"

"And cut like them!" shouted Sandusky—Gracie at the switchboard sniffed.

"There's been some misunderstanding, Mr Ben-

der," Dickinson's unhappy murmur started down
the aisle and died.

"Scene two," said Joe Murphy.

"Let's not shout at each other, Sandy, please,"
said Peter Bender. "How can you, Dickinson, and
you, Nicholls, and the rest of you, align yourselves
with such rot? And you, Miss Pierce, a pretty girl
like you—how would you like your boy-friend to
find you, Miss Pierce, down on the sidewalk carrying placards on your shoulders like a sandwich
man? Why my God, my dear, you're too charming
to go in for such stuff as that! Joe, you *can't* have
thought this thing through, why your wife would
be fearfully upset, and I can't blame her. . . . Gee,
listen, these are damn tough times, friends, for all
of us, no one knows it better than I—do you think
I *enjoy* cutting salaries? I cut them so I can afford
to run this office, so you can all keep your jobs. . . .
Well, say, it's a free country, I'm the last guy in the
world to try and coerce you into staying against
your will. I'd hate like hell to see any of you leave,
but you know I can fill your places easily, I can get
college professors to write copy and débutantes
to sell it—while you people will have a hard time
finding work anywhere else. But that's not the
point." Here Peter Bender plunged his hands into
his pockets and faced them honestly. "The point
is it's still a free country, you're free, every one of
you, to stay and keep your jobs, or free to go and
jeopardize your families' safety—and perfectly free
to go and make damn fools of yourselves on the

street. But gee, listen, folks," he swept his hand, boyishly earnest, through his hair, "I guess I'm just a dumb guy, just a sentimental fool, I thought you all were happy here, and now—*organizing* against me! behind my back! well, gosh! I couldn't feel worse if my own sisters and brothers hired a lawyer instead of coming simply to me. . ." (You could hear Miss Pierce, still blushing from her compliments, gently blow her nose, and Betty Carlisle herself was swallowing hard.) "And what do you think of yourself, Mildred Curtis, don't you feel you've undertaken a pretty grave responsibility, playing upon people's sympathies and getting them to risk their jobs?"

"I sure do," said Mildred Curtis, steely-eyed. "And I'll tear up our list of demands any time they ask me to."

"No, No, No!" shouted a number of voices in the office, but definitely, thought Betty, standing by, her senses as keen as though she were counting votes, definitely not more than half. The top staff of the super-mice looked as though it felt itself rather foolish, Dickinson was pawing the ground like an embarrassed pony, and Joe Murphy was scowling with his cigar gone dead in his mouth.

"No, listen, folks," said Peter Bender, talking in the voice he had used with the little errand-boys, at once stern and very kind, "remember this is the fifth year A.D.—After Depression. There are 400,-000 families in New York City alone living on relief, figure five to a family it comes to about two million—and where is this strike or whateveryou-callit going to land you, except out on the streets with the rest of the unemployed? . . . No, seriously, friends, I'm shocked, and hurt, and really surprised—but most of all I'm concerned as hell for all of you. I'd hate like the devil to see any of you become officers in the army of the unemployed." (The art man suddenly departed for the Men's Room, and although he had left his hat on his desk he did not reappear that afternoon.)

"There's another point I'd like to make," continued Peter Bender, sad and urbane, "if you'll permit me to grow a little sentimental—a point about good sportsmanship. Probably the most decent thing that ever happened in this country is the show-down made by the depression. Some of us, at the first hint of bum luck, bumped ourselves off. Couldn't take it. A lot of others suddenly showed they had guts; met with reverses and took it in their stride.

"Well, I consider that we're having a show-down right now in this office." Peter Bender looked about him, so noble himself, thought Betty, that he raised them all for one minute, to his level. "I think I can spot the quitters from the stickers already, the ones that can take it. . . . Why my God, Miss White, Gracie!" he cried, turning to her so swiftly that she started, "aren't you ashamed of making so much of one little tough break? Why my God, my dear girl, last week I got socked as hell in the stock market, but you don't see me picketing Wall Street, do you?

Do you advise me to picket the Stock Exchange, Gracie, tell me? How about it, Miss Pierce, will you pose as my starving child? Why, my God!" Peter Bender laughed easily, and then harder, and then allowed himself to shake with his laughter as though he couldn't control it. Betty Carlisle joined in, as heartily as refinement would permit, pretty soon Miss Pierce was laughing too, and Dickinson started coughing till you couldn't tell whether he was laughing or clearing his throat. Nicholls was giving Miss Pierce excited little glances as though he wanted to date her up, and one or two of the others were hiding their laughing faces from Mildred Curtis. Betty Carlisle was almost drunk with admiration for handsome Peter Bender; he really is a leader, a leader of men, she said to herself, while her shoulders shook with laughter and her legs shivered with a sort of thrill.

"Now as for you, Gracie," said Peter Bender, pulling himself out of his laughter, "as for you, my dear, I think you've been misled. You don't want all your friends to lose their jobs on account of you, do you, Gracie?"

"No, Mr Bender," said Gracie weakly.

"And you don't want to lose your own job, Gracie, do you? I think you've got a little sister partly dependent on you, well, you don't want to let her down like that, do you, my dear?"

"That's not fair," shouted Mildred Curtis. "Don't let him bully a weakling like that, you ought to be ashamed, Mr Bender—"

"And here's your good friend calling you a weakling, Gracie," said Peter Bender gently. "Now look, I don't know a darn thing about this communism, but I do know a thing or two about plain old-fashioned friendship. How good a friend do you think Mildred here can be to you, Gracie, wouldn't a good friend rather lend you some of her own salary than get you to risk all of your own?" Peter Bender put his hand on Gracie's shoulder.

"Swine," muttered Joe Murphy in admiration.

"I don't know, Mr Bender," sobbed Gracie, "I didn't know it would be like this, I didn't mean to start any trouble—she started it, Mildred did, she said, she promised me—"

"Gracie! pull yourself together!" Mildred Curtis swept to the switchboard with Sandusky, mute and passionate, close behind her. "Gracie! You know you said you couldn't live on what you make, twelve dollars a week, my God! and two sisters! And we're all in practically the same boat, Gracie, don't you see, most of us have been cut already, and the rest of us will be—if we don't stand together and protest right now. Don't give in, Gracie, remember all you said this morning, you don't want to let your fellow-workers down, do you, Gracie? We've all sworn to fight for you."

"I don't want to f-f-fight," sobbed Gracie.

"And nobody will make you fight, Gracie," said Peter Bender kindly. "Come now, my dear, you're all unstrung for nothing. Look up, Gracie, there's a good girl. Now look, I didn't know you were in such a spot with all those sisters and everything, suppose we promise you a nice Christmas present, a bonus, will that be all right, Gracie?"

The whole office went up in arms at that, Sandusky leading the storm. "Don't give in to that, Gracie! For God's sake where's your pride? Are you going to let us down, Gracie, for a lousy little bonus, it won't be more than twenty-five dollars, Gracie, Gracie, Gracie!"

"I—I promised Mildred," muttered Gracie. Then she lifted her head from her hands and saw the whole office staring at her. Terror and a kind of hysterical joy seemed to dawn in her at once. So many people staring at her! Betty saw her weak, red eyes float from face to face, waver between Mildred's and the boss's, and then she gathered strength enough to speak. "I promised her," said Gracie, urging her telephone-girl voice out in a kind of high-pitched nasal defiance, "I did promise her, but she never told me there'd be all this fuss, and anyway like you said, what kind of a friend can she be to go and let me lose my job and all?"

"Gracie!" The whole office seemed to breathe her name, typewriters, filing-cabinets—the very walls, as though a member of the staff were dead before their eyes.

"I can't help it," cried Gracie, sobbing again, "everybody tells me what to say, and all I want . . . oh, I want to go home, Mr Bender, I don't want to fight, please Mr Bender, let me go home. . ."

"Certainly, Gracie, that's the wisest thing you can

do," said Peter Bender. "Poor girl, you've had a bad day of it—look, Miss Carlisle, help her find her things. . . ." Gracie tried to rise, and Mildred Curtis fastened her hands about her wrists. (Betty Carlisle leaped forward at the boss's order but Sandusky blocked her way.) "Let go of her, Mildred, she's sick," said Peter Bender reproachfully.

"Gracie, you're not really quitting?" said Mildred in a low, harsh voice.

And Gracie, trembling, sobbing, fidgeting, crying out that she didn't want to lose her job, suddenly freed one hand and in a frenzy of helplessness, like a baby in a tantrum, reached up and struck Mildred Curtis a blow full across the mouth. Mildred fell back, stunned, while Gracie, more frightened than ever, put her erring hand behind her back. Sandusky let go of Betty and ran to Mildred, and Betty, righteous and brave, led the trembling telephone-girl to the elevator. The door clanged after her with a curious air of finality.

"All right, ladies and gents, break it up for God's sake—" Peter Bender was speaking briskly, "quit standing around looking like Amateur Night at the local movies, we've got fifteen minutes to closing time and anybody that hasn't checked in at my office by then is out cold, this is no Union Square." (He was moving quietly toward the private office.) "How about it, friends? A snifter or a bowl of soup on some nice breadline?" He clapped his arm around Dickinson and gave him a hearty boost toward his private door. "Come on there, Miss Carlisle will shake up drinks for anyone that's got the sense to admit he just woke up with dyspepsia this morning . . . this way, folks, I'd hate to think I was never going to see you people again. . . . Remember, it's 1934 . . . step on it, Dickinson, come on there, Nicholls, Miss Pierce, Murphy, all of you—there's thirteen minutes to go, all aboard that's staying aboard. . . ."

There were murmured shouts of "Scab!" "White collar slave!" "Rat!" as Dickinson went as far as the impetus of the boss's push could carry him. Then he turned, hiding his head behind one shoulder and looked mutely at his fellow-mice, at his boss, and at last, very humbly, at Betty Carlisle, who smiled kindly back to him (he really did look, she thought, more like a rat than a mouse) and then proceeded, like a rat in reins, to work his way to the private office. "Come on, folks!" cried Peter Bender, genial and grim; "twelve minutes to go—"

"Comrades!" The strong, inarticulate Sandusky had found his voice. "Don't let him bully you, it doesn't matter about Gracie, it's better if we get rid of the scabs in the first place. I propose we knock out all mention of Gracie and go on with the strike as planned. As Mildred said before—"

"Eleven minutes," said Peter Bender, baring his wrist watch. (Miss Pierce slid a step or two toward Dickinson.)

"As Mildred said before," Sandusky's voice had grown thick with emotion, "we're all in the same boat, either now or tomorrow, as Gracie—only some of us have got guts!" He turned to look at Mildred, but Mildred was standing with her hand to her mouth where Gracie had struck her, looking like a blind girl. "Stand by, Comrades—"

"Ten minutes," said Peter Bender.

"Don't listen to him," shouted Sandusky hoarsely, "he can't do anything if we all stick together and hold out against him. Nicholls, come back, Mister Nicholls, Mister Dickinson—*you'll* stick by us, won't you, Joe?"

But Joe Murphy, with that dead cigar in his mouth, was reaching for his hat. "Nope—show's over, Sandy, far as I'm concerned. Count me out, I'm like Gracie, I've got no guts; I want my job, my filthy, God damned, boot-licking job. I don't sneak through the can like our artist, I go out like an advertising man." He pulled his hat theatrically over one eye. "Your martyr has quietly folded her tents and gone home—and now exit your advertising man." He started for the door. "Never trust an advertising man, Mildred, they can write a good list of demands for you, but they've all got million-dollar wives and grand pianos to support. . . ."

"Drink, Murphy?" said Peter Bender cordially.

"No thanks, Bender, I can buy my own poison," Joe Murphy bit on his cigar. "My congratulations, by the way, you're as lousy as I am, Bender. . . . So long, all of you that've got guts—the rest of you I'll see tomorrow and the next day and the day after, at half-past nine." He clicked his heels and saluted bitterly. "Partridge and Murphy, the Monitor

Boys." The door slammed after him and they could hear him whistling "Onward Christian Soldiers" as he waited for the elevator to take him the way Gracie had gone.

"Nine minutes," said Peter Bender. "Come on, Miss Carlisle, you're wanted to make drinks."

Betty Carlisle's head was high as she stepped through the aisle of workers at Peter Bender's side. If anything, the glances full of hate that she received from the dwindling mice made her drunker, prouder, recklessly gay. They're all so jealous they're about to pop, she thought drunkenly—even that Mildred. "There's a pretty nasty name for female scabs, Miss Betty Carlisle," the youngest checker called out after her, and Betty let her nostrils quiver a little, like Peter's, and felt more aristocratic than ever. And then Peter Bender led her into the private office.

Dickinson was standing by the window with his back to them when they came in, and his whole body looked weak and dejected, as if it had slipped inside his suit. Miss Pierce was wandering on the terrace admiring the fine city view, and Nicholls was standing, a little embarrassed, pretending to examine Peter Bender's lithographs. "Where's all the gayety song and dance?" cried Peter Bender, shutting the door smartly on the Mouse-Trap. "Come on, Dickinson, snap out of it, round up the glasses and ice, Miss Carlisle, Miss Pierce stand by and look pretty—"

"It's certainly mighty lovely in here, Mr Bender,"

said Miss Pierce shyly. "I didn't ever really have a chance to take my time and look around before."

"I agree it's pleasanter than the inside of a cell," said Peter Bender, pouring highballs all round. "Which is where you *might* be headed for—"

"Oh, you wouldn't have sent us all to jail, Mr Bender, would you really?" cried Miss Pierce gayly. "Oh Mr Nicholls, do you believe him, do you really?"

"To jail, Mr Bender!" cried Dickinson, trembling bravely as though he had just realized what a brave thing he had done in escaping it.

"Sure thing," said Peter Bender cheerfully. "Well, bottoms up!" The door opened shyly, and two more stenographers stood shyly in the frame. "Oh Mr Bender, we'd like to explain, it wasn't altogether clear to us, I was just telling Julie—" "To hell with it," cried Peter Bender, "have a drink instead— we've six more minutes."

There they all were drinking with the boss and you could see *they* weren't used to it, thought Betty Carlisle warmly. To show them all, and Peter Bender, and herself too, that *she* was, Betty hoisted herself upon Peter Bender's desk and sat there swinging her handsome legs, in their long, fine chiffon hose. Over the top of her glass she gave Mr Bender excited little looks, and she felt the intimacy between them growing, till she was proud and happy enough to sing.

"I dunno, I dunno, Mr Bender," said Dickinson, who could hardly swallow his drink, "I dunno just how I feel about it, Mr Bender, I didn't feel quite right then, not loyal to you or anything, and I don't feel quite right now—I guess I must be soft, Mr Bender," said Fred Dickinson, sighing deeply.

"Soft!" cried Peter Bender. "Why, my God, I'm soft as hell myself! I'm a hell of a sentimental chap when it comes to personalities, personal troubles and all that kind of thing—but causes! heaven preserve me from causes and fanatics, they leave me ab-so-lutely cold! Now take that little Mildred Curtis, does she give a tinker's damn for Gracie? No, certainly not, she was *using* Gracie for her own ends—and playing on your sympathies for her own ends too—"

"She don't come of a good family at all," said Miss Pierce, wiping her mouth very nicely.

The door opened again, and they heard Fleetman, the cosmetics copy man, with one hand on the knob—"can't help it, Mildred, two kids, you know—" and then he stood inside: "I—" began Mr Fleetman, "I don't quite know what to say, Mr Bender—"

"All right, all right, don't bother saying it," said Peter Bender, "the drinks are on the house." The clock jumped and everybody saw that it was three minutes to five, a nearby church-clock began to chime ahead of time. The two recruits from the stenographers' contingent glanced nervously at the door as though they feared that Mildred Curtis might burst in. "I just want to tell you all," said Peter Bender, rising, glass in hand, "now that we're all here together, how deeply and sincerely I appreciate your loyalty. I won't forget it either." It was two minutes to five and Peter Bender spoke more rapidly. "Honestly, on the whole I'm glad this thing happened, it's a show-down sure enough." Again the door opened, and this time the younger checking-boy slunk through; one of his eyes was newly blacked, and it was clear that he had been crying. He stood there sullen, in an agony of embarrassment; he was there, but he was not going to admit it in so many words. Peter Bender hurried on, one hand on the checking-boy's shoulder. "From now on there will be perfect harmony in the office, because everybody that's staying on has learnt a lesson, and has proved himself—" The churches were chiming five o'clock all up and down Fifth Avenue, the office clock recognized the time at last, the hand jumped and stood still. "I think you people had better run along now," Peter Bender said.

"Do we, do we have to go through *there*?" said Dickinson, pointing to the outer office.

"No, no, go out my private door, you won't be seen," said Peter Bender impatiently. He shook hands gravely with each one of them, only the youngest checker slinking out with his right hand over Sandusky's black eye. "Christmas is coming, and so is prosperity," he promised them quickly, as voices rose in the outer office, "and you will find that I won't forget the people who stood by me in a crisis."

Dickinson's frightened tail had scarcely trembled through the private exit when the door of the Mouse-Trap, on the last stroke of five, burst open. Three stood there, Mildred Curtis, Sandusky, and Mr Partridge's part-time boy.

"Am I to understand," began Peter Bender, smiling tentative but grim, his sleeve rolled up above his wrist-watch.

"There are just a few things we feel like telling you, Mr Bender," said Mildred Curtis, giving Betty Carlisle a look that Betty said afterwards gave her the creeps, sort of, it was so funny. "We feel like telling you what we think of your—"

"I've had enough of your feelings," said Peter Bender, preparing to shut the door. Sandusky, in-articulate again with anything but his muscles, lunged forward with his fists raised, Mr Partridge's part-time boy and Mildred Curtis held him back, and Peter Bender, smiling, poked him out and slammed and locked his door. Then he and Betty Carlisle stood still and looked at each other warmly in the locked room, and Betty thought that every-one in the world was leaving them together, her breath came and went with excitement as the voices (was Mildred Curtis sobbing? no, it sounded rather like Sandusky) died in the Mouse-Trap, the final steps were heard, the elevator outside rose again, and carried the last people in the world away.

"Oh my dear, my dear!" cried Peter Bender, "I hope you know how swell it was. Oh my God, I haven't had such a good time since the War! And did we rout them, baby! and did we scare them! and did we get rid of just the ones we wanted to get rid of! I feel swell, baby, swell! Come and kiss papa, honey, quick!"

He grew before her eyes into a giant of a man, his virility somehow enhanced, as a general's must be returning home after victory. She felt he could do anything in the world he wanted, have anything in the world he looked at, and when he caught her in his arms and began dancing with her about the empty office, Betty Carlisle felt that she would give him anything he asked for. "You were marvelous," she whispered, "I admired you so—and slamming the door in their faces at the end, I nearly died!"

"And how you stuck by, baby, you were wonderful too, you can take it in your stride yourself." He kissed her with a new and violent passion. "Let's have music and drinks."

He turned on a little radio in the wall and poured them both high-balls, which he set with a pitcher of cracked ice and a bottle of whiskey on a little modernistic table beside the divan. She had a vision of him standing there and looking at her for a moment before he switched off the lights and threw open the door to the terrace, so that the fading light of city afternoon cast a dull yellow shadow on their faces. He led her to the couch and sat beside her, kissing her and drinking, laughing, holding her high-ball to her lips.

"I got such a thrill, baby," he whispered, "seeing

you there beside me all afternoon, like a swell little partner." Such heady happiness leapt in Betty's heart that she wanted to tell him that she loved him. "You're a swell-looking gal, kid, and you've got brains as well as legs," he whispered. "You know how to live, you know what it's all about—don't you, Betty? don't you?" She lay quiet, feeling in her bones that her life was about to be settled. "It doesn't happen often, Betty, does it, that two people are so able to think alike, and enjoy things together, like we do." He pressed closer, and she caught the scent of his expensive shaving-lotion mingling with his country-club tweeds. "I'm just nuts about you, baby," he whispered gayly.

They lay there kissing each other for a long, slow time. "You've got such a soft beautiful mouth," he said, "you sure learned how to kiss back there in Topeka, how were the Kansas boy-friends, not so slow, eh?" "Oh no, I—" she murmured but he stopped her by kissing her again. "We could have such a swell time together, baby, I knew it the first time I saw you, such a swell old time together, if only you—God damn that orchestra! I hate those twangy Negro blues, wouldn't you think they'd learn something new!" He left her to change the radio station, and Betty lay there still and frightened.

"Turn it off altogether, Peter," she said shyly. "Oh no, I like a little music," he said crossly, fiddling in the dark with the knobs and the buttons. "There, there we are, I've got the real thing now, to hell with Harlem! This is the Biltmore, honey, now we can relax and imagine we're in a suite upstairs."

He came back and lay beside her, taking her in his arms. "Oh Peter, don't, oh please don't!" whispered Betty Carlisle, all her Kansas training—and something else besides, some unnamed fear—sending the tears to her eyes.

"Why not, baby, I'm nuts about you, honestly. . ."

She lay there paralyzed, Betty Carlisle did, unhappily acquiescent as though she were taking dictation from the boss. A funny kind of gloomy cold wind blew in from the city through the pent-house door—they were so terribly high up! thought Betty, thinking of the nineteen floors and the elevator rising and falling and carrying the city's mice to and from their work, above the city's roof-tops.

"The wind," she said faintly, struggling for time, "won't you please shut the door?" "Are you cold, baby, with *me* here?" he whispered tenderly, and gathered her more closely in his arms. "No, I'm not cold, it scares me, the wind does—it makes me nervous, sort of." "My God," he said, "what's the matter with you anyway—turn off the music, close the door—can't you take a bit of wind in your stride, Betty? Kiss me, honey," he said irritably.

"No, no, no," sobbed Betty Carlisle—but Peter Bender was the boss, and soon he was kissing her till she couldn't talk—Peter Bender was the boss, and he could take everything in his stride, music, wind,

other people's fear—and love; and it was not at all
long before Betty Carlisle, who had never let the
Kansas boys take liberties, had let the boss take the
final liberty with her, on the evening of the day
they had settled the strike together.

"You won't be sorry, baby," he was whispering,
soft as air, "you'll never be sorry, honey, I'll help
you out, I heard what the little Curtis said this afternoon, and I hadn't realized it before, I'll see to it
you have plenty of nice clothes, baby, honestly I
will—"

She lay there paralyzed, Betty Carlisle did, not
exactly taking in his words but hearing the meaning just the same. All at once there was a terrific
gust tearing up from the street nineteen floors below; the terrible volume banged against the pent-
house door and sent it leaping and shuddering inside the room. "Please shut the door, please, please,"
said Betty Carlisle, almost sobbing now, for the
wind seemed to threaten something, her own peace
of mind maybe, coming as it probably did all the
way from home in Kansas, blowing across prairies
(like all the young stenographer-receptionists who
were too pretty to stay home, who fled with their
fitted suit-cases year after year—and what became of
them all, she wondered! scattered in offices and
pent-houses above Fifth Avenue and God only knew
what happened in their heads and hearts as those
fitted suit-cases, those gifts from home, wore out!)
blowing across prairies and coming through the

narrow city streets and rising to the nineteenth floor. . .

"God damn it!" cried Peter Bender—and jumped from the couch with his shirt-tails flying to buck that Kansas wind. He set his shoulders against the door and pushed and shoved and cursed, and he would get it just so far when the wind from home would develop a sense of humor and fling it back in his face. Betty Carlisle sat up on the couch and felt the wind cool on her cheeks, and she began to laugh a little at Peter Bender's antics. "God damn this thing!" he shouted like a puny giant above the gale, his expensive voice breaking with anger; but for all his bank-accounts and tennis muscles, thought Betty Carlisle, struggling into the jacket of her tailleur, for all he had been able to slam the door in the faces of the striking mice, he couldn't do a thing against the wind. . .

"Where are you going?" he shouted to her as the wind roared between them. "Wait a minute, where are you going?"

"Home," Betty Carlisle cried back in a defiant nasal Kansas twang—and not caring any more that her tailleur was mussed or her silk stockings wrinkled, or even if she looked more like a stenographer than a receptionist.

"You little fool," he shouted back, pushing against the door, "don't be such a little fool, if you're going to take it this way, how in hell are we going to have any fun, how are we even going to get along in the same office, one of us will have to look for another job—" and he abandoned the door and gripped her by the shoulders.

But Betty Carlisle had grown desperate, and kicking and struggling, she pitted her good basket-ball muscles against his tennis-and-golf-and-whiskey wrists and gave him a kind of half-Nelson that her brothers had taught her in Topeka, before she realized she had lost her job and crept out and down the stairs like a mouse to catch the elevator from the eighteenth floor.

1934

Missis Flinders

Missis Flinders

* This story, originally conceived as a unit, later became the final chapter of "The Unpossessed." It is here reprinted as it properly belongs with any collection of the author's short-stories. —The publishers.

"HOME you go!" Miss Kane, nodding, in her white nurse's dress, stood for a moment—she would catch a breath of air—in the hospital door; "and thank you again for the stockings, you needn't have bothered"—drew a sharp breath and turning, dismissed Missis Flinders from the hospital, smiling, dismissed her forever from her mind.

So Margaret Flinders stood next to her basket of fruit on the hospital steps; both of them waiting, a little shame-faced in the sudden sunshine, and in no hurry to leave the hospital—no hurry at all. It would be nicer to be alone, Margaret thought, glancing at the basket of fruit which stood respectable and a little silly on the stone step (the candy-bright apples were blushing caricatures of Miles: Miles' comfort, not hers). Flowers she could have left behind (for the nurses, in the room across the hall where they made tea at night); books she could have slipped into her suit-case; but fruit—Miles' gift, Miles' guilt, man's tribute to the Missis in the hospital—must be eaten; a half-eaten basket of

231

fruit (she had tried to leave it: Missis Butter won't you . . . Missis Wiggam wouldn't you like . . . But Missis Butter had aplenty of her own thank you, and Missis Wiggam said she couldn't hold acids after a baby)—a half-eaten basket of fruit, in times like these, cannot be left to rot.

Down the street Miles was running, running, after a taxi. He was going after the taxi for her; it was for her sake he ran; yet this minute that his back was turned he stole for his relief and spent in running away, his shoulders crying guilt. And don't hurry, don't hurry, she said to them; I too am better off alone.

The street stretched in a long white line very finally away from the hospital, the hospital where Margaret Flinders (called there so solemnly Missis) had been lucky enough to spend only three nights. It would be four days before Missis Wiggam would be going home to Mister Wiggam with a baby; and ten possibly—the doctors were uncertain, Miss Kane prevaricated—before Missis Butter would be going home to Mister Butter without one. Zigzagging the street went the children; their cries and the sudden grinding of their skates she had listened to upstairs beside Missis Butter for three days. Some such child had she been—for the styles in children had not changed—a lean child gliding solemnly on skates and grinding them viciously at the nervous feet of grown-ups. Smile at these children she would not or could not; yet she felt on her face that smile, fixed, painful and frozen, that she had put there, on waking from ether three days back, to greet Miles. The smile spoke to the retreating shoulders of Miles: I don't need you; the smile spoke formally to life: thanks, I'm not having any. Not so the child putting the heels of his skates together Charlie Chaplin-wise and describing a scornful circle on the widest part of the sidewalk. Not so a certain little girl (twenty years back) skating past the wheels of autos, pursuing life in the form of a ball so red! so gay! better death than to turn one's back and smile over one's shoulder at life!

Upstairs Missis Butter must still be writhing with her poor caked breasts. The bed that had been hers beside Missis Butter's was empty now; Miss Kane would be stripping it and Joe would come in bringing fresh sheets. Whom would they put in beside Missis Butter, to whom would she moan and boast all night about the milk in her breasts that was turning, she said, into cheese?

Now Miles was coming back, jogging sheepishly on the running-board of a taxi, he had run away to the end of his rope and now was returning penitent, his eyes dog-like searching her out where she stood on the hospital steps (did they rest with complacence on the basket of fruit, his gift?), pleading with her, Didn't I get the taxi fast? like an anxious little boy. She stood with that smile on her face that hurt like too much ice-cream. Smile and smile; for she felt like a fool, she had walked open-eyed smiling into the trap (*Don't wriggle, Missis, I might injure you for life, Miss Kane had said cheerfully*) and felt the spring only when it was too late, when she waked from ether and knew like the thrust of a knife what she had ignored before. *Whatever did you do if for, Missis Flinders, Missis Butter was always saying; if there's nothing the matter with your insides —doesn't your husband . . . and Won't you have some fruit, Missis Butter, her calm reply: meaning, My husband gave me this fruit so what right have you to doubt that my husband. . .* Her husband who now stumbled up the steps to meet her; his eyes he had sent ahead, but something in him wanted not to come, tripped his foot as he hurried up the steps.

"Take my arm, Margaret," he said. "Walk slowly," he said. The bitter pill of taking help, of feeling weakly grateful, stuck in her throat. Miles' face behind his glasses was tense like the face of an amateur actor in the rôle of a strike-leader. That he was inadequate for the part he seemed to know. And if he felt shame, shame in his own eyes, she could forgive him; but if it was only guilt felt man-like in her presence, a guilt which he could drop off like a damp shirt, if he was putting it all off on her for being a woman! "The fruit, Miles!" she said; "you've forgotten the fruit." "The fruit can wait," he said bitterly.

He handed her into the taxi as though she were a package marked glass—something, she thought, not merely troublesomely womanly, but ladylike. "Put your legs up on the seat," he said. "I don't want to, Miles." *Goodbye Missis Butter* Put your legs up on the seat. I don't want to—*Better luck next time Missis Butter* Put your legs *I can't make out our window, Missis Butter* Put your "All right, it will be nice and uncomfortable." (She put her legs up on the seat.) *Goodbye Missis But.* . . "Nothing I say is right," he said. "It's good with the legs up," she said brightly.

Then he was up the steps agile and sure after the fruit. And down again, the basket swinging with affected carelessness, arming him, till he relinquished it modestly to her outstretched hands. Then he seated himself on the little seat, the better to watch his woman and his woman's fruit; and screwing his head round on his neck said irritably to the man who had been all his life on the wrong side of the glass pane: "Charles street!"

"Hadn't you better ask him to please drive slowly?" Margaret said.

"I was just going to," he said bitterly.

"And drive slowly," he shouted over his shoulder.

The driver's name was Carl C. Strite. She could see Carl Strite glance cannily back at the hospital: Greenway Maternity Home; pull his lever with extreme delicacy as though he were stroking the neck of a horse. There was a small roar—and the hospital glided backward: its windows ran together like the windows of a moving train; a spurt—watch out for those children on skates!—and the car was fairly started down the street.

Goodbye Missis Butter I hope you get a nice

roommate in my place, I hope you won't find that Mister B let the ice-pan flow over again—and give my love to the babies when Miss Kane stops them in the door for you to wave at—goodbye Missis Butter, really goodbye.

Carl Strite (was he thinking maybe of his mother, an immigrant German woman she would have been, come over with a shawl on her head and worked herself to skin and bone so the kids could go to school and turn out good Americans—and what had it come to, here he was a taxi-driver, and what taxi-drivers didn't know! what in the course of their lackeys' lives they didn't put up with, fall in with! well, there was one decent thing left in Carl Strite, he knew how to carry a woman home from a maternity hospital) drove softly along the curb . . . and the eyes of his honest puzzled gangster's snout photographed as "Your Driver" looked dimmed as though the glory of woman were too much for them, in a moment the weak cruel baby's mouth might blubber. Awful to lean forward and tell Mr Strite he was laboring under a mistake. *Missis Wiggam's freckled face when she heard that Missis Butter's roommate . . . maybe Missis Butter's baby had been born dead but anyway she had had a baby . . . whatever did you do it for Missis Flind. . .*

"Well, patient," Miles began, tentative, nervous (bored? perturbed? behind his glasses?).

"How does it feel, Maggie?" he said in a new, small voice.

Hurt and hurt this man, a feeling told her. He is

a man, he could have made you a woman. "What's a D and C between friends?" she said. "Nobody at the hospital gave a damn about my little illegality."

"Well, but I do," he protested like a short man trying to be tall.

She turned on her smile; the bright silly smile that was eating up her face.

Missis Butter would be alone now with no one to boast to about her pains except Joe who cleaned the corridors and emptied bed-pans—and thought Missis Butter was better than an angel because although she had incredible golden hair she could wise-crack like any brunette. Later in the day the eight-day mothers wobbling down the corridors for their pre-nursing constitutional would look in and talk to her; for wasn't Missis Butter their symbol and their pride, the one who had given up her baby that they might have theirs (for a little superstition is inevitable in new mothers, and it was generally felt that there must be one dead baby in a week's batch at any decent hospital) for whom they demanded homage from their visiting husbands? for whose health they asked the nurses each morning second only to asking for their own babies? That roommate of yours was a funny one, Missis Wiggam would say. Missis Wiggam was the woman who said big breasts weren't any good: here she was with a seven-pound baby and not a drop for it (here she would open the negligée Mister Wiggam had given her not to shame them before the nurses, and poke contemptuously at the floppy parts of herself within) while there was Missis Butter with no baby but a dead baby and her small breasts caking because there was so much milk in them for nothing but a . . . Yes, that Missis Flinders was sure a funny one, Missis Butter would agree.

"Funny ones", she and Miles, riding home with numb faces and a basket of fruit between them— past a park, past a museum, past elevated pillars— intellectuals they were, bastards, changelings . . . giving up a baby for economic freedom which meant that two of them would work in offices instead of one of them only, giving up a baby for intellectual freedom which meant that they smoked their cigarettes bitterly and looked out of the windows of a taxi onto streets and people and stores and hated them all. "We'd go soft," Miles had finally said, "we'd go bourgeois." Yes, with diapers drying on the radiators, bottles wrapped in flannel, the grocer getting to know one too well—yes, they would go soft, they might slump and start liking people, they might weaken and forgive stupidity, they might yawn and forget to hate. "Funny ones," class-straddlers, intellectuals, tight-rope-walking somewhere in the middle (how long could they hang on without falling to one side or the other? one more war? one more depression?); intellectuals, with habits generated from the right and tastes inclined to the left. Afraid to perpetuate themselves, were they? Afraid of anything that might loom so large in their personal lives as to outweigh other considerations? Afraid, maybe, of a personal life?

"Oh give me another cigarette," she said.

And still the taxi, with its burden of intellectuals and their inarticulate fruit-basket, its motherly, gangsterly, inarticulate driver, its license plates and its photographs all so very official, jogged on; past Harlem now; past fire-escapes loaded with flower-pots and flapping clothes; dingy windows opening to the soot-laden air blown in by the elevated roaring down its tracks. Past Harlem and through 125th street: stores and wise-cracks, Painless Dentists, cheap florists; Eighth Avenue, boarded and plastered, concealing the subway that was reaching its laborious birth beneath. But Eighth Avenue was too jouncy for Mr Strite's precious burden of womanhood (who was reaching passionately for a cigarette); he cut through the park, and they drove past quiet walks on which the sun had brought out babies as the Fall rains give birth to worms.

"But ought you to smoke so much, so soon after —so soon?" Miles said, not liking to say so soon after what. His hand held the cigarettes out to her, back from her.

"They do say smoking's bad for child-birth," she said calmly, and with her finger-tips drew a cigarette from his reluctant hand.

And tapping down the tobacco on the handle of the fruit-basket she said, "But we've got the joke on them there, we have." (Hurt and hurt this man, her feeling told her; he is a man and could have made you a woman.)

"It was your own decision too," he said harshly, striking and striking at the box with his match.

"This damn taxi's shaking you too much," he said suddenly, bitter and contrite.

But Mr Strite was driving like an angel. He handled his car as though it were a baby-carriage. Did he think maybe it had turned out with her the way it had with Missis Butter? I could have stood it better, Missis Butter said, if they hadn't told me it was a boy. And me with my fourth little girl, Missis Wiggam had groaned (but proudly, proudly); why I didn't even want to see it when they told me. But Missis Butter stood it very well, and so did Missis Wiggam. They were a couple of good bitches; and what if Missis Butter had produced nothing but a dead baby this year, and what if Missis Wiggam would bring nothing to Mister Wiggam but a fourth little girl this year—why there was next year and the year after, there was the certain little world from grocery-store to kitchen, there were still Mister Butter and Mister Wiggam who were both (Missis Wiggam and Missis Butter vied with each other) just *crazy* about babies. Well, Mister Flinders is different, she had lain there thinking (he cares as much for his unborn gods as I for my unborn babies); and wished she could have the firm assurance they had in "husbands", coming as they did year after year away from them for a couple of weeks, just long enough to bear them babies either dead-ones or girl-ones . . . good bitches they were: there was something lustful besides smug in their pride in being "Missis". Let Missis Flinders so much as let out a groan because a sudden pain grew too big for her groins, let her so much as murmur because the sheets were hot beneath her—and Missis Butter and Missis Wiggam in the security of their maternity-fraternity exchanged glances of amusement: SHE don't know what pain is, look at what's talking about PAIN. . . .

"Mr Strite flatters us," she whispered, her eyes smiling straight and hard at Miles. (Hurt and hurt . . .)

"And why does that give you so much pleasure?" He dragged the words as though he were pounding them out with two fingers on the typewriter.

The name without the pain—she thought to say; and did not say. All at once she lost her desire to punish him; she no more wanted to "hurt this man" for he was no more man than she was woman. She would not do him the honor of hurting him. She must reduce him as she felt herself reduced. She must cut out from him what made him a man, as she had let be cut out from her what would have made her a woman. He was no man: he was a dried-up intellectual husk; he was sterile; empty and hollow as she was.

Missis Butter lying up on her pillow would count over to Missis Wiggam the fine points of her tragedy: how she had waited two days to be delivered of a dead baby; how it wouldn't have been so bad if the doctor hadn't said it was a beautiful baby with platinum-blond hair exactly like hers (and hers bleached unbelievably, but never mind, Missis Wiggam had come to believe in it like Joe and Mister Butter, another day and Missis Flinders herself, intellectual sceptic though she was, might have been convinced); and how they would pay the last instalment on—what a baby-carriage, Missis Wiggam, you'd never believe me!—and sell it second-hand for half its worth. I know when I was caught with my first, Missis Wiggam would take up the story her mouth had been open for. And that Missis Flinders was sure a funny one. . . .

But I am not such a funny one, Margaret wanted, beneath her bright and silly smile, behind her cloud of cigarette smoke (for Miles had given in; the whole package sat gloomily on Margaret's lap) to say to them; even though in my "crowd" the girls keep the names they were born with, even though some of us sleep for a little variety with one another's husbands, even though I forget as often as Miles—Mister Flinders to you—to empty the pan under the ice-box. Still I too have known my breasts to swell and harden, I too have been unable to sleep on them for their tenderness to weight and touch, I too have known what it is to undress slowly and imagine myself growing night to night. . . I knew this for two months, my dear Missis Wiggam; I had this strange joy for two months, my dear Missis Butter. But there was a night last week, my good ladies, on coming home from a party, which Mister Flinders and I spent in talk—and damn fine talk, if you want to know, talk of which I am proud, and talk not one word of which you, with your grocery-and-baby minds, could have understood; in a régime like this, Miles said, it is a terrible thing to have a baby—it means the end of independent thought and the turning of everything into a scheme for making money; and there must be institutions such as there are in Russia, I said, for taking care of the babies and their mothers; why in a time like this, we both said, to have a baby would be suicide —goodbye to our plans, goodbye to our working out schemes for each other and the world—our courage would die, our hopes concentrate on the sordid business of keeping three people alive, one of whom would be a burden and an expense for twenty years. . . . And then we grew drunk for a minute making up the silliest names that we could call it if we had it, we would call it Daniel if it were a boy, call it for my mother if it were a girl—and what a tough little thing it is, I said, look, look, how it hangs on in spite of its loving mother jumping off tables and broiling herself in hot water . . . until Miles, frightened at himself, washed his hands of it: we mustn't waste any more time, the sooner these things are done the better. And I as though the ether cap had already been clapped to my nose, agreed offhandedly. That night I did not pass my hands contentedly over my hard breasts; that night I gave no thought to the nipples grown suddenly brown and competent; I packed, instead, my suit-case: I filled it with all the white clothes I own. Why are you taking white clothes to the hospital? Miles said to me. I laughed. Why did I? White, for a bride; white, for a corpse; white, for a woman who refuses to be a woman. . . .

"Are you all right, Margaret?" (They were out now, safely out on Fifth Avenue, driving placidly past the Plaza where ancient coachmen dozed on the high seats of the last hansoms left in New York.)

"Yes, dear," she said mechanically, and forgot to turn on her smile. Pity for him sitting there in stolid New England inadequacy filled her. He was a man, and he could have made her a woman. She was a woman, and could have made him a man. He was not a man; she was not a woman. In each of them the life-stream flowed to a dead-end.

And all this time that the blood, which Missis Wiggam and Missis Butter stored up preciously in themselves every year to make a baby for their husbands, was flowing freely and wastefully out of Missis Flinders—toward what? would it pile up some day and bear a book? would it congeal within her and make a crazy woman?—all this time Mr Strite, remembering, with his pudgy face, his mother, drove his taxi softly along the curb; no weaving in and out of traffic for Mr Strite, no spurting at the corners and cheating the side-street traffic, no fine heedless rounding of rival cars for Mr Strite; he kept his car going at a slow and steady roll, its nose poked blunt ahead, following the straight and narrow—Mr Strite knew what it was to carry a woman home from the hospital.

But what in their past had warranted this? She

could remember a small girl going from dolls to
books, from books with colored pictures to books
with frequent conversations; from such books to
the books at last that one borrowed from libraries,
books built up of solemn text from which you took
notes; books which were gray to begin with, but
which opened out to your eyes subtle layers of gently
shaded colors. (And where in these texts did it say
that one should turn one's back on life? Had the
coolness of the stone library at college made one
afraid? Had the ivy nodding in at the open dormitory windows taught one too much to curl and squat
looking out?) And Miles? What book, what professor, what strange idea, had taught him to hunch his
shoulders and stay indoors, had taught him to hide
behind his glasses? Whence the fear that made him
put, in cold block letters, implacably above his desk,
the sign announcing him "Not at Home" to life?

Missis Flinders, my husband scaled the hospital
wall at four o'clock in the morning, frantic I tell
you. . . . But I just don't understand you, Missis
Flinders (if there's really nothing the matter with
your insides), do you understand her, Missis Wiggam, would your husband? . . . Why goodness,
no, Mister Wiggam would sooner . . . ! And there
he was, and they asked him, Shall we try an operation, Mister Butter? scaled the wall . . . shall we
try an operation? (Well, you see, we are making
some sort of protest, my husband Miles and I; sometimes I forget just what.) If there's any risk to Shirley, he said, there mustn't be any risk to Shirley.

. . . Missis Wiggam's petulant, childish face, with its sly contentment veiled by what she must have thought a grown-up expression: Mister Wiggam bought me this negligée new, surprised me with it, you know—and generally a saving man, Mister Wiggam, not tight, but with three children—four now! Hetty, he says, I'm not going to have you disgracing us at the hospital this year, he says. Why the nurses will all remember that flannel thing you had Mabel and Suzy and Antoinette in, they'll talk about us behind our backs. (It wasn't that I couldn't make the flannel do again, Missis Butter, it wasn't that at all.) But he says, Hetty, you'll just have a new one this year, he says, and maybe it'll bring us luck, he says—you know, he was thinking maybe this time we'd have a boy. . . . Well, I just have to laugh at you, Missis Flinders, not *wanting* one, why my sister went to doctors for five years and spent her good money just *trying* to have one. . . . Well, poor Mister Wiggam, so the negligée didn't work, I brought him another little girl—but he didn't say boo to me, though I could see he was disappointed. Hetty, he says, we'll just have another try! oh I thought I'd die, with Miss Kane standing right there you know (though they do say these nurses . . .); but that's Mister Wiggam all over, he wouldn't stop a joke for a policeman. . . . No, I just can't get over you, Missis Flinders, if Gawd was willing to let you have a baby—and there really isn't anything wrong with your insides?

Miles' basket of fruit standing on the bed-table,

trying its level inadequate best, poor pathetic inarticulate intellectual basket of fruit, to comfort, to
bloom, to take the place of Miles himself who would
come in later with Sam Butter for visiting hour.
Miles' too-big basket of fruit standing there, embarrassed. Won't you have a peach, Missis Wiggam
(I'm sure they have less acid)? Just try an apple,
Missis Butter? Weigh Miles' basket of fruit against
Mister Wiggam's negligée for luck, against Mister
Butter scaling the wall at four in the morning for
the mother of his dead baby. *Please* have a pear,
Miss Kane; a banana, Joe? How they spat the seeds
from Miles' fruit! How it hurt her when, unknow-
ing, Missis Butter cut away the brown bruised cheek
of Miles' bright-eyed, weeping apple! Miles! they
scorn me, these ladies. They laugh at me, dear, almost as though I had no "husband", as though I
were a "fallen woman". Miles, would you buy me
a new negligée if I bore you three daughters? Miles,
would you scale the wall if I bore you a dead baby?
. . . Miles, I have an inferiority complex because
I am an intellectual. . . . But a peach, Missis Wiggam! can't I possibly tempt you?

To be driving like this at mid-day through New
York; with Miles bobbing like an empty ghost (for
she could see he was unhappy, as miserable as she,
he too had had an abortion) on the side-seat; with a
taxi-driver, solicitous, respectful to an ideal, in
front; was this the logical end of that little girl she
remembered, of that girl swinging hatless across a
campus as though that campus were the top of the

earth? And was this all they could give birth to, she and Miles, who had closed up their books one day and kissed each other on the lips and decided to marry?

And now Mr Strite, with his hand out, was making a gentle righthand turn. Back to Fifth Avenue they would go, gently rolling, in Mr Strite's considerate charge. Down Fourteenth Street they would go, past the stores unlike any stores in the world: packed to the windows with imitation gold and imitation embroidery, with imitation men and women coming to stand in the doorways and beckon with imitation smiles; while on the sidewalks streamed the people unlike any other people in the world, drawn from every country, from every stratum, carrying babies (the real thing, with pinched anæmic faces) and parcels (imitation finery priced low in the glittering stores). There goes a woman, with a flat fat face, will produce five others just like herself, to dine off one-fifth the inadequate quantity her Mister earns today. These are the people not afraid to perpetuate themselves (forbidden to stop, indeed) and they will go on and on until the bottom of the world is filled with them; and suddenly there will be enough of them to combine their wild-eyed notions and take over the world to suit themselves. While I, while I and my Miles, with our good clear heads will one day go spinning out of the world and leave nothing behind . . . only diplomas crumbling in the museums. . . .

The mad street ended with Fifth Avenue; was left behind.

They were nearing home. Mr Strite, who had never seen them before (who would never again, in all likelihood, for his territory was far uptown) was seeing them politely to the door. As they came near home all of Margaret's fear and pain gathered in a knot in her stomach. There would be nothing new in their house; there was nothing to expect; yet she wanted to find something there that she knew she could not find, and surely the house (once so gay, with copies of old paintings, with books which lined the walls from floor to ceiling, with papers and cushions and typewriters) would be suddenly empty and dead, suddenly, for the first time, a group of rooms unalive as rooms with "For Rent" still pasted on the windows. And Miles? did he know he was coming home to a place which had suffered no change, but which would be different forever afterward? Miles had taken off his glasses; passed his hand tiredly across his eyes; was sucking now as though he expected relief, some answer, on the tortoise-shell curve which wound around his ear.

Mr Strite would not allow his cab to cease motion with a jerk. Mr Strite allowed his cab to slow down even at the corner (where was the delicatessen that sold the only loose ripe olives in the Village), so they rolled softly past No. 14; on past the tenement which would eventually be razed to give place to modern three-room apartments with In-a-Dor beds; and then slowly, so slowly that Mr Strite must surely be an artist as well as a man who had had a mother, drew up and slid to a full stop before No. 60, where two people named Mister and Missis Flinders rented themselves a place to hide from life (both life of the Fifth Avenue variety, and life of the common, or Fourteenth Street, variety: in short, life).

So Miles, with his glasses on his nose once more, descended; held out his hand; Mr Strite held the door open and his face most modestly averted; and Margaret Flinders painfully and carefully swung her legs down again from the seat and alighted, step by step, with care and confusion. The house was before them; it must be entered. Into the house they must go, say farewell to the streets, to Mr Strite who had guided them through a tour of the city, to life itself; into the house they must go and hide. It was a fact that Mister Flinders (was he reluctant to come home?) had forgotten his key; that Missis Flinders must delve under the white clothes in her suit-case and find hers; that Mr Strite, not yet satisfied that his charges were safe, sat watchful and waiting in the front seat of his cab. Then the door gave. Then Miles, bracing it with his foot, held out his hand to Margaret. Then Mr Strite came rushing up the steps (something had told him his help would be needed again!), rushing up the steps with the basket of fruit hanging on his arm, held out from his body as though what was the likes of him doing holding a woman's basket just home from the hospital.

"You've forgotten your fruit, Missis!"

Weakly they glared at the fruit come to pursue them; come to follow them up the stairs to their empty rooms; but that was not fair: come, after all, to comfort them. "You must have a peach," Margaret said.

No, Mr Strite had never cared for peaches; the skin got in his teeth.

"You must have an apple," Margaret said.

Well, no, he must be getting on uptown. A cigarette (he waved it, deprecated the smoke it blew in the lady's face) was good enough for him.

"But a pear, just a pear," said Margaret passionately.

Mr Strite wavered, standing on one foot. "Maybe he doesn't want any fruit," said Miles harshly.

"Not want any *fruit!*" cried Margaret gayly, indignantly. Not want any fruit?—ridiculous! Not want the fruit my poor Miles bought for his wife in the hospital? Three days I spent in the hospital, in a Maternity Home, and I produced, with the help of my husband, one basket of fruit (tied with ribbon, pink—for boys). Not want any of our fruit? I couldn't bear it, I couldn't bear it. . . .

Mr Strite leaned over; put out a hand and gingerly selected a pear—"For luck," he said, managing an excellent American smile. They watched him trot down the steps to his cab, all the time holding his pear as though it were something he would put in a memory book. And still they stayed, because Margaret said foolishly, "Let's see him off"; because she was ashamed, suddenly, before Miles; as though she had cut her hair unbecomingly, as though she had wounded herself in some unsightly way—as though (summing up her thoughts as precisely, as decisively as though it had been done on an adding-machine) she had stripped and revealed herself not as a woman at all, but as a creature who would not be a woman and could not be a man. And then they turned (for there was nothing else to stay for, and on the street and in the sun before Missis Salvemini's fluttering window-curtains they were ashamed as though they had been naked or dead) —and went in the door and heard it swing to, pause on its rubbery hinge, and finally click behind them.

1932

The

Friedmans'

Annie

The Friedmans' Annie

FRAMED by the little window in the swinging-door, the Friedmans make for Annie a round picture of three people blindly poking at their food, hidden from one another behind spread-out newspapers. Mr Friedman has been quick today; already his chair is pushed back from the table, his paper stands on his chest, his napkin lies soaking in what is left of his coffee. Now Annie watches Mister Robert's slowly emptying cereal dish: she likes to time herself so that while Mister Robert is impatiently pushing forward his empty cereal dish she can slip his bacon neatly around his left shoulder and, darting to his right, remove the cereal dish without causing him a second's delay. Of course Miss Mildred is ready for coffee—but let her wait, Annie never hurries for Miss Mildred, it is not ladylike to have a job and Annie wants Miss Mildred to know that she knows it. . . . Mrs Friedman's place at the head of the table is still empty; behind it the goldfish swim from one end of their bowl to the other: will it be one of her sick days, so that for company all day long Annie will have her high voice talking into the telephone, Well you know, it comes and goes, it gets better and worse. . . .

Annie wipes the sweat that rolls down her face. New York in Summer is hot and lonely. In the big rooms beyond the kitchen the furniture is covered with flowery cotton, the pictures are heavily veiled, the curtains camphored and rolled away in the closets—the Friedmans' old Elsa, bringing her baby spent two Spring days in helping. The rugs are gone; Mrs Friedman's weary, hurrying footsteps (when she is well) can be heard all over the house, sharply tapping the bare floors. It seems that everyone except the Friedmans is away for the Summer; the dumbwaiter shaft is almost silent now. The Allens' Bertha, that wild one, sent a post card from the Seashore; the Goodkinds' Elsa is in the Mountains; almost the only one left is that Greenhorn, the Golds' Lisa, who cries down the shaft from the fourteenth floor because she is homesick. Annie is ashamed that the Friedmans are not going away; she is ashamed of what people must be saying, the milkman, and the Allens, and the Allens' Bertha. And it is all Miss Mildred's fault: a job she has to have, like any common person! Annie has heard Mrs Friedman sighing to her sister, Mrs Rosenbloom; Mrs Rosenbloom always snaps back, She don't get it from *our* side of the family! Yes, it is lonely without the Allens' Bertha, she misses her jolly *Achtung!* Annie! have you given Mrs F. her orders for the day? . . .

But today is Thursday! On Thursdays Annie's hair is in curlers from Wednesday night; she does her work all day long with her hair tied up in a bandana which presses the little bumps against her head and reminds her constantly of Thursday night and Joe. For on Thursday nights the Friedmans eat early and Annie, in a fine black dress that once belonged to Mrs Friedman, goes with Joe to Trommer's beer garden in Brooklyn. That Joe! if only he would not be always after her about getting married . . . with his forty dollars (hardly the price of a coat! Mrs Friedman says) every Saturday. . . .

Mister Robert was ready. Annie snatched the bacon and glided into the dining-room, passing the swinging-door from her shoulder to her elbow so that it would swing quietly back to its place. Last night Mister Robert came into the kitchen with his tuxedo jacket over his pajamas and knocked things about in the ice-box until Annie came out with a coat thrown over her nightgown and made coffee for him while he teased her about Joe Schmidt and said, A plumber always sleeps with his tools and an extra toilet lid under his pillow, and, When you lived on a farm, Annie, how could you tell which was you and which was the cow; Annie had giggled till she could hardly talk, Mister Robert was a jolly one, not like Miss Mildred. (That boy has never given me a moment's trouble, Mrs Friedman used to say to her sister Mrs Rosenbloom.) But today he had forgotten, and when Annie accidentally grazed his sleeve with her hand he drew his arm back sharply, and with his eyes still fastened on the newspaper began blindly chasing the bacon on his plate.

Ya, it is lonely in the Summer, thinks Annie, back on her side of the swinging-door, and it will be a long time before evening and Joe. But tonight will come and Joe will come, and after he has stopped being angry about getting married, they will drink beer and be jolly under the trees at Trommer's.

Mr Friedman picks his watch off the table and without looking at his children sticks his paper under his arm—and comes briskly toward the kitchen. Annie stands modestly waiting, with one hand on her hip, her behind stuck out a little, like Mrs Friedman—she is no Greenhorn any more to stand with her hands dangling and her feet far enough apart for a milking-stool between them!

Well, Annie, said Mr Friedman cheerfully, and she knew it was something unusual—generally he called her Elsa or What's-your-name—looks like another hot day, what? Annie blushed and swayed her shoulders, Mr Friedman was nice and jolly like Mister Robert. Mrs Friedman's going to stay in bed today, Annie, and I know I can count on you to take good care of her. Oh yes, Mr Friedman, I'll do everything. Yes, I know you will, Annie, you're a good girl, you take care of all of us. Oh, and by the way, Annie . . . He looked at her helplessly. His eyes shot up toward her Thursday bandana and glanced away again. Of course I know, Annie . . . He was silent, twisting his watch-chain. Of course, Mr Friedman said, looking out of the window, I know today is Thursday, but you could have Sunday although it's not your Sunday—you see there'll be some people dropping in to see her tonight—I mean

—I hate to ask it, Annie. . . . Don't worry yourself,
Mr Friedman. I'll stay in, said Annie.

Mr Friedman stood there smiling and blinking,
Oh thank you, Annie, that's mighty nice, that's—
mighty nice; suddenly he held out a dollar bill,
tickling her hand; Buy—buy yourself something, he
said. Oh no, Mr Friedman, no thank you—Annie
put her hands behind her back. Then Mr Friedman was in a great hurry, he put the bill back in his
pocket (Annie wondered if it meant one of Mrs
Friedman's hats—maybe that black satin one with
the rose—instead!) and said, Well what you say goes,
you're the boss around here, Annie! and started to
go out.

Annie stood there suddenly frightened, thinking
how mad Joe would be—with his What do they
think you are anyway, a horse, do they think they
own you?—but Mr Friedman was waiting for her
to laugh at his joke, so she laughed and flapped her
dishcloth at him coyly and he rushed out with a
Yes, sir, you're the boss, Annie! and Annie was left
alone with a long day before her and no Joe at the
end, and really, she thought, maybe it would be
better if I just marry Joe right away . . . but Ach!
look at me standing here dreaming like a Greenhorn
with Mrs Friedman sick. . . .

Annie set the breakfast tray gently on the table
in Mrs Friedman's bedroom, for halfway down the
hall she had heard her high voice at the telephone,
Well, it comes and goes. . . . As she silently

straightened brushes and little boxes on the dressing table, she watched in the mirror Mrs Friedman propped on one elbow, with her free hand smoothing the long lacy skirts of the telephone doll. Do you mean to tell me, Mrs Friedman said, Am I in my senses, Mrs Friedman said, and she rolled her eyes to the ceiling with that look of pain she used to have when Annie was a Greenhorn and wasted time heating soup-plates or forgot, the last thing at night, to turn down the covers on the Friedmans' beds; Well, Mrs Friedman said, shaking her head at the telephone, if that isn't the limit, and she expected you to believe it, say, people don't starve as easy as all that, no such luck—and then she gave the little groans and oh my's and don't tell *me's* that Annie loved to hear.

Annie hovered about the dresser hoping Mrs Friedman would talk to her and at last, when she hung up the receiver and replaced the doll, she turned to Annie with a sigh. Annie, did you ever hear such a thing! Remember that devil Katie from the Swedish Agency, that took such advantage my sister had to turn her out without a character? She's been bothering my sister all Summer to take her back, says she can't find another place without a character. (Of course she can't, but it would be a *crime* to give her one.) Well! this morning that devil has the crust to come back pretending she's *starving* and *faint* right outside my sister's door! Not that I believe she really fainted . . . have you ever heard of such cheek? And the idea! as if anybody could

starve in a big city like this—my goodness, this is
1930, not the year 1!

Annie stood with the duster in her hand and
rolled her eyes shyly to the ceiling. Such cheek, she
murmured as she gave an elegant little flip of the
duster along the foot of Mrs Friedman's bed. Oh,
it just discourages you, said Mrs Friedman sighing
deeply, such treatment in return for every kindness;
it was different when I was young I can tell you that,
Annie, you girls today have it mighty easy; my
mother's girl got up at five and worked all day and
never had a night off, and you wouldn't believe
what they paid her! A girl knew her place in those
days—and there was no *starving* either! Well get
back to work now, Annie, you'd chatter all day if
I didn't stop you . . . no use your wasting time just
because I'm flat on my back. . . .

Annie went singing down the long hall, singing
inside of herself of course, because only a Greenhorn sings out loud anywhere but the kitchen or
her own room, and Annie had come a long way
from being a Greenhorn like that foolish Katie . . .
from the days when Mrs Friedman didn't trust
her to open the Linen Closet and had to keep telling
and telling her, remember this, remember that . . .
those awful first nights when there seemed to be a
hundred Friedmans instead of only four, and her
serving-cap, shaking like a bug in her hair, threat-
ened to fall off and splash in the gravy . . . the
first time the Friedmans had Company . . . how
the other girls laughed at her up on the roof on

wash-day because she was afraid to go near the edge
. . . how everyone said Greenhorn, Greenhorn
. . . how stupid she had been when she had murmured *Leider,* I am sorry, that first morning when
Mrs Friedman told her And no small children,
think of that: *Leider,* the Greenhorn said! No,
Annie could hardly believe she had been so dumb—
crying for home in her little room at night . . .
praying . . . writing letters to her mother . . .
dreaming all the time how she would sail back in
the First Class with her pockets filled with money
. . . actually longing, just imagine, for the days
when she was nothing but an ignorant country
girl, leading a cow through the village street and
chewing a blade of grass. . . .

There goes Mrs Friedman's telephone again . . .
Oh yes, my dear, it's got the better of me again. . . .
How nice to have Mrs Friedman sick and in the
house all day. . . . *It comes and goes.* . . . Annie
lifted the statue of the lovely lady with a dress falling off one shoulder and dusted the table under it
(Don't neglect what you can't see!)—such a fine
piece! could she and Joe ever have a thing like that
in their house?

No, Annie was no Greenhorn any more and she
didn't like it when Joe or the Allens' Bertha teased
her about those days; sometimes Joe puffed out his
cheeks and rubbed them red, That's how you used
to look Annie! and Bertha would say, Will I ever
forget your face Annie the first time you saw a nig-

ger—it was only poor old Albert, but you sure thought he was a devil out of hell. . . . Ach, so long ago, can't you forget? I didn't know any better, Annie would tell them—and she no longer asked her mother in letters what was doing on Saturday nights at home . . . those Greenhorn dances, imagine, jumping up and down, swing to the left, swing to the right . . . how hard it was to find anything to write her mother about, after all how could that old-fashioned old German woman in her wooden shoes, who had never even seen a subway or a movie, understand this smart new Annie who powdered her face . . . who had a fine room to herself with curtains crossed like the curtains in Mrs Friedman's own bedroom, a clean little room, papered with pink roses like the inside of a cardboard box for ladies' handkerchiefs . . . who was trusted every day to polish the grand silver that stood in rows on the sideboard. . . . Catch Annie going back to Germany! no, sir, not even in the First Class, not even with her pockets filled with money, no, no, Annie is an American now, she will never milk a cow again, New York is her home and she wears high heels even with her uniform, makes over Mrs Friedman's old hats for herself and knows about saving money in the bank and buying bargains and keeping a fellow waiting like any American girl, and when she goes out on Thursday nights and alternate Sundays she looks more like a lady than Miss Mildred who leaves her crêpe de chines hanging in the closet and goes to work in old sweaters with glasses sliding down her nose!

Oh, but she was smart, that Annie! You couldn't fool her, she knew how to do things right—how to dress, how to work, how to save her money. Na, that stupid old bear of a Joe, with his Let's get married tomorrow, Annie. . . .

Mrs Friedman, did you ring? Yes, Annie, I was thinking you might as well go over my room. It won't bother you, Mrs Friedman? Well yes, of course, but I don't want anything neglected just because I'm flat on my back, I'm not one to let my own suffering interfere, just work quietly Annie and don't chatter, I'll lay still and rest. . . . Yes, sir, what do you think of that devil Katie? Starving's out of date, I told Mrs Rosenbloom to tell her. Some of these ignorant girls just don't know when they've got it good, a place in a liberal American family, every advantage. . . . O that telephone, your friends don't do you any favor calling up when you're sick, no I'll answer, Annie! . . . Hello, hello, oh Mamie, I was wondering why I didn't hear from you, well, you know, it gets better and worse . . . I can't complain . . . it comes and it goes . . . if I'm alive Mamie!

Mrs Friedman sighed; Annie, Annie, it's a relief to have you around the house instead of some Greenhorn *schlemiel*—I've taught you a good German word, na, Annie? and don't forget I've taught you everything else you know, don't you be in a hurry

with that young man of yours! you know a good
berth when you see one, don't you Annie; you're
nobody's fool; you know what side your bread is
buttered on, don't you, Annie. . . And rolling her
eyes to the ceiling she said in a low voice as if to
somebody else, Nobody knows what I suffer, not
even the doctors. . . .

And Annie felt proud that Mrs Friedman made
jokes with her, and wasn't she a smart American
girl to know which side of her bread was buttered,
and she felt terribly sorry for Mrs Friedman's suf-
ferings—Mrs Friedman said it was something ladies
her age get; Annie couldn't remember her mother
ever having it, but she knew it must be something
terrible; Mrs Rosenbloom had it, too, and when
she came with Mr Rosenbloom for a visit in the
evening the two Ladies would lie back and talk
about it together, and Mr Friedman and Mr Rosenbloom would pick up their handkerchiefs and
open and close windows and bring them glasses of
water and keep saying unhappily, Why don't you
stop worrying, why don't you take things more
easy, and Mrs Friedman and Mrs Rosenbloom
would look at each other and shake their heads and
sigh, O you men, what do you know about it, where
would you be if we let things slip, oh don't tell us
what we should do and what we shouldn't . . . oh,
but Annie had it nice here and Mrs Friedman was
almost like a mother to her and such a fine, smart
Lady. . . .

The telephone rang again and Mrs Friedman

sighed and slipped off the telephone doll and talked quietly with her eyes on the wall, and then she began to speak mysteriously and glance at Annie out of the corner of her eye. Then she said softly into the phone, Wait a minute, it has six ears, and she put her hand over the mouth of the instrument and said Don't you think you better look at the biscuits Annie—and Annie knew that she must be talking about Miss Mildred again, and went and waited in the kitchen until Mrs Friedman called and she could go back to her again.

Oh, Annie loved these busy mornings, best of all she liked them when Mrs Friedman in a bungalow apron and with her hair pinned back behind her ears followed her around the empty apartment with a duster and chatted about bargains and how everything picked up soot from the river boats until Annie almost forgot that Mrs Friedman was her Lady. But it was nice, too, when Mrs Friedman was in bed, directing things with a hand to her side like a sick queen, Don't forget *under* things, Annie; I hope Mr Papenmeyer is prompt with that meat; be careful with those flowers, Annie; my, they certainly look real, everybody wants to know where I got them, but I'd be ashamed to tell 'em they were so cheap—and Annie forgot about Joe and got down on her knees and scrubbed till her face was purple.

And at the end of the morning she brought Mrs Friedman a jelly omelet and blushed all over when Mrs Friedman said, Oh, Annie, you're a treasure, what would I do without you! and wished Joe could

have heard her being praised like that. Then Mrs
Friedman said, Hasn't that devil sent the meat yet,
Annie? and Annie said, Not yet, and Mrs Friedman
said, Isn't that the limit, just when I'm flat on my
back, and Annie said shyly, It's the most terrible
thing I ever heard, and together they rolled their
eyes to the ceiling, Mrs Friedman with her head
leaning back against the pillow and Annie standing
over the foot of the bed with Mrs Friedman's jelly
omelet on a large tray in her hands.

But now the morning was over and Mrs Friedman was asleep with one arm over her face, and the
dirty lunch dishes were piled in the sink and the
kitchen was far away from the bedroom and very
empty and the long afternoon was beginning just
as it did every day, only when Mrs Friedman was
well she came into the kitchen in a fine black coat,
gave a quick look around and walked smartly out,
slamming the door behind her—but whether Mrs
Friedman was sick or well, it was always lonely in
the afternoons.

The dining-room looked gloomy and dead
through the window in the swinging-door. When
there was no longer work to be done in those big
rooms beyond the kitchen, they seemed too strange
to enter alone. . . . It didn't seem right, after the
nice busy morning together, Mrs Friedman falling
asleep at the other end of the house . . . now there
was nothing left awake except those silly goldfish
swimming from one end of their bowl to the other

. . . if it was Winter Annie would rap on the dumb-waiter for a little company with the Allens' Bertha.

Oh yes, the afternoons were lonely, and it was too bad that she wouldn't be going out tonight with Joe to Trommer's (after all it *was* her night out) and what was she to do this long afternoon by herself before Mr Papenmeyer sent the meat and vegetables? A letter from her mother lay on the chiffonier in her room, but it would only make her sadder because everything at home was bad and her mother always wrote if Annie was so grand now, why couldn't she send them more money? So Annie put the letter away in a drawer and got out the bedjacket she was making for Mrs Friedman's birthday present—nobody crocheted like Annie, Mrs Friedman said—but it didn't do at all, and at last she gave it up and sat down with a sigh on her bed . . . *I wish I was married.*

Yes, it would be nice to have your own house with Joe and to save up for a radio and to have babies (two, like Mrs Friedman, not thirteen like her mother in the old country)—oh yes, it would be fine to have Joe all the time in the same house, the same room, at night in the same bed. Twenty-eight she was, and at home if a girl was not married at twenty-eight the children followed her down the road singing songs and laughing—and a girl's mother was after her all the time. But what did they know there, Annie thought,—in America everything is different, why the Allens' Bertha said it wasn't so bad in America if you never got married, the only thing is to

have enough money, she said, and have a good time.
. . . Well, that was all right for Bertha—she hated
babies and she said all men were alike and she'd
like to see the one worth tying up with. . . . But it
was different with Annie, Annie wanted to get married all right—some day—and Joe was a good man
. . . maybe he was right when he said Annie got
these stuck-up ideas about forty dollars from Mrs
Friedman and when he said Mrs Friedman took
advantage of her (after all, Thursday *was* her night
out!) and God knows there were nights when Annie
couldn't sleep for wanting Joe.

Yes, these afternoons were lonely, and Annie sat
on that white bed for a long time without moving,
and then she looked up at the trunk (filled with
things she was saving for her trousseau) that hung
on a shelf over her head and suddenly she remembered what that queer one, Miss Mildred, had said
to her once. Miss Mildred had marched into Annie's
kitchen one day, I've never seen your room Annie,
would you mind letting me see it? She looked
around without touching anything. So this is what
they give you, well, well, like a palace only a little
more like a coffin with your toilet in a closet and
your trunk hanging over your head on a shelf, isn't
that just too lovely; did you ever stop to think, Annie, that that trunk might fall down on you some
day and it would be nobody's fault but your own?
And suddenly Miss Mildred looked at her with her
shiny glasses, Why don't you get married, Annie?
Believe me, if I could find a man who'd take me out

of this house and not put me in another just like it,
I wouldn't be here another night! You mustn't talk
like that behind your mother's back, Annie began,
but Miss Mildred stalked out of the room. Now
Annie sat and looked up at that trunk above her
head and shuddered . . . and then she had a feeling that she just wanted to lie down and cry.

But no—only a Greenhorn like the Golds' Lisa
cried!—her eyes would be red while she was waiting
on the table and Mr Friedman would come out
with one of his jokes about Somebody—Somebody's
Sweetheart hasn't been around lately, or Somebody looks like the Niagara—and Mister Robert
would scream with laughter. . . .

But how mad Joe would be tonight! Nowadays,
he was mad at so many things, at Annie and the
Friedmans and his job and America, that sometimes
Annie was scared of him, he was so changed. So jolly
he had been when she first met him, at a dance hall
that the Allens' Bertha and her sailor-friend had
taken her to, always so cheerful, always talking
America this, America that: he clapped his hand
over her mouth when she spoke in German. You
are finished with all that, he said, you must become
a real American, and he walked with an American
newspaper and a little dictionary in his pocket.
They went to the movies in those days, American
movies and American down-town dance halls, never
to Trommer's, never to any place that reminded
them of Germany. Annie was ashamed because Joe
was so much more American than she was, she cut

off her hair, she bought herself silk stockings, she asked the Allens' Bertha to buy her powder and gloves. But nowadays he said if he could make forty dollars a week he'd just as soon live in Germany, he said America's not such a grand country after all, there's a lot of Jews and rich people here the same as any other country and the people that have the money keep it. . . .

As crazy as Miss Mildred he sounded sometimes, thought Annie, like the time she had stalked into the kitchen with her hat and coat still on and said to Annie, Well, Annie, where do you think I've been today? and Annie said, I don't know, Miss Mildred, where? Miss Mildred said, loudly, Down to Fourteenth Street, where the men without jobs were shouting for food and work, what do you think about that? Annie said slyly, Aaaaaah, those Reds they make me sick, they ought to go right back to Europe and leave us alone, what do they want making trouble in this country anyway? Your mother says— Miss Mildred cut her short: Annie, you make me so sick I want to kill you. . . .

Well, Joe wasn't shouting in the streets yet, but neither did he talk any more of getting raises and saving money, no, all he wanted to do now was to get married and keep his same old job, and if he didn't care any more, how would he ever make more than forty dollars? And it was Joe in the old days who was so set on waiting. We got to wait, he used to say, we got to have a regular American home—now he said what was the use, and they might as well live together while they were young in any kind of a place, instead of Joe living in a dirty furnished room and Annie in what Joe called a closet off Mrs Friedman's kitchen.

The bell rang and Annie wiped her hands and ran to the door and let in Mrs Rosenbloom. Even in the Summer Mrs Rosenbloom wore a long black cape and Annie had slapped Joe in the face once for saying she looked like a beetle. She stepped in and asked Annie in a whisper how Mrs Friedman felt and when Annie said, Better, she threw up her hands and said Thank God in a big deep voice, and then she frowned, If she's so much better she had no right to send for me, God knows I don't feel too good myself and nobody would believe how upset I was when that Katie—a girl ought to be put in prison for scaring a person out of their wits! I gave her a cup of coffee too, I'm too soft-hearted, I should have sent her about her business at once. I never would have come today if my sister hadn't phoned —leaving my *schlemiel* to spoil the dinner. Ah, Annie, I wish there were two of you!

Annie was happier in the kitchen now. She picked up Mrs Friedman's bed-jacket again and started to crochet briskly. It was nice thinking of the two Ladies chatting in the bedroom about their sickness; Mrs Rosenbloom would take off her shoes and lie down on Mr Friedman's bed and the two Ladies would lie there side by side, shaking their heads and sighing, Oh yes, it comes and goes, and then they would talk about that devil Katie for a little while and Mrs Friedman would say how she didn't know what would become of Miss Mildred and Mrs Rosenbloom would say . . . and then they would lie there shaking their heads because nobody knew how sick they were. . . .

Sick! Joe said (Joe had it in for Mrs Friedman) she's a big strong woman and she makes *me* sick, that's the only thing that's the matter with her. No Annie, you can't expect a man to wait forever, he said, and he called Mrs Friedman such bad names that Annie had to tell him to just take his hat off of her clean white sink and *get,* but it wasn't her sink Joe would say, it was Mrs Friedman's and what was she but a goddam Jew no more American than they were—and sometimes he would take his hat and go and Annie would be afraid he had left for good. But Mrs Friedman always laughed. Don't worry, Annie, he'll be back, and if he isn't there's plenty of fish in the sea for a smart girl like you— and sure enough (Mrs Friedman was a wonder!) he always came back on her next evening off.

Joe was wrong to talk against Mrs Friedman. Didn't she stick up for Joe herself? Didn't Mrs Friedman say he was better than the other fellows she had had because he spoke good English and she wasn't going to have her kitchen filled with rough foreigners who were taxi-drivers and what-not, and they didn't mean any good to Annie either, You can bet your last red cent on that, you don't hear Italian fellows talking about getting married, do you? Annie had had an Italian fellow once, and she certainly didn't hear him talk about getting married, she didn't hear him talk about anything because it was when Annie was new and they couldn't understand each other's English so they just met in the park and made love—Mrs Friedman put an end to that when the dirty dago telephoned and asked for Annie Friedman, Annie said it must be her cousin from Newark and Mrs Friedman said, Oh, and he talks with an Italian accent, does he? and went back to the phone and gave that fellow a piece of her mind. . . . No, I know what's best for you, Annie, keep Joe as a steady and be engaged to him and then when he's made enough money . . .

What with Joe coming, and everything to worry about and Joe sure to be angry all over again—thank goodness the Ladies were inside, lying side by side, peacefully talking about this and that, shaking their heads and sighing. . . . She would surprise them! She would bring them a tray of tea and buttered toast before Mrs Friedman thought of asking. She carried the tray briskly down the long hall while the Ladies' voices got louder and louder, and then, when she stood in the doorway they suddenly stopped (they must have been talking about Miss Mildred again!) and Mrs Friedman said quickly Ah here's Annie with tea, Annie you're an angel! And when she was halfway down the hall again with empty hands she heard them start all over again, and she hated to hurry away from the friendly buzz of their voices which died down so that when she stood again in the doorway of the lonely kitchen there was no sound except the hum of the frigidaire, and it was lonely and there was nothing to do but to think again of Joe.

That Joe! a girl couldn't get him out of her head —Maybe he was right—it wasn't fair, it wasn't natural, to keep a man waiting. . . .

But whenever she went to Mrs Friedman with her mind half made up Mrs Friedman shook her head and sighed, Annie, Annie, you don't know when you're well off; an independent girl like you earning good money and having plenty of freedom and what do you want to do but throw it all away just because a man lifts his finger; I don't say Joe isn't a good boy he is, God forbid I should keep anybody from doing what they want, but I'm just giving you the best advice I can; after all you are a young girl and your mother isn't here; now come, come now, Annie, what would the Ladies say Saturday afternoon if they didn't find Annie's cookies, and look at Elsa, Annie . . . but don't think I couldn't get another girl tomorrow and cheaper, too, so just let me know when you're going; well, what do you say? Well what could Annie say when Mrs Friedman was ready to hurry her right out of the house tomorrow and get in some new girl, some Greenhorn that would burn the vegetables and forget to baste the meat, so Annie said she didn't mean right away, she meant maybe in a couple of months maybe in the Fall or something like that. And Mrs Friedman said, angrily, Look here, Annie, you can't run off and leave me in the lurch like that; I'm surprised, Annie, after all I've done for you; have you no sense of gratitude I took you in when you were absolutely *green*? . . .

Now Mrs Rosenbloom was going, Annie heard her call out Goodbye, goodbye, and she hurried out to open the door for her. Mrs Rosenbloom held her cape around her throat and said, Annie compared to what I feel my sister is in Paradise, don't tell her, I wouldn't have anybody worry for worlds, but if Mr Rosenbloom knew what I went through he'd send for a million big doctors from Germany . . . Well I'm coming back after dinner . . . if I'm alive . . . nobody should worry about me. . . .

And now the vegetables had come and there were the butter-balls to roll and Annie began to feel a pleasant hurry in her bones, for dinner was coming and the Friedmans were coming and everything must be perfect because everybody counted on Annie. As for Joe . . .

It was nice waiting on them at dinner without Mrs Friedman there, Annie felt that she was taking Mrs Friedman's place because she cut up the meat in the dining room and served it herself, and Mr Friedman said, What's for dessert, so I should know how much to eat? and when Annie said Ice-box cake, Mr Friedman and Mister Robert opened their mouths and patted their bellies like little boys. Miss Mildred, of course, sat there as glum as ever, picking at her food as though nothing was good enough for her!

While she was cutting up the meat on the sideboard for seconds, Annie heard Mister Robert say, Gee I forgot about mother's being sick, I made a date tonight, who's going to stay in? and Mr Friedman said, What's-her-name said she'd stay, and Miss Mildred butted in, Why do you make her stay in on her one night out, that isn't fair, father, and Mr Friedman said, Oh, for heaven's sake, Mildred, if the girl doesn't mind why should you? and Miss Mildred said in her disagreeable way That's just it, she *ought* to mind, and Mister Robert screamed Socialist! and threw a piece of bread at her and Annie felt like laughing when it splashed into her plate. Come, come, Robert, said Mr Friedman, is that a way for a man to treat his sister, and then he made a funny noise as if he were choking and wiped his eyes with his napkin and Annie could see he was laughing himself, and she couldn't help laughing too. Fools! said Miss Mildred and didn't eat another thing, just sat there with her glasses shining like crazy and looking as disagreeable as she possibly could.

Mr Friedman and Mister Robert got very jolly after that, kidding Annie every time she handed them anything, and Mr Friedman said, Oooooo look at Somebody's hair tonight and Mister Robert roared, Do I have to? Annie just shook with laughter! Then Mr Friedman put out his hand and pulled the ends of her apron so it came off and dragged on the floor while she was passing the coffee, and Mister Robert said, Papa, papa, I'll tell on you, undressing young women when your wife's sick in bed, and Annie escaped through the swinging-door with the apron crumpled in her hand, laughing and blushing like sixty!

So by the time Annie had cleared the dining-room and brought Mrs Friedman her supper on a tray (Mister Robert and Mr Friedman sat on the edge of her bed handing her things and being very quiet while she sat up and held her side and said she really couldn't complain, except for that pain in her side and a little difficulty in breathing and an appetite like a bird—Miss Mildred stood in the window with her back to everybody and played with the cord of the shade) she was feeling so jolly and important that she hardly cared what Joe said when he came. After all, Mrs Friedman knew best. No, sir, the Friedmans' Annie is no Greenhorn, she knows how to treat a fellow the same as any American girl!

So when the kitchen door-bell rang she stuck out her behind defiantly and opened the door.

Joe came in with a big smile on his face that slowly got smaller and smaller. Hello, he said, pulling at her apron, what's the big idea, going to a masquerade? Joe, said Annie crossly, can't you find time to shave before calling on a lady? Oh, I'm calling on a lady, are I, said Joe throwing his hat on the kitchen table; well, leave me tell you you don't look like

one, not in that rig; what's the big idea? Now Joe,
said Annie, grabbing his hat off the table and hanging it neatly on a nail, how many times have I got to
tell you . . . And by the way, Joe (Annie rubbed
the nails of one hand on the inside of the other, as
she had seen Mrs Friedman do), I won't be able to
go out with you tonight, Mrs Friedman's sick.

Sick is she, growled Joe, tapping his pipe so the
burnt tobacco flew all over the floor, what's the
matter with the old hag? Now you know perfectly
well Joe Schmidt, she's not at all strong and she's
not so young, and she's got something the matter
with her ladies of her age get . . . Say, who're you
fooling, said Joe, I knew plenty of dames in the old
country that age and they weren't too sick to milk
cows every day, and he laughed nasty and said I suppose only Ladies get it? So Annie said very snappy,
Well, they get it in this country, that's all.

Joe stood there stuffing his pipe angrily. At last
he spoke in German. Annie I've had enough of this,
he said, it's Mrs Friedman this and Mrs Friedman
that and I'm sick of it—listen, Annie, she's a big,
strong woman, she can have less rooms and do her
own dirty work—you don't have to spend your life
taking care of other people's houses. Annie said,
How can you be so common, Joe, this is my home
and I do my share in it just like Mrs Friedman does
hers, and what do you want, do you want her to
stop entertaining? . . . Look here, Annie, I'm not
going to wait around until Mrs Friedman dies
and then you'll think you have to cook for that fat-

headed son of hers. . . . Now, Joe, do we have to go over all this again; you don't know how nice Mrs Friedman is to me; why she told me only today I'm like one of the family. . . . The one that does the work, Joe said; aaaaaaah, the old hag, she makes me sick. . . .

Excuse me, Joe, that's Mrs Friedman's bell, she wants her tea; I'll be right back. . . . Annie, you listen to me, do you hear? . . . Now, Joe, shut up a minute and don't drop your ashes on my nice clean floor, I'm going to give Mrs F. her tea; and Joe said, Well, pour it down her neck, the dirty old Jew.

When she came back Joe was sitting on the kitchen table with his feet on a chair, smoking his pipe. Thanks, I'm making myself right at home, he said, I'm just crazy about this wonderful sofa you have in your lovely parlor. If you think, he said, kicking the chair, that I'm going to get out of here just because they asked you to stay in tonight . . . I'm going to stay right here in this goddam kitchen and talk to you; things can't go on like this, do you hear, Annie, I'm not going to be a monkey any more.

Sssshh Joe, don't shout like that in my kitchen. *Your* kitchen! he roared, that's a hot one, that is. He spoke more quietly. All right, Annie, I won't shout, only let's talk it over; are you listening to me, Annie, and will you please, for God's sake, stop washing those dishes while I talk?

Joe, I might as well get them out of the way, it don't look nice. . . .

Oh, don't it look nice, Joe mimicked her angrily

with his little fingers crooked. Pfui, you sound just like Mrs Friedman!

Joe . . .

If you don't listen to me, I'll shout like hell, I'll shout so everybody can hear, I don't give a damn for your lousy Friedmans. . . . But he sat down quietly. Oh, Annie, he said, you ought to marry me pretty soon, it isn't natural for a man, Annie. . . . *Are they calling you again? What do they think you are, a horse?*

Annie was too frightened to move; she thought Mrs Friedman would get right out of bed and come down the hall and say, Now march, young feller, the way she had to the delivery boy who got fresh when Annie was new and hadn't learned to say Knock your block off. I'll be right back, Joe, she said soothingly, I guess she wants a hot-water bottle before the Company comes, and she ran down the hall and felt awful when Mrs Friedman said, What's your hurry, Annie, the outside of this bottle is all wet, and if Joe can't talk more quietly he'll have to go, where does he think he is anyway, and then she ran back to the kitchen.

Annie, can't you see, it just makes me sick, Annie, to see you running around waiting on a lot of people instead of getting married to me, Joe said; listen, Annie, don't you like me any more? Annie put her arms around his neck. Of course, silly, you're my boy. Joe began kissing her, but all the while she kept one eye open to stare through the window in the swinging-door. Annie, Annie, Joe whispered, we'll be married soon, ya Annie? we'll have a little house of our own, ya, please, Annie? There was a loud ring and Annie jumped away and smoothed her skirt. Joe grabbed her, but Annie pulled herself away, Excuse me Joe, that's my bell, and ran out to open the door and let in Mr and Mrs Rosenbloom, who whispered, How is she, Annie? oh my poor sister, if she knew how I was feeling myself!

Joe was standing in the kitchen with his hat in his hand and he said, I'm going, Annie, that's all there is to it, this is the end; every time I get started talking you run away and do something for those people, I'm sick of it, I'm *through*. . . . He put on his hat and buttoned up his coat and tapped his pipe as if each thing was the last, but Annie knew what to do. She reached up and started to tickle him under the arms and he kept trying to push her off and keep from laughing. And then all of a sudden he was kissing her again and saying she must marry him right away. See, Annie, I can't wait for you any more, sweetie; that's what it is, I've waited nearly four years and it makes a man sick; ow, stop tickling, Annie. . . . Then he wasn't able to speak any more. He reached up under her skirt with one hand and Anne felt his hand playing with her garter, and she got excited. But all the time her ears were straining for the sound of bells, and she giggled nervously. . . .

Then a bell rang, very sharply. Annie pushed him away and bent down with trembling hands to fasten her garter, and Joe asked in a dazed voice, What

was that? My doorbell, of course, Annie answered in
a shaky voice, and as she stood up Joe put his hands
around her neck and said, I dare you not to answer,
until suddenly the bell rang again and Joe let her
go.

It was the Mandelbaums and the Steins who had
met in the elevator and they all came in pointing
their fingers at one another and saying, No *we*
caught *you,* and as soon as they got inside they were
very quiet and the two Ladies said, How is she, Annie? and Mrs Stein stayed in back of Mrs Mandelbaum on purpose to smile at Annie and say, I'd like
to steal you Annie, but I guess I haven't got a chance,
have I? Annie ducked her head to hide how red
her face was, but she felt very pleased and she stood
there swaying her shoulders modestly until she
heard Mr Friedman kissing Mrs Mandelbaum and
saying, Aha, look what the cat dragged in, what did
you bring your husband for, Mamie? and then she
went slowly back to the kitchen.

She found Joe sitting and staring ahead of him
angrily and she wished suddenly that he would go
home, she was tired of seeing him there and fighting
with him and going through everything all over
again and the Company inside laughing and scraping chairs excited her and she wanted to watch
them through the swinging-door.

I'm sick of this, Annie, Joe started all over again.
You listen to me, Annie. . . .

You listen to me, Joe Schmidt, said Annie, tossing her head, what do you think I am anyway, a Greenhorn, that I should get married just because a man lifts his finger, look at me, independent, making my own money, I should throw it all away just because . . .

All right, Mrs Friedman, Joe said, very nasty. Ach, be yourself, Annie. You didn't use to talk like that. What's the matter with me anyway, why shouldn't we get married? Now, Joe, we've been over all this; you know very well we want to wait until we have enough money to do everything nice. . . . But we won't starve on forty dollars. . . . Mrs Friedman says times are hard, and you might lose your job . . . and you'd be satisfied to make forty dollars the rest of your life. . . . Why not? forty dollars is a lot of money, it's more than your father in the old country ever heard of or mine either; you get these crazy ideas from your Lady, I tell you; I don't want to live like them, I don't want to marry a Mrs Friedman. . . . But Joe, look at Elsa, what a hard time she had. . . . What do you mean hard time? She ain't starving and she's got a nice fat baby, and she doesn't have to live in somebody else's house. . . . But she hasn't any other hat to wear, Winter and Summer, but the one Mrs Friedman gave her three years ago. . . . Christ, Annie, it's not so long ago that you never heard of anything but a handkerchief to cover your head. . . . Shut up, I'm no Greenhorn any more. . . . And I tell you I wish you were, you were a lot nicer to me in those days. . . .

Annie could hardly sit still she was so impatient
and she began to listen for the men's voices in the
parlor. It sounded like the beginning of a card game,
very jolly and friendly. She wished she had thought
of making cookies to surprise Mrs Friedman . . .
and she itched to be at the window of the swinging-
door. . . .

Don't you see, Annie, you've got ideas in your
head? why my God, have sense . . . Oh, for Christ's
sake, Annie, let's get *out* of this damn house tonight,
we'll get married in the morning—oh, for Christ's
sake, Annie, can't you see what a fool you are, can't
you see Mrs Friedman don't give a damn for you?
. . . I can see you have no manners, Mr Schmidt,
and I wish you'd go home, I'm sick and tired—what
do you think I am, anyway, you must think I'm
crazy; how could I leave Mrs Friedman in the
lurch? . . .

Mr Friedman called loudly Elsa, Annie, What's-
your-name, are you going to let us all starve?

Joe swore and pounded his fist on the top of the
washing-sink. Annie got up without looking at him
and filled three large trays with glasses and plates
and napkins and ginger ale and carried them one
at a time through the swinging-door. She set a glass
of ginger ale before Joe, and he threw it in the sink.
She didn't look at him. She hurried in to Mr Friedman and the gentlemen who were sitting around
the green card table waiting for her.

Annie always fed the gentlemen first, she knew
the ladies could wait, and it was fun passing them

things that they took with the wrong hands because all rules were off when the ladies were not in the room, and Annie didn't bother about left shoulders or anything—and fat Mr Mandelbaum winked at her and said he was winning all Mr Friedman's money, and Mr Friedman roared and said Elsa's too smart to believe that, Moses! Then she carried the last tray in to the ladies and was helping them daintily when suddenly she remembered Joe sitting angry alone in the kitchen and she got so frightened —maybe he might get really mad and leave once for all and she'd never—and she began to tremble and hurry. . . . But Mrs Rosenbloom stopped her to ask the recipe of her ice-box cake, Maybe my *schlemiel* can learn to make it, she said, and Annie had to stand in the doorway and tell it to her three times before she could get away.

Well, did you feed the pigs? Joe said as soon as she got back to the kitchen. Annie are you going to spend the rest of your life feeding the pigs? Oh, but Annie was sick and tired of the whole thing. She rolled her eyes to the ceiling like Mrs Friedman: You talk like an ignorant foreigner, and please remember this is Mrs Friedman's kitchen.

That's something I never forget, said Joe savagely. And I tell you what, Annie Schlemmer, I'm sick of this business, I'm not going to hang around any more, I'll get another girl, a nice girl that thinks forty dollars is a lot of money. . . .

Aaaaach, you and your other girls! So go and get

one, a fine girl you'll get, one that's too dumb to
want a decent coat to her back—

You make me sick with your coats! he shouted,
what the hell do I care? . . . In America a fellow
wants his girl to have a nice coat, said Annie tossing
her head, a decent fellow would be ashamed . . .
Well, I'm not that kind of a fellow, Joe said. I'm
the kind that's ashamed to hell to have my girl cooking for a lousy Jewish outfit and eating what's left
over and saying thank you every time they step on
her neck, that's what. . . . Annie held her head in
the air and tapped one foot on the floor as Mrs
Friedman did when she was scolding a delivery boy.
Any decent fellow, she murmured, any gentleman—

Pfui! said Joe, shut up, you make me sick, you do,
talking like Mrs Friedman and getting so stuck
up and ladylike; I'm through with you, see, I'm
through. I'm not going to be a monkey all my life—
a fellow can't make love to his girl because a couple
of fat old Jews want a glass of ginger ale! Pfui! I'm
through, I swear to God I'm through, and I'm never
coming back. . . .

Well, just let me know when you're going, said
Annie, still tapping her foot, I don't have to worry,
I can get someone else easy. . . .

All right, I *will* go! shouted Joe. He stood up and
slapped his hat on the back of his head just as he
used to, before Annie taught him better. So long,
he said carelessly. Annie stood there dully without
saying anything. Goodbye, I said! Joe said loudly.
Annie stood there without looking at him. Good-

bye, Annie, Joe said in a fierce voice, aren't you even going to kiss me goodbye? Annie didn't move. All right, don't! said Joe. Annie heard the doorknob rattle. But when she turned round, there was Joe standing at the door looking at her and twisting the knob with a hand behind his back. Go already, she said, and she gave him a little push with her hand. The door closed behind him.

Annie went into her own room and kicked off her shoes and sat down on the bed. She felt like crying—but she was no Greenhorn to go crying her eyes out after a man. . . . Anyway he'd come back. . . . But suddenly she put her head in the pillow and cried like any Greenhorn.

Outside they were saying goodbye. Miss Mildred had brought the company to the door and Mr Stein was saying, Well, Mildred, it's pretty late for us working-men, isn't it, and Mrs Stein said, Try and tear you away from a card game though and then she said, Did I tell you my son sent his regards, Mildred? and Mrs Mandelbaum said, You won't be working long, Mildred, before you know it you'll be getting married, and Mrs Rosenbloom said, Married! and then her troubles begin; come on, Al, I can't stand here talking all night; goodnight, Mildred, you don't look well, dear, and take care of your poor, poor mother—Al, come along, can't you see I'm dying on my feet?

Annie thought she'd better go to Mrs Friedman and see if she wanted anything; it would be nice just to say a word to somebody before she went to bed. Outside the bedroom door she heard Mrs Friedman and Miss Mildred talking in loud voices. For *my* sake, then, Mrs Friedman was saying angrily, what's the matter with you; you're twenty-three years old; three times she said her son asked for you; would it have hurt you . . . Annie stepped into the room and Mrs Friedman said sharply, And what's the matter with you, Annie, with that sour face, are you going to worry me, too? Oh, it's nothing, Mrs Friedman, Annie said sniffling, only Joe—he went away again. And he'll come back again! said Mrs Friedman; my God, don't air your troubles; what do you want me to do about it? Miss Mildred looked at them with her eyes very bright behind her glasses. Why don't you advise *Annie* to get married mother, you don't even have to find a man for her! Mrs Friedman said bitterly, Do you compare yourself with Annie? Oh no, certainly not, said Miss Mildred laughing in a nasty way, I should say not; oh my goodness, no, why Annie's *pretty*—and she's five years older!

That'll do now, Mildred! Annie I'll have to have a hot water bottle, nobody knows what I'm suffering. Wait a minute—I almost forgot, Mildred will you get that black hat of mine out of the closet? That's a pretty cheap trick, said Miss Mildred, a pretty . . . Mildred, will you do as I say? said Mrs Friedman. No! you can do your own dirty work! said Miss Mildred and stalked out of the room. Annie felt ashamed that she had brought her troubles to Mrs Friedman when God knows she had troubles of her own with that crazy one! Just help yourself to that hat Annie, said Mrs Friedman pathetically, it's in the corner there . . . and my hot water bottle please. Nobody knows . . .

There was sobbing behind the closed door of Miss Mildred's room and Annie hurried with her new hat past the parlor in which Mr. Friedman was yawning and folding up the card table. In the kitchen she turned her new hat round and round in one hand, while the water for Mrs Friedman's hot water bottle splashed into the sink, and the hat looked funny to her. After a while, she saw what was funny about it. It was Mrs Friedman's old black hat all right, but there were a couple of loose black threads on the side where the flower had been . . . still, it was a fine hat all the same. . . .

1930

The answer

on the

magnolia tree

The answer on the magnolia tree

I

THE magnolias must have burst at dawn! Linda woke up with a start of joy, her room filled like a bowl with the scent of them. At first when she opened her eyes it seemed there was a cloud in the room. But it was only mist, early morning mist, and she could see it rise, and thin, and climb the side of Lookout Hill, away on the edge of the campus. What was left of it blew very rapidly past her window and each second revealed more brightness. At last the six o'clock sun gleamed unhampered, still low, still a little cold, twisted through the curtains, the baby-green ivy, before it fell in a shower of speckles over Linda's bed. It was a lovely, hungry Spring morning—perilously lovely, as if each moment it might end; yet each moment it grew lovelier. And the birds! all the birds in the world, Linda thought, gathered on the campus of Magnolia Hall, lived in its trees, in the ivy that covered the walls. At this moment the maids in the attic had the best of it, for there were nests directly under the eaves; but later the birds would hop down in time for breakfast, to scream in through the French doors which opened from the dining-room onto the garden; and then later still they would strut about the ground and twitter in the classroom windows, their cocky heads on one side, mimicking the algebra teachers. Down the corridor outside her door went the night-watchman, tramping his last round. Six miles they said he walked, each night—but he was a fat man; strange; a fat man living his waking hours in the night, walking out his life to punch time-clocks on every floor, to see that there were no fires, to check up on occasional rumors of Lady Macbeth—the crazy old librarian—of strange men peering in the Library windows; his shoes squeaked past Linda's door. Ah, it was fine to be Linda! It was Spring; she was seventeen; she was Linda—at the Dance two nights before she had worn her first evening gown with a train, and a little velvet ring inside the hem to hold round her wrist when she danced. Next year she would be at college—in a few weeks she would float like a bride down the aisle of Juniors (Sudie her partner, and Jean coming behind with Aster), through the garden you saw from the dining-room, to the smooth Graduation Sward; her parents weeping proudly on little camp-chairs under the trees, the Duchess nodding, proud and ugly, with the Faculty; the magnolias, finished by then, smiling and waving for the last time to the Class of '35. Oh, the happiness was almost too much to bear! It was Spring and she was Linda; she had got an A from Miss Laurel in English; she was learning to do swan-dives, so the Oranges would take the pennant from the Greys; the watchman's boots squeaked; she had found a nail-polish that did not peel; the magnolias were out at last, she believed in God. The curtains fluttered, danced, lifted with the light Spring breeze—and paused, held their breath in expectation of the bright, bright day. . . .

And then she remembered. Something was wrong with today. Linda was an outcast, Linda must not go to classes, or to meals; Linda must not speak to the other girls, for at the Dance two nights before. . . Linda could not leave her room until the Faculty Committee and the Student Council (damn Natalie Freeman!) had settled on her punishment. Sometime after tea.

She had a moment of panic. What if they expelled her? What would Daddy say! Was it one of the serious times, or one of the times when he would roar with laughter? What exactly had the Duchess meant when she called Linda before her desk (yesterday morning, when Natalie had "told") and talked—her buck teeth dancing—about "implications"? "Do you understand the implications, child—of staying out all night with a young man—on a *golf* course?" (How angry and yet how frightened the big teeth had looked—almost hurt!) Linda had wanted to say something funny, like "implications of immortality"—it was odd, but the silly paraphrase haunted her all through the interview. "What you did was a disloyal thing to your School," the Duchess said, her teeth trembling. Disloyal to the School! In spite of her seventeen years, in spite of having spent the night with a young man—on a golf course!—Linda's blood had run cold. For she loved Magnolia Hall.

She thrilled to the basketball songs as she thrilled to "My Country 'Tis of Thee" or the sound of a parade, or the feel of the cold water in the swimming-pool after the first dive. "Not to speak of jeopardizing your own character," the Duchess said, playing with her big blue and white beads that looked like a string made of her own eyes and teeth; "are you engaged to that Thomson boy?" (The Duchess had bent, as if embarrassed, and touched the head of her little gray cat, which had wandered into the office.) Engaged! Linda had almost giggled. She wanted to run and tell Sudie and Jean and Betty Fleet and Aster. Engaged—when she was still struggling with Miss Armstrong's binomial theorem, when Daddy still laughed at her in the holidays for coming to dinner with a smudge on her nose! And anyway, to Edgar Thomson! Good Lord! To *Ed*-gar! Co-*loss*-al! Still. . .

Still, how did you know when you were in love? How could Miss Laurel (College Entrance English) *know* that she was in love with Mister Hendragin, her fiancé, and for goodness' sake how could even Mister Hendragin love old Lorelei? (Miss Laurel was *thirty-one*.) Probably Mister Hendragin was the only man who had ever kissed her—they all knew he *did* kiss her, for Lorelei had taken a little vacation from chaperoning the Dance and come back with definite magnolia leaves in her hair—and her eyeglasses in his pocket! (Colossal!) But *Sudie* was never sure she was in love with anyone till she had stopped being in love with them; Aster was always in love with her brother's friends, older men of around twenty-five; Gwennie was in love with everybody, and Jean never talked about things like that. The dormitory maid was in love with one of the chefs—she had got all the spaces in her mouth filled in with nice false teeth, as soon as the snow had melted, showing the beginning of crocuses in the garden.

The seven o'clock gong sounded, rolling musical and faintly out of tune, blending and struggling with the library chimes, up the stairs, along the corridors. The sun was high and warm, the birds merry; if you looked long enough at the side of Lookout Hill you thought the dormitory was a ship, listing gently. Vague sounds of rising—in Spring it was easy to get up early—Caroline Siller, for instance, running to the John to get there ahead of her roommate; a window slamming on the floor above, up on Faculty Hall, Miss Engle's room. Rubber heels padded outside Linda's door; Smithy and the Halloran, probably, who both had crushes on the gym teacher—you got an extra star for walking the Half-Mile Circle before breakfast (and both of them Greys, thought Linda, I bet there's not an Orange walking.) And a wild scramble for the stairs, for somehow, one didn't know why, it was thrilling to arrive first in the big empty diningroom; it meant luck all day. A door slammed. *"Jeannie! Rush! We'll be first! Colossal!"* It was Sudie.

Only Linda was not rising. Her breakfast would

be brought her later, by the nurse. She wondered if
they would miss her in the dining-room; if they
would put their heads together over the prunes and
talk about her; if they would try to pump the Freeman and other Student Council girls about her fate.
She wondered what the Faculty were thinking of
her—M'sieur; Miss Armstrong, who smelled of algebra and eau de cologne; Miss Graham who carried
her handkerchief in her bosom; Miss Engle, who
always sneezed in the Spring—Miss Winsey, Lady
Macbeth, the Duchess. . . . She wished, wished,
wished she were getting up with the others; running
to breakfast; living through the long slow day, the
long drowsy classes ("Linda! are you paying attention? well! you are not going to find the answer
outside on that magnolia tree!"), the cooking labora-
tory in the afternoon, sneaking crumbs and yawning, longing for the tennis court. . . . It seemed to
her that these common things would never happen
to her again, that she was already out of School,
she missed it like an alumna of five years' standing;
she was years older than these friends of hers flying
to breakfast, she was no longer an Orange, no longer
a child. . . . Oh why, why, why had not Linda returned like the others after the Dance, checked in
with Miss Engle, on corridor duty that night, at one
o'clock? Why had Linda left the "ballroom"—the
ballroom being the gym, of course, Linda herself
had been one of the Decoration Committee, had
climbed a ladder and draped the basketball court,
under Miss Winsey's direction, with the School

colors, Orange and Grey—taken Edgar's arm, walked calmly out the School gates—her long white evening dress catching on everything!—and gone like a bewitched girl, straight to the forbidden golf-course? and winked over Edgar's shoulder at a tipsy moon? and stayed there, all night long, until the embarrassing morning light? Oh why, why, why? And what would they do to her? Still, it would be COLOSSAL to be kicked out of School for love. . . . Linda sprang out of bed to look at the magnolias.

II

Now we shut the win-dow, now we find clean stock-*ings*, now we brush our teeth, said Miss Engle very kindly to herself; now we choose a dress (no, not that one, *that* we save for tea, dress-up tea today with a visiting lecturer from somewhere), now we hunt through the pile of modern history pages for our comb. . . . For otherwise it would have been too lonely to get up at all. It was different for Armstrong and Graham, across the corridor. Armstrong was Graham's "wife" and Graham was Armstrong's "wife". They shared the cutest two-rooms-and-a-bath, with dolls and teddybears thrown on every horizontal surface. They had a car, bought with their joint savings. They had little jokes between them. Abbreviations that nobody else understood. Glances. Smiles. They had each other. They could call in to one another (Engle heard them sometimes, across the hall): "Lazy Mary, will *you* get up, will *you* get up, will *you*. . ." or "Say, Armie, what are you going to wear? I thought my peach. . ."

But Engle roomed alone. Engle had to talk to herself for company. There had been almost nobody left to room with, it had been so late last year when the Duchess decided to have Engle back. Nobody left hardly but the cooking teacher, who had an inferiority complex so that you had to use the word "culinary" in every sentence—or Miss Winsey, whom the Faculty suspected of being "queer", like so many athletic directors; and of course Lady Macbeth, as the students called her, who was not "queer" but downright crazy—and as old as the Duchess, with whom indeed she had gone to Magnolia Hall, some forty years ago. So Engle took the room opposite Armstrong-and-Graham's, and dropped in there as often as she could.

And now we powder our nose, she told herself brightly (it was really a very fine day) and then we will run over and see if Armstrong and Graham are ready for breakfast. . . .

But there was a patter of bare feet down the hall. "Eng-le! Eng-le!" It was Chambie, little Miss Chambers, Engle's assistant, stopping outside Engle's door, looking like an ad for very chic underthings. Chambie—in very brief shorts, with her hair up in curlers—didn't look much older than some of the Seniors. She wasn't really—Chambie was twenty-six to Miss Engle's thirty-six. She stood there with her head on one side, eyeing Engle with the look of a spoiled baby. Engle would have loved Chambie for being so pretty, if she hadn't happened to hate her for the same reason. "Engie, darling! are you doing anything *very* special tonight?"

Why yes, Engle wanted to say, I have a date with M'sieur; or Clark Gable; or the night-watchman. Doing anything special! A special Faculty meeting, probably, to discuss the Linda case; or a little special coaching on the Boston Tea Party; or a special fire-drill! And Chambie knew it very well, Chambie standing there with a Date shining in her eyes, nodding from each curler on her head. And the knowledge gave an extra filip to Chambie's joy, she couldn't help it; for Chambie, even at twenty-six, had had enough of these long School evenings to understand them.

"Oh all right, I'll take your damn corridor duty, Chambie," said Engle irritably.

"Engie! you angel! how did you guess! You see, Jerry phoned, he's in town. . . ." But Chambie's elaborate gratitude was ritual. Even the Duchess (almost!) would have taken over corridor duty to make a Date with a Man possible.

"Run along, you fool!" said Engie, both irritable and good-natured. "And you can have my long black gloves again, I'll clean them for you," she called after Chambie, down the hall.

And now we will call for Armstrong, said Engle, alone again—but it didn't work; she couldn't seem to go, not yet. She went and stood for a moment in the window, painfully breathing the balmy air, sickening almost with the odor of magnolias. The door at the end of the hall slowly opened; slow and cautious footsteps moved mysteriously past her room—Lady Macbeth, safely out of the way. But still Engle lingered. She could hear sounds from Armstrong-and-Graham's room; the last of Lady Macbeth's lonely 1890 footsteps; voices of students returning from an early walk—"Greys forever, yay, yay, Grey!"—voices gone suddenly sharp and high like children's. There was a weeping way inside Engle's soul, somewhere at the core. There was moisture in her eyes, a twitching in her throat. Are we really never going to have it?—and a funny little sound happened somewhere. Those damn magnolias! Engle said (humorous, at her own expense); they always give us hay-fever, every Spring. . . .

III

Still breathless from the race downstairs, Sudie beat Jean to the Best Table, the one beside the corner windows, furthest from the Faculty Tables. "Oh, open the windows!" cried Jean, "for heaven's sake open all the windows!" She was right; they were all stifling; stifling from too high spirits left over from the Dance. The waiting-maids and Miss Whitson, the housekeeper, helped them throw open the French windows, and the whole big bare dining-room was flooded with Spring. The flowers in the garden outside were scarcely brighter than the gleaming high-lights on the plain cups and saucers, in the maids' eyes, in the dancing sunshine flecking the walls. Never had dishes clinked so merrily. Never had there been so many birds. And oh, the Dance! *You're the top! you're the*—still floated in Sudie's head (for that matter she had been living in a song, one song after another, in a dream, ever since her sixteenth birthday in the Fall). But Sudie felt melancholy as well as gay. For she had a problem. Why *hadn't* she kissed Malcolm at the Dance? or in his car, afterward? or out on the golf-course—like Linda! She was distressed; but the song persisted, the dream persisted, just as it did through classes (how she ever passed a course, when she hadn't heard a word all year! hadn't understood a line she'd read, scarcely even felt what she touched with her fingers!)—making everything vague, everything unreal—and at the same time terribly real and beautiful!

"Prunes again!" said Jean, almost singing. "I hate them—bring me three portions, Sarah, ask Miss Whitson. My God, I'm eating so much I'll weigh a ton, I'll be as fat as Florence, I'll burst out of my graduation dress—*and* the cream, please, Sudie!"

You're the top! you're the— She might be eating prunes or figs, she might talk or she might keep silent—nothing mattered; everything mattered. But Sudie thought she must be queer. She had *planned* to kiss Malcolm. Before the Dance she had been terribly warm and excited (for weeks before, in fact—living through classes and meals in a dream of the Dance). She was never cool, like Jean. She rested, she bathed, she curled her hair, she rested again. *You're the tower of Pisa*—and when she did come to dressing at last, she did every detail with devoted care. And all the time she had been dreaming she would kiss Malcolm that night. She had thought of Malcolm and the blood pounded in her temples—it still did; even now, pushing away her prunes, drawing her cereal bowl closer. *You're the top. . .*

"Good-morning, children. What, prunes again?" It was Natalie, with her cool, superior air, Natalie, who had "told" on Linda. "Well, thank heaven I've got two board members right here. I can give you your orders right now, Sudie and Jean." Natalie was editor of the Yearbook, as well as chairman of practically everything else. "You'll have to take Linda's place, and try to get ads in the Village. The Yearbook needs another hundred dollars. The first place to try is the Florist, then the tea room, the camp stool place where we got our chairs for the Dance, and Prosser's of course. . ."

Sudie wasn't listening. You could count on Jean to remember and explain details, Jean was good in algebra, Jean didn't curl her hair, even for a dance. Sudie thought of Linda enviously. Linda might be frightened today, she might be in a panic up there in her room awaiting punishment (that hateful Natalie Freeman!)—but at least Linda couldn't be ashamed. *You're the top. . .* "Of course you can sit here, Florence, you fool!" (Poor Florence, always humble, always squeezing herself in and out of places, because of her fat!) *You're the—* And here were Betty Fleet and Betty Crail, Midge Paine, Rusty, Frances, Gwennie (*Gwennie was not a virgin!*)—and then the Best Table was full, and Aster had to go and start a new table by herself, where she sat making faces and looking foolish till she was joined by the rest of the School, waking up. *You're the—* Oh, the preparations Sudie had made for the Dance! And standing before the bureau mirror, all dressed at last, she had *felt* so beautiful she wanted to kiss herself. "My darling!" she dreamed Malcolm saying (she said it for him, while Jean was taking her turn in the bath), "you look like a princess, an angel, you're so different from all these others, different from Jean, more sex appeal than Linda, more beautiful even than Gwennie! Susan, may I kiss you?" All this time she would hold her head delicately lifted, her lashes (a pity they were so short) fluttering; and then suddenly Malcolm would sweep his arms tightly about her, tight, tight, tight . . . and the dream that Sudie lived in, the dream would break, *let* the dream break. . . .

"What are you going to *do* to Linda, Natalie?" Jean was asking, and poor fat Florence, who shared everyone's worries, shook her head with solemnity and awe.

"But you should *see* the magnolias down the road!" cried Smithy and the Halloran, pushing in all rosy from their half-mile walk and shouting breathlessly so that Miss Winsey—just seating herself at the Faculty Table—should look down and smile. "They're all *out!*" cried Smithy, taking her place at the Next Best Table and holding her shoulders as nearly like Miss Winsey as she could.

"You know we can't discuss that, Jean," said Natalie coldly—hateful prig, thought Sudie, sitting there complacent and safe, just worrying about yearbooks and marks and committee meetings; conceited old scholarship girl. "Two stars for the Greys!" shouted the Halloran, "there wasn't an Orange out walking." "They ought to segregate the Juniors," said Jeannie in disgust. *You're the top! you're the—* And what had happened, Sudie thought disconsolately (forgetting for a blind moment whether she was an Orange or a Grey), what had happened when she actually came downstairs, knowing her dress was perfect, knowing every hair on her head was perfectly curled! What had happened was that she was barely able to talk to Malcolm! that her hands went icy cold (and yet sweaty, too) even while she greeted him; that she trembled so when she danced with him that she tripped and tried to lead him, as though she were dancing with Jean in the Senior Smoker! And finally when Malcolm got her outside, into that strange night air, which was warm like swimming in the moonlight, which was fragrant with the odor of magnolias about to spring into life—when Malcolm put his arms about her, Sudie had turned cold all over, like her hands, as cold as ice. Something happened—perhaps the dream intervened, became stronger than reality; but all Sudie wanted was to get back, get back in-

side the ballroom, under Miss Engle's and Miss
Laurel's eye. It was true he hadn't called her "My
darling" or any of those things, but he *had* said,
joking and passionate, "You're the cream in my
coffee, kid—" and he told her she looked colossal.
Out on the tennis courts he tried to kiss her, but
Sudie (oh, coward, coward!) had wriggled so
sharply that he had to let her go. "Don't you ever
neck, at *all*?" he said, amazed. And Sudie said coldly,
"Let's go back, please. We aren't supposed to miss
more than one dance at a time." Colossal! Sudie
could scarcely swallow her third piece of toast, she
was so disgusted with herself.

The whole dining-room had filled by now, the
Faculty tables were laughing and chatting as though
Spring had hit them too. Sudie wondered what the
Faculty could find to laugh about; what people
thought about, *dreamed* about, anyway, after they
were twenty-five, after dances no longer interested
them. Miss Chambers must have been cute; but of
course she was getting old. Miss Engle was impossible—terribly kind and all that—but sharp-nosed
and precise. Miss Armstrong looked like a horse,
like a stallion. "Tell them," Natalie was saying,
"that if they don't buy space, we will boycott
them—" (Oh, don't *listen* to her, Sudie thought,
we ought to boycott *her* for "telling.") At the door
stood Miss Whitson, in white as always, with her
face neither that of a maid nor a teacher, gazing and
gazing to see if everybody had enough prunes,
enough bacon. The trained nurse, then Miss Win-

sey (whom they were all sure had a secret love affair, so handsome she was, so breezy, altogether too charming—though a bit stiff from so much hockey —for a teacher)—and next to Miss Winsey the Duchess, her big teeth looking as though she would take a bite into the fine Spring day, the Duchess presiding over the lot of them. The funny teachers, neither young nor old, neither girls nor women, neither women nor ladies—but falling somewhere, in all those categories, between the students and the Duchess. "Don't you see, you sell them *space*," said Natalie. Oh, shut up, thought Sudie, in bewilderment. And all the faces blurred into a warm sea and she wasn't sure she was eating eggs or cereal, and Natalie's voice continued and then Jean's interrupting, and all the voices in the room formed a hazy song in Sudie's ears (*You're the tower of Pisa, you're the*), for all the din, and scents, and brightness were not enough to break through Sudie's year-long dream.

IV

Linda heard them singing in Assembly. "Lead kindly light—" their voices slurred and pleaded, they were wringing every ounce of tragedy out of the words, the melody—but their voices held the quality of April, Linda knew well how they would all be standing there in solemn rows, the little black hymn books in their hands, not even laughing at the Duchess' enormous teeth leading them in

song—and how the next minute, they would burst
out, the harmony gone, laughing and shouting and
worrying down the halls, finding their books, looking for pencils, clustering like bees about the post-
office. She felt a thousand years older than any of
them, up here in her room at this unaccustomed
hour. "A-mid the darkling glo-oom. . . ." A strange
feeling of being suspended in time and place took
hold of Linda, as though this odd day of awaiting
punishment were to last forever. "Lead thou me
oo-on. . . ." The last note, lingering on the air,
floating up to her on the lightest breeze, became a
breath. She closed her eyes. Why, why had Linda
gone with Edgar to the golf-course? and lain in his
arms through the whole night? Why, Linda? she
could see the boring little eyes of Natalie Freeman,
who had brought such a funny boy—non-college—
to the Dance, asking this question. Why, Linda?
asked the Duchess, asked her father, asked the entire Student Council, backed by the Faculty Committee: why? And the bright sun asked it too, stream-
ing reproachfully over the sill; and the voices of
her friends, singing in Assembly, and the fragrance,
the still, heavy fragrance of the new magnolia blossoms. Because I am in love, she answered them all,
and herself too, proudly. She felt Edgar's hand, like
the breeze, gently moving over her cool bare arms,
stopping time from moving, holding the moon in
its place in the sky, the branches of the tree overhead stood still in a trance. . . . "Edgar, I love
you," she whispered now, as she had not thought of

doing then; "I love you, Edgar, I love you, love you, love you—Linda, I love you, I love you, Linda . . ." And because Edgar was not there she drew her own hands over the outline of her brow, and cheeks, and lips, and they felt very beautiful to her.

The bell rang for classes.

V

"Now look here," said Miss Laurel, in Room 23, the English Room, "I don't like to lecture you children first thing in the morning, especially on such a lovely Spring day. But this is something—something I can't swallow," she said, feeling her prerogative, as an English teacher, to use all the slang she wished. "Listen to this, the end of Aster's paper. Aster has been describing an automobile trip to the shopping district, which is delayed by the car's halting beside some city slums. Now listen carefully, and see if this makes you as sick as it does me: (She glanced over the top of her glasses, and saw the rows of young faces, very like sunflowers, she thought, bright and puzzled, terribly eager and terribly dumb):

" 'I saw a shabby-looking boy walking down the street with his arm about a poorly-dressed girl. I could imagine their coarse conversation. I looked into the windows of the miserable flats and saw dirty dinner dishes standing about on the tables, and the beds unmade. I heard filthy babies wailing. At last the lights changed and the car moved on, and I offered up a prayer of thanks to God that I was not one of those filthy beings, born to squalor and ugliness, living like savages.'" Miss Laurel looked up, triumphantly. "There, now! Does everybody see what's wrong with that?"

"Two 'filthies'," said Midge Paine eagerly.

"Too many I's," said Edith Whitney.

"The last sentence is trite," said Betty Fleet, using Miss Laurel's favorite word of criticism.

"No, no!" Miss Laurel looked at them, really surprised—and rather hurt. "Aster, don't *you* see anything wrong with it, now that you hear it read?" Good God, you stand here, day after day, she thought, and talk your head off and your heart inside out—and all they think of is passing college entrance exams.

"Too many adjectives?" said Aster blindly.

Oh, her joy in the day was spoilt! Miss Laurel thought, adjusting her glasses. "Listen, let me read you the last sentence again," she said quietly. (For they were children, after all; they must be given every chance.) " 'and I offered up a prayer of thanks to God that I was not one of those filthy beings, born to squalor and ugliness, living like savages.' Is there *nothing* in those words that makes your hair stand on end?" said Miss Laurel desperately. Next year, please God, she thought (meeting their dumb, puzzled eyes, their shining, well-fed faces), next year I shall teach in a public school, where the kids are human; next year Peter Hendragin and I . . . "Natalie?" she pleaded. For Natalie's face was

not like the others; it was keen, sharp, discontented
—intelligent; Natalie knew how to think, and Natalie was not rich. "I don't know, I really don't,"
said Natalie Freeman, her face closed, her voice
cold. And Miss Laurel shook her head in despair.

The class sat quiet and uneasy. Not one of them
dared to look out of the windows, or at the black-
board, or anywhere but Miss Laurel's face. Miss
Laurel knew they thought she was awfully clever
and shabby, and that although she was invariably
kind, they were more afraid of her than of the other
teachers. The others—Miss Armstrong, Carola Graham—were what children expected teachers to be,
a kind of superior continuation of their cast-off
governesses; their whole lives were spent at Magnolia Hall, in service, almost, to the Duchess, to
the students. But Miss Laurel led her own life, both
intellectually and sexually; and she thought the
girls sensed it and unconsciously resented it.

"Well, I'll tell you what's wrong," she said now,
grimly. I will tear down their crêpe de chine minds,
I will destroy their million-dollar illusions, I will
run arrows into their platinum hearts. "Aster—"
she looked straight into Aster's eyes, wide and blue,
like a baby's, "Aster, how about offering a prayer
—or even a dime—not to God, not for yourself—but
for these 'filthy beings living in squalor and ugliness?' " There was a ripple of relaxed laughter over
the classroom, at Aster's expense. "No, it's not
funny," said Miss Laurel in what she felt to be a
terrible voice; she couldn't help it; she was furious;

she hated them, sitting there in their smug, expensive, careless clothes; "it's horrible. Listen, Aster, and the rest of you; how do you *know* that what the shabby-looking boy is saying to the poorly-dressed girl is 'coarse'? How do you know he isn't very sweetly and tenderly in love with her? How do you know he isn't holding his arm about her very gently, because she is tired from working behind a counter all day, and that he isn't saying, Darling, it's too bad your mother is so sick, and my father is so old that we have to support them and we can't get married. How do you know the girl isn't saying to him, Darling, don't feel badly about losing your job, I'll support you till you find another. . . . And suppose he *was* being 'coarse'?" Miss Laurel heard her voice grow shrill. "Haven't you ever heard a Harvard boy being 'coarse'? Haven't you ever seen a Harvard boy drunk, disorderly, selfish, beastly?"

Miss Laurel caught her breath. All of the girls in the rows facing her had lost their sophistication and become frightened kids in school. Aster's eyes had filled with tears, but whether from fright or from contrition it was hard to say. But still they were all moved, moved by something; they were children; they were vulnerable, malleable. What couldn't one do with children! if it weren't for their parents, for what their parents represented. Miss Laurel warmed to her subject and her class.

"And whose fault is it," she went on, "whose fault, that most of the people in the world, the great majority, must live in such misery and squalor as Aster describes? Why, it is the fault of the few, the lucky and selfish few. . ." Were they merely listening, as though to a dullish lecture, those wide, moist eyes so trustingly fixed on her? No, they *were* moved, Miss Laurel decided again. You could see drops of intelligence falling into them, painfully, like grains of salt. "Aster," said Miss Laurel, "should have offered her prayer *to* these people, for forgiveness! Or she should have prayed for intelligent enlightenment." She thrilled to the joy of being a teacher, a teacher in the proudest meaning of the word. Aster was openly wiping tears—that might be for her marks; but the rest, the rest of them sitting there in their smug, expensive clothes, were transfixed! (Natalie staring, not at Miss Laurel, but into space, as though she saw a ghost.) Seventeen, eighteen, daughters of the wealthy, of the worldly, and here was Ernestine Laurel, her brain clear, her soul angry, talking to them, moving them, shaking them down to thinking on a real, harsh level.

She talked to them gravely now, less angrily.

And then it was impossible, it would have been anti-climactic, to go back to sentence structure, or themes about canoe-trips. She would treat them, for once, as adults. There were thirty minutes more to her period, but Miss Laurel stood up and faced them now, as though she were their friend. "Please try to think about these things," she said quietly. "Don't forget them. They're true, they're the truest things there are. And now I think we'll dismiss the class."

They sat on, silent for a moment, incredulous as always, like children, of any break in their routine. And then they got up and marched solemnly out of the class. Miss Laurel saw their grave departing backs, their sunburned bare legs sturdy and frank down to their fashionable bright-colored tennis socks. She thought again how the children of the rich, like well-watered stock, would make the finest citizens—if only they could be made to see the light. So strong, so clean, so healthy, so *young*—she loved her little class, filing quietly out of her room.

Miss Laurel sat down, emotionally exhausted. She found she was trembling. She was longing for Peter, to tell him. She felt great, important. Her eyes drifted through the window, to the voluptuously budding magnolia tree outside; to the wide sweep of campus beyond, rolling with its pleasant, rural, country-club air to the athletic fields, the tennis courts. Ah, the great luck of the rich! Some day such fine ivy-colored buildings would house the children of the poor, all children alike; all children were created equal. . . . Footsteps crunched the gravel outside the English Room window; through the branches of the magnolia tree Miss Laurel caught a flash of color, four bare legs—a tennis racket; green socks, pink socks—and then when the figures emerged from behind the magnolias, Aster and Betty Fleet (Miss Laurel could see them plainly now) broke into a run and raced each other to the tennis courts.

VI

Library clock played three-quarters of its tune, suspended the last note, letting it zzzzing on the air losing its shrillness, dying away, you couldn't quite tell when it left off and became air. Muffled by the closed window the last notes of the tune played in and out of Natalie's ears, the final note, held too long, humming in her head like the sound of a bee or a dentist's drill. I must read, I must work, I must not think, thought Natalie, in horror of herself. What kind of awful girl was she growing into? First, reporting Linda; of course it was her duty as Chairman of the Council—but oh! if she had only skipped that duty, just this once! And then, to sit silent in Miss Laurel's class, not to answer when she *knew* the answer! knew it surely as well as Miss Laurel— and there she had sat, Natalie Freeman, scholarship girl, a worse snob than any of them, and let Miss Laurel carry the whole burden of poverty on her shoulders alone. Oh Natalie, Natalie! Denying her own mother (home scrubbing dishes, scrubbing clothes all day, so Natalie could wear the proper dresses—and still of course they weren't proper!), denying her own father who kept writing and writing, "If my little girl isn't happy at the School, she must write and tell us the truth, we can send you to a good school, baby, even if not a fancy one like

Magnolia Hall." Ah, shut the window on the cool Spring day! shut the window on Magnolia Hall, with its beauty, its ease, which Natalie (Editor of the Yearbook, Chairman of the Student Council) never can possess, belong to! Shut the heart to Miss Laurel's pleading, to the pleading of her own childhood, her own knowledge, the poverty she knew so well. Forget the boy, poor Roger Dunn (if Roger hadn't danced so badly, if Roger hadn't sounded so obviously a Night School student, a non-college boy, if Roger hadn't worn such uncollegiate clothing—would Natalie have reported Linda for staying out all night? oh, be honest, Natalie Freeman, daughter of the poor!)—forget Roger, whose father owned the grocery store at home, forget his "different" vocabulary, his "different" way of dancing, his honest, clean, *poor* smell; forget his curiously adult air among all those smooth, shiny, sophisticated college "men," Roger, who was a man yet whom one could only describe as a "boy"; forget your own feelings, Natalie, your feeling of relief as you bid him goodbye, as you hurried him away to what—standing lamely among those smart coupés and rumble seats —he described as his Dad's old "rattle-trap." Forget it, forget it . . . you will never forget it; the smell of poverty is in your nostrils, the din of scrubbing in your ears, the shadow on your shoulders. . . . You will never forget the look on Roger's face as he said, "Gee, Nat, I'd like to come up again to your graduation—*if I can scrape up the dough.*" You will never forget your mother, wiping her hands on her apron (though they were perfectly dry) when she came to the door to see you off to Magnolia Hall on a scholarship. "Don't *you* see what's wrong with this, Natalie?" "No, Miss Laurel, no, I don't." Oh Natalie, Natalie! Oh shame, shame, shame.

She saw them playing tennis through the branches of the magnolia tree, laden with the heavy white blossoms—Aster and Betty Fleet, her roommate. She saw their bare legs, Aster's fat, running and leaping over the court, their sneakers flying, their red balls spinning. Her own game was rotten, rotten; she was too good at committees, at passing exams, at winning scholarships, to be any good at tennis; she had not spent her childhood's Summers watching her father winning—or even losing—his club matches; the feel of the game was not in her blood, her muscles found it foreign. Miss Winsey said she was heavy on her feet—and passed on to correct Linda's serve, Betty Fleet's forearm. Miss Winsey said kindly, "Look, my dear, *spring, spring, spring* from the ankles, from the toes. Let your wrist go so —like this. You're too stiff. Too slow. Look. Watch me smash this one. See?" But only the rich girls, the girls who wore linen sun-back suits and threw them into the wash after one day, could *spring, spring* from the ankles, from the toes. . . . Natalie could only bend low over a book; remember the dates of the Norman invasions; report good tennis players for staying out all night with a man, a "college man". . . .

VII

Are we really never going to have it, Miss Engle moaned to herself through her third-hour class, are we really going to miss all that? What she meant was: a husband; a home; a kitchen; self-respect; a telephone, a butcher, a bridge-club, of one's own —someone to wake up with in the mornings. She let herself live with various men in various houses, during her Modern History classes. Now it was a rich broker, now a poor poet; but in any case, when the stock market crashed, or when all the magazines in the world sent back her husband's poems, Marcia Engle could say, with all the rich and generous untapped love in her soul: Anyhow, we have each other, darling. We . . . we . . . *we*! To say "we" and to mean two people; two separate living wholes, who yet could come together, worry together, *have each other darling*. There would be two tooth-brushes in the bathroom, two combs on the shelf, two glasses on the table—Miss Engle, Mr-and-Mrs-Somebody-or-other, would have exactly, neatly, miraculously, two of everything. In the mornings he would call to her from the other bed (the broker, the poet, the *companion*), "Hey there, Lazy Mary. . ."

"But why, *why* do you think Oliver Cromwell. . ." she nodded at Betty Fleet. "Of course you don't know! you are not going to find the answer on the tennis courts!"

What was there, she thought, looking into the
bright and empty faces, of Betty Fleet, of the girl
behind her, of all the children in the shining rows,
what distinctive thing was there about youth? *Real*
youth—not being still "young at thirty-five", not
"not being taken for one's age." But being eighteen
and proud to be taken for it, never having earned
a cent, never having endured this particular kind
of loneliness. . . . Even Gwennie, whose hair was
bleached, who wore mascara on her eyes to morning classes, who knew more about men than her
teachers, looked young, *was* young; fresh, dewy—
all of them; some of their faces were hard, some of
them were cold; but all of them were young, with
this terrible, mobile, ruthless youngness, that smote
one to the heart, that made one ache, made one long
in an awful way for what could never come again.
For what had never altogether been, thought Miss
Engle, sighing; for her own youth had been not so
carefree. Still there had been hope, there had been
time, for anything to happen. Suddenly she felt
young again, ridiculously young and sweet. She remembered standing in the History office, at the
University; an undergraduate; plain, perhaps,
rather poor—but still young, still terribly, rav-
ishingly, uncompromisingly young—twenty. The
weather must have been exactly like this. "My
wife," Professor Mellish was saying, whimsical and
charming, "my wife does not know the first thing
about the causes of the Civil War." He had put his
hand on her shoulder. "I think you, little Marcia

Engle," he had said, "I think *you* understand everything." She had gone out, happy enough to cry. She had gone up and shaken hands with him at her graduation exercises; and smiled, feeling charming, at his wife, his old wife who must have been twenty-nine.

So she smiled now, rather charmingly, at Betty Fleet. "My dear child! Think twice. What were his *motives*? What was he trying to *achieve*?"

How she had stood there, the merry graduation breeze lifting the ruffles of the white dress she had made herself. Flowers, her brother had sent her flowers, nodding in her arms like so many fresh, unwithered testimonials to her youth. She had hoped Professor Mellish and his wife would think a swain had sent them. "I shall always think of you as being young, with the whole world before you," Professor Mellish had said—his last words; with a warm little clasp of her hand while his wife had turned to greet a friend. All at once the vision mocked: "always young, the whole world". . . But it had happened yesterday! Fifteen years had flashed by in a day! What had she been thinking of, to let them go like that! Had she expected her youth to last forever? Had she dreamily, year after year, postponed the things she should have seized? Yet what could she have done? what *should* she have done? Grasped Professor Mellish by the arm and shaken it, cried out "Yes, yes, I am young now but I shall not always be, and what are you going to do about *that*?" Stopped the earth from turning one day until Marcia Engle could figure out how to find happiness? They were gone, gone, those fifteen years, gone in a flash, and forever!

"Pencils!" said Miss Engle bitingly. Fourteen young heads bowed in submissive rows before her. "Pencils!" said Miss Engle—and they gasped; they forgot the sun, and the magnolias, and their incredibly lucky boon of youth—they merely gasped and wetted their pencils with bright pink little tongues and held them obediently above fresh sheets of paper. "It would seem that Spring," said Miss Engle—hating herself for the brief sadistic pleasure she derived, "that Spring has gone to your heads. We will have a quiz."

VIII

"Oh! I—I just thought I'd change into my peach," said Graham, backing guiltily away from the window as Armstrong—she had not expected her so soon—dropped her blue-books on the bed.

"I really only dismissed them three minutes earlier," said Graham, holding her petticoat between her knees as she smoothed the pleats of the peach dress.

"Of course I suppose it's rather silly," said Graham pleadingly, "only in this hot weather and all. . ."

"And anyway," said Graham, not quite meeting Armstrong's eye in the mirror, "anyway, I'll be all ready for tea, I won't have to change again."

They stood side by side before the bureau, these two friends who had roomed together seven years, each gazing stolidly at her own image in the mirror. Generally their gaze would cross, as Armie did up her back hair, as Graham ran a wet finger across her eyebrows; generally they chatted, and smiled, and lent each other advice about too much powder. But today they were silent. With the same motion (in this uncomfortable silence) they patted their noses with powder, skimmed their lips with rouge, swayed forward for closer inspection, and reared back, questioning. At the same instant they fluffed bits of hair over identical spots above their temples; turned left, turned right, each giving herself that suspicious side-glance that means the winding-up of the process. Not once did their eyes meet, to hold friendly confab in the glass. But without seeing anything but her own image, Graham knew how Armie must be looking: severe, unsmiling, scornful—yet perhaps with a quivering lower lip. From years of habit Armie, when she was finished with it, transferred the eau de cologne from her "side" to the invisible boundary line which separated their toilet articles, their "sides": for seven years, Armie on the left, Graham on the right. Mechanically Graham reached for the bottle. Their fingers touched, drew back; they didn't speak. Unhappily Graham splashed herself with their favorite scent.

But the feel of the peach dress was refreshing, that last side-glance at the mirror sweet. Graham was drawn, weak and happy and willess, against her better judgment, to the window. Ah! Through the heavy blossoms of the magnolia tree she caught a glimpse of a slender figure—M'sieur Laval, the French teacher—mounting to his classes from his little room in the village. "So beautiful today," Carola Graham murmured, a little breathless. (Armie was still silent behind her.) M'sieur Laval wore no hat. The slight breeze went through his thin hair and lifted it in little French wisps above his ears. The air blowing in was sweet and warm; the birds lusty; on Mondays M'sieur Laval lunched at the School. "I think it's very foolish," said Carola Graham defiantly, "to save and save a new dress, half the time they wear out in the closet before you get a chance to use them." Turning, bold in the new peach dress, she met Armstrong's canny eye.

"Sometimes," said Armie coldly, "I think you are as bad as Chambie—or as loony as Lady Macbeth. And anyway," she added cunningly, "I think it is our turn to sit with the Duchess today, and leave ze leetle Frenchman to the *ozzer* vultures."

You couldn't beat Armie, thought Graham, sighing, and turning her back on all that was French and male. She sighed; but it was not unpleasant, this bossing, this scorn, of Armie's. It was warm, protective, safe—and exclusively Carola's.

IX

By mid-day, by lunch-time, it seemed that the sky had cracked wide open. The sun shone, the breeze

blew, the birds sang, as though all of them had just
been released, as the girls had been, from algebra
and Latin classes, as though they had reached the
apex of their careers. And yet that noon had a quality too that it was impossible to imagine ever end-
ing, it had a forever quality as well as a fleeting one.
Impossible for Linda, up in her room and writing
feverishly in her diary of love, and Edgar, and herself, to imagine growing older by so much as a minute. Impossible for Miss Whitson, the housekeeper,
to remember her tragedy of being neither servant
nor teacher—as she stood at her post in the dining-
room and watched the child, Betty Fleet, whom for
some reason she had picked to love all year. And
impossible for Natalie Freeman, who had cried a
bit from self-pity, who had come down like a non-
scholarship girl with her arm around her room-
mate, to feel poor, to feel mean, to feel anything in
fact but hungry.

At the Best Table Sudie pushed her mashed potatoes into mountains and ravines and ate meatballs
in an absent-minded dream; Jean and Betty Fleet
practiced their forearm using their forks for rack-
ets; Gwennie's incredible blonde hair shone like
a halo, as bright as the sun. The entire Next Best
Table was engaged in testing their individual electricity by lifting spoons with the tips of their middle-
fingers and thumbs, till Aster started an epidemic
of dropping them with a clatter to the table, which
proved just as much fun. At the long Faculty Table
the breezy gym teacher ate nothing but raw vege-

tables, the "culinary" teacher ate everything that came to the table with passionate abandon; around M'sieur Laval there was a gentle eddying of love, innocent and guileless, and Lady Macbeth sat with a Greek wreath of braids about her temples and the look on her plain face of a handsome woman. Even Miss Laurel sat with a smile, allowing herself to be seduced by the richness, the last-minute glory and gayety, the merry ring of knives and voices—and even, perhaps, the pleasant, unfamiliar warmth of a man's voice in their midst. And over it all, at the Chief Faculty Table, the Duchess and her teeth presided, benign and ugly and big and kind. The Duchess—bowing her head to her breast for grace, being first ahead of Armstrong and Graham and little Miss Chambers to pick up her spoon, to put down her spoon—the Duchess sat at the Chief Table and loved her School; "her girls" for being so young and coming from such nice families, and "her teachers" for being so plain, so respectfully gay, so timidly "at their ease" with her—and for waiting to see when she picked up her spoon, put down her spoon, and if she would laugh at their jokes.

"It's as if," wrote Linda in her diary, "I had a thousand little bugs inside me, all squirming and wriggling and pushing me up and holding me down at the same time. Everything's so beautifull today, is that because I'm in love, or am I in love because everything's so beautifull. Everything's ahead of me and yet I've got everything in the world I want or will ever have right now in the palm palme palm of my hand. I feel good enough to forgive Natalie Freeman because the poor thing is so plain and I feel terrably sorry for people who are old or ugly because what can they possibly have ahead of them? I think I will kill myself the day I am thirty, it would be too awful to be old."

"Carpe diem," said Lady Macbeth suddenly at the Faculty Table, and M'sieur Laval looked up from pouring chili sauce on his meat-ball in faint surprise, his soft French eyebrows delicately raised. "My goodness, Macbeth," said Miss Laurel; and she and Engie exchanged a little glance of amusement.

Miss Whitson stood, a little self-conscious—she never got used to standing before them all, with her arms folded, in her white uniform—and looked with love at Betty Fleet, and hoped she was getting the best of everything, the best meat-balls, the creamiest potatoes, she hoped Betty Fleet liked green peas. There was nothing very particular about Betty Fleet —her blondish hair strained back by a round comb, and her face spattered with adolescent spots—there were prettier children at Magnolia Hall, and plainer; she was just an ordinary child, with stocky legs and a rather loud voice, and it was perhaps because there *was* nothing special about her that Miss Whitson had picked her out, at the first lunch of the year, to love.

"But the point is," said the Duchess in a low voice, "if we *dropped* her, there'd be trouble. Linda's *mother* is an alumna of Magnolia Hall, and her *father* is a fraternity brother of one of our trustees. Not, of course," said the Duchess, fingering her glass beads, "that I would let *that* stand in my way, if I really thought anything, if I really thought she, I mean," said the Duchess, horribly embarrassed, "if I didn't think she was really a *very* good girl." And little Chambie sat up very straight, not daring to think of her Date tonight with Jerry lest the Duchess read it in her eyes.

"who was probably *the* smoothest man at the Dance, I said no, I can't go up to Princeton without my room-mate, haven't you got a room-mate too. . ." "Oh, it was colossal, because then *he*. . ." "certainly he's a fairy, did you ever see a French teacher who wasn't, Sudie?" "Still, I'd like to know what they *do*" "*do,* you fool, they don't do *anything,* that's just it—" the Best Table burst into roars of laughter, while Sudie sat, feeling hot and silly, mixing her peas into the mashed-potato canyon. "All the same, tennis or no tennis," said Natalie, regaining her confidence, "those ads have to be got, this afternoon." "Have you people any extra chili sauce?" asked Edith Whitney, leaning over from the Next Best Table.

"We all know," wrote Linda in her diary, "that Gwennie"—and then she crossed out Gwennie and put G—, for you never know in a boarding-school, "that G— is not a virgin and we all envy her because at dances she's not the least scared of boys and goes right up and says anything she pleases to a strange boy even if they haven't spoken to her. So we all

envy her but sometimes I wonder if G— doesn't
envy us a little bit too, I mean suppose she really
fell in love with a boy some day. I can't figure anything out. I can't figure Myself out, least of all. I
mean, I am in love with Edgar and how I wish he
would write to me today or call me up Long Distance from New Haven but if he did I know exactly
what would happen, I would snap at him over the
Long Distance and afterward I would think he was
a collossal fool and stop being in love with him.
Dear God, must my love always be so selfish? Some
day I want a family of my own, I would like to be a
good unselfish mother with a lot of children who
simply adored me!!!!!! there I am being selfish
again!! because if they didn't adore me. . . Oh
God, now I am frightened of something, I don't
know quite what of. But whenever I get a glimpse
of my own Mother being a person a real person like
Myself, getting into evning dresses and all and not
being just My Mother, I get terrably scared, I get a
hollow feeling in my tummy like when Bobby and
I were kids and used to scare each other telling each
other there were wolves in the nursery and all of a
sudden we'd holler and nobody would here us.
That just proves what a baby I still am. But I don't
feel like a baby at all, not with all these feelings of
insects crawling up and down my legs on the inside
and pushing and pulling me seven different ways at
the same time. I get worried about things like this
too. When I think of Edgar and I know I'm in love
with him I think right away of Jack and Fred and

Eddie and wonder and hope that knowing I'm in love with Edgar will make them fall in love with me!!!! Oh dear God is that awful!! It makes me feel like pshycology class when Dr Chapman stood there and said women were either born Mothers or born prostitutes. My God if Edgar knew I had thoughts like these. Well then why didn't I let him go all the way? At the last minute I thought of Daddy and of Bobby too. Daddy would laugh if it wasn't so serious but of course Mother wouldn't understand or she would pretend not to, she always pulls down the shades eTc for those kind of subjects. Sometimes I simply hate Mother oh God I'll be sorry I said that. Oh Edgar Edgar Edgar why don't you call me up call me up Long Distance Edgar call me up call me up dear God make him call me up make him invite me to the prom up there God I am so selfish and so petty is this what Miss Laurel calls free association, she'd *die* if she ever saw this. . ."

"They tell me," said Chambie very grave and careful to sound "at ease" in the Duchess's presence, "that at Ann Matthews Hall they let the Juniors smoke now—of course," Chambie said with a mature little laugh, "*I* don't see what's the use of keeping girls in a school if you're not going to use *discipline*—so important to their characters and all," finished Chambie lamely, for a glance at Armstrong convinced her that no one was being much impressed. "Those beads are so becoming," said Graham, leaning across to the Duchess and striking a fitter note; "didn't you say, from Florence?" (Oh

Jerry, you could take me out of this, prayed Chambie to her baked apple; God, make Jerry want to marry me, save me from being an old maid, a schoolteacher, God, God, God. . .)

Miss Whitson stood with a little smile on her face, watching how Betty Fleet flung back her hair and twisted it under the round comb, how Betty Fleet reached too far and got tickled by her neighbor when she tried for the bread two places away, how nicely Betty Fleet wiped her little rosy mouth with her napkin. For some reason, for no reason, everything that Betty Fleet did stood out for Miss Whitson, and although Betty Fleet did not know it at all, she had lived and moved all year in a frame of love provided by the housekeeper, who watched her on the tennis courts, watched her going to classes, watched her with her hair curled and her hair uncurled, watched her get thin before the holidays and plump and tan in Spring. . . .

"Oh, he's colossal! and Linda says dances like nobody's business" "do you suppose that's what they were doing on the golf-course" "oh you *pig*" (Screams of mounting laughter) "my new white dress, and Daddy wrote and said that was the last thing this year and no more money and then he wrote P.S. here's a check for twenty dollars don't tell mother" "Oh colossal" "colossal" "colossal"

Oh, their voices, thought Miss Laurel, listening to the high clear chatter, not a word of which reached the Faculty Table. As smooth as silk, their voices, and soft—but hard too, harsh (remembering their cruelty of the morning, how they had let her down, how they had spat upon the poor!) harsh like the ringing of steel skates on ice, expensive skates on artificial, imported ice. . . . "Is it not that the gels work less hard because of the weathair," said M'sieur Laval to Miss Engle, who—trying to be light, trying to be charming, had nevertheless found herself reporting in detail, like a teacher, how she had had to give them a quiz this morning. "The weather's pretty hard on the faculty too, M'sieur," she answered gayly—but no, it was not charming, it was not gay, it was deliberate and eld-erly-coy; Engie grew silent and sad. "Merci beau-coup, M'sieur," said Lady Macbeth, accepting the sugar and smiling dreamily.

"Yes, from Florence, from the Ponte Vechio," said the Duchess, little drops of spray falling from the spaces between her teeth, "my married niece . . . of course we shall have to make an *example* of Linda, and I *think*," said the Duchess, playing with her beads, "that we should not allow much talk among the students about the whole unfortunate, the whole unfortunate—" "Incident," supplied Armstrong accurately. "Oh of course not," said Graham eagerly. "Oh of course not," murmured Chambie, wondering what it was she was saying Of course not, to. And then they all put down their spoons because the Duchess had.

"Miss Flam the nurse has just been here bringing my lunch," wrote Linda. "The minute she opened the door I wanted to laugh, she looked so funny standing there, and I wanted to scream at her Hey Flammie, have you ever had a lover? Imagine!!! Collossal! Only nobody would have believed me except Sudie. It's funny Miss Engle sometimes talks about her brother and the fun they used to have and I just can't believe that the *Engles* were ever kids like Bobby and I rolling around on a nursery floor and talking about oh all sorts of things that certainly would have made Mother leave the room!!!!?! Oh Edgar Edgar Edgar whatever happens to you for the rest of your life you'll never have anything happen to you like Linda falling in love with you even if it turns out only to be for one night. I wonder if Edgar is a virgin I wouldn't be surprised. Why did we say goodbye such a funny way. It's funny after that long night on the golf-course, I really think *implications of immortality* is clever I wish I knew what it meant—but after that long night of almost being lovers except that we had our clothes all on (I'll have to throw this page down the John and it's really too bad I'd like to show it to Sudie first but it would be terrable if They found it) and being so close, and yet I don't think Edgar understands me, he never asks me what I think about anything—and then in the morning the minute it got light it was so terrably embarrassing and we were both so sort of bashful sneaking back to the School and shaking hands instead of kissing, I didn't want to ever see him again we were really both ashamed of something, I wonder if we would have been ashamed if we had gone the whole way, I

wonder how I would be feeling now, I wonder if
it's true a boy can tell it about a girl the minute he
looks at her, you can tell it about Gwennie or *can*
you, doesn't she tell it to you first—oh that's simply
disgusting, I'm getting terrable again guess I'll eat
'my last meal' . . . oh God oh God, tell Linda
what it's all about. . . ."

"*Look* at Macbeth!" cried Sudie suddenly. "Oh
colossal!" cried Jean. They all looked and saw the
Medusa-like white braids crawling about her large
head. They saw the paisley dress that Lady Macbeth had made herself on the Greek model, with an
Empire waist that allowed her lax old belly to slope
like a tent beneath it. They saw the thong sandals
she had sent to Sears Roebuck for because they
looked Grecian. And they saw her smiling, shrug-
ging her shoulders, being French as well as Greek.
"Colossal!" cried Jean, and Sudie, and Gwennie
and all the others. And something caught them in
the middle so they laughed and laughed and could
not stop laughing, stuffing their napkins into their
mouths, their brows bursting with sweat, tears of
joy springing to their eyes. And when they began
to stop, the Next Best Table caught it and started
it up again and it would sweep the whole group like
a gale, till they rocked in their chairs and swung to
and fro, and the other tables caught it, and the maids
began giggling, and at last even the Faculty, not
knowing what they were laughing at, began to
smile and shake and quiver and sway in their
chairs, the Duchess laughed (Armstrong and Gra-

ham and Chambie following her lead), and finally
Lady Macbeth herself, innocently joyful in her own
secret way, smiled kindly over her bi-focals, as
though she extended the palm to Cæsar and Na-
poleon, both at once.

X

Sudie and Jean had managed to get on the bus to
the Village hatless and wearing only their tennis
socks, against all rules. They couldn't help giggling
at all the funny people in the bus, hicks from the
Village and the funniest colored woman with a huge
market-bag. Jiggling on their laps were notebooks
and slips of paper for the storekeepers to sign, that
Natalie had ruled and typed for them. Of course
it was really fun, skipping tennis and going off like
this—but somehow the minute the big bus shook its
way out of sight of the campus, Sudie began to feel
scared.

It was as if what they were going to do, sell advertising space for the Yearbook, weren't, somehow,
quite *nice*. It seemed dangerous. Sudie had a clear
feeling that her mother wouldn't like it. It was all
right for Jean; Jean was good in algebra, Jean remembered things and would be calm and business-
like in the Village, and not frightened, she would
know just what to say to people. But Sudie felt a
little lonely, even beside Jean, already; a little as she
had out on the tennis-court with Malcolm, dying to
get back inside the School. The campus seemed so

far away. All these people in the bus were strangers; and although they looked quite pleasantly and with amusement at Jean and Sudie, Sudie somehow didn't like it—she wished they had worn stockings and were not so conspicuously girls from Magnolia Hall. She wished she were safely back in her room, in the library, on the tennis-courts, with a nice kind teacher's eye upon her. The strangers in the bus suddenly made her a stranger too, a stranger to herself; she couldn't imagine what she was doing there. And it was queer about the song too, *You're the top,* the song which accompanied her dream—it no longer flowed; it came spasmodically, whole bars were lost. It felt either as though she were coming out of her dear dream into a reality that was hateful —no, for this was not reality; it felt rather as though she had got into the wrong dream by mistake. But all the time she went on giggling with Jean (who was suddenly a stranger too) about the funny people and the funny houses that they passed.

"Now," said Jean, as they climbed out of the bus, "you take Prosser's, and I'll tackle the camp-stool place, then we'll meet right here and catch the three o'clock bus in time for tea and the charm-woman, I'd hate to miss the charm-woman. . . ."

Sudie stopped dead in her tracks. "You mean— *alone?* You mean we've got to *separate,* Jean? Oh Jeannie, I'm scared to *death,* I'd rather *die.* . . ."

"Idiot," said Jean briskly, "what do you think, the man isn't going to bite you! Why, you've been in their store a thousand hundred times, you've bought sneakers, and tennis socks, and bandanas, and ski-pants—*don't* be a baby!"

The dry-goods store did not look the haven it was when you merely dashed in for sneakers, or tennis socks, or bandanas, or ski-pants. It looked like a foreign place, dull and frightening—what was it Lorelei had lectured them about this morning? And Sudie to be going in, not dashing about with a five-dollar bill in her purse and all of Magnolia Hall behind her, not to advance politely to the saleswoman and kindly make a purchase—but Sudie going in, *to make her way,* to ask a favor, something she couldn't simply pay for—Sudie to *sell something*! Like other people, the kind of people one didn't know, like *grown-ups.* Sudie wondered if grown-up people went around all the time with that empty lonely feeling she had now in the pit of her stomach. Perhaps they did, only when they were about twenty-five they forgot they had it or got used to it, like having false teeth. She stood there and pretended to be looking at the window display, and then she stood there and pretended to powder her nose. And nothing would have driven her in but that she turned round at that minute and caught sight of Jean at the top of the hill, about to enter the camp-stool place, and Jean waved and beckoned and put her hands on her hips in disgust until Sudie gave up and went in the door.

XI

"The Theory of the Leisure Class" was propped on the table before Natalie; each sentence sank with precision and righteousness into her brain, meeting there with the mellowed synthesis of previous sentences melted together into meaning. A thin veil of satisfaction lay between her and her reading; she was proud of reading a book which their sociology teacher had considered too difficult to put on the "prescribed" list, and had recommended to her in conference. And she was proud too that she need not play tennis this afternoon, as though it were not merely because she was "out" for physical reasons. "The largest manifestation of vicarious leisure in modern life. . ."

Out-of-door shouts from another world floated, far-off and crazy, through the half-closed window; the veil of satisfaction trembled, shot through with sound. Natalie wrinkled a corner of her term paper lying beside her, marked with an A and "Shows an excellent grasp of the subject" in Miss Engle's thin Spencerian. "These duties are fast becoming a species of services performed, not. . ." Library chimes again, cheerful, triumphantly playing all four quarters of the tune; pregnant silence; tonnng; tonnng. Dentist's drill again, the second tonnng spinning, fainter and fainter, in her brain long after it had died in her ears, it must be gone, no, I can still feel it like a mosquito—it's gone. I'm supposed to be brilliant, Natalie thought, and I hate it. She returned to the book: "As fast as the household. . ."

"Hya, Nat." The words fell in with a shock. It was Betty Fleet, freshly showered, dripping in the doorway, one sunburned shoulder sticking out of the towel. "*Studying*, Nat? A day like this?"

"Not studying: I'm reading."

Glowing room-mate standing still, towel falling from gleaming body, mouth open like faintly wondering, very sweet baby. "*Reading*?" Natalie grimly enjoyed the sensation she had caused. "Oh, you're 'out' today, aren't you? don't you feel well?"

Betty Fleet choosing a fresh linen dress, dropping the last one into the laundry bag; bending double to examine a black-and-blue spot on her thigh. Oh read on, read on, Natalie. Why doesn't Betty Fleet notice the term paper marked "A"?

"Natalie! An A! God you're wonderful. And from Engle! Colossal! Oh, it's terribly hot in here, Natalie. Mind if I open the window all the way?" Immediately the out-of-door sounds rushed in and a breeze ran over the table, lifted the top sheet of the A theme, contemptuously dropped it again. Like Betty Fleet, thought Natalie. But she's noticed it. Now I can put it away.

Dressed again, hair pulled back under the stupid round comb, Betty Fleet stands for a moment with her arms around her room-mate. "You're so smart, Nat, gosh! Remember when we found we'd be room-mates? How we stared at each other and wondered? I knew I'd like you though. But you must of thought

I was a colossal nut! Papa says what I don't know
would fill about a million books. Coming down,
Nat? not even to *watch*?" Betty Fleet is in the door
again, nobody knows how she moves, how she gets
from one place to the next one, one moment her
arms are friendly and warm about your neck, the
next they are cradling a tennis racket. A moment
more and Betty Fleet will be flying down the gravel
path, between the magnolia trees. "Oh, it's *colossal*
out-of-doors, Nat!"

"Yes, colossal."

"Well, see you at tea then—don't forget the
charm-woman. So long, Nat."

"So long, Fleet."

Light steps tramping down the hall; steps stop;
words float back. "Going over tennis?" "Sure."
"Hurry up then, you fool. Whistle blows two minutes." Double steps tapping down the hall. Steady
tapp-it tapp-it tapp-it of rubber heel-and-toe on
cement walk beneath the window, voices high and
false cutting the thin air "Then hurry, you fool,
we've got to be back to dress for tea, it's dress-tea
today, the charm-woman," "Did you ever *smell* such
weather?" Natalie hitched her chair closer to the
table. "That is to say, since vicarious—" Library
bells, full and rich with that unbearable window
wide open, flung up by Betty Fleet, ringing first
quarter.

"But already at a point in economic evolution
far antedating the emergence of the lady"—she
scribbled a note in her note-book: "Roger says con-

ception of lady arose from pride of economic freedom in upper classes, i.e., must wear wrap instead of buttoned coat in order prove not carrying family wash, etc." Roger again! Poor Roger! Had he seen how Natalie was ashamed of him at the Dance, had he known that her dress was borrowed from Betty Fleet, her slippers from Caroline Siller? And her manner from—God knows whom! "But already at a point in economic. . ."

Natalie pushed the book forward on the table, dropped her head on her hands. Little dark world made of sweating hands and glasses cutting into bridge of nose; ears are still in outside world, peeping Toms sticking out on both sides of my head, why can't I take them in like snails, but you can't, you can close your eyes but you can't make your ears stop thinking. ("Thirty love! Net ball!" float in from that other world.) Voices outside losing their separateness, merging, sweet distant song, like shell held to ear, going round and round in Natalie's brain, ears going to sleep at last, room warm, faint breeze on back of neck, quieter, quieter . . . soft high shouts from far-off tennis court. . .

"Finals! Natalie Freeman versus Betty Fleet assisted by Linda who plays every other game. Games are, said Miss Winsey—looking at her whistle, looking at her watch—games are five to one, favor Fleet-Linda. All right—serve! Natalie! called Miss Winsey. I'll give 'em an ace, thought Natalie, and did—three of them and then after winning a simple volley, took her first love game. And then it was Linda serving and Natalie won easily on that, and then Fleet again, and then Miss Winsey said the games were five all. Natalie started serving again, and served for four games straight which brought them to seven all. Then it was eight-seven favor Natalie, and all the girls began to scream, Come on Natalie, come on Freeman, show 'em what you've got, and Natalie served a pair of aces, and then they volleyed for ten minutes straight, at the end of which Natalie was panting and at last Natalie sent the ball first down the left alley to Linda, then down the right to Fleet, and finally straight down the middle, and when Fleet and Linda returned a soft one, up to the net rushed Natalie, *spring, spring* from the ankles, from the toes—smashing down on the ball and winning the point, the game, the set, the match, the championship—and then she kept right on running till she had leapt the net (which she had never been able to do before) and shaken Linda and Betty Fleet by the hand and received a cup from the Duchess so large she could scarcely carry it. "I didn't know you were so nice," Linda kept saying through the rounds of applause and cheering, "I didn't know you were so nice." And there was Natalie's mother (rather dim, so you didn't have to worry about her dress) and her father, and Roger Dunn, who came slowly through the crowd with an indistinct smile on his lips, saying "I bet you're the only scholarship girl that ever won a cup—" and Natalie, looking about in terror

lest anyone had heard him, dropped the huge cup
and woke up.

XII

The fat woman's face changed, seemed to lose
its kindness, the face of the woman who had sold
Sudie socks, and shirts, and ski-pants, when Sudie
asked to see the manager. Sudie was speaking in a
voice she knew was not her own; and when the
woman pointed to the private office back of the
"stocks" Sudie got there with a walk that was not
hers either.

Mr Prosser was sitting at his desk in the little
"office," which was nothing but a compartment
made of beaverboard, behind the selling part of
the store. Mr Prosser shifted his cigar at Sudie, and
recognizing her as a Magnolia Hall girl, started to
smile as she came in, and swept a pile of women's
underwear to one side on his desk. "Well, little
lady, and what can I do you for?"

Sudie felt that she had blotted out the sun and
sweetness of Spring forever by coming here, where
the air was stale with cigars and bargains, musty
with unsold goods. She felt that she stood on dangerous ground. She watched Mr Prosser's smile
change as she shyly explained her errand. It was not
that it walked off his face—it actually seemed to
grow; but it lost its ingratiating quality and became
assured. It was as though they had changed places,
Mr Prosser and Sudie; it was now Sudie who came

with something to sell, Mr Prosser who could grow petulant and toss his head if he wished to. "And so of course," concluded Sudie vaguely, "we thought of you because all our girls buy so much here, socks and all, and we knew you'd be glad. . ." She wound up by trailing off. She was not sure of any of her facts, and the fundamental reason for the ads was somehow not clear to her, there had been so much talk and she had never really bothered to listen. When she said "socks" she became acutely aware of her own, and wished she had not bought them here, from Mr Prosser, and wished anyway that her legs were not bare in his presence.

"Well, take a load off your feet, sit down," said Mr Prosser, still smiling hugely and enjoying himself.

Sudie thought it would not be polite to refuse to sit down. There was only one chair beside Mr Prosser's, and that was drawn up to his desk, beside his. Sudie sat down on the edge, and then, because that left her bare legs too much in evidence, wriggled back against the slats, from where she sat uncomfortably and gravely smiling up at Mr Prosser.

"Now," said Mr Prosser, "you've told me the price, but you haven't said the different sizes. And you haven't told me can I use cuts or photos. And you haven't told me when this Yearbook is coming out. And you haven't—"

Sudie knew sickeningly that although Mr Prosser would say yes in the end, she would have to endure his miserable adult banter first, for as long as he chose to deliver it. It was a sort of price that he put on his doing her a favor—Magnolia Hall was at his mercy for once.

"Cuts?" she inquired, like a stupid little girl playing up. "Just what do you mean, cuts, Mr Prosser?"

"Well now, look here," said Mr Prosser largely. Out came pencils, six-inch rules, a pad of fat white paper. Mr Prosser began to draw. To measure. To bring his chair closer to hers so that she smelled the tobacco on his suit. Till his jokes came heavily into her ears. Till she was painfully conscious of her breast, rising and falling the more painfully for the knowledge, directly beneath his eyes. Till she felt the faint pressure of his thick knee against her bare leg and was afraid to move it lest Mr Prosser be really a kindly old man who was unaware of the contact, and Sudie merely a dirty-minded little girl.

"So you see it makes a difference, eh, you see?" said Mr Prosser. "It makes a difference the size of the cut, the kind and everything, you see? Little business-woman! Now take photos—suppose I decide. . ." But his voice was lower as though he did know that their knees were touching. Now, *now* was the time to move away, under pretext of crossing her knees and getting out her handkerchief. "And if I want a border, or want it mounted," said Mr Prosser—and though Sudie had accomplished the miracle of escape a thousand times in pantomime in her mind, she still sat with her trembling knee against his. *Now* perhaps, as he turned from her a little to relight his cigar. Hurry, Sudie—but Sudie went on sitting there, as still as a statue. "Then of course you should be able to say to your prospects exactly about the kind of type. Suppose I should want some in italics, suppose. . ." Mr Prosser himself had shifted; definitely he was moving his chair back, as though to give his belly more space; there was a cool spot on Sudie's knee where Mr Prosser's knee had been. Now, now was the time to move, now or never, said a faint voice in Sudie's ear. She sat in a delicate agony of suspense; there were so many seconds in which to move; the seconds dragged; they flew. And all at once it was too late to move, forever too late, for Sudie didn't *want* to move, she would rather have died than not have Mr Prosser's knee against her own again. The knee came back; it had given her a full twenty seconds to escape, and now it came back with assurance, came and rested firmly against her own as though it knew its place—and the rest of Sudie disowned her knee, and despised it, but nevertheless it had become the center of her body, of the world, all sensation was born in it from the touch of Mr Prosser, and Sudie sat locked in horrified fascination at the curious changing of the blood in both her temples.

"So you see, business-woman," said Mr Prosser, whose voice disowned *his* knee too, "you come to me without a very clear proposition. But what should you know, eh? what should you care? You smile, and we do anything you say. We buy space in your Yearbook, we don't know when it is coming

out, you will forget to send us proofs—but what of
it, eh? Well, well, now we will see what we can say
in this ad of ours."

Mr Prosser bent over his paper again and Sudie
who could not bear to look at his face, who could
not bear to look down at herself, sat there terrified
and dumb—and prayed that it would never end.
Sudie who had not let a nice boy, whose mother
knew her aunt, so much as kiss her, here was Sudie
with a stranger's knee pressing on her own, and
praying it would never end. Was this another kind
of dream? Was this the end of all dreams? This experience that Sudie was having came under no classi-
fication, compared with nothing she had ever felt
before. Oh, if life, or not life but *whatever it was*
could go on like this forever—helpless, choking,
secret. . . And then suddenly it was over; something was over; the feeling had gone dead, her knee
numb. And Mr Prosser seemed to feel it too, for he
spoke to her in a stale voice now, withdrawing his
knee, handing her his slip of paper. Sudie accepted
his check, his reproof, his farewell, and made her
way blindly through the outer store to the street
where the sun was waiting for her, her song, her
dream, and Jeannie with a bag of apples.

XIII

Miss Laurel was holding her English conferences
on the deserted hockey field, under a magnolia.
Tell me, God, she said (between Edith Whitney

and Aster), is this real? She meant the heavy, blossom-laden tree above her; the fresh grass laid beneath; the wide peaceful arc of the sky swimming cloudlessly miles above the campus. Because if this is real, she thought, what of the city, and the crooked dirty streets, what of the stock market—but what, even, of the Public Library, the hospitals and what (going farther) of Peter Hendragin's social revolution? What of these girls—and you can't help loving them, despite their flimsiness, their showiness, their shallowness, because they are children (the group with their arms stretched, lying like starfish under the sun, at the other end of the field; the two girls swinging up from the bus-stop, waving a bag of apples; Aster running toward her from the tennis courts, stumbling a little, looking a little frightened because she was late)—if these girls are real, then what of the public school children with their bright peaked little faces, their bright peaked little minds? Still, it was natural for children to grow up in safety, to grow straight and healthy and beautiful—and yet if one counted on these fine-looking children with their creamy skins, where would be your Dostoievskys, your Karl Marxes? And would it be better. . . . But here was Aster!

And what was she saying, her blue eyes large and tremulous? Miss Laurel tried to stop her, to tell her that she must not apologize, if she thought poor people were ugly and mean in the morning she must stick to it now, out here in the sun, under this magnolia tree; if that was what she really thought. But Aster went on, tears in her blue eyes.

"But did you really mean it, Miss Laurel, I never understood it before, my father, you see he and mother are divorced, my father says if I spend a lot of money, the more money I spend, that is the way I can show I still love him, even though I live with mother—I send him expense accounts each week and I have to spend a lot to show him. And I never knew, I never dreamed—of course I've passed slums before, driven through them on the way to theater, but I never dreamed that—" here Aster drew a deep, gasping, frightened breath—"Miss Laurel, do you honestly mean that *more than half* the people in the world, that *most* people, are poor? I feel as though my father lied to me. . ."

XIV

Miss Winsey's tennis players were flying back across the hockey field in their shorts and sun-backs, to get ready for the dress-up tea. Behind them Miss Winsey, like a small erect shepherd, put one sturdy leg after another—Smithy and the Halloran each clinging to an arm. Two girls coming up from the bus-stop madly waved a bulky paper bag—cut across the field to join two comrades: Sudie and Jean hatless and barelegged, defying all rules—shouting to Betty Fleet and Aster, still in their tennis clothes.

Natalie, seated on the window-sill waiting for the tea-bell, saw them. Below her the campus stretched, shadows growing longer; afternoon sunlight, warming through sheets of coolness, picking out patches on trees, on buildings, flecking the gravel paths that ran between magnolias. Oh I love this place, I love this place, thought Natalie, I'm the only one here intelligent enough—and outside of it enough —to see its beauty, the others are all a part of it, unconscious inheritors; I love it; the campus, the library clock, the trees, the paths, the air—even the silly traditions. It's so solid, so sure—for everyone but me. Is that because my mother didn't come here and carve her initials on the library steps, like Betty Fleet's and Linda's? Is it because my clothes are not the same? No, it is deeper than the clothes, as though I were of a different race, the Poor, the unlucky majority. . . . Below came the four girls, eating apples—they were laughing and their voices floated sweetly upward. Jean, at the end of the row, finished her apple; looked curiously at it, turning it round in her hand, and nibbled at the core. Without pausing, she lifted it high over her head and flung it as far as she could. One by one, each girl finished her apple, turned it round in her hand, nibbled, flung it as far as she could with careless power. They continued all the while their conversation, their laughter, their light patter-patter walk. The girl on the end opened the paper bag and passed them each another apple. . . . Oh God, thought Natalie, I never could eat an apple like that; no dull, earnest scholarship girl. . . She leaned out of the window as far as she could: "Did you get the ads?" she called coldly.

Miss Engle, pressing her long black gloves for Chambie to wear tonight, saw them too. She rested her elbows for a moment on the ledge of the window, in the Faculty pressing-room. A sudden pain constricted her chest; she had never seen anything so beautiful as the four girls coming up the walk, eating their apples and flinging them away. One wanted to lift one's hand and cry "Stop!" to all the world; to cause this hour in the afternoon to remain the same, forever; to retain its beauty, to make it permanent, to make it the only thing in existence. Just this campus, rolling and stretching, miniature world, criss-crossed by winding paths beaten into the earth by generations of youthful feet. . . . The girls have entered the dormitory. But they have left their presence, sublimely unconscious, symbolic; the ground is hallowed where they flung their apples. Girl-nibbled cores of apples falling like blessings on sweet-green earth, rolling, skipping, bouncing, coming to rest at roots of trees, unnoticed, rotting slowly, beaten by rain deeper into the earth, decaying in dampness, fragrant, fertile, melting into the earth, becoming earth, blessed cores of apples flung in carelessness by bare girl-arms. . . . Oh if she could only warn them, thought Miss Engle in a panic; warn them that what they had would leave them! yet she had the wit to sense that consciousness would spoil it, was not a part of youth. No one over twenty could eat, could fling, an apple, in that way—and then turn, lust undiminished, to the next one. Just as they flung their apples so must they fling their youth. The bell rang for tea. And now we will put the gloves away, and then we will go downstairs, being careful not to crush the frills in the back of our nice clean dress, said Engie to herself—and listen to the lecture.

XV

The charm-woman, dressed in beige, accessories pastel, sat with her ankles crossed, on the leather lounge beside the Duchess. She never stopped smiling and tilting her head from one side to the other, being charming, as one student after another was introduced, as they brought her tea, and little cookies, as the lounge filled up with nicely dressed girls who had put on stockings in her honor. "They have the charm of good-breeding," said the charm-lady to the Duchess, "the natural charm of being well brought-up." She spoke in the accents of a Pennsylvania woman who has stopped in Charleston, purposefully. "I do think they are nice, polite little girls," said the Duchess affectionately. She loved her girls, loved them en masse like this, when they came down, scrubbed and shining like children, and yet soft and fashionable like young women —though she was terrified of them individually. And she loved a certain loyalty in them, for whatever they felt about these dress-up teas, disturbing their tennis and their swimming, they came before strangers always with their very best manners, and however nervous or embarrassed they were with the Duchess personally, they always managed, before a visitor, to convey an atmosphere of "being at ease" with her, as though they would live up to the catalogue. The Duchess felt that they were all conspirators.

The Duchess's teachers, too, were in the conspiracy. They came and flocked about the Duchess, "at ease" and yet respectful, and pretending a charming, playful camaraderie among themselves. They looked fresh and bright too, a generation beyond the students, and just one social rung beneath them —they were still young, but not flamboyantly so; they were tastefully dressed, but not expensively— altogether a suitable, modest, becoming background for the girls, as they sat smiling at their pupils of half an hour ago, receiving tea, and pleasantries, and deference, because they were not under twenty years of age but variously above it.

"But I find everyone so absolutely delicious," said the charm-lady, who had been to Paree as well as Charleston.

"I think the girls are about settled," said Armstrong, nodding to the Duchess.

"I think the girls are about ready," said the Duchess to the charm-lady. The Duchess nodded twice to Gwennie, who stood out, apart from her friends, waiting for this signal and (virgin or no virgin) shyly twisting a lock of her bleached-gold hair. Gwennie's friends poked her from the rear and

Gwennie took a step or two forward, blushing, and spoke in her odd raucous voice.

"We are all very glad to have Miss Bracket with us again, the old girls remember her from last year and how much we all enjoyed her very instructive and charming little talk on how to be charming and we are all very glad to welcome Miss Bracket back with us again this year and we are all sure that the new girls as well as the old girls will find Miss Bracket's talk, Miss Dawn Bracket is known all over the country for her helpful talks on charm she gives a keen analysis as well as many helpful hints, will find Miss Bracket's talk both helpful instructive and beneficial. And interesting. Miss Bracket."

And Gwennie, moving her long sophisticated, wicked legs under her hostess frock, went back with the awkwardness, Miss Engle thought, of a new-born lamb; the grace of gaucherie, of unawareness—the charm, in short, Miss Engle knew, of youth. The Faculty suspected Gwennie of having "affairs" with the mottled-complexion fraternity boys who were always driving down for her on date nights; and yet Gwennie, like the others, was a child, Gwennie, who already knew men, sat on the stairs among her comrades, blushing, gulping, making faces behind her handkerchief. Her exquisitely shod feet shot out from under her dress—unexpectedly big and flat and—pigeon-toed! And here *we* sit, Miss Engle thought, at our age, ready to laugh at the charm-lady—yet all agog for helpful hints: we members of the Faculty.

"It's just lovely," said the charm-lady, standing with her hands at a very soft round cushion of a breast, "just lovely to be back at Magnolia Hall, I have such happy memories of my last year's visit. As I look about me," the hands fell away and from one of them there unfurled a long orchid georgette handkerchief which she moved about like a flag, "I recognize many bright faces, and I find myself thinking," the head went on one side to prove this phenomenon, "how can I tell all these bright and happy young faces, these gracefully unfolding Buds, anything they don't know—about Charm." Soft laughter from the girls as they draw their feet up under them on the stairs and on the floor, and feel sleepy and good and comfortable.

"But," said the charm-lady earnestly—and the orchid banner waved, "Charm is not merely a thing one is born with or without, Charm can be studied, acquired. By one and all. And it is the first duty of every young lady, as it must be her first wish, and her parents' first wish, to be attractive. It is even a practical necessity—for making the right friends, a happy marriage, and valuable contacts."

Oh, of course, the Duchess thought, Miss Bracket is a little old-fashioned, a little finishing-school, but we have her every year, it is a tradition, the girls laugh at her but they listen also—*and* there is certainly something in what she says. And the Duchess looked about her, from the great bowls of magnolias that the girls had placed on the piano and the mantel, to the girls themselves, sitting in a shaft of sunshine—and she thought of her favorite lines from Longfellow: Standing with reluctant feet, Where the brook and river meet . . . Ah, maidenhood, thought the Duchess.

"To begin with, let me assure you," said the charm-lady, holding the banner to her cheek, "that *the lady* has returned—and I for one am heartily, heartily glad. The day of the swaggering, boyish girl, aping the men in her clothing and her manner, is gone forever. I for one wave it a happy farewell. Yes, the *lady* is in vogue again. Frills, furbelows, perfume, languor. But let us talk a little of the practical points, the fundamentals.

"When you enter a room," said the charm-lady, her voice rising pedantically, "what do you do? Do you enter boldly, rush up to people you know? No. I am sure you do not. But perhaps you do not know just what you should do. Do not merely *enter;* you must—*make an entrance.* Stand for a moment in the doorway." Miss Bracket did a pantomime of *making an entrance.* Fingers delicately outspread, a mixture of shy confusion and polished poise, the handkerchief floating. "Look about for your hostess. Pause. Take your time. Ah, you have found your hostess, caught her eye. Now you advance—not quickly; give people a chance to notice you, to admire you. Then advance toward your hostess, like this, body a little forward from the waist, you are eager but restrained, hands out gracefully in greeting, smiling always—not too much, just a cordial flicker of a spontaneous smile. You smile more brightly when you are introduced, still leaning a little forward, so. You give yourself, do you see; you are not holding back; you are gi-i-iving yourself, to each person you meet."

Ah, *this* the girls cannot swallow without laughter. They make the briefest motions toward one another, suggestive of lewd "gi-i-iving"; they smile with their eyebrows, and a trained ear like the Duchess's, like the teachers', can detect an epidemic of snorts aborted in the throat.

The charm-lady catches it too, and takes it on the chin. "You may laugh. Yes, yes, it sounds funny to me too." She laughs girlishly, Charm winning out over irritation. "But how would you like to be a wall-flower at a party? to be ignored by the handsome young gentleman that is the catch of your débutante season? to be 'taken up' by the wrong crowd just because you have no poise?" The charm-lady has won the second round; the word "wall-flower" caught all their attention, and they watch her furtively now.

"And never neglect," the charm-lady warns them, "never neglect the mousy little woman in brown who sits quietly in a corner. Nine times out of ten it is she, she of all the showy people present who owns the best estate on Long Island; whose face is not familiar to you because she refuses to be photographed, but whose name will spell dignity, culture, fine family. Perhaps it will be she, next month, or next year, who will give the great ball of the season, or her nephew who will be the most talked-of young man of the year. *Never* neglect a contact. *Never* forget a name or a face. Always make some little association with each new name, so that you can make the proper remark on being introduced, or at your second meeting: 'Ah, did you enjoy your stay in Newport?' or 'Ah, I see your dahlias got a first in the Flower Show.' Remember this: a party, a social gathering, is not primarily for a good time; it is a move, a step, in the great social game—and you must make each step as carefully as you would make a move in chess."

Oh my God, thought Miss Laurel, amused no longer, but outraged, furious, that such stuff should be offered to children. Even though they laughed, something of the silky poison would make its way down their vulnerable throats, lodge forever in their susceptible minds. But silly though it sounds, thought the Duchess, rocking in approval, there is *something* in it, after all.

" . . . and never argue, don't disagree with people, especially with the *men,* my dears—you will find that though the men profess to admire a woman with opinions, they seldom fall in love with them. Don't have too definite opinions on any subject, for too much thinking makes lines in the face, furrows . . . leave it to the men to do the thinking, the worrying, the money-making, it is women's first duty to be charming. . .

"Because, girls—let me remind you again—*the lady* is back, to stay. Oh it is true, I assure you. I don't advocate," the charm-lady said, "that you all go in for swooning, like our grandmothers. But be silly, be helpless—take a leaf out of the book of our southern belles, who never, even during those awful days of dressing mannishly, lost their Charm, their feminine allure. It is not a bad thing, not at all, to occasionally—returning to our grandmothers —drop the handkerchief. The poor little post-war flapper would have rushed to pick it up herself, her head would have collided with the gentleman's —except that in those days the *gentleman* might not have been gentleman enough to stoop for it! Try it, girls. Surprise a gentleman who is not paying you sufficient attention, by letting your handkerchief slip to the floor—your dainty, scented, feminine kerchief. If the gentleman does not immediately bend down for it" (the charm-lady sensed a joke somewhere in the air), "just let it lie there; look at him with your eyebrows raised—so—a mixture of helplessness and indignation—and wait. He will respect you all the more for it. I speak most earnestly to you on this subject, because though you are all young now, still Buds—you are about to flower in the social world, and I want you to unfold your petals with charm and grace, so that your blooming will bring you the greatest joy, the greatest security. . ."

The girls clap long and loud. The Duchess is grateful. They keep on clapping and the Duchess, waking from a dream of the gentle days in which one did drop handkerchiefs and curtsey, becomes suspicious, lifts a hand and stops them. The charm-lady smiles and bows repeatedly, waving her scented handkerchief. The girls get up, stretch impercep-tibly (their tennis-and-hockey muscles tired from so much sitting), move slowly, demurely, past the teachers, out of the lounge. Anyone knowing them as their teachers do, knows that the minute they are out of sight, there will be an epidemic of dropped handkerchiefs, raised eyebrows, position three of gi-i-iving; that upstairs they will drop on their beds and burst into shouts of explosive laughter, calling each other Buds, in their voices that are raucous as the voices of adolescent boys and soft as the cries of children. All the same, thinks the Duchess, there *is* something in it; and nobody laughs when—as she rises to say goodbye to Miss Bracket—her handker-chief slides off her lap and slips to the floor. Arm-strong rushes to pick it up. . .

XVI

"I don't *know* why, all I know is I *couldn't* go back to the dormitory after the Dance, I couldn't have slept," said Linda miserably. Now that they have given her her punishment and she knows that she will not be expelled but is only to miss a few date-nights, now that Natalie and her fellow-mem-bers of the Student Council are gone, Linda's de-fiance has disappeared. She is frightened, wishing she had not—in a mood of recklessness—smeared her lashes with mascara; her eyes sting, and she is afraid to cry. "I just don't know," she said mournfully to the Duchess.

"You are facing, you are at the time of life, everything is very important now, Linda, at your age," said the Duchess, fidgeting with her beads. Both of them looked out, embarrassed. The magnolia blossoms outside the Duchess's office window hung heavy in the setting sun. "I always think of Longfellow's fine words," said the Duchess softly. "Standing with reluctant feet, where the brook and river meet—from his beautiful poem called 'Maidenhood.' Standing with reluctant feet—at your age, all you young girls—where the brook and river meet, that is you, Linda, do you see, that is where you are, at the crossroads, standing with. . ." The Duchess looked back, guiltily; Linda's eyes still strayed outside. "Linda! are you taking this seriously, are you paying attention? Well! You are not going to find the answer on the magnolia tree. . . ." Linda's eyes swing back. "When I tell you," said the Duchess sternly, "that what you did is a dangerous, a very easily misconstrued, the implications—" the Duchess is playing with her beads again, her large teeth helpless and embarrassed—"do you know what I mean, Linda, the implications—" There is a delicate crash; a miniature volcano. The Duchess's fingers have at last burst the string about her neck, and the beads, which resemble her own eyes and teeth, bounce down the bosom of her dress, and roll and sputter gayly to every corner of the room.

XVII

They were dressing Chambie for her date in town. Miss Armstrong lent her earrings and then said she looked like hell without a scarf—"Remember the *lady* is back—" said Engle, giggling—and lent her a pink chiffon, which she had never worn. Then Graham came up from tutoring the College Preps, and seeing Chambers standing there in everybody's clothes shrieked that Chambie must wear her black velvet hat and carry her little black velvet bag. Engle, who was taking Chambie's corridor duty, and had spent the half hour after dinner pressing Chambie's pink silk slip, stood in the door of Armstrong-and-Graham's room with her long black gloves over her arm.

Chambie stood there feeling a little stiff, for Armstrong had made her wear a girdle. She looked in the mirror over and under and among their solicitous hands, and she knew that they had beaded her lashes too thickly, she knew she should not be wearing both Armie's earrings *and* the scarf, she knew that Engle's long black gloves were out of place. But a wave of love came over her for these friends who were all older than she and who must stay here in the great female shell of a dormitory, in spite of the Spring air and the warm breeze and all the men in the cities. "But not, *not* the rhinestone clip in my hat," she pleaded in spite of herself; "you know Jerry, it's just as likely to be the movies as not!"

"Then you must drop your handkerchief!" cried Graham gayly, "*then* he won't dare to take you to the movies." They all laughed; and then they were suddenly silent for a minute, while Macbeth passed by with her curious, cat-like secret tread, on the way downstairs to the Library. "She gives me the creeps," said Engle, shuddering; "I'm sure she's nuts." "Give us about twenty more years of it," said Armstrong quietly, "and who won't be." And Engle turned her head sharply and disappeared, for there was a racket from the floor below, in the corridor she was watching for Chambie.

"If you could have seen the night-watchman's face!" said Chambie, to get them all laughing again —and told them, for the second time, exaggerating it, how Engie had brought her her slip, all ironed, and how she had stepped out in it without a kimono, to go across to the Johnny, and bumped right into the watchman who was making his first round.

"An auspicious beginning," said Armie dryly, "for the rest of your evening, my dear. . . . Come here, your hair is down, in back."

"Better be careful," said Graham, laughing, "or they'll be campussing you like Linda. My, I never saw a child look so frightened."

"Frightened!" said Armie scornfully. "She was as defiant as—if you ask me, she was disappointed that she wasn't expelled. Sitting there and looking out the window while they talked to her. I wouldn't mind knowing just what *did* go on there out on that golf-course. . . ."

"Well, in this Spring weathair—" began Chambie merrily, but a glance from Armstrong stopped her.

Engle was in the door again, still holding the long gloves. "Here you are, chicken, don't leave them on the train. The noise below is a quiet little party in the Senior smoking-room—I rather suspect in Linda's honor, though she's not supposed to speak to anyone tonight, and I didn't *exactly* see her. . . . Don't forget to check in, Chambie, by breakfast time—and don't sneak in the Library window or Macbeth might take you for a man." Engie put her arm awkwardly on Chambie's shoulder. "Have a simply wonderful time, little one—for all of us; and save a few cookies and gin for old aunt Engie. . . ."

"I guess I'd better go—my train," said Chambers, rather wistfully. Now that she was all dressed up she felt reluctant to go to town and face the unpredictable world of men, she felt it would be fine and peaceful to spend the evening here, in Armstrong-and-Graham's room, all of them manicuring their nails and talking about men behind their backs, instead of boldly facing them. She looked up, and there were her three older friends standing, gazing at her, with the oddest mixture of pride, and love, and hate—the hate involuntary, Chambers knew, unconscious, unadmitted; she was their product, and their representative tonight, to the world of men, of fun, of gayety. And by chance they were all three standing, rather wistful, with their arms clasped across their bosoms, the way she remembered her own teachers standing, when she was

a child, years ago, before she had thought of being
a teacher herself—and all at once they looked very
old to Chambie, as though she were that child again.
And she saw them even older, looking as they would
in three years, five, ten, at Macbeth's age and the
Duchess's, if they didn't find some man. . . . And
she thought of Jerry with relief and joy, she felt
glamorous compared to Armstrong and Graham
and poor old Engle, she felt that she must escape
quickly before their old-maid air contaminated her
(she would take off the earrings on the train, stuff
the long black gloves in Graham's bag). She thanked
God in her heart for Jerry, jumped up and hugged
old Engie, blew a kiss to Armstrong, waved Graham's own bag at Graham—and was out, dancing
down the hall, hoping that the Seniors in the smoking-room would catch a glimpse of her in the gym
teacher's moiré coat. . . .

XVIII

The dormitory was going to bed.

The Duchess's grey kitten had paid its last visit
to the magnolia trees.

On his first round the night-watchman had collided with Miss Chambers in her pink silk date
slip. On his second he encountered no one but Miss
Engle, making *her* rounds, and an occasional student dashing across a corridor in her pyjamas.

On the main floor only three people are left awake
and alive: in the library, Miss Macbeth, copying

catalogue cards, and Natalie Freeman, studying there by special permission; and of course the Duchess, whose "suite" occupies the wing of the building bordering on the garden which leads to Graduation Sward.

"Sit still now! You've *been* out," said the Duchess sternly to the little grey kitten—restlessly stretching his legs again before the door. Red jack on black queen. Red seven on black eight. Black five—no, no place for it. The Duchess pushed the cards aside. She couldn't understand that Linda-child. And her mother a Theta at the Duchess's own Alma Mater. But she *had* been moved by the Duchess's words, of that the Duchess felt sure. Standing with reluctant feet, where the brook and river. . . And then her beads! Still, they couldn't have expelled the child. Too much influence there. Too bad, thought the Duchess, she had not invited Armstrong and Graham and one of the others in for a rubber of bridge . . . still, best to preserve the lines, even though they *were* (as the catalogue put it) all one happy family. Ah well, that Charm lecture may have been a bit old-fashioned, my girls may have laughed, my Faculty (Miss Laurel was something of a Communist, or so she feared) may have looked superior; still there *is* something to be said. . . And she put her head on one side and smiled Charmingly as though she were gi-i-iving her big teeth to someone. "Isn't there, Kitten, isn't there? You may come and sit on my lap—oh it's a dood ittle titten, it is, it *is*." The kitten smelled faintly of magnolias.

"Darling Peter" (wrote Miss Laurel): " . . . and so the day ended at last, but it was a lesson to me. There is *no use* my teaching these girls anything, if they must go home and unlearn all I have taught them. I asked one girl today (the one I told you, wrote about the poor) what she was going to do when she got out of school? She looked blank. I said, I mean, do you think of earning your living? *Oh no,* she said—and Peter, she looked horrified, and amused, and patronizing, as though I'd committed a ridiculous social blunder—which I suppose I had. And another thing, Darling Peter—I have decided that we simply must not let a little thing like your being broke stand in our way another year. It's too ridiculous, my darling—you just must swallow your silly masculine pride and let me keep us till you have found steady work. What if we won't have much? It would be better to be together. I can't stand it here, now that Spring has come—what our pansy French teacher calls the 'weathair'. I shall get like Miss Engle, the one I told you talks to herself, or the Librarian who looks hopefully for men under her bed every night. I feel so sorry for them all—and for myself too! It is not natural for a woman (or for a man either, Darling Peter!) to go to bed alone at night and wake up alone in the morning. I want to wake up with you, not just *some* mornings, but all mornings, even mornings when I don't want to! that's nature and human nature too. If you could see, and feel, and *smell* this great woman-filled dormitory. On a night like this (I told you the damn magnolias were out) it positively reeks of suppressed desires. I think the magnolias are laughing at us, looking in the windows and laughing—perhaps they're even trying to call us out, to teach us some lesson. Darling Peter. . . ."

"Girls!" Miss Engle stood in the door of the Senior Smoker. "Altogether too much noise. It's quiet hour for the Juniors, you know—after ten." (It *did* look like Linda's kimono cord trailing under the hastily-closed door of the John—but let it go; it was Spring; they were young.) "Oh Miss Engle, we *can't* keep quiet, we're practicing *Charm!*"—ingratiating her, but mocking too, mocking the fact that she was old, old and finished. Jean and Aster and Betty Fleet, all of them, in fresh pyjamas like gay little boys, threw an avalanche of handkerchiefs at each other's pink, bare feet. Miss Engle looked at them and smiled reluctantly. The little points of breasts beneath their pyjama jackets —something about them hurt her; and hurt her *for* them, too. They were so transient! Like the magnolias. Like the Spring. Like Miss Engle's youth. . . .

"Come on out, you fool, she's gone!" hissed Sudie, "and anyway your tail's been showing the whole time—" Betty Fleet bent and tugged at Linda's bathrobe cord. "I can't, you fools—" there was a smuggled giggle from the John—"I'm where the *brook and river meet.*" Gwennie gave a hoarse laugh in her voice like a boy's before it has changed, Jean gave a rapid interpretation of "standing with reluctant feet," and all of them screamed with laughter. From down the hall came Miss Engle's "Shh—shh."

"I wonder," said Graham softly, "what Chambie's doing now—she must be there. He's met her train, they've stood there talking about what they'd do—and now. . ." "You'd think it was *your* date," said Armstrong; "pass me the red pencil, Carola, I don't think I can conscientiously pass this paper." "But what *do* you suppose they're doing," persisted Graham dreamily. "Oh, those Seniors—" Engle, on another rest from corridor duty. "If you ask me," said Armstrong coldly, "they're not even at the movies. They're at *his hotel*." "Armie—do you really think—" "Think," said Armie, "I *know;* didn't you hear what she said about Linda—and the weathair?" And they were all three silent, thinking respectfully of the fate of their scarf, their earrings, and their long black gloves—until Armie picked up the manicure set and began to work on her nails.

The dormitory is a vast empty shell, thought Natalie in the Library; the dormitory rises above me, so many cubicles filled with sleeping girls or girls talking about their dates—what do I care if their mothers came here when they were our age, the Library is my palace, Macbeth is my attendant; I alone have special permission to use the Library this late at night (she swallowed the knowledge that she would not have dared to up and face the girls, so soon after Linda's punishment.) These nights are precious, Natalie thought, precious nights of being alone and learning, I shall never forget them, I *must* never forget them—the back of old Macbeth bending over her files, the musty odor of text-books, the smell of the white magnolias. . . . Just then the Library clock struck twice, and Natalie, nodding to Miss Macbeth, picked up her notebooks and pencils and walked proudly through the dark, deserted halls.

Oh dear, thought Miss Winsey, entering her room, the maid has put my dolls in all the wrong places again! There is a row of cushions along the side of Miss Winsey's bed; leaning up against them, in an order she knows and loves well, is a row of dolls, one of them dressed like a sailor, and teddy bears, and toy dogs, and a big Winnie-the-Pooh. Miss Winsey straightens the rakish little sailor and takes away a scottie from his side; the Winnie belongs there. Miss Winsey looks for a minute into her mirror, framed with snap-shots all around the edges —snaps of herself and other girls in shorts, taken at the Camp where she works as counselor every Summer—and then walks to her desk where she stands frowning over a sheaf of papers. The mysterious Miss Winsey, who the Faculty think is "queer," whom the girls suspect of having secret love affairs, stands there, her lovely head like a flower on the erect stem of her neck—and sighs, and shakes her head. Miss Winsey is worried. Things look bad for the Greys. The only chance they have now is if they win the track meet, for it is clear that the Oranges (now that we know that Linda will be here) are going to win the swimming—and then the 1935 pennant—unless, of course, the swimming meet is scheduled for a day when Linda is "out". . . .

In the smoking-room six girls in pyjamas are copying Linda's model "impulsive letter"—the one you send to boys who have not written last to you—addressed to six or more boys at New Haven, Princeton, and Cambridge. The letter reads: "Dear Bill (or Jack, or Eddie, or Malcolm): This is an impulsive letter, and I wouldn't dare write it to anyone but you, knowing *you* will understand. I am all alone up in my room, everyone else in the School has gone to sleep, and it is four o'clock in the morning. I just feel like writing—to you. Most people would spoil the mood—of course I may be wrong (?) but I feel as though you wouldn't. . ." Gwennie is writing it to three different boys; Sudie has written it to Malcolm; Betty Fleet, with ointment on her face where the spots are, is writing it to Aster's brother, whom she has never met, on a dare. Linda stands over them, proud of her composition and her disciples, but ready to duck into the John at the first sound of Miss Engle's footsteps. *"That'll* get them," says Gwennie, running her tongue over the glue on the third envelope; "but wouldn't it be colossal if the Princeton prom is the same weekend as the Lehigh thing?" "Oh, colossal," said Jean, yawning; Jean had no one to write the letter to, so she is doing the algebra homework, her own and Sudie's. "That letter," says Linda, "was responsible for Edgar, my little Buds." "You be careful there,

Brooklet," said Gwennie, shrieking again, "or you'll corrupt us all." "Do the Duchess again for us, Linda—" "I bet if Natalie wasn't an Orange, you'd have been expelled" "Nat's all right, she *had* to do it," said Betty Fleet hastily. "But I almost *died*," said Linda, "when she kept on quoting, when the brook and . . . and then I forgot and started counting the magnolias on the tree outside. . ." "single standard, of course I believe in it, but how would you like it if your own *mother*" "guess I'll write to mine, I need some money" "what's that other way of stating the binomial theorem, Jean?" "but you can believe in God without going to Church" "and if the Greys don't win the swim" "but I wonder if boys feel the same as we do about those things" "I *wish*," said Gwennie, "that my Bob would call me up, *right now*—I'd ask him" (shouts of laughter) "and *I* wish," said Sudie, yawning, "that the Dance was still ahead of us, *you're the top, you're the tower of Pisa*. . ." "So we could all be Charming and gi-i-ive ourselves," said Aster, catching her yawn; "well, this little Bud is going to be-e-d—shall I throw the letters down the stairs?" "Wonder if the night-watchman censors them all," said Betty Fleet, yawning till the round comb quivered. "I wonder how long the magnolias last," said Linda at the window; "I can't seem to remember any Spring but this."

But the night-watchman thinks nothing of the letters, nothing at all. It is his duty to collect them for the early morning mail; and it is the custom of

the girls not to leave them in the corridors, outside
their doors, but to take the trouble (as well as the
risk) of throwing them down the stairs, so that *he*
must take the trouble of stooping to pick them up.
No one knows why this is; it is simply a custom of
Magnolia Hall. And the night-watchman is used to
the shower of letters—but he has not the slightest
interest in their addresses or in who wrote them,
there the girls are wrong. All he cares about is the
colors of the envelopes, white, grey, beige; for some
reason he rather likes the colors. And there is one
other thing he likes to do, though for the life of
him he couldn't tell you why, and would rather be
caught dead than found doing it; he cannot pass
a single one of the dozen water-coolers on his nightly
hike of six miles, without reaching out a hand and
tapping the top of each keg twice—no matter what.

Ah, my girls are going to bed, thought the Duchess, watching from her wing, and seeing the lights
snap out in the little dormitory windows, one after
the other. The Duchess sighed over the glassful of
broken beads. Then she dropped into bed and
switched off her light. The Duchess sighed. More
lights were going out in the dormitory windows,
the Faculty windows were growing dark too, the
maids' windows up in the attic. . . The School was
going to bed. Only the kitten was still restless,
pacing the floor, the scent of magnolia blossoms in
his fur. . .

Miss Winsey touched her toes for the fiftieth
time, breathed deeply, relaxed, bent her knees

twenty times, breathed deeply—and suddenly decided, with the odor of the night air too strongly in her lungs, to leave out the back-stretching exercise and go straight to bed. "And so, Darling Peter," wrote Miss Laurel, "the dormitory is going to bed, and I shall too. I love you, dear, and I look forward to seeing you Friday, as soon as my grammar class is out." She lay on her side in the dark, leaning on one elbow, staring out through the window onto the peaceful campus, rolling and rolling under the waning moon; I wish, she thought, for the sake of falling asleep, they could turn off the magnolias at night. They think I am crazy, thought Macbeth, making unfortunately certain that there was nothing like a man under her bed, or in her closet, or even (at the last moment) in the waste-basket under her desk; but there is definitely a man prowling about the grounds at night—very likely that French teacher, that M'sieur Laval; they will see. "Are you asleep, Armie?" called Graham softly. There was a moment's silence; Graham was disturbed; Armie had been irritable all day—ever since she had changed her dress for M'sieur, and then the Chambie business. Then Armie answered, briefly, "No; why?" "Oh, I just wondered; I just—wondered," said Graham; but Armie sounded as lonely as Graham felt. It is something about their skins, thought Engle, and the way they hold their heads, the way they move, their voices—but most of all it is their expressions, she thought; rather stupid, rather dewy, their mouths moist and ripe and half open, as though they expected life, in the form of strawberries, to fall gently in their mouths; as though they expected their youth to last forever; as though they thought the magnolias would never die; that, my dear, is youth, she said grimly to herself. "Hop on the foot of my bed, kitten," said the Duchess; "tum on there, you lazy, restless, dood-for-nothing titten—" and the kitten leaped up with a sigh. Take off the scarf, take off the earrings, take off your long black gloves, said Chambie's boy-friend in Graham's dream; I want to kiss you and hold you and love you, he said, and Graham stirred gently to let him into the bed beside her. You'll not find the answer on the magnolia tree, said Armstrong harshly to Linda, in her dream; give me the red pencil, Graham, I cannot in all conscience allow this thing to go on—and Armstrong groaned a little in her sleep. And now we turn out our light, said Engle, obeying herself; and lay in the flood of magnolia-scented moonbeams until she sneezed from their odor.

Miss Whitson, in her little room under the eaves, in the servants' quarters, sighs and tosses on her bed, while two floors below, Betty Fleet, who had forgotten to take off her round comb, flings it sleepily on the floor, and lies with her eyes closed and the moonlight glistening on the ointment covering the little round spots on her face. Natalie is studying in the John.

The night-watchman's shoes squeak in the silence; they pause; he is tapping the water-cooler—twice. His chest expands with relief.

Where the brook and river meet. . . She shouldn't have laughed at the Duchess's words, thinks Linda, for foolish as they were, they *did* mean something. "Where the brook and river meet," "implications of immortality"—both phrases, equally meaningless, meant something, meant the same thing maybe. Linda shivers in her pyjamas at the window. The breeze comes up, holding the scent of the magnolias, no longer as fresh as it was in the morning. And the moon, riding the sky, not full as it had been two nights before, out on the golf-course with Edgar, but waning, slipping, a part of it gone already. Linda herself is two days older. *Pay attention, Linda! you will not find the answer on that magnolia tree!* But the wind sighs; the night-watchman's boots squeak; the moon will go down and the world will grow dark. And the magnolia blossoms, even before graduation time, will have faded and fallen; those special magnolia blossoms never to live again. Oh this moment, this one moment—with the moon at that particular point above Lookout Hill—I must remember it forever, forever! But already the moon has slipped downward, she cannot remember the spot. Sadness, like a terrible song without words, hurts in Linda's chest. *How long do magnolia blossoms last, Sudie? I can't remember any Spring but this. . .* Perhaps the answer *is* on the magnolia tree.

1935

A life
in the day
of a writer

A life in the day of a writer

O SHINING stupor, O glowing idiocy, O crowded vacuum, O privileged pregnancy, he prayed, morosely pounding X's on his typewriter, I am a writer if I never write another line, I am alive if I never step out of this room again; Christ, oh, Christ, the problem is not to stretch a feeling, it is to reduce a feeling, *all* feeling, all thought, all ecstasy, tangled and tumbled in the empty crowded head of a writer, to one clear sentence, one clear form, and still preserve the hugeness, the hurtfulness, the enormity, the unbearable all-at-once-ness, of being alive and knowing it too . . .

He had been at it for three hours, an elbow planted on either side of his deaf-mute typewriter, staring like a passionate moron round the walls that framed his life—for a whole night had passed, he had nothing or everything to say, and he awoke each morning in terror of his typewriter until he had roused it and used it and mastered it, he was always afraid it might be dead forever—when the *telephone* screamed like an angry siren across his nerves. It was like being startled out of sleep; like being caught making faces at yourself in the mirror —by an editor or a book-critic; like being called to account again by your wife. His hand on the telephone, a million short miles in time and space from his writing-desk, he discovered that he was shaking. He had spoken to no one all the morning since Louise—shouting that she could put up with being the wife of a non-best-seller, or even the wife of a chronic drunk with a fetish for carrying away coat-hangers for souvenirs, but not, by God, the duenna of a conceited, adolescent flirt—had slammed the door and gone off cursing to her office. Voices are a proof of life, he explained gently to the angry telephone, and I have not for three hours heard my own; supposing I have lost it? Courage, my self! he said, as he stupidly lifted the receiver and started when nothing jumped out at him. All at once he heard his own voice, unnaturally loud, a little hoarse. *I wish to report a fire,* he wanted to say, but he said instead, roaring it: *Hello.* The answering *Hello sunshine,* came from an immeasurable distance, from America, perhaps, or the twentieth century—a rescue party! but he had grown, in three long hours, so used to his solitary island! And though he was a writer and said to be gifted with a fine imagination, it was beyond his uttermost power to imagine that this voice addressing him was really a voice, that since it was a voice it must belong to a person, especially to the person identifying herself as Louise.

Ho, Louise! he said, going through with it for the purpose of establishing his sanity, at least in her ears if not actually in his own: he spoke courteously as though her voice were a voice, as though it did belong to her, as though she really were his wife; *now,*

darling, don't go on with—But then he discovered
that she was not going on with anything but being
a wife, a voice, an instrument of irrelevant torture.
How goes the work, she said kindly. What in hell
did she think he was, a half-witted baby playing
with paper-dolls? *Oh, fine, just fine,* he answered
deprecatingly. (I'm a writer if I never write another
line, he said fiercely to his typewriter, which burst
out laughing.) *Well, look,* she was saying, *Freddie
called up* (who in hell was Freddie?), and then her
voice went on, making explanations, and it seemed
that he was to put away his paper-dolls and meet her
at five at Freddie's, because Freddie was giving a
cocktail party. *Cocktail party,* he said obediently;
wife; five. Cocktail party, eh—and a dim bell
sounded in his brain, for he remembered cocktail
parties from some other world, the world of yesterday; a cocktail party meant reprieve from typewriters, rescue from desert islands; and it might also
mean Betsey—he cocked a debonair eye at his typewriter to see if it was jealous—Betsey, who, along
with half a dozen coat-hangers, had been the cause
of this morning's quarrel! *Yes, your wife for a
change,* came the off-stage tinkle over the telephone
again; *and you might try taking her home for a
change too, instead of someone else's—and by the
way, my treasure, don't bring those coat-hangers
with you, Freddie has plenty of his own.*—*Right
you are, my pet,* he said, feeling smart and cheap
and ordinary again, *right you are, my lamb-pie, my
song of songs, ace of spades, queen of hearts, capital*

of Wisconsin, darling of the Vienna press—But she had got off, somewhere about Wisconsin.

He looked, a little self-conscious, about his now twice-empty room; aha, my prison, my lonely four-walled island, someone has seen the smoke from my fire at last, someone has spied the waving of my shirttails; at five o'clock today, he said, thumbing his nose at his typewriter, the rescue plane will swoop down to pick me up, see, and for all you know, my black-faced Underwood, my noiseless, portable, publisher's stooge, my conscience, my slave, my master, my mistress—for all you know it may lead to that elegant creature Betsey, whom my rather plump Louise considers a bit too much on the thin side . . . ah, but my good wife is a bit short-sighted there, she doesn't look on the *other* side, the bright side, the sunny side, the side that boasts the little, hidden ripples that it takes imagination, courage, to express; the little hiding ripples that the male eye can't stop looking for . . .

He seated himself again before his typewriter, like an embarrassed schoolboy.

Black anger descended upon him. It was easy enough for her, for Louise, to put out a hand to her telephone where it sat waiting on her office desk, and ring him up and order him to report at a cock-tail party—Louise, who sat in a room all day surrounded matter-of-factly by people and their voices and her own voice. But for him it was gravely an-other matter. Her ring summoned him out of his own world—what if he hadn't written a line all morning except a complicated series of coat-hanger designs in the shape of X's—and because he couldn't really make the crossing, it left him feeling a little ashamed, a little found-out, caught with his pants down, so to speak—and a little terrified, too, to be reminded again that he was not "like other people." He was still shaking. She had no right, damn it, no damn right, to disturb him with that sharp malicious ringing, to present him with the bugbear, the insult, the indignity, of a cocktail party —she, who was proud enough of him in public (Bertram Kyle, author of *Fifty Thousand Lives*, that rather brilliant book), although at home she was inclined to regard him, as his family had when he refused to study banking, as something of a sissy.

Still, when you have accepted an invitation to a party for the afternoon, you have that to think about, to hold over your typewriter's head, you can think of how you will lock it up at half-past four and shave and shower and go out with a collar and a tie around your neck to show people that you can look, talk, drink, like any of them, like the worst of them. But a party! Christ, the faces, the crowds of white faces (like the white keys of the typewriter I had before you, my fine Underwood), and worst of all, the voices. . . . The party became abnormally enlarged in his mind, as though it would take every ounce of ingenious conniving—not to speak of courage!—to get to it at all; and as he fell face downward on his typewriter, he gave more thought to the party than even the party's host was likely to do, Freddie, whoever the devil "Freddie" was . . .

O degrading torture, lying on the smug reproachful keys with nothing to convey to them. He remembered how he had once been afraid of every woman he met until he kissed her, beat her, held her captive in his arms; but this typewriter was a thing to master every day, it was a virgin every morning. If I were Thomas Wolfe, he thought, I should start right off: O country of my birth and land I have left behind me, what can I, a youth with insatiable appetite, do to express what there is in me of everlasting hunger, loneliness, nakedness, a hunger that feeds upon hunger and a loneliness that grows in proportion to the hours I lend to strangers . . . If I were Saroyan I should not hesitate either: But I am young, young and hungry (thank God), and why must I listen to the rules the old men make or the rich ones, this is not a story, it is a life, a simple setting down in words of what I see of men upon this earth. No, no, I am not Saroyan (thank God), I am not Thomas Wolfe either, and I am also not Louise's boss (ah, *there's* a man!). And I cannot write an essay; I am a natural liar, I prefer a jumbled order to chronology, and poetry to logic; I don't like facts, I like to imagine their implications. O to get back, get back, to the pre-telephone stupor, the happy mingled pregnancy, the clear confusion of myself only with myself . . .

And so Bertram Kyle opened up his notebooks. He felt again that the story he had outlined so clearly there, of the "lousy guy" whom everyone thought was lousy including himself, but who was so only because of a simple happening in his childhood, might be a fine story; but it was one he could not do today. Nor could he do the story (which had occurred to him on a train to Washington) of the old lady, prospective grandmother, who went mad thinking it was her own child to be born. Nor could he do the story—partly because he did not know it yet—which would begin: "He lived alone with a wife who had died and two children who had left him." Perhaps, he thought bitterly, he could never do those stories, for in the eagerness of begetting them he had told them to Louise; too often when he told her a story it was finished then, it was dead, like killing his lust by confiding an infidelity.

And so, desperately, he turned to those thoughtful little flaps in the backs of his notebooks, into which he poured the findings in his pockets each night; out came old menus, the torn-off backs of matchbooks, hotel stationery that he had begged of waiters, ticket-stubs, a time-table, a theatre program, and odd unrecognizable scraps of paper he had picked up anywhere. The writing on these was born of drinking sometimes; of loneliness in the midst of laughing people; of a need to assert himself, perhaps, a desire to remind himself—that he was a writer; but more than anything, he thought, for the sheer love of grasping a pencil and scratching with it on a scrap of paper. "If I were a blind man I should carry a typewriter before me on a tray suspended from my neck by two blue ribbons; I think I *am* blind"—he had written that on a tablecloth once, and Louise was very bored.

"It is always later than you think, said the sundial finding itself in the shade"—from the back of an old match-box, and undoubtedly the relic of an evening on which he had strained to be smart. A night-club menu: "Dear Saroyan: But take a day off from your writing, *mon vieux,* or your writing will get to be a habit . . ." Another menu—and he remembered the evening well, he could still recall the look of tolerance growing into anger on Louise's face as he wrote and wrote and went on writing: "Nostalgia, a nostalgia for all the other nostalgic nights on which nothing would suffice . . . a thing of boredom, of content, of restlessness, *velleities,* in which the sweetness of another person is irrelevant and intolerable, and indifference or even cruelty hurt in the same way . . . linking up with gray days in childhood when among bewilderingly many things to do one wanted to do none of them, and gray evenings with Louise when everything of the adult gamut of things to do would be the same thing . . ." (At that point Louise had reached down to her anger and said, "All right, sunshine, we come to a place I loathe because you like to see naked women and then, when they come on, you don't even watch them; I wouldn't complain if you were Harold Bell Wright or something . . .") "In order to make friends," he discovered from another match-box, "one need not talk seriously, any more than one needs to make love in French"—and that, he recalled tenderly, was plagiarized from a letter he had written to a very young girl, Betsey's predecessor in his fringe flirtations. "A man's underlying motives are made up of his thwarted, or unrealized, ambitions," "The war between men and women consists of left-overs from their unsatisfactory mating." "But the blinking of the eye"—this on a concert program —"must go on; perhaps one catches the half-face of the player and sees, despite the frenzied waving of his head, a thing smaller than his playing, but perhaps the important, the vital thing: like the heart-beat, at once greater and smaller than the thing it accompanies . . ." "We are not so honest as the best of our writing, for to be wholly honest is to be brave, braver than any of us dares to be with another human being, especially with a woman." "*At bottom one is really grave.*"

He was pulled up short by that last sentence, which was the only one of the lot that made sense. "At bottom one is really grave."

Suddenly he raised his head and stared wildly round the room. He was terrified, he was elated. Here was his whole life, in these four walls. This year he had a large room with a very high ceiling; he works better in a big room, Louise told people who came in. Last year he had worked in a very small room with a low ceiling; he works better, Louise used to tell people, in a small place. He worked better at night, he worked better in the day-time, he worked better in the country, better in the city, in the winter, in the summer . . . But he was frightened. Here he was all alone with his life until five o'clock in the afternoon. Other people (Louise) went out in the morning, left their life behind them somewhere, or else filed it away in offices and desks; he imagined that Louise only remembered her life and took it up again in the late afternoon when she said good night to her boss and started off for home —or a cocktail party. But he had to live with his life, and work with it; he couldn't leave it alone and it couldn't leave him alone, not for a minute—except when he was drunk, and that, he said, smugly surveying the scattered coat-hangers, relic of last night's debauch, that is why a writer drinks so much. Hell, he thought, proud, I'm living a life, my own whole life, right here in this room each day; I can still feel the pain I felt last night when I was living part of it and Louise said . . . and I can still feel the joy I felt last week when Betsey said . . . and I can feel the numbness and the excitement of too many Scotch-and-sodas, of too perfect dancing, of too many smooth-faced, slick-haired women; I can remember saying *Listen—listen* to anyone who would or would not, and the truth of it is I had nothing to say anyway because I had too much to say . . . Hell, he thought, my coat-hangers lie on the floor where I flung them at three this morning when Louise persuaded me that it was better not to sleep in my clothes again, I have not hung up my black suit, I have not emptied yesterday's waste-basket nor last week's ashtrays (nor my head of its thirty years' fine accumulation) . . . everything in my room and in my head is testimony to the one important fact, that I am alive, alive as hell, and all I have to do is wait

till the whole reeling sum of things adds itself up or
boils itself down, to a story . . .

There seemed now to be hunger in his belly, and
it was a fact that he had not eaten since breakfast
and then only of Louise's anger. But the turmoil in
his insides was not, he felt, pure hunger. It came
from sitting plunged in symbols of his life, it came
because he did not merely have to live with his life
each day, but he had to give birth to it over again
every morning. Of course, he thought with a fierce
joy, I am hungry. I am ravenously hungry, and I
have no appetite, I am parched but I am not thirsty,
I am dead tired and wide awake and passionately,
violently alive.

But he lifted his elbows now from his typewriter,
he looked straight before him, and he could feel
between his eyes a curious knot, not pain exactly,
but tension, as though all of him were focused on
the forefront of his brain, as though his head were
a packed box wanting to burst. It was for this moment that, thirty years before, he had been born;
for this moment that he had tossed peanuts to an
elephant when he was a child; that he had by a
miracle escaped pneumonia, dropping from an air-
plane, death by drowning, concussion from football
accidents; that he had fallen desperately and permanently in love with a woman in a yellow hat whose
car had been held up by traffic, and whom he never
saw again; that he had paused at sight of the blue in
Chartres Cathedral and wept, and a moment later
slapped angrily at a mosquito; that he had met and

married Louise, met and coveted Kitty Braithwaite, Margery, Connie, Sylvia, Elinor, Betsey; for this moment that he had been born and lived, for this moment that he was being born again.

His fingers grew light. The room was changing. Everything in it was integrating; pieces of his life came together like the odd-shaped bits of a puzzle-map, forming a pattern as one assembles fruits and flowers for a still-life. Listen, there is a name. Bettina Gregory. Bettina is a thin girl, wiry, her curves so slight as to be ripples, so hidden that the male eye cannot stop searching for them; she drinks too much; she is nicer when she is sober, a little shy, but less approachable. Bettina Gregory. She is the kind of girl who almost cares about changing the social order, almost cares about people, almost is *at bottom really grave*. She is the kind of girl who would be at a cocktail party when someone named Fr— named Gerry—would call up and say he couldn't come because he was prosecuting a taxi-driver who had robbed him of four dollars. She is the kind of girl who would then toss off another drink and think it funny to take old Carl along up to the night-court to watch old Gerry prosecute a taxi-man. She is the kind of girl who will somehow collect coat-hangers (I give you my coat-hangers, Betsey-Bettina, Bertram Kyle almost shouted in his joy) and who will then go lilting and looping into the night-court armed to the teeth with coat-hangers and defense mechanisms, who will mock at the whores that have been rounded up, leer at the taxi-driver, ogle the red-faced detective, mimic the rather sheepish Gerry—all the time mocking, leering, ogling, mimicking—nothing but herself. Frankly we are just three people, she explains to the detective, with an arm about Gerry and Carl, who love each other veddy veddy much. She must pretend to be drunker than she is, because she is bitterly and deeply ashamed; she must wave with her coat-hangers and put on a show because she knows it is a rotten show and she cannot stop it. It is not merely the liquor she has drunk; it is the wrong books she has read, the Noel Coward plays she has gone to, the fact that there is a drought in the Middle West, that there was a war when she was a child, that there will be another when she has a child, that she and Carl have something between them but it is not enough, that she is sorry for the taxi-driver and ashamed of being sorry, that *at bottom she is almost grave*. In the end, Bertram Kyle said to anybody or nobody, in the end I think . . .

But there was no reason any more to think. His fingers were clicking, clicking, somehow it developed that Gerry had muddled things because he was drunk so that the taxi-man must go to jail pending special sessions, and then Bettina and Gerry and Carl take the detective out to a bar someplace; explaining frankly to waiters that they are just four people who love each other veddy veddy much . . . and, perhaps because they all hate themselves so veddy veddy much, Carl and Gerry let Bettina carry them all off in her car for a three-day spree which means that Gerry misses the subpoena and the taxi-driver spends a week in jail, earning himself a fine prison record because he stole four dollars to which Carl and Gerry and Bettina think him wholly and earnestly entitled, and perhaps in the end they give the four dollars to the Communist party, or perhaps they just buy another round of drinks, or perhaps they throw it in the river, or perhaps they frankly throw themselves . . .

And is this all, Bertram Kyle, all that will come out today of your living a life by yourself, of your having been born thirty years ago and tossed peanuts to elephants, wept at the Chartres window, slapped at mosquitoes, survived the hells and heavens of adolescence to be born again, today—is this all, this one short story which leaves out so much of life? But neither can a painter crowd all the world's rivers and mountains and railroad tracks onto one canvas, yet if his picture is any good at all it is good because he has seen those rivers and mountains and puts down all that he knows and all that he has felt about them, even if his painting is of a bowl of flowers and a curtain . . . And here, thought that thin layer of consciousness which went on as an undercurrent to his fingers' steady tapping, here is my lust for Betsey, my repentance for Louise, my endless gratitude to the woman who wore a yellow hat, my defeatism, my optimism, the fact that I was born when I was, all of my last night's living and much that has gone before . . .

The room grew clouded with the late afternoon

and he cigarettes that he forgot to smoke. His fingers went faster, they ached like the limbs of a tired lover and they wove with delicacy and precision because the story had grown so real to him that it was physical. He knew that his shoulders were hunched, that his feet were cramped, that if he turned his desk about he would have a better light—but all the time he was tearing out sheet after sheet and, with an odd accuracy that was not his own at any other time, inserting the next ones with rapidity and ease, he typed almost perfectly, he made few mistakes in spelling, punctuation, or the choice of words, and he swung into a rhythm that was at once uniquely his and yet quite new to him.

Now each idea as he pounded it out on his flying machine gave birth to three others, and he had to lean over and make little notes with a pencil on little pieces of paper that later on he would figure out and add together and stick in all the gaping stretches of his story. He rediscovered the miracle of something on page twelve tying up with something on page seven which he had not understood when he wrote it, the miracle of watching a shapeless thing come out and in the very act of coming take its own inevitable shape. He could feel his story growing out of the front of his head, under his moving fingers, beneath his searching eye . . . his heart was beating as fast as the keys of his typewriter, he wished that his typewriter were also an easel, a violin, a sculptor's tools, a boat he could sail, a plane he could fly, a woman he could love, he wished it were something he could not only bend over in his passion but lift in his exultation, he wished it could sing for him and paint for him and breathe for him.

And all at once his head swims, he is in a fog, sitting is no longer endurable to him, and he must get up, blind, not looking at his words, and walk about the room, the big room, the small room, whether it is night or day or summer or winter, he must get up and walk it off . . . *Listen, non-writers, I am not boasting when I tell you that writing is not a sublimation of living, but living is a pretty feeble substitute for art. Listen, non-writers, this is passion. I am trembling, I am weak, I am strong, pardon me a moment while I go and make love to the world, it may be indecent, it may be mad—but as I stalk about the room now I am not a man and I am not a woman, I am Bettina Gregory and Gerry and the taxi-driver and all the whores and cops and stooges in the night-court, I am every one of the keys of my typewriter, I am the clean white pages and the word-sprawled used ones, I am the sunlight on my own walls—rip off your dress, life, tear off your clothes, world, let me come closer; for listen: I am a sated, tired, happy writer, and I have to make love to the world.*

Sometimes it was night when this happened and then he must go to bed because even a writer needs sleep, but at those times he went to bed and then lay there stark and wide awake with plots weaving like tunes in his head and characters leaping like mad chess-men, and words, words and their miraculous combinations, floating about on the ceiling above him and burying themselves in the pillow beneath him till he thought that he would never sleep and knew that he was made . . . till Louise sometimes cried out that she could not sleep beside him, knowing him to be lying there only on sufferance, twitching with his limbs like a mad-man in the dark . . .

Louise! For it was not night, it was late afternoon, with the dark of coming night stealing in to remind him, to remind him that if he were ever again to make the break from his life's world back to sanity, back to normalcy and Louise, he must make it now, while he remembered to; he must leave this room, stale with his much-lived life, his weary typewriter, he must shake off his ecstasy and his bewilderment, his passion, his love, his hate, his glorious rebirth and his sated daily death—and go to meet Louise; go to a cocktail party . . .

He was shocked and terrified when he met his own face in the mirror because it was not a face, it was a pair of haggard, gleaming eyes, and because like Rip Van Winkle he seemed to have grown heavy with age and yet light with a terrible youth. He managed somehow to get by without letting the elevator man know that he was crazy, that he was afraid of him because he was a face and a voice, because he seemed to be looking at him queerly. On the street Bettina appeared and walked beside him, waving her drunken coat-hangers and announcing,

"Frankly there is nothing like a coat-hanger," while Gerry leaned across him rather bitterly to say, "If I hear you say frankly again, Bettina, frankly I shall kill you." But they walked along, all of them, very gay and friendly, despite the tax-driver's slight hostility, and then at the corner they were joined by Carl with the detective's arm about him, and Carl was saying to anybody and nobody that they passed —"Frankly we are veddy veddy mad." And they came at last to Freddie's house, and there Bertram Kyle stood for a moment, deserted by Bettina and Carl and Gerry—even the detective was gone—hiding behind a collar and a tie and frankly panic-stricken. The door opens, he enters mechanically— good God, is it a massacre, a revolution, is it the night-court, a nightmare? . . .

But he pushed in very bravely and began to reel toward all his friends. "Hello, I'm cockeyed!" he roared at random. "Hell, I've been floating for forty days, where's a coat-hanger, Freddie, frankly, if there's anything I'm nuts about it's coat-hangers, and frankly have you seen my friends, some people I asked along, Bettina Gregory, Gerry, and a detective?" He saw Louise, ominous and tolerant, placing her hands in disgust on her soft hips at sight of him. Frankly, he shouted at her, frankly, Louise, I am just three or four people who love you veddy veddy much, and where's a drink, my pearl, my pet, my bird, my cage, my night-court, my nightmare— for frankly I need a little drink to sober down . . .